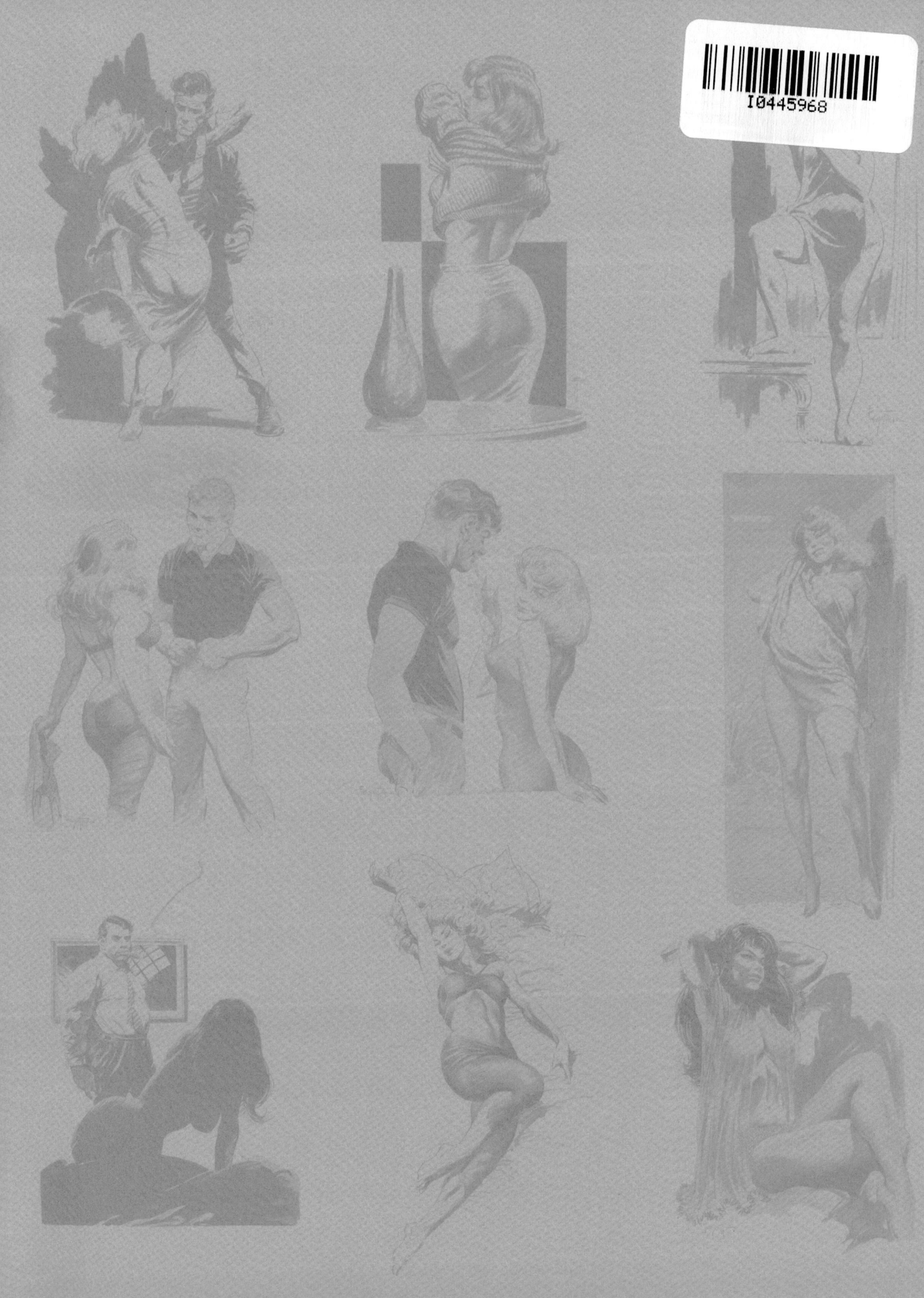

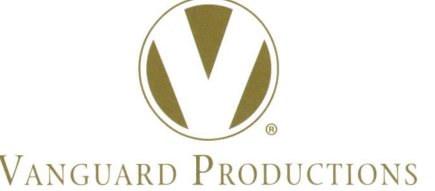

The Sensuous Frazetta

VANGUARD PRODUCTIONS

THE SENSU

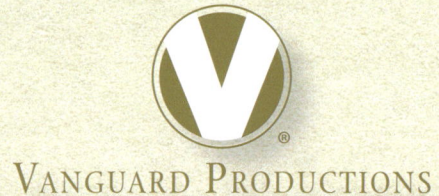

VANGUARD PRODUCTIONS

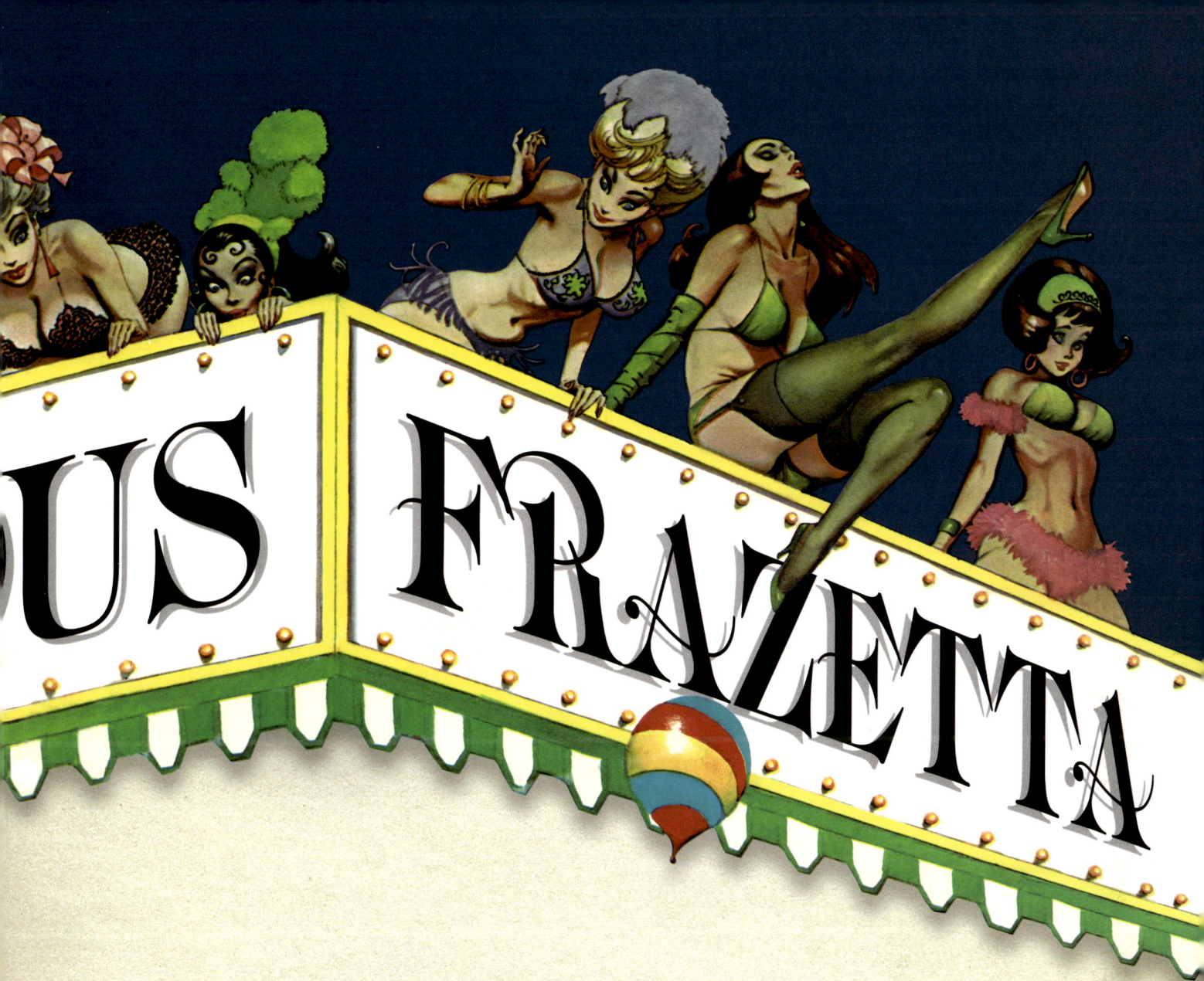

...US FRAZETTA

BY
J. DAVID SPURLOCK
— & —
FRANK FRAZETTA

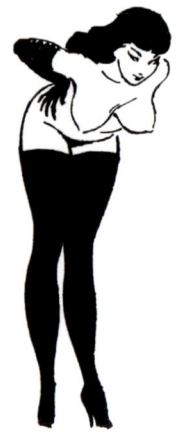

TEXT, EDITING & ART DIRECTION
J. David Spurlock

DESIGN, PRODUCTION & CAPTIONS
Patrick K. Hill

—

Special thanks to:

The Frazetta family, Leigh McMillan, Joseph Michael Linsner,
Andrew Steven, Gary Groth, Russ Cochran, Dr. Dave Winiewicz,
Sammy Bailey, Fershid Bharucha, Topper Helmers, Rich Dannys, Sandy Plunkett,
Larry Ivie, Brent Frankenhoff, and Peter Koch.

—

—

Frontis: Illustration #4 from *Perfumed*, Midwood, 1963.
Title Spread: "The Night they Raided Minsky's" (uncensored version).

—

Vanguard Editorial Office, N. Miami Beach, FL 33162;
Vanguard books are distributed by Ingram and DCD.
Vanguard Publishing, Vanguard Press, Vanguard Frazetta Classics and Vanguard Comics are trademarks of
Vanguard Productions, LLC. Vanguard Productions is a registered trademark. All © & ™ works appear for
scholarly and historic purposes and are the properties of their respective owners.
Collective copyright, as well as editorial & image modifications are
© Vanguard Productions, 2016.

DLX Slipcased HC w/ Bonus Folio ISBN-13: 978-1934331767 $69.95
Trade Hardcover ISBN-13: 978-1934331750 $39.95
Trade Paperback ISBN-13: 978-1934331743 $24.95

www.VanguardPublishing.com

1st Printing Spring 2016 • 2nd Printing September 2021
Printed in China

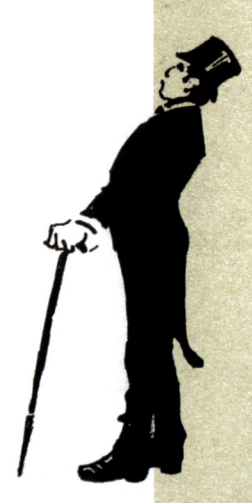

TABLE OF
Contents

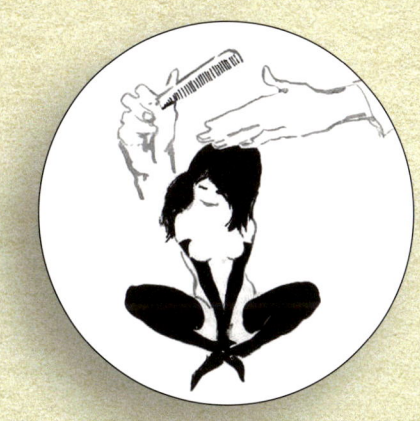

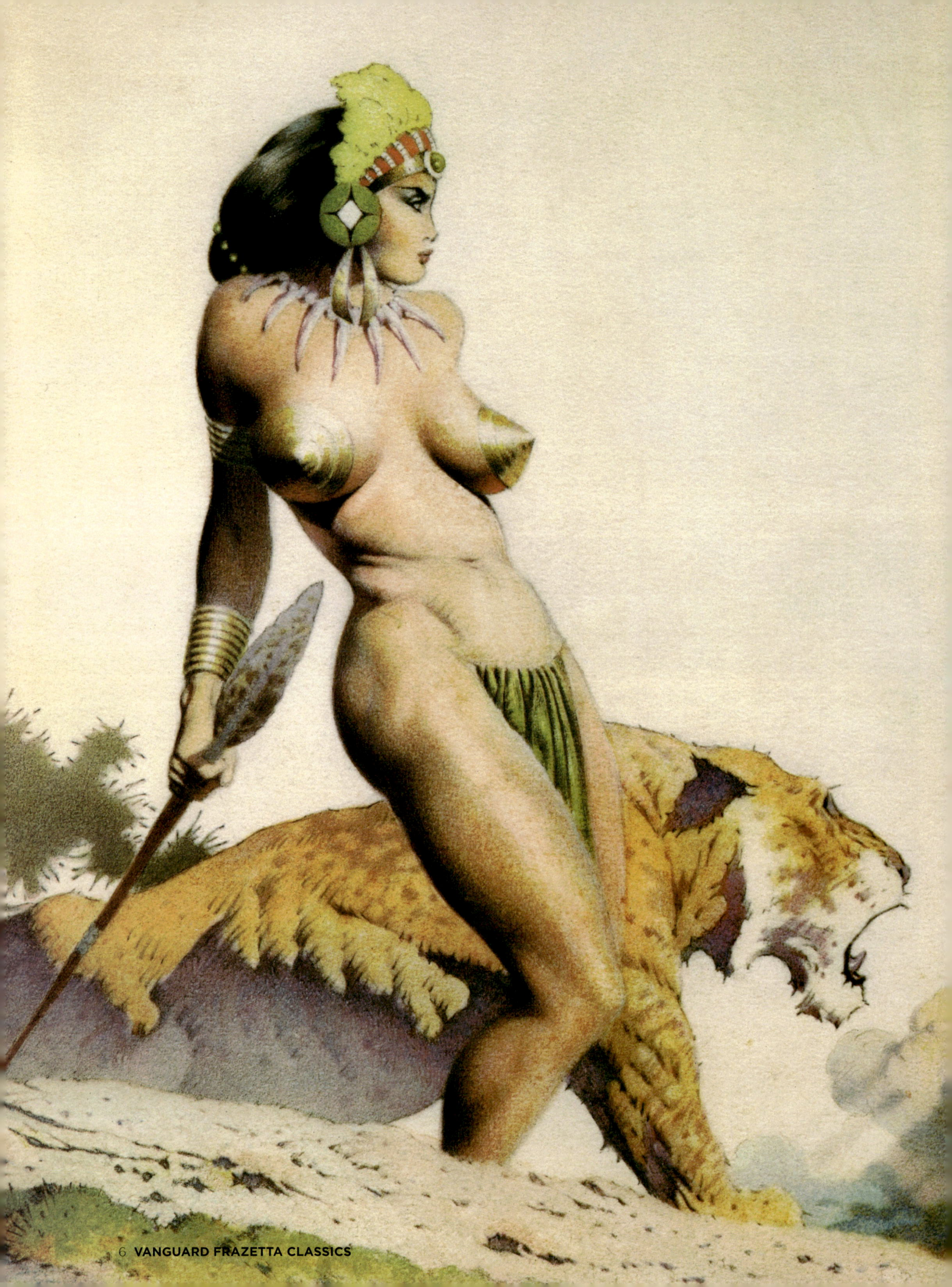

FOREWORD
THE SENSUOUS FRAZETTA

JOSEPH MICHAEL LINSNER

Art is a lie which tells the truth.
— **PABLO PICASSO**

"The one who wins is the one who wants it the most." — Sun Tzu, The Art Of War.

Without a doubt, in the realm of fantastic art the king is Frank Frazetta. He was the best simply because he wanted it more. The emotional content of his work was deeper that anyone who had come before him. Just as Elvis brought new levels of passion to popular music, Frazetta explored the depths of his own heart with an exciting new honesty. He didn't just want to slay the dragon and save the princess — he wanted to make love to her forever once the threat was behind them. When he drew a triumphant John Carter walking towards a reclining Dejah Thoris, you knew what fire burned in his blood. It radiated off of the page and you felt it.

William S. Burroughs said that a creative person can only depict what is in front of their senses at the moment of creation. It has to become real for the artist otherwise it won't translate to the page. When he painted, Frazetta made love with color and shadow, caressing every crease of flesh, every tensed muscle. His girls were real creatures he breathed life into. Because he felt it, we lucky viewers get to feel it, all through the alchemy of his art.

Is his work just the expression of an untamed libido? No. Frazetta has never done a piece that I would've hesitated to show my own mother. He holds his female protagonists in the highest regard. There is deep carnal desire, but there is also admiration and respect. Frazetta women are strong creatures who are in touch with their own sexuality. A glow of innocence shines in their eyes, but they always stand tall and they are never victims. Even the girl leaning against Conan's leg in his ultimate Conan painting THE BARBARIAN radiates power. I'm sure he wouldn't have it any other way.

Frazetta girls are real — I've seen them. Their beauty doesn't line up with the contemporary concepts of beauty. Their style and grace come from a deeper, more primal spot where hourglass figures never run out of time. The Frazetta girls I've seen aren't afraid to get their hands dirty. Personally, I've seen more women appreciate Frazetta girls than other fantasy females because of their earthiness. They seem more genuine, even though they are actually quite exaggerated.

In 1976, the master himself said, "A woman can be sensuous and erotic in typical, mundane movements, and I try to capture that precise motion or pose when she is at her most sensuous. I do exaggerate a lot in my work, but I find I have to exaggerate least when I paint women."

And yet in 1982, after trying to bring a his work to life in the animated epic 'Fire and Ice,' where actors were hired and then traced (rotoscoped) Frazetta went on to revise his opinion. "I'm not against a very slender, shapely woman at all. But I found that in the interpreting of it, when putting it onto the canvas or paper, it doesn't read well. You have to exaggerate in order for it to even look like you would imagine it. In other words, if I see a very slim, shapely woman walking down the street, now, you know we can respond to that. She's slim and graceful and wonderful. But if you actually draw that figure, it just doesn't create any effect on you. You're not getting the movement, you're not getting the dimensions; it simply doesn't work. I found out how much I exaggerate when I was making that movie."

"We found that in order for it to be exciting even in the slightest, she had to be extreme… If you take someone like Cindy Crawford and just trace her, just so that it's an outline, you know what? You'll ho-hum it to death. Whereas if you trace something that's really outrageous, more like a Marilyn Monroe, that barely works… So I've found that they have to be very extreme in order for you to look at the painting or drawing and really be impressed. Exaggeration is necessary for it to read well, to capture your mind's eye."

Frazetta was a genius at lacing his creations with subtle details which anchored his wild fantasies in a familiar reality. The tiny way a strap

● ● ● ● ● ● ● ● ● ● ●

QUEEN KONG detail: Originally produced in the early-1970s for, and based on a concept by Frazetta's friend, Wally Wood, as a proposed mature comics magazine cover — sometimes referred to as POW — to be released by Warren Publishing. Wood dropped the project when the first pay check failed to arrive. The piece ultimately saw print as the cover to Eerie #81, released toward the end of 1976 with a cover date of February 1977. When Warren failed to return the original art to Frazetta, it marked the end of the artist's relationship with the publisher.

will bite into skin, or a dimple in the muscles on the back of a girl's thigh. A great irony is that these are the exact elements which much modern photo retouching wants to erase. They take out the folds in the skin, take out evidence of a bikini biting into real flesh. Photoshop nightmares fill American advertising — what fantasy world are they after, I wonder? Frazetta's women were real, and yet they came to life straight out of one man's imagination.

I learned how to draw women from Frazetta's girls. I'm still learning! His work is an artistic battery which I constantly return to for recharging. Every time I go back to it I find something new, and come away enlightened. Through his work, Frazetta was a truth teller. He expressed something untapped in the human psyche; desires and urges laying dormant in the subconscious. His overwhelming lusts and fierce angers became ours, and he expressed emotions many of us are afraid to acknowledge in ourselves. Frazetta, born and raised in Brooklyn, fought his battles in the steel canyons of New York. He emerged triumphant because he was able to tap his inner barbarian, his primal core, and capture that on the page.

Over the years, I made multiple visits to the Frazetta museum to pay

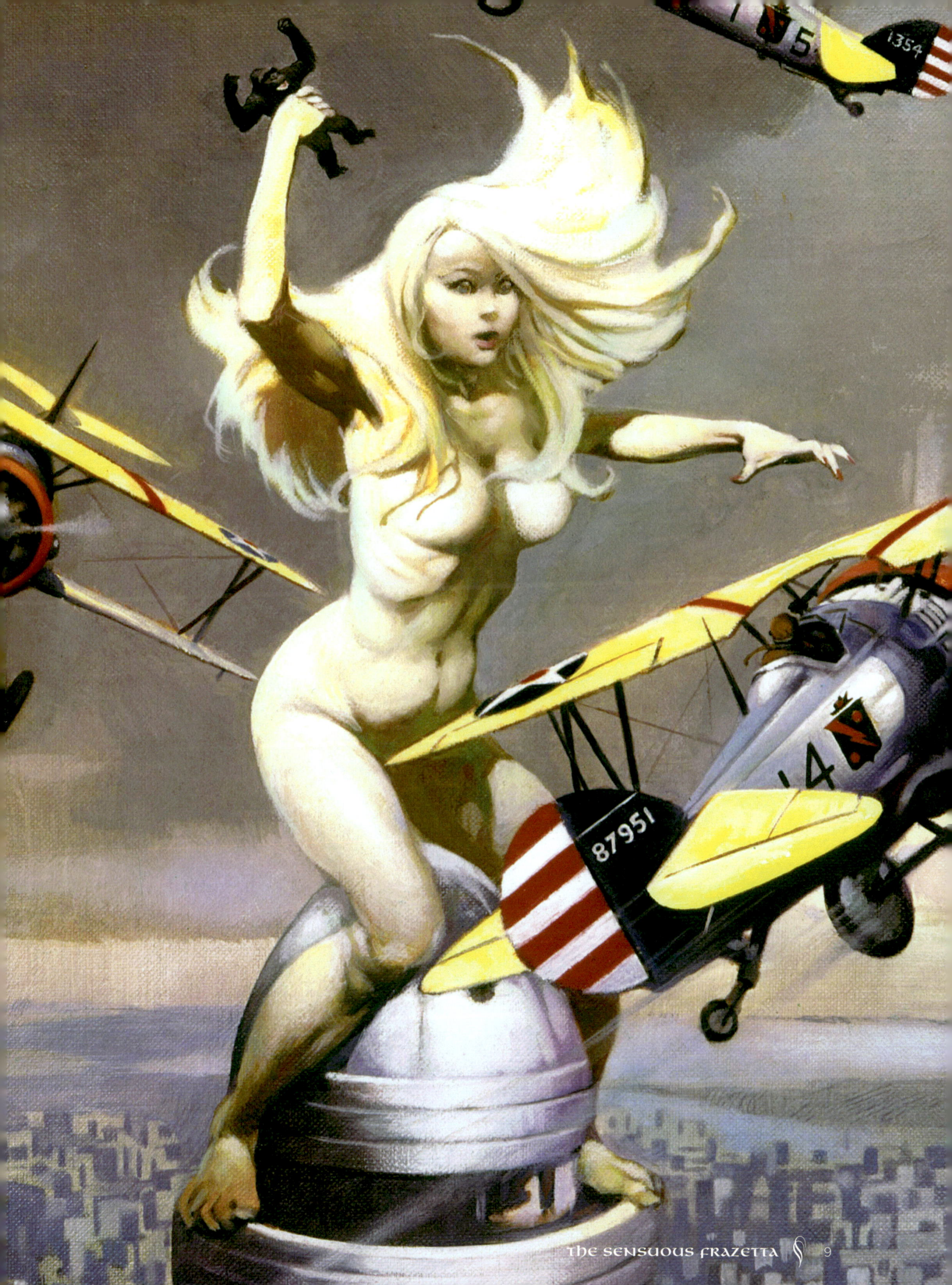

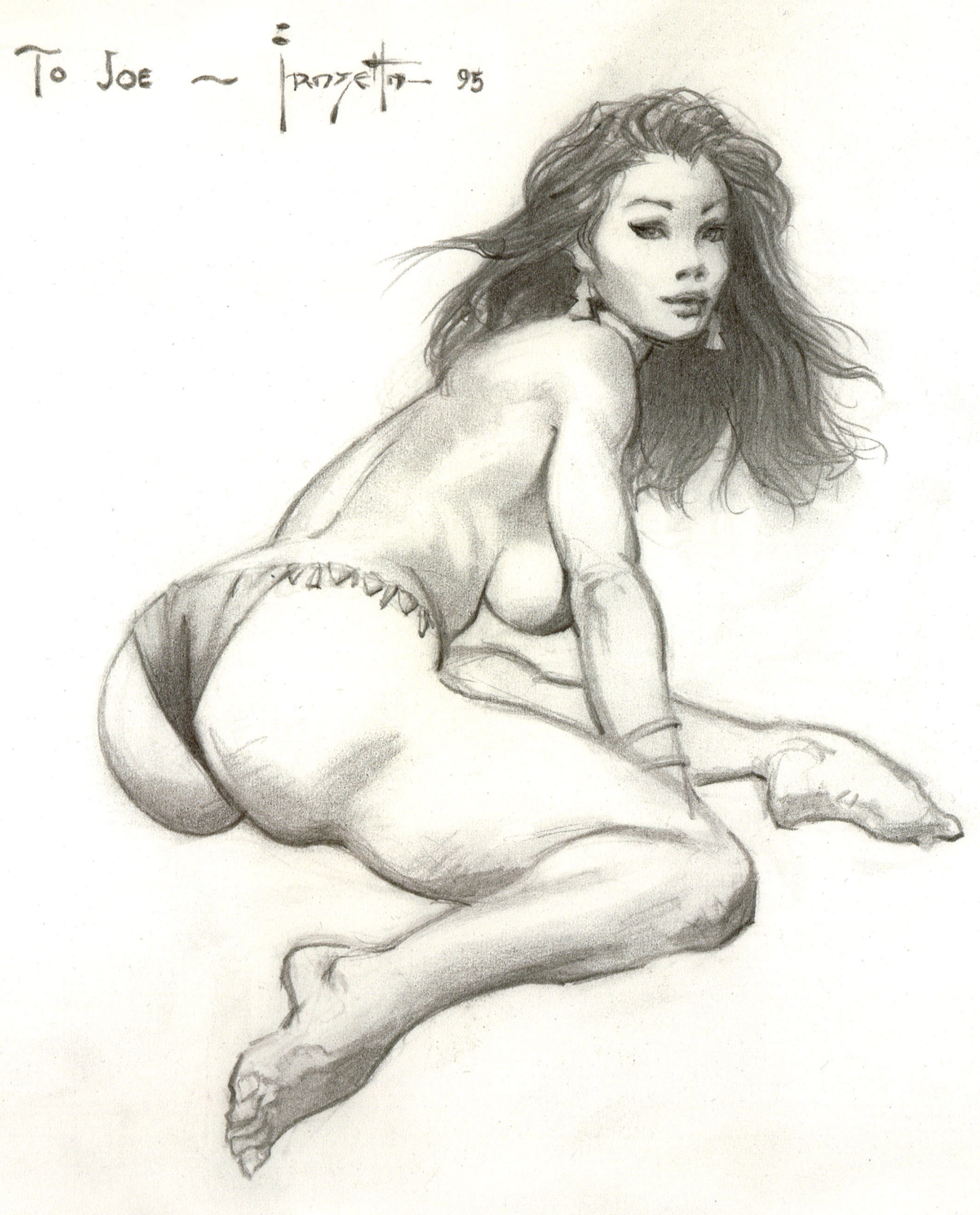

To Joe ~ Frazetta 95

my respects and see the masterpieces in all of their glory. I was lucky enough to meet his lovely wife Ellie, who was very warm and friendly. Sadly, I never got to meet Mr. Frazetta, who passed away in 2010. He was my artistic hero — without a doubt my very favorite artist. I do have a tiny spark of personal contact with him though. As a thank you for the success of my first card set, my publisher at Comic Images, Hank Rose, got me a wonderful Frazetta pencil drawing (he also published the Frazetta card sets). It's inscribed 'To Joe ~.' It hangs in my studio, and every time I pass it, I get a big smile on my face.

I'm looking forward to finally getting a printed copy of this book. A singular volume focusing solely on 'the sensuous Frazetta' is long overdue. The achievement of his work is acknowledged in many arenas, but he needs to be recognized as one of the great artistic masters of the female form. A master pin-up artist, right next to Vargas, Elvgren and Petty.

I hope that young people are still discovering the work of Frank Frazetta. The reality of his fantasy is something that our society could use right now — the emotionally pure heart of it.

"…There is such a thing as poetic, ecstatic truth. It is mysterious and elusive, and can be reached only through fabrication and imagination and stylization." — Werner Herzog

In a world where photographs are no longer incontrovertible evidence in court, where computer generated effects saturate every major movie, we need the exaggerated truth of Frazetta's work. The fantastic is all around us, we just have to open up and feel it. Frazetta's art provides a key to that door which separates fantasy from reality. It grounds our base emotions on earth and lifts our spirits up to the stars. Where a Frazetta girl, who looks just like Dejah Thoris, is waiting to lead the way…

Joseph Michael Linsner
November, 2015

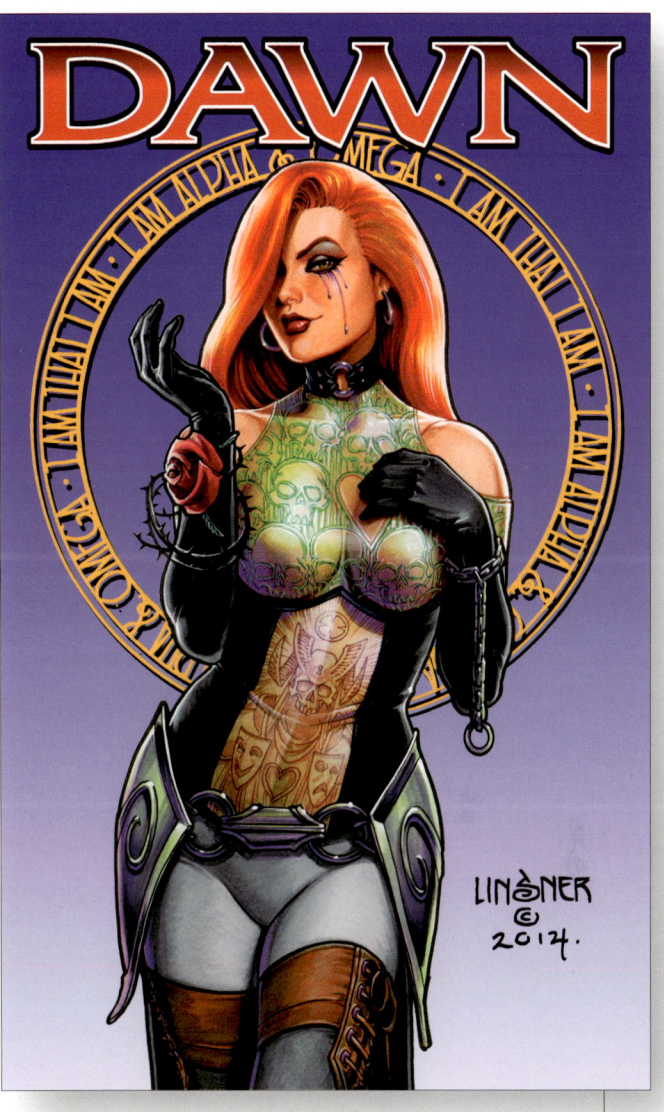

Artist and writer **Joseph Michael Linsner** *has been drawing the adventures of his most famous creation, Dawn, for 27 years. He has painted covers for every major comic publisher, bringing Wolverine, Spider-Man, Killraven, Witchblade, Conan, Red Sonja and many others to life. His most recent project is Dawn & Vampirella — a very special project for Joe since Vampi was designed by Mr. Frank Frazetta.*

*OPPOSITE:
Linsner's inscribed
Frazetta drawing,
1995.*

*ABOVE:
A 2014 Dawn
cover design.*

THE SENSUOUS FRAZETTA 11

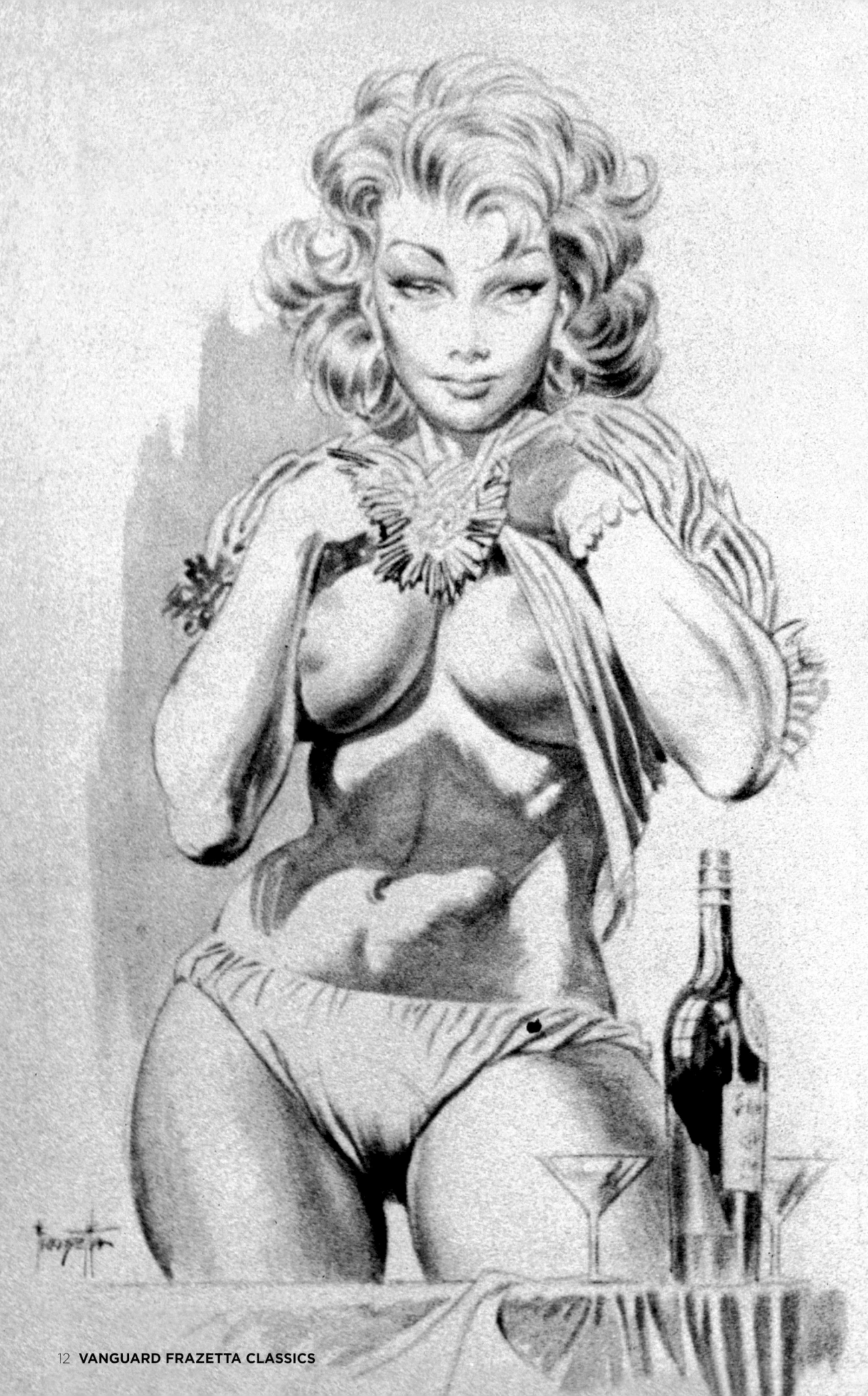

CHAPTER ONE
BETWEEN THE SHEETS
PAPERBACK INTERIORS

As much as his famed monsters, beasts, and barbarians; his Tarzan, Conan, Death Dealer, and King Kong paintings; from Vampirella to *Weird Science*; to Edgar Rice Burroughs' Pellucidar and Dejah Thoris, Princess of Mars; no one is more renowned for exquisite renderings of exotic women than the world's greatest heroic-fantasy artist, Frank Frazetta. From his earliest comic-book work until the day he died, Frazetta imbued nearly every work of art with a unique sensuality. Despite competition from such brilliant artists as Alex Toth, Wallace Wood, Jay Scott Pike, and Matt Baker, Frazetta's 1950s romance comics (included here) were the most sensuous of all mainstream romance comics. As he moved from comic books to newspaper strip work, his *Johnny Comet* and *Li'l Abner* art, likewise teamed with bodacious beauties.

Most people are unaware that there was a brief period, in the early 1960s, between Frazetta leaving comics and his coming to fame as an innovative oil painter of barbarians, in which he was primarily producing risqué pin-up style art for men's magazines and paperback books. Few among the growing Frazetta fan base knew of these — or what titles or covers to look for — at the time; resulting in their becoming rare collectors' items, which now sell for $200 to $400 each. By the time Frazetta had become a superstar in the late-1960s via his *Creepy* magazine, Conan, and Tarzan work, fanzines were popping up like wildflowers. These were usually very low-budget, one-color, mimeograph or pulp paper affairs; often unauthorized by copyright holders, and had little distribution other than mail order. One such cheap, early-1970s newsprint fanzine collected 21 of Frazetta's 26 rare men's paperback illustrations under the apropos title, *The Sensuous Frazetta* — inspired by the hugely successful contemporaneous book, *The Sensuous Man*.

OPPOSITE: Previously unpublished, circa 1962 drawing, believed to be an outtake for a Midwood paperback.

THIS PAGE: The 1970 Science Fiction Book Club edition interior from A Princess of Mars *(Nelson-Doubleday, Inc.).*

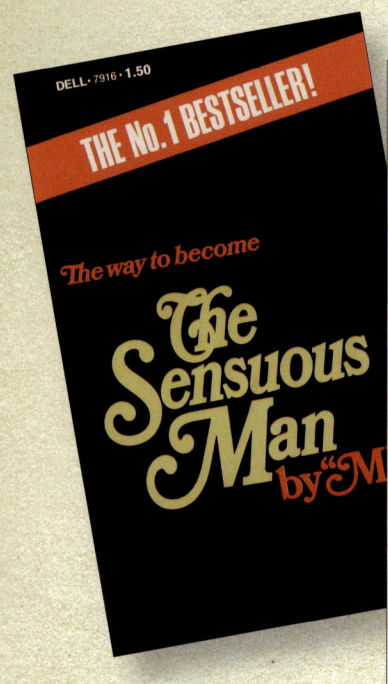

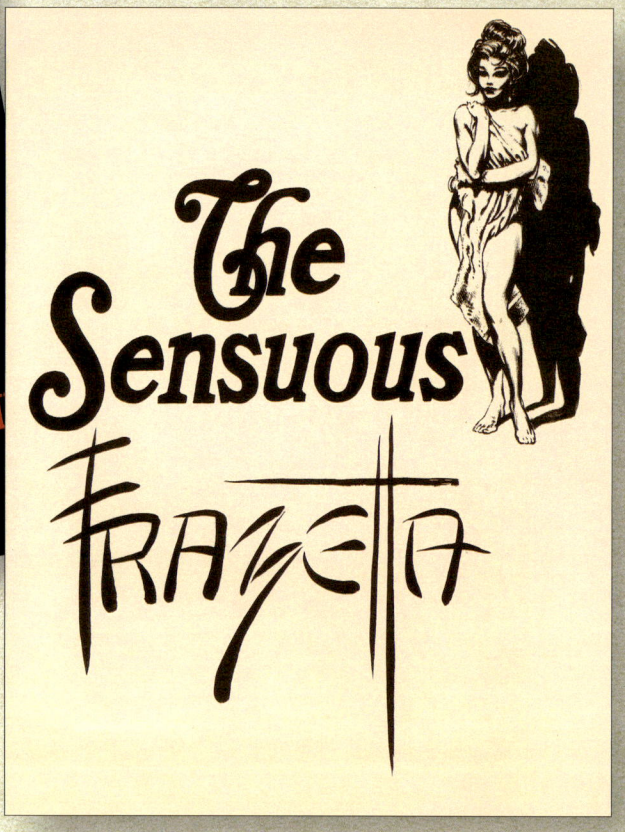

Until now, only the most ardent collectors achieved acquisition of the very elusive grail items from the short period of Frazetta's men's magazine and risqué paperback book illustrations — the Tower/Midwood paperbacks alone tend to sell for $250 to $400 each as of the time of this writing. In this, Vanguard's glorified revival, we have significantly expanded *The Sensuous Frazetta* concept from the original 20-something pages to nearly 200 big, quality art-stock pages in full color. With state-of-the-art reproduction techniques, we've included every single one of these men's magazine and book illustrations, plus previously unpublished preliminary art, a chapter of Frazetta's most flirtatious movie poster works, and the most seductive romance comics ever — including the legendary "Untamed Love"— collected for the first time with its original, vintage color intact; all to create the most complete tome ever of rare, vintage Sensuous Frazetta.

*TOP:
The 1973 unauthorized fanzine,* The Sensuous Frazetta, *featuring 21 Midwood drawings.*

RIGHT: Perfumed *and* Pampered, *Midwood's 1963 illustrated paperback, featuring ten "naughty" drawings, with captions from the text.*

FRAZETTA

Pampered,
Illustration #1

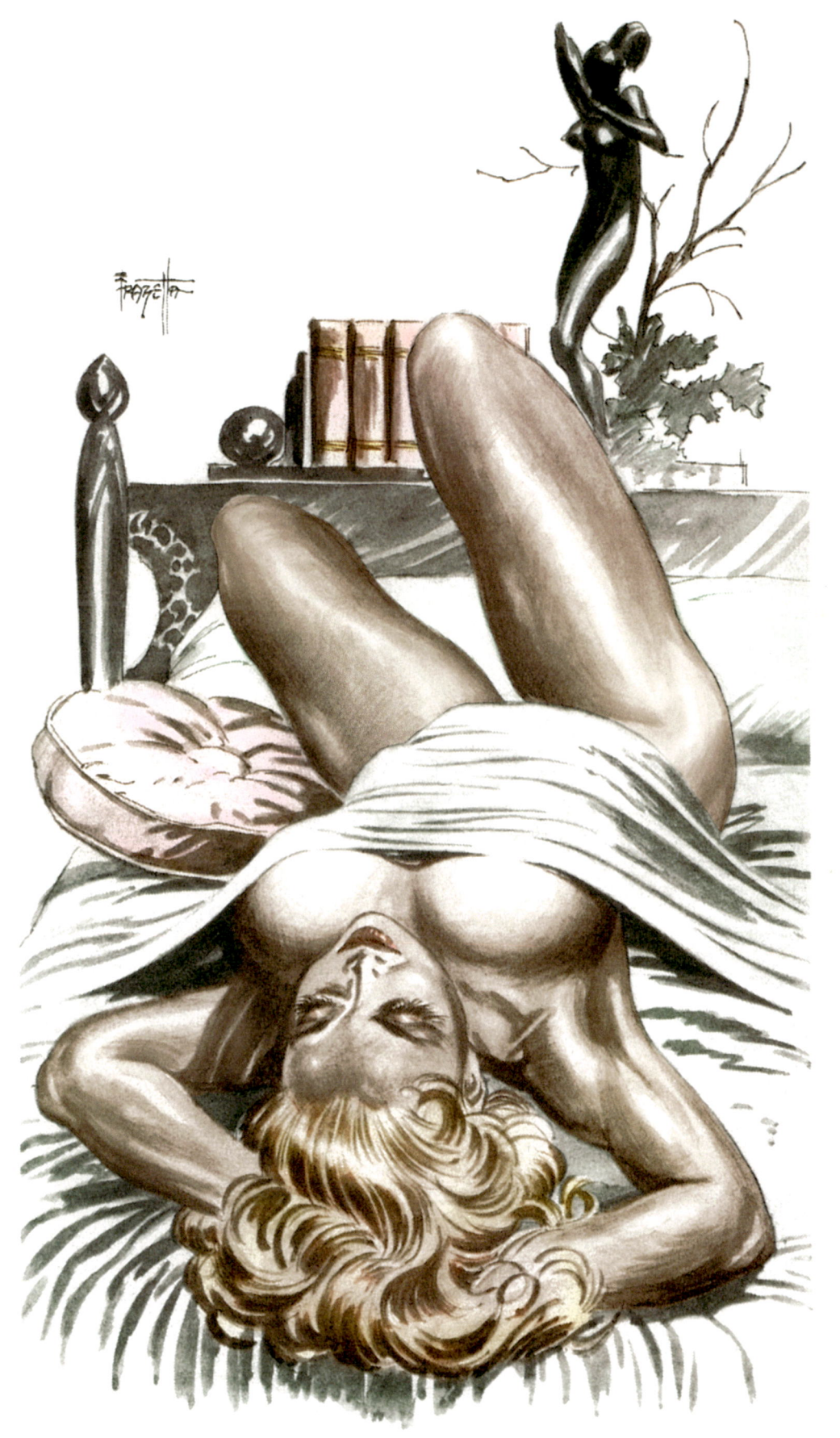

In 1962, after working for nine years as a well-paid, but uncredited "ghost" artist, penciling the *Li'l Abner* newspaper strip for Al Capp, Frazetta abruptly quit, inspired by Capp wanting to cut his pay in half.

Along with some magazine illustrations, Frazetta broke into the pin-up art genre with *Perfumed/ Pampered*, a 1963 book of soft-core prose fiction for Midwood/ Tower Publications. He produced ten interior illustrations in ink wash, depicting curvaceous females in titillating poses.

Two other double novels followed, with eight illustrations in each. Unfortunately, Midwood/Tower did not hire Frazetta to paint covers, for which they had both photographers, and a proven stable of artists, most notably, Paul Rader. Though Frazetta only worked with Midwood/Tower

RIGHT: Harry Shorten went from creating cartoon features and developing Archie Comics *to launching his own book, magazine and comics publishing endeavors including Midwood/ Belmont/Tower.*

BELOW: Paul Rader's cover for The Mark of a Man, *1963.*

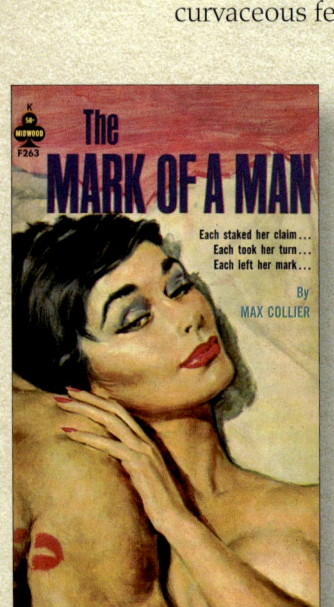

for a short time, the company's story is interesting, though little known or understood.

From the January 22, 1991 obituary by Maria Elena Fernandez for the *Florida Sun Sentinel*: "Cartoonist Harry Shorten, creator and former editor of *Archie* Comics and creator of the syndicated [newspaper cartoon] *There Oughta Be A Law*, died on January 14 of stroke complications. He was 76. Mr. Shorten moved from Rockville Centre, NY to Pompano Beach in 1982 after he retired from Midwood/Tower Publications, the company he founded in 1958. The publishing company produced comic [books,] pocketbooks and magazines, including *Afternoon* TV, one of the first soap opera magazines. After Mr. Shorten graduated from New York University in 1937 with a bachelor's degree in geology, he played professional football for two years, said Linda Lemle Goldberg of West Hartford, Conn., his daughter. Mr. Shorten created *There Oughta Be A Law* in the 1940s as a free-lance artist [/writer],

Continued on Page 24

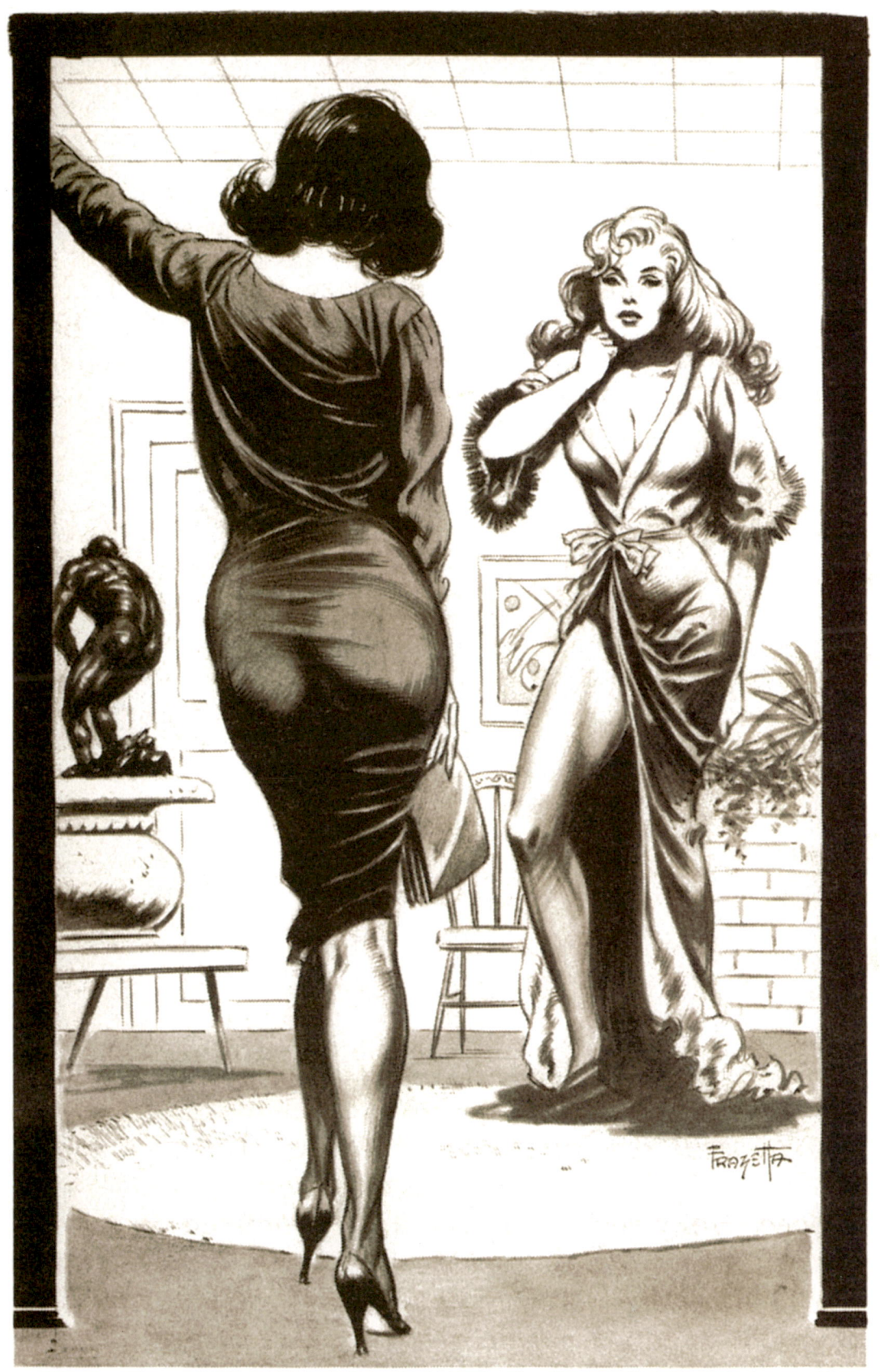

I pushed the door open and came face to face with my husband's mistress, the girl I had come to punish… and somehow, all I could think of was that she was the most beautiful creature I'd ever seen.

Pampered,
Illustration #2

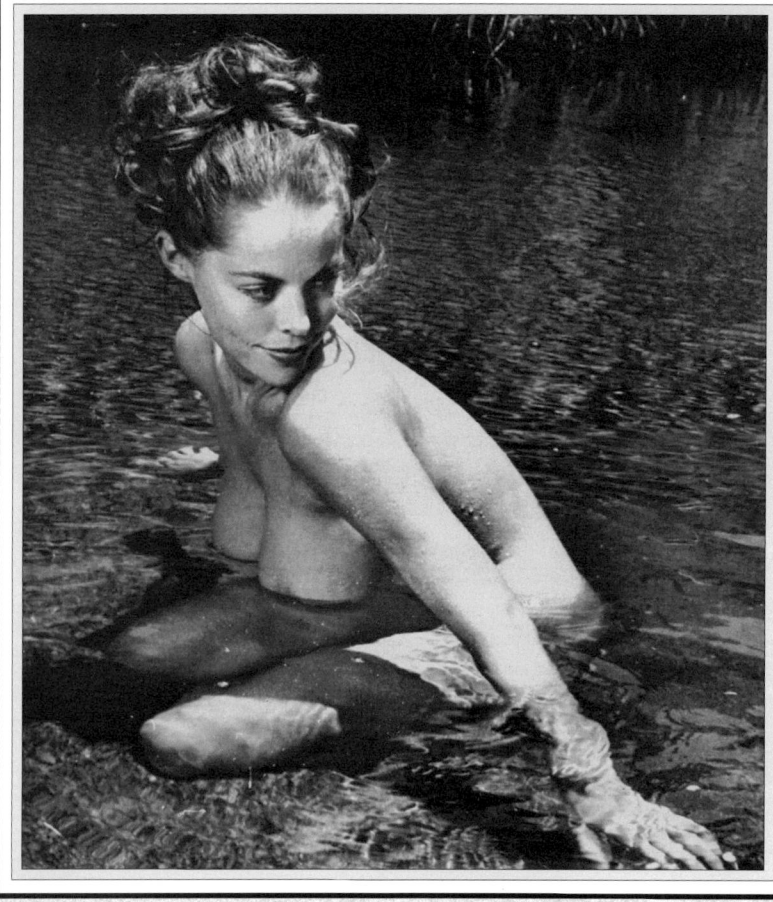

Frank Frazetta had an amazing visual memory that might be considered somewhat "photographic." This, along with his years as a comic book artist, helped him develop the ability to create amazingly convincing art without the need of photographic reference which, is a tool of nearly every illustrator. Frazetta's tendency to not use photographs has led to the over-simplified idea that he never used photographs. But he did occasionally and one of his favorite inspirations was the popular model Diane Webber as seen in this illustration (opposite) and related published photo of Webber.

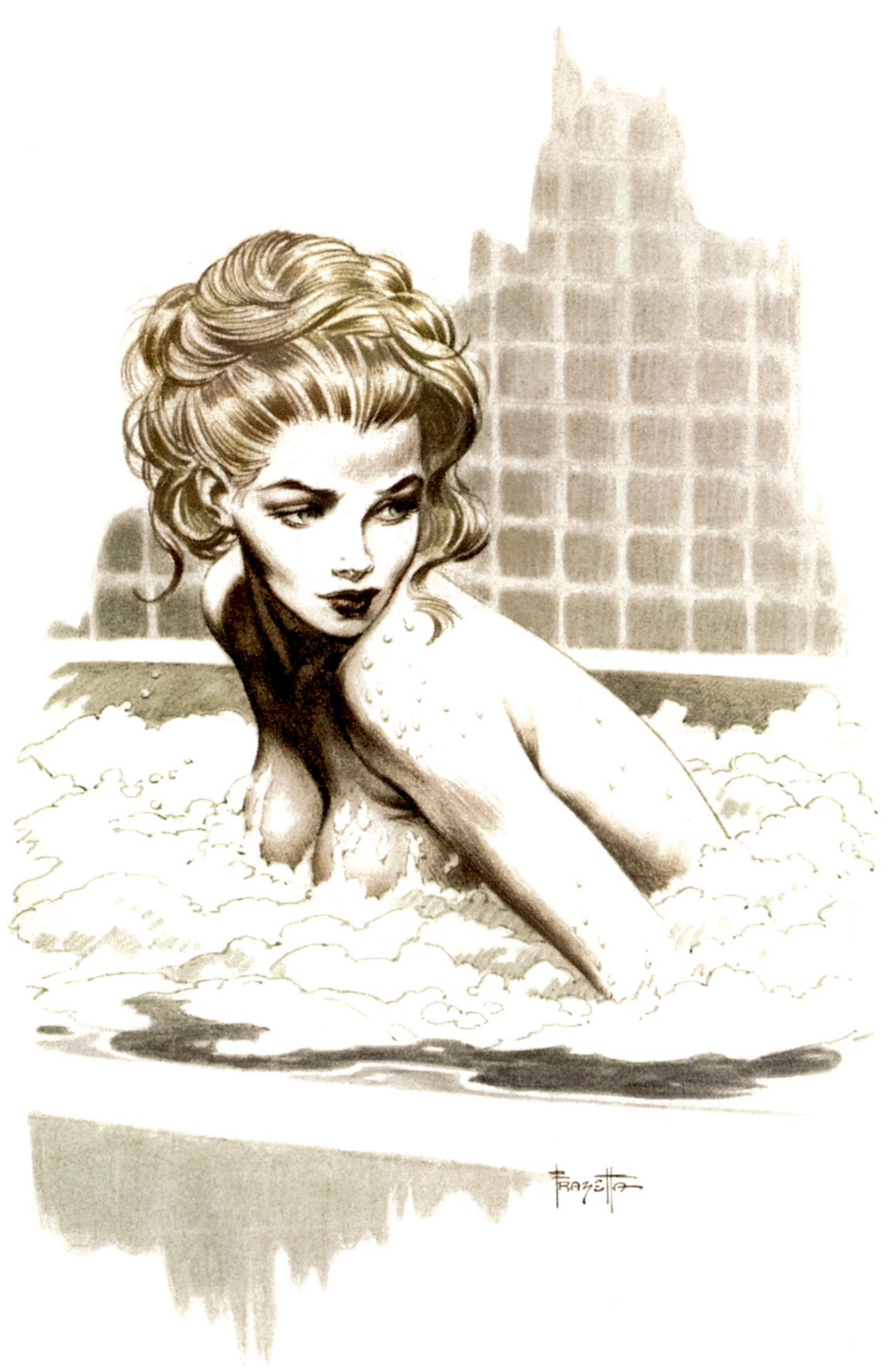

Under the surface of the water, her body looked like shimmering cream.
I found myself understanding why my husband wanted her.
I found myself understanding how anyone, male or female, would want her.

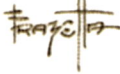

*She stood on the bathmat, patting herself gently with the towel,
her luscious body glistening, her lovely face flushed and glowing.
Something happened inside me and I began moving toward her…*

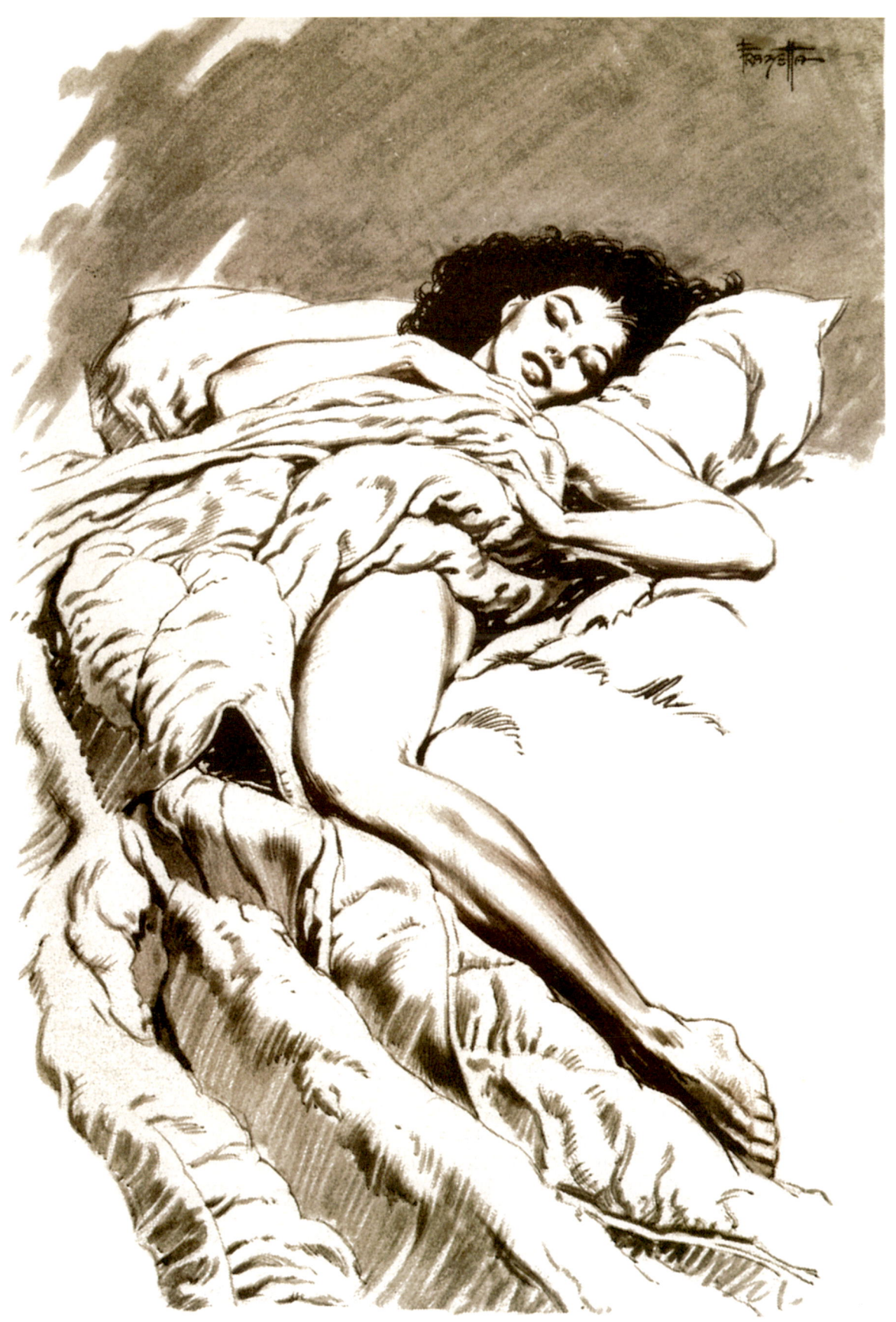

She started toward the bed and I had to close my eyes. Somehow I knew that it would have been too much to bear to see as well as to feel what was to come. I waited, my heart pounding, my body throbbing, for the first touch of her hand…

Pampered,
Illustration #5

Frazetta

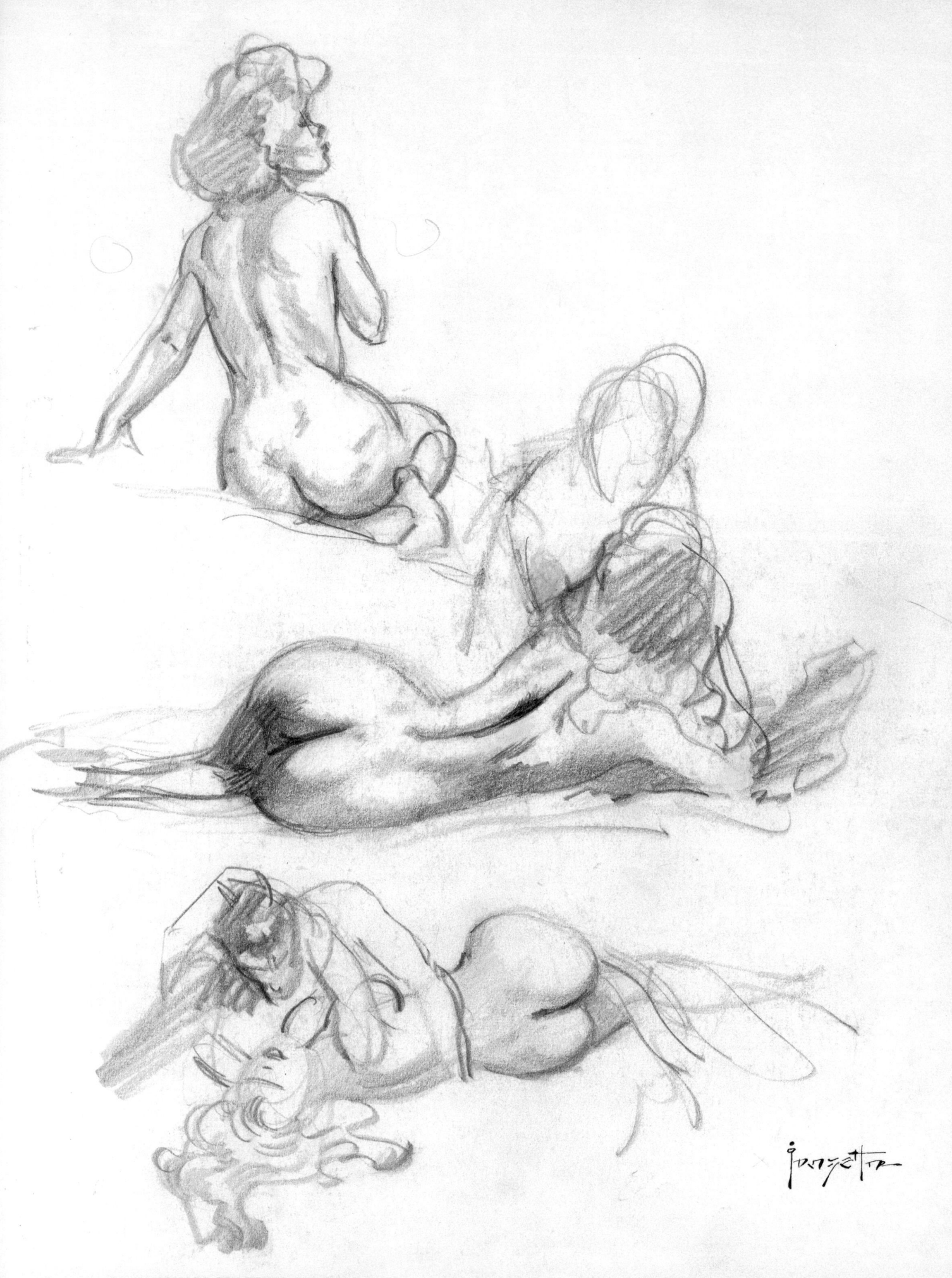

FRAZETTA

THIS PAGE:
Perfumed,
Illustration #1

OPPOSITE:
Rough drawings for this series (11″ x 13.5″)

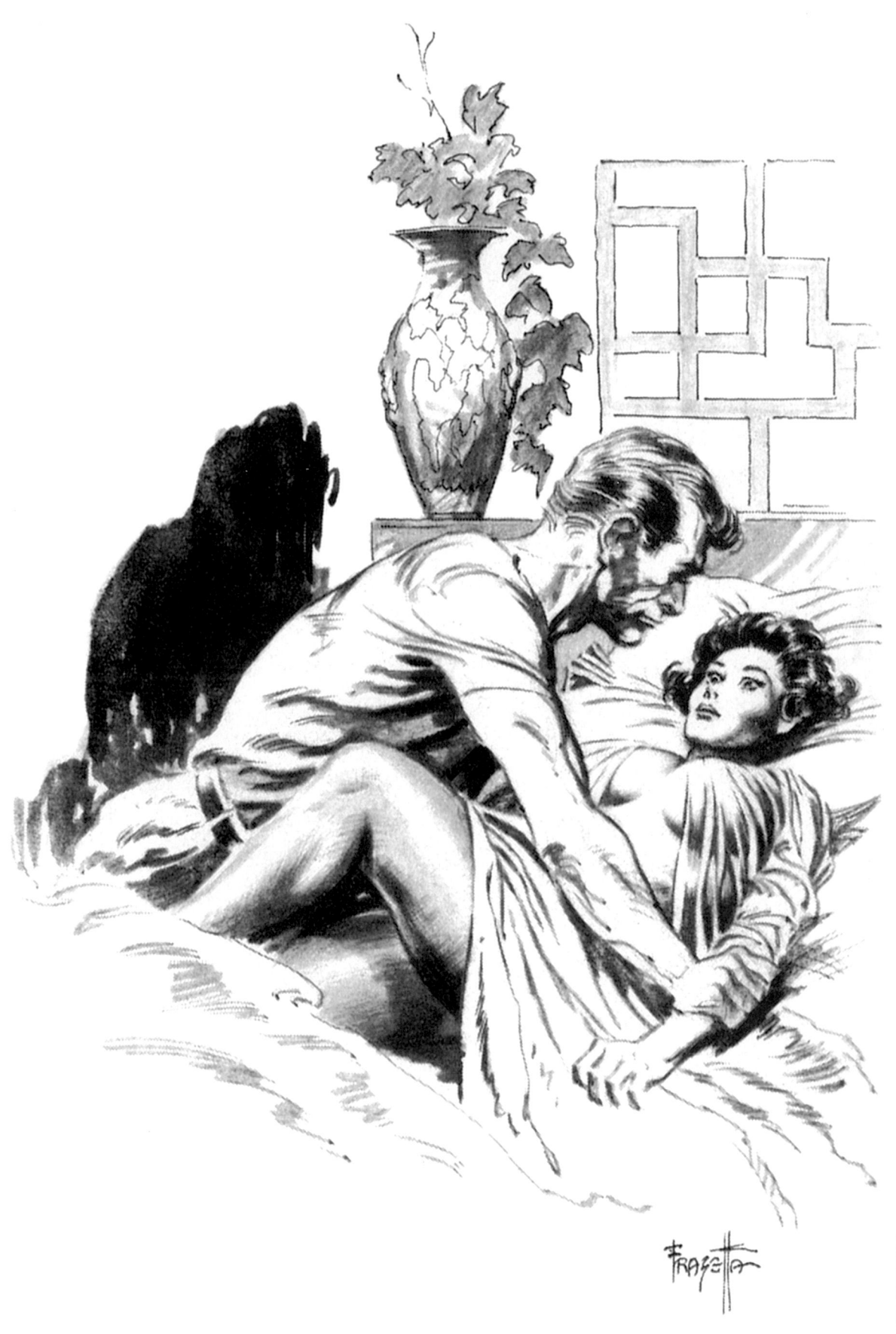

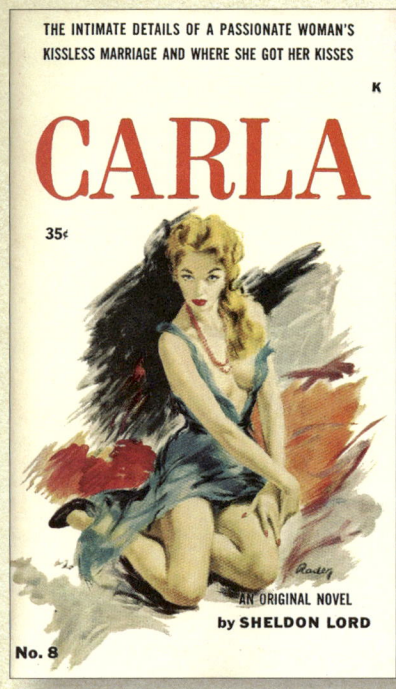

THE INTIMATE DETAILS OF A PASSIONATE WOMAN'S
KISSLESS MARRIAGE AND WHERE SHE GOT HER KISSES

K

CARLA

35¢

AN ORIGINAL NOVEL
by SHELDON LORD

No. 8

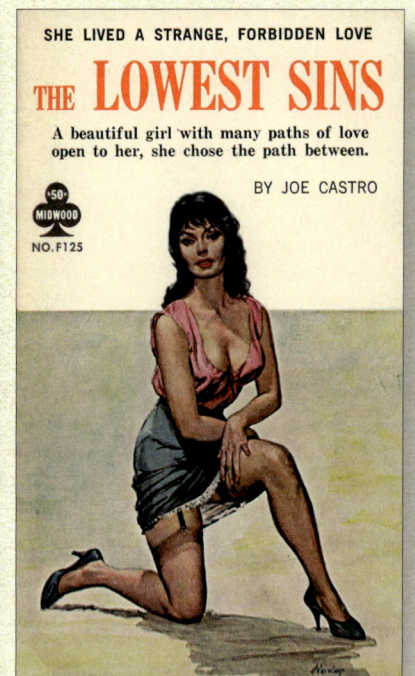

SHE LIVED A STRANGE, FORBIDDEN LOVE

THE LOWEST SINS

A beautiful girl with many paths of love
open to her, she chose the path between.

BY JOE CASTRO

50¢ MIDWOOD

NO. F125

...continued from Page 16

then joined MLJ Publications, where he worked on the *Archie* character that grew to fame through comics and television."

On his website, paperback book dealer/ expert Lynn Munroe wrote, "Harry Shorten came from the Midwood section of Brooklyn, NY. With his partner, artist Al Fagaly, Shorten made his fortune with a comic strip called *There Oughta Be A Law.* Shorten thought up the ideas and Fagaly would do the drawings. Looking around for somewhere to invest all the money he was making from his cartoon, Shorten decided to become a paperback book publisher. He looked at the success of Beacon Books, a series of slick cheap throwaway

melodramas and sexy romances with flashy girlie art covers marketed to men and published by Universal Distributing. Shorten figured he could do the same, and, in 1957, at 505 8th Avenue in Manhattan, he started a paperback book line named for his old neighborhood." While most of the risqué Midwood/Tower books are considered kitschy trash, and the authors tended to write under pennames, a number of Midwood/Tower writers eventually became stars including Donald E. Westlake, Robert Silverberg, Gil Fox, Lawrence Block, and Julie Ellis.

Midwood/Tower writer Gil Fox said, "Shorten's… first editor was Elaine Williams, who wrote as Sloane Britain.

ABOVE: Rader covers for Carla (1958) and The Lowest Sins (1961).

RIGHT: Elaine Williams was Harry Shorten's first editor, who wrote as Sloane Britain. Insatiable *and* Meet Marilyn *(both from 1960).*

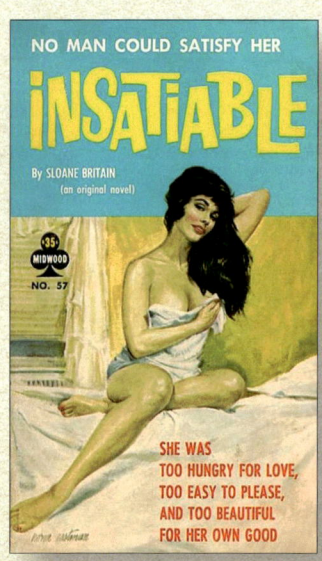

NO MAN COULD SATISFY HER

INSATIABLE

By SLOANE BRITAIN
(an original novel)

35¢ MIDWOOD

NO. 57

SHE WAS
TOO HUNGRY FOR LOVE,
TOO EASY TO PLEASE,
AND TOO BEAUTIFUL
FOR HER OWN GOOD

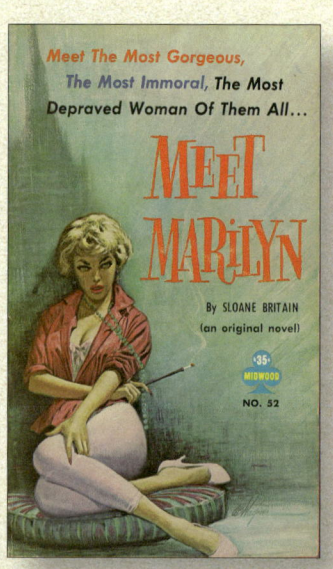

Meet The Most Gorgeous,
The Most Immoral, The Most
Depraved Woman Of Them All...

MEET MARILYN

By SLOANE BRITAIN
(an original novel)

35¢ MIDWOOD

NO. 52

Continued on Page 28

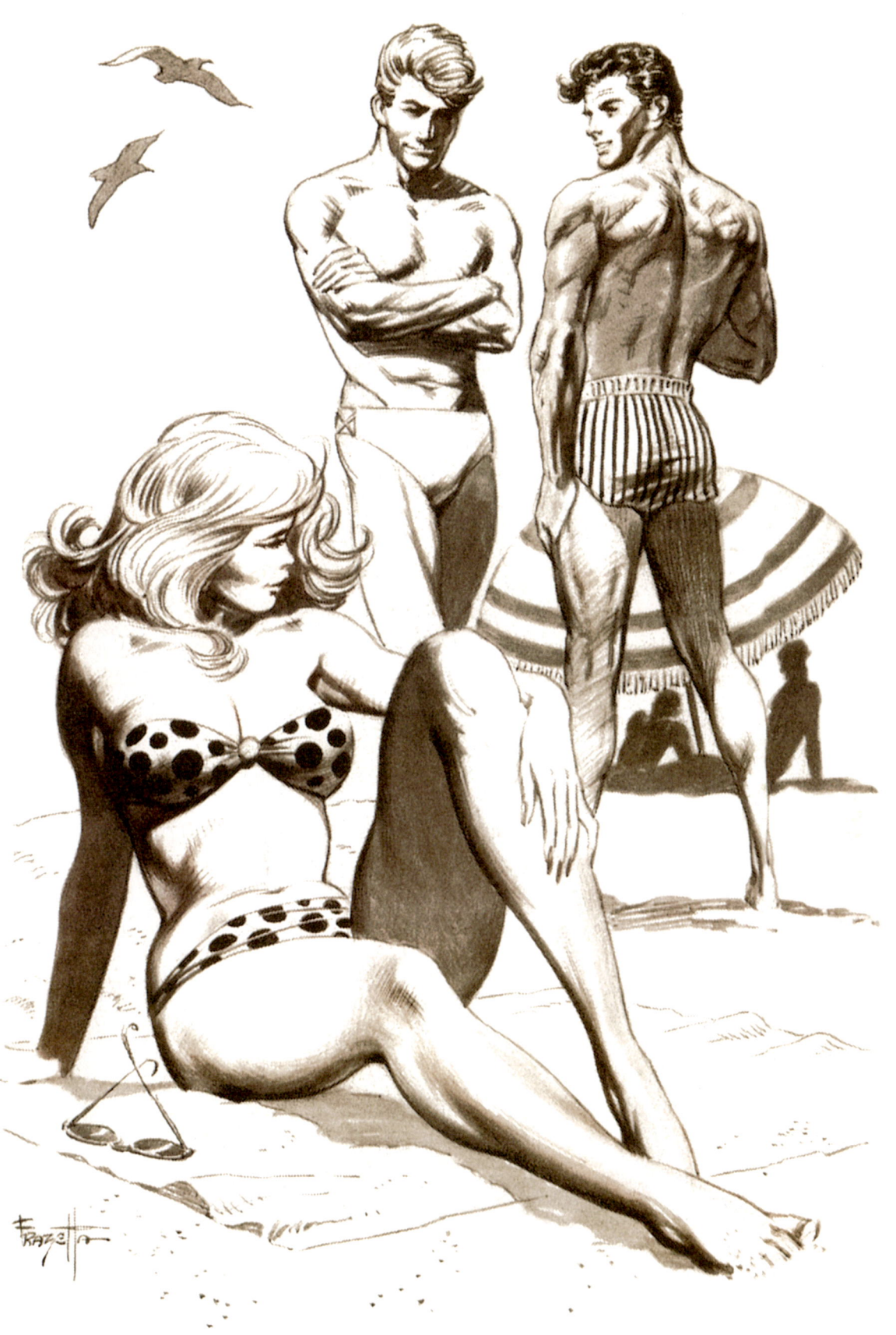

The hunger was growing with each passing day. How much longer would I be able to fight it? Temptation surrounded me. The young men at the lake, so strong, so clean, so eager… so available.

Perfumed,
Illustration #2

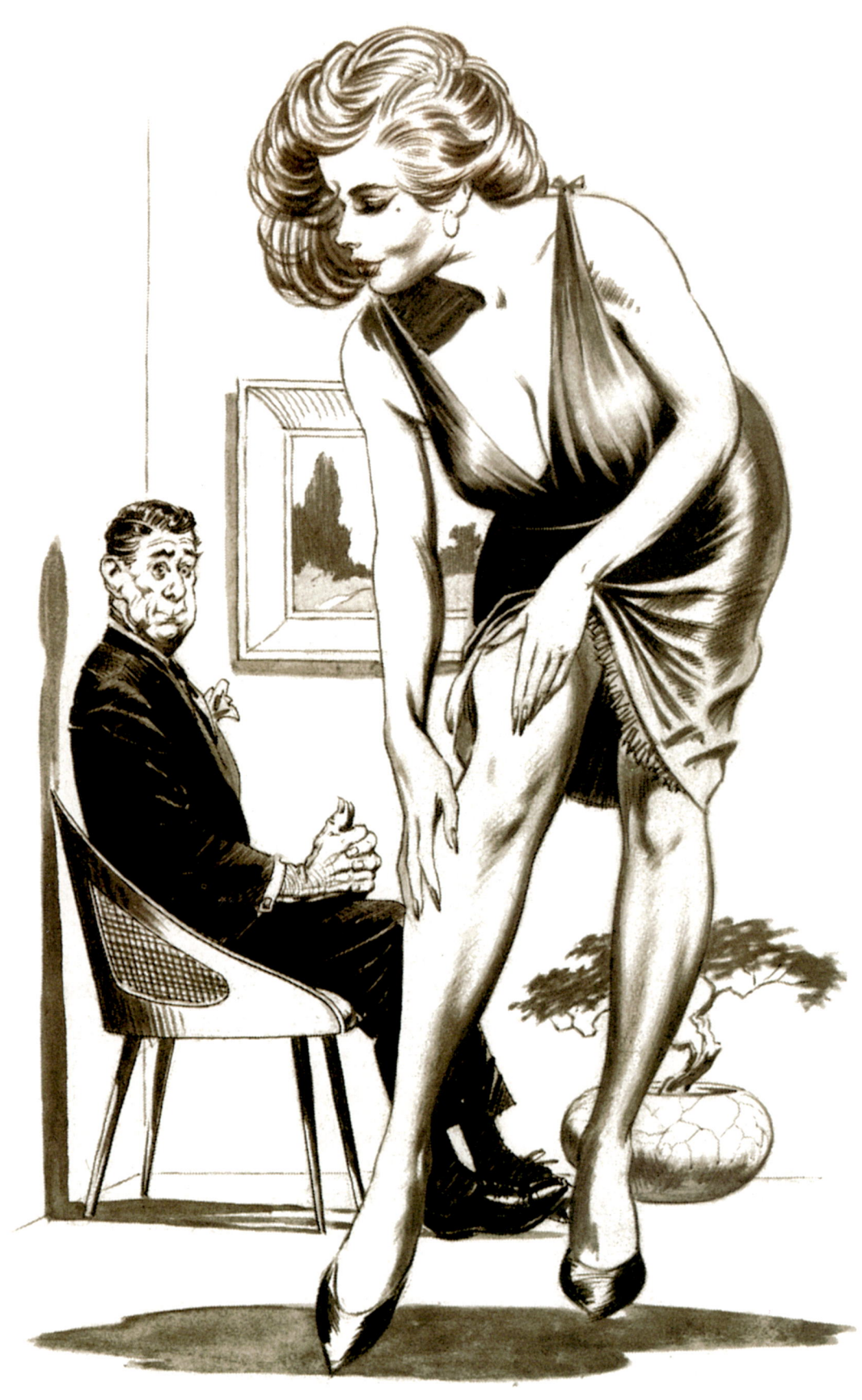

*Vera smiled with amusement as she lifted her dress to smooth the sheer stocking,
forcing the timid little man to follow each sensuous movement of her fingertips.*

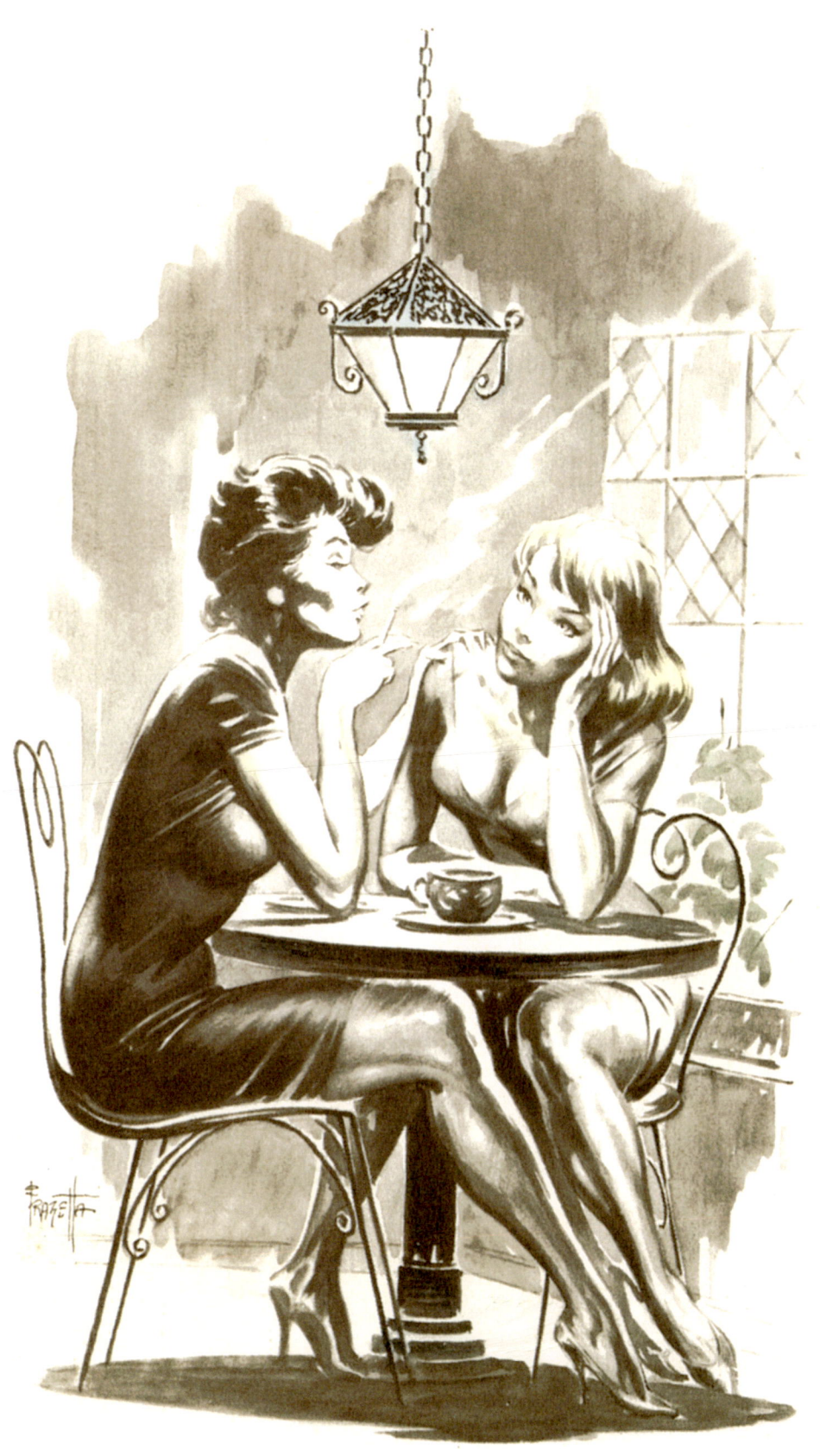

As Nina leaned forward the light stroked her shoulder and slipped into shadow over the soft curve of her breast.

Imitation Lovers, *Illustration #1.*

...continued from Page 24

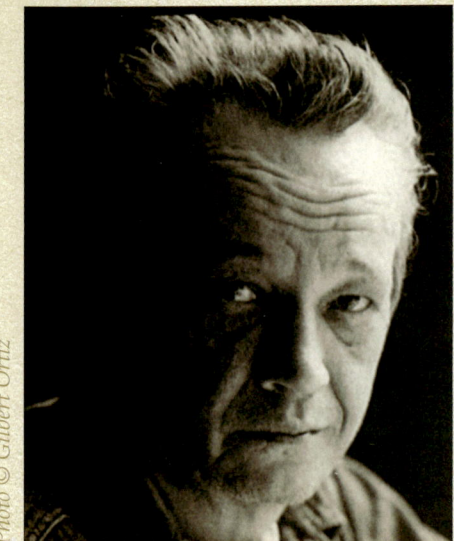

Photo © Gilbert Ortiz

art director. Soon after Frazetta moved on to better work with movie posters and oil paintings for paperback book covers, Dugger was replaced (at least as editor) by John Plunkett and the line expanded from just the risqué Midwood line in 1964, to add the Belmont-Tower line of non-fiction, historical adventure, mystery, and science-fiction.

Also added was the Tower Comics line headed by one of Shorten's old Archie associates, Samm Schwartz and one of Frazetta's old EC Comics colleagues, Wallace "Wally" Wood. Wood served as freelance creative director, editor, writer, and artist over the Tower adventure comics which were primarily Wood's own creations, The *T.H.U.N.D.E.R. Agents.*

Continued on Page 34

Her family refused to accept the fact that she was a lesbian, and she committed suicide. Marshall Dugger was Harry's right hand man, his art director, and a drunk. Every once in a while Harry would have to go out and get Dugger out of trouble someplace." Toward the end of his tenure, around the time of Frazetta's Midwood work, Dugger worked as the editor as well as

ABOVE:
Wallace "Wally" Wood, Frank Frazetta's friend from EC Comics, *Johnny Comet, Witzend,* etc.

RIGHT:
Tower's *Tippy Teen* comic. Harry Shorten's friend Samm Schwartz oversaw the comic intended for the Archie audience; Wood's *T.H.U.N.D.E.R. Agents* #1.

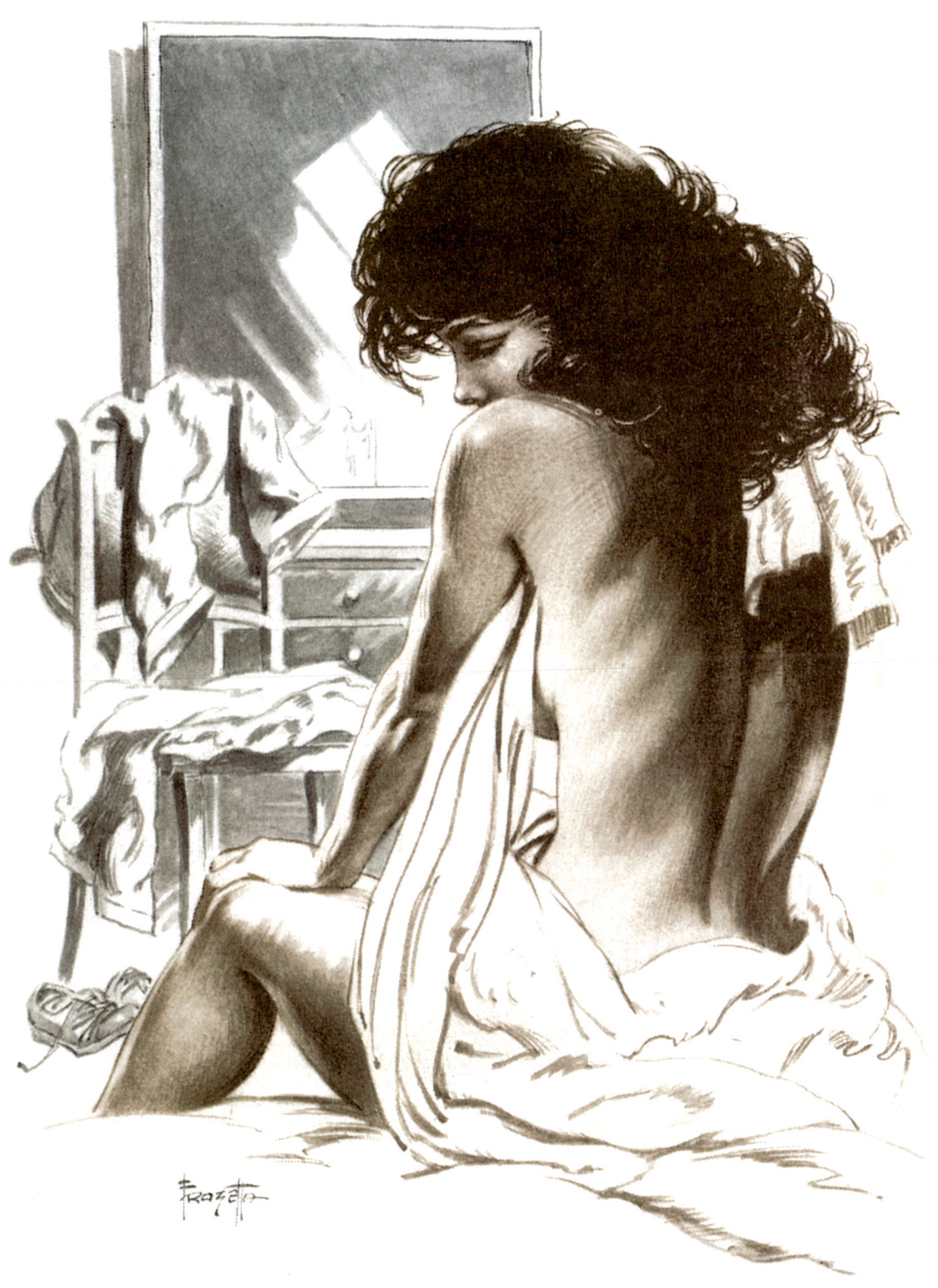

How could she have allowed it to happen? What had possessed her?
A cheap motel… three men… strangers…

Perfumed,
Illustration #5

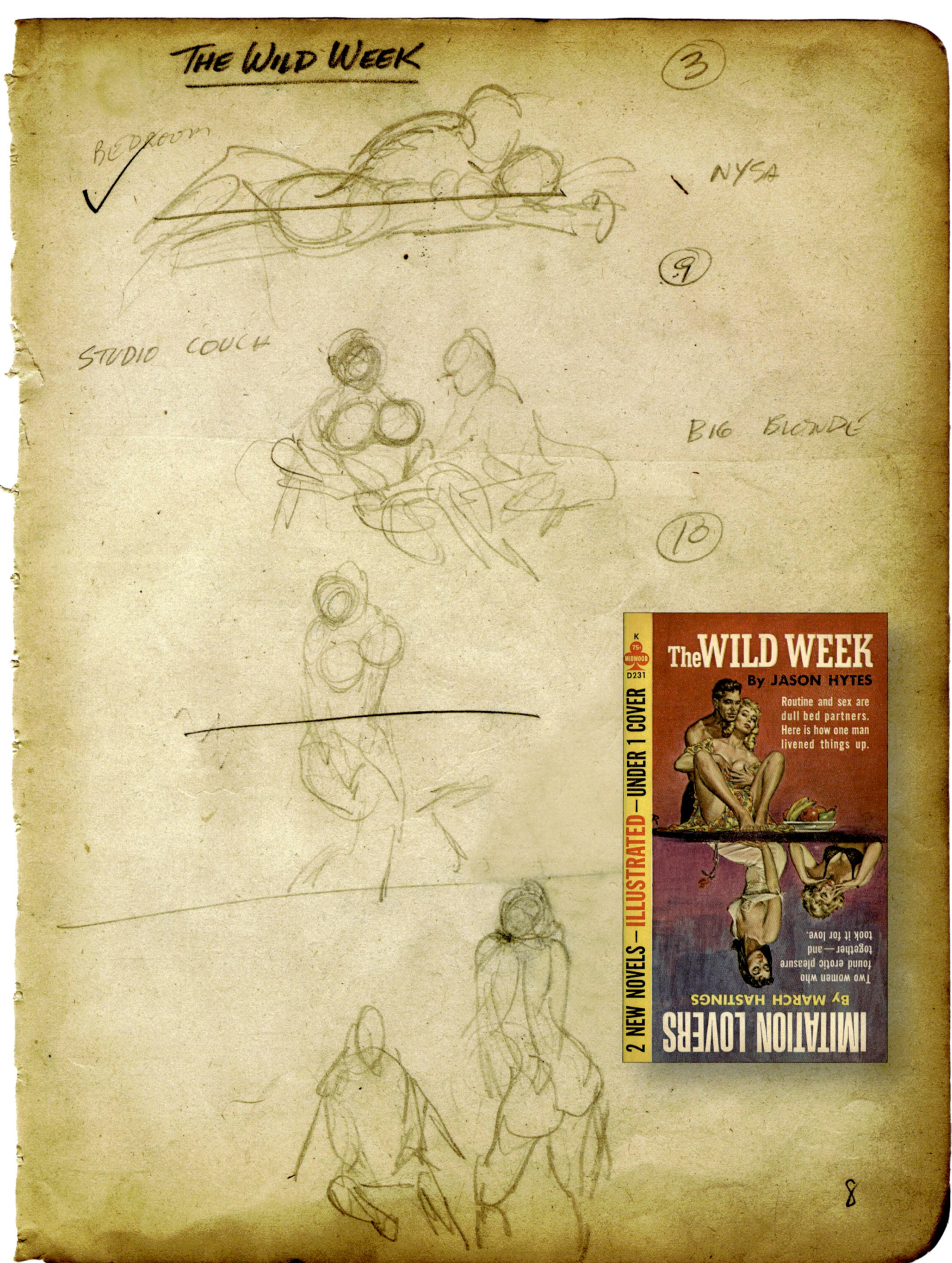

THE WILD WEEK

③

BEDROOM

NYSA

⑨

STUDIO COUCH

BIG BLONDE

⑩

8

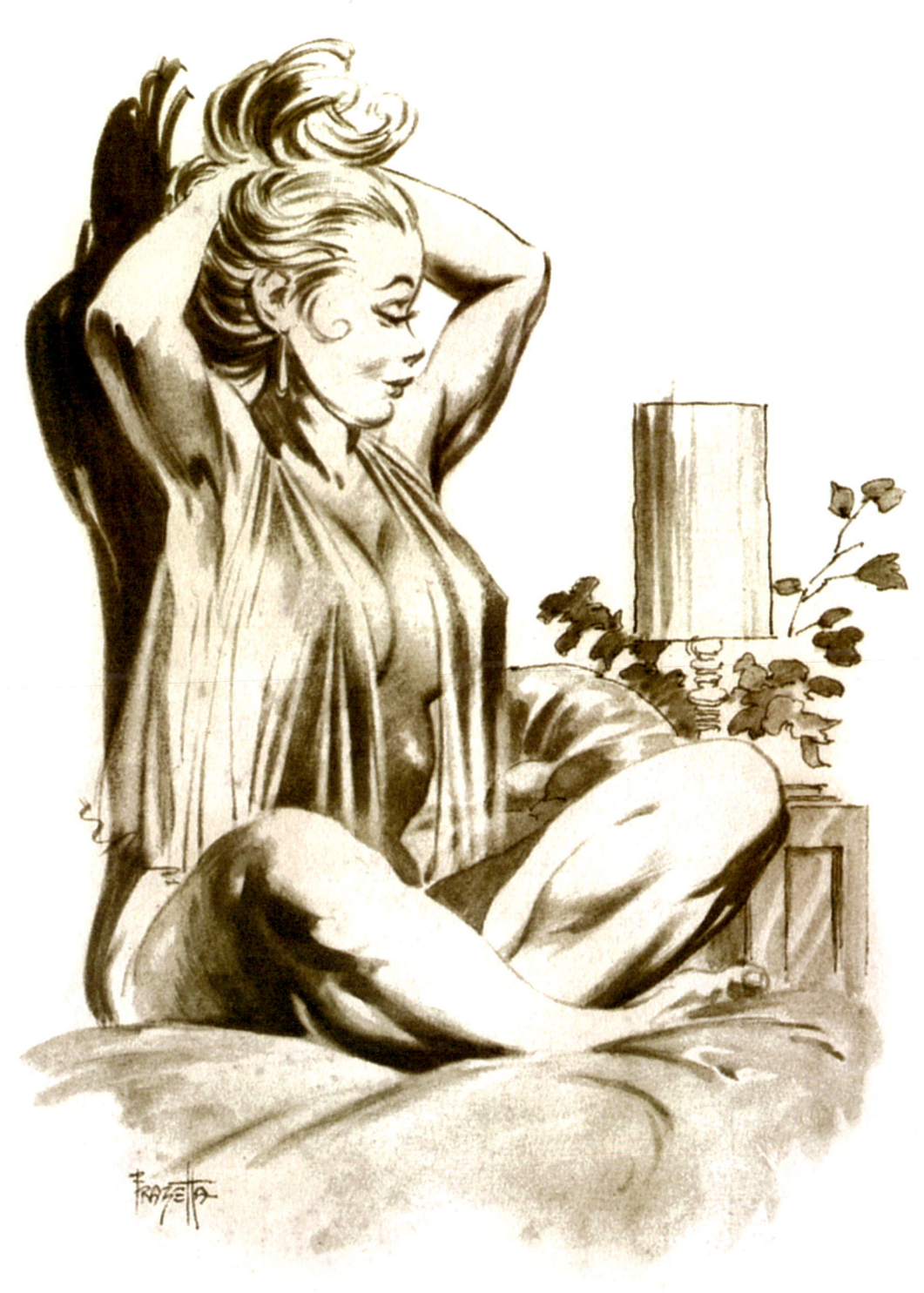

*As she sat there fixing her hair, the pose struck
him as being excitingly innocent.*

OPPOSITE
The Wild Week
and Imitation
Lovers,
*Midwood's
1963 illustrated
paperback,
featuring eight
more drawings,
with captions
from the text;
a preliminary
sketch page for
this title.*

THIS PAGE:
The Wild Week,
Illustration #1.

P, 22"
11
DRESSED
P, 26
NAKED BOTH
P. 26.
PATTI.

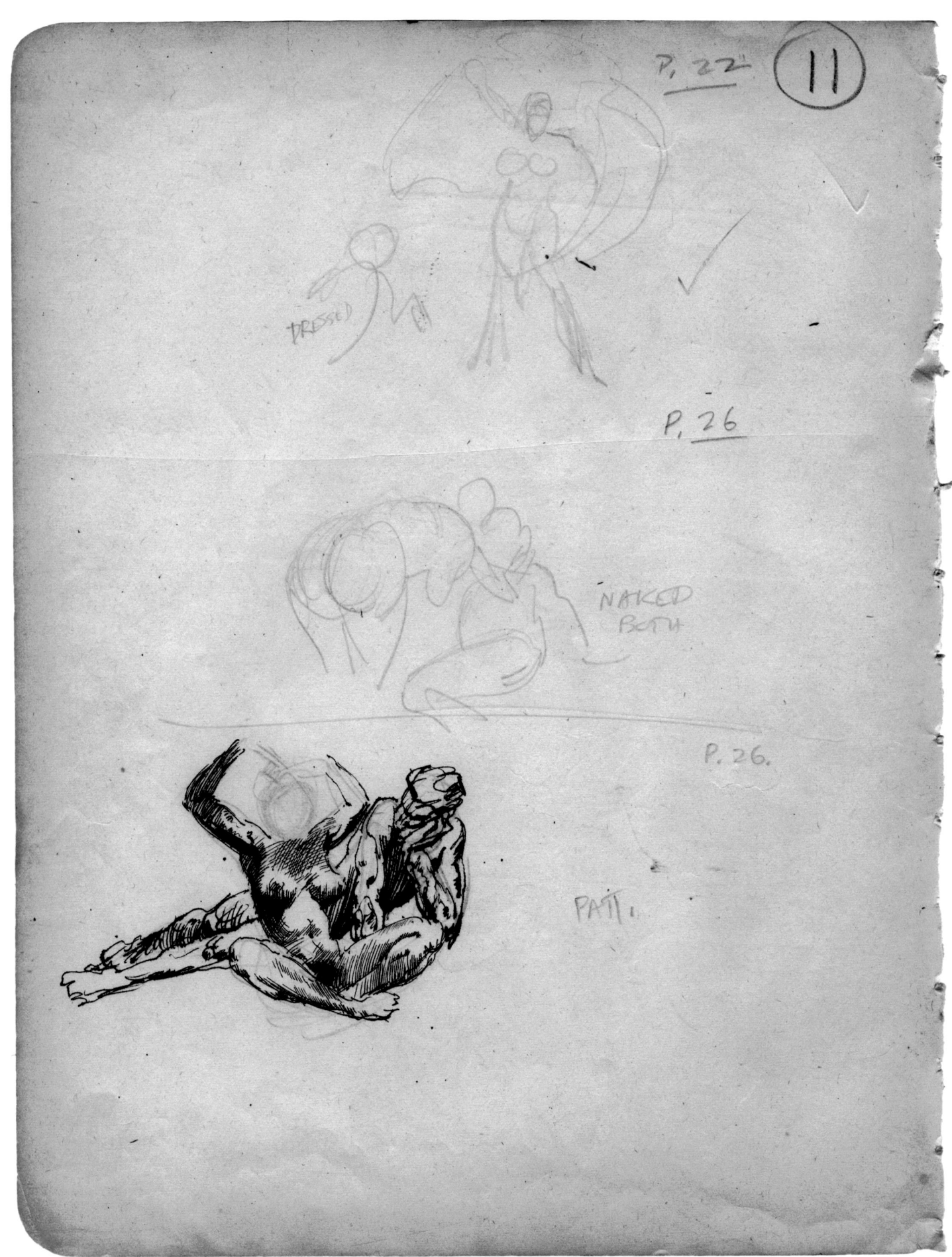

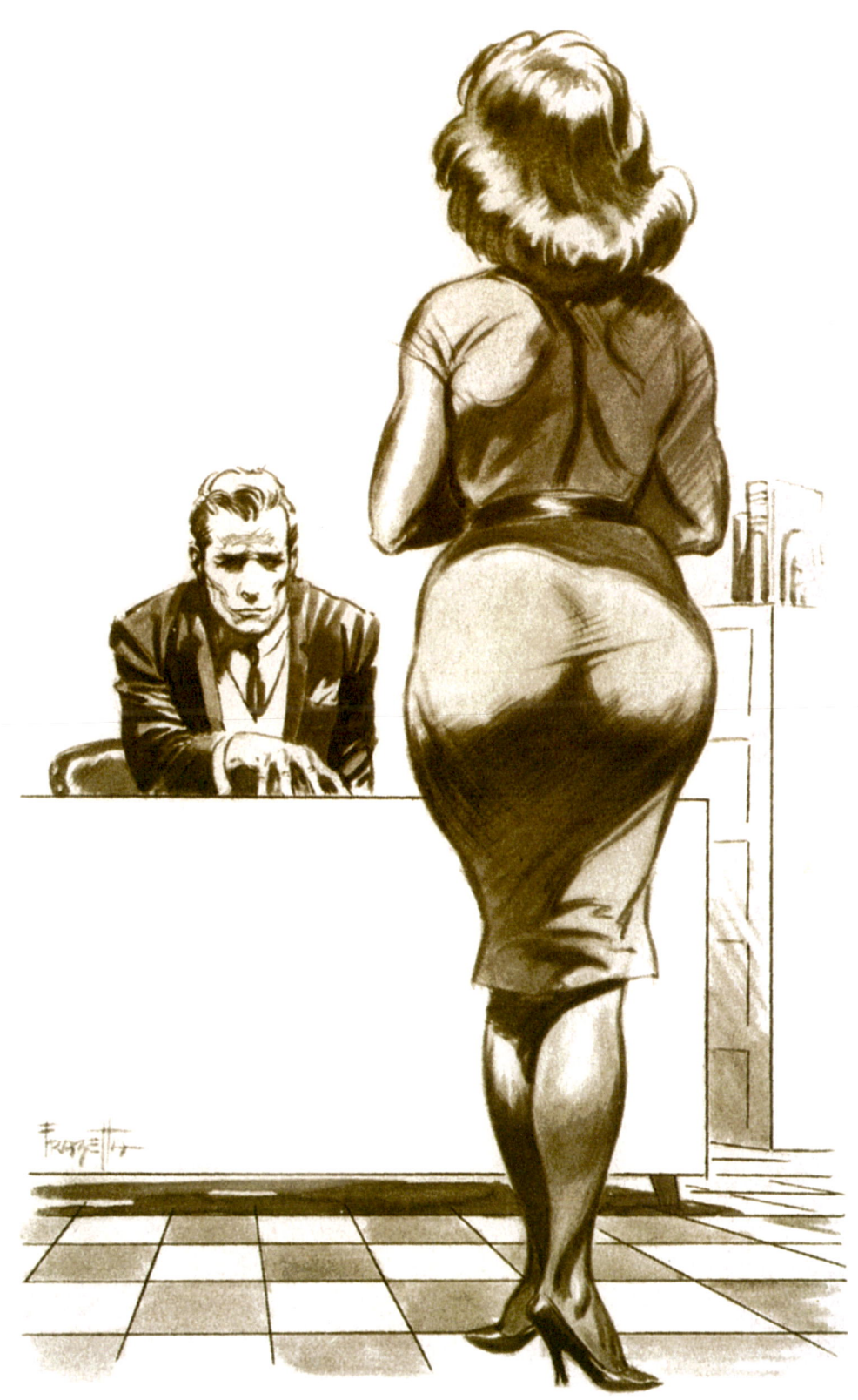

Richard looked up at her — she was a big girl — her hips and thighs sturdy in their roundness...

OPPOSITE:
a preliminary sketch page for this title.

The Wild Week, *Illustration #2.*

...continued from Page 28

From late 1965 through 1969. Schwartz primarily looked after Tower's *Tippy Teen* humor comic book, which was designed to sell to the same audience as *Archie*.

Munroe: *"Around 1970 there were sweeping changes in the content of 'adult paperbacks' in America as a direct result of certain decisions made by the Supreme Court about what constituted pornography. What were tame paperbacks in the Sixties became something else in the Seventies. At the same time, for unrelated reasons, Paul Rader stopped supplying Midwood covers."* Gil Fox said, "Harry [Shorten] never had any involvement with the Mafia. [Midwood and] the adult book business collapsed [in the early 1980s] when the Mafia came in and took over the bookstores and said they would only sell books by their own publishers. And they started printing and selling absolute garbage."

> •••• 66 ••••
> *When you start doing pornography, there ain't no way it can be in good taste. And for the most part it isn't beautiful. There's a difference between sexuality and pornography. Pornography is just plain dirty. Sex can be beautiful. You can suggest it and you can do it so it's not explicit and yet it's sensuous as hell. You can get great joy out of it and you'd probably be more stimulated by that than some trashy stuff.*
>
> — FRANK FRAZETTA

A sensual energy was inherent in everything Frazetta did. If an assignment was not meant to be sensuous, Frazetta would either find a creative way to insert sensuality into it or he would have little interest in the job and try to finish it as quickly as possible. The artist told this author, "I like to get juicy" — which has a double meaning; relating to a lushness in his art but also, that he would warm up to doing a job by doing some personal art that was even more sensual than his published works. Discussing the sensuous side of Frazetta's work with his wife, Ellie, she would quickly say, "Those were men's magazines, my husband doesn't do pornography."

Frank likewise, saw a great difference between producing art that was filled with beautiful, sensual people and pornographic art which is designed solely to physically arouse.

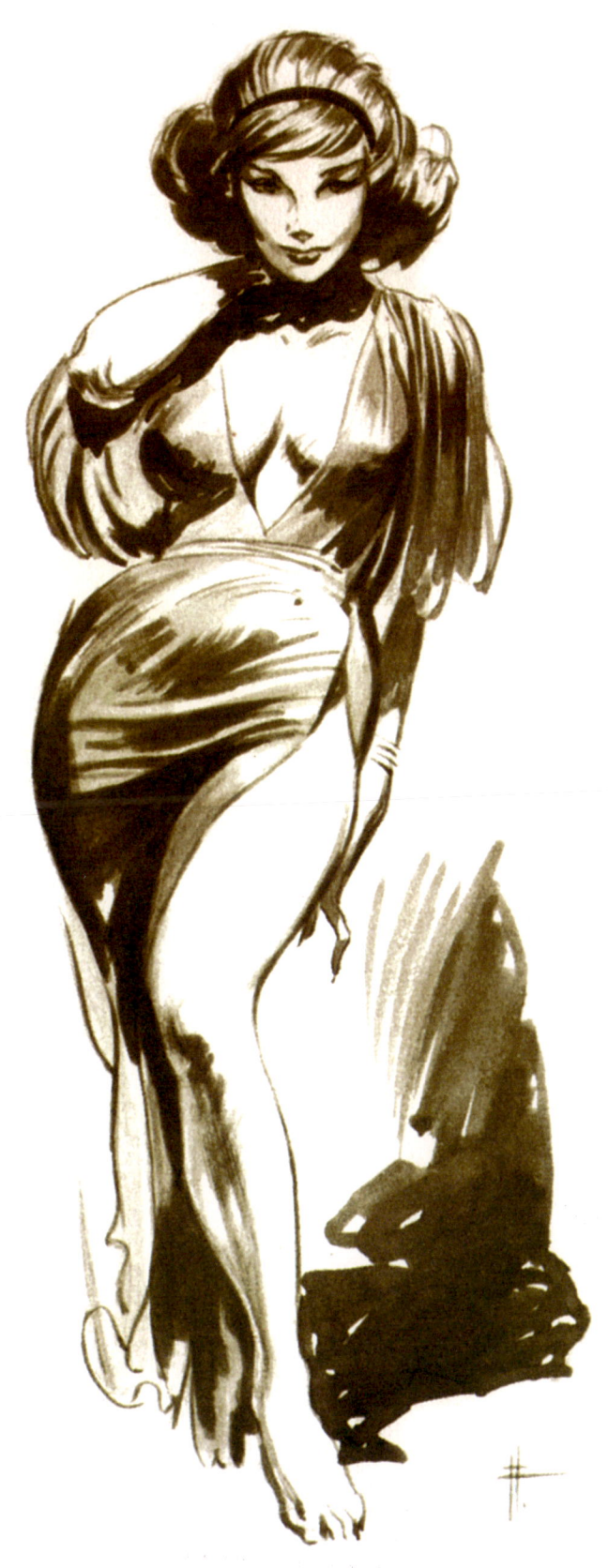

*Patti glided toward him, an elusive half smile on
her glistening lips...*

Frazetta was a true artist and even when he was producing art for comic books, to be reproduced as solid black line art, he would put in subtle, unnecessary tonality in the original art, knowing it would not reproduce but also knowing the actual art was more beautiful for it. Likewise, when producing tonal art for black and white reproduction, some artists' originals reveal slight hues of color — or at least, an aged patina. Unfortunately, the vast majority of the original art to Frazetta's early-to-

• • • • • 66 • • • • •

I [draw and paint] beautiful women, so damn pretty. Everybody likes to dream — and if ya have 'em in your brush, why not? Funny thing about my girls — I'm an ass man. Not a breast man. Oh, I love incredible breasts. But... [the] ass, that brings out the animal in me. They told me, 'Frank, you paint all those hairs. You just don't have to.' They don't know I separate the camel's hairs on my brush and load each hair and just swirl on the hair — ha!

— FRANK FRAZETTA

Interviewed by Donald Newlove in 1977 for Esquire *magazine.*

mid-1960s men's magazine and sensuous paperback art, is not known to have survived. Without the original art to shoot from, here, we incorporate the finest, state-of-the-art techniques to reproduce from the very rare, 1960s published artifacts. But, in an effort to better emulate the subtleties, warmth, and slight chroma of the lost Frazetta originals, we have enhanced the tent of the paperback illustrations here — some more than others. We hope you enjoy the effect.

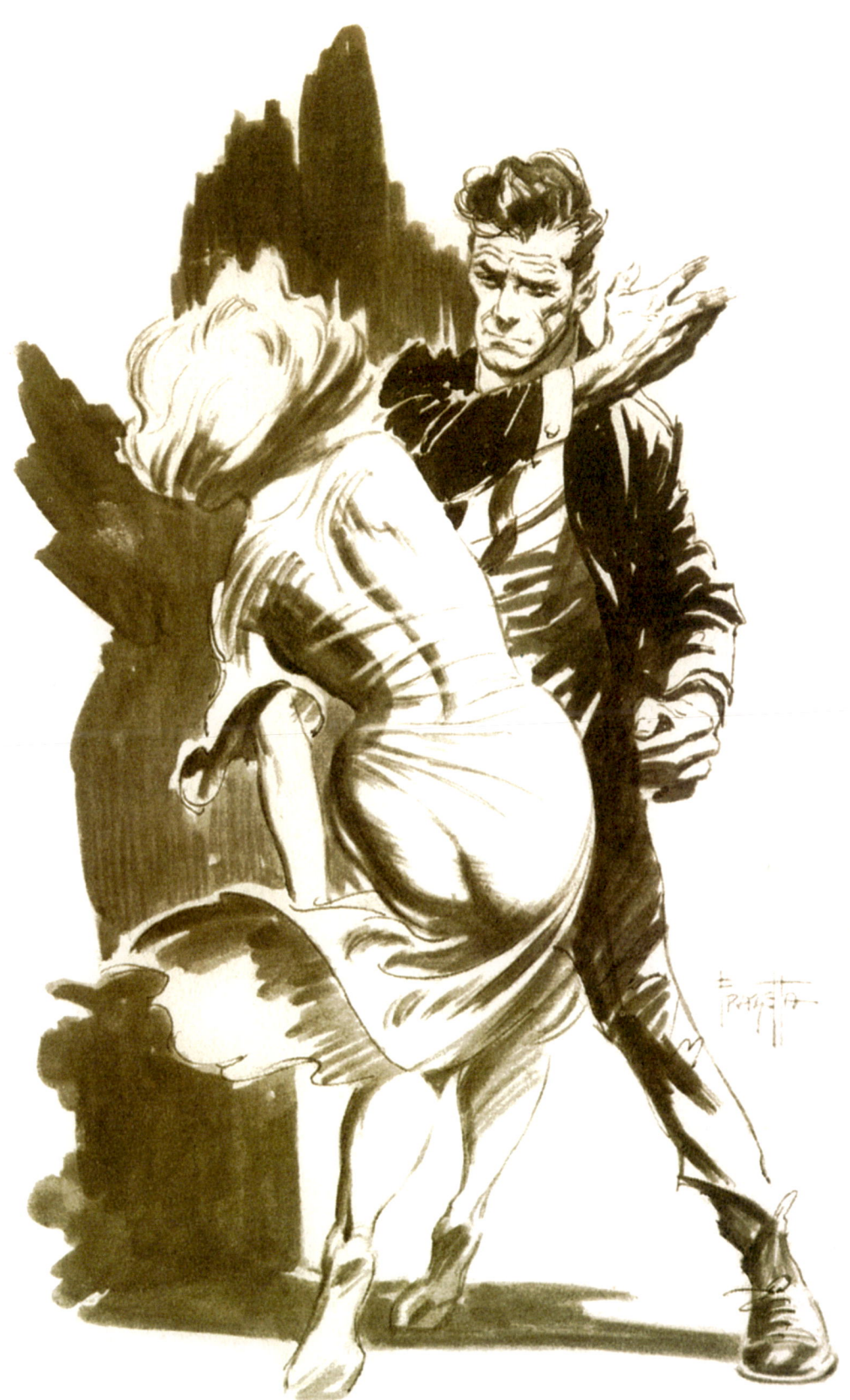

The sound of the blow echoed sharply. Patti stumbled away from him, her robe sliding free of her thrusting breasts...

The Wild Week, *Illustration #4.*

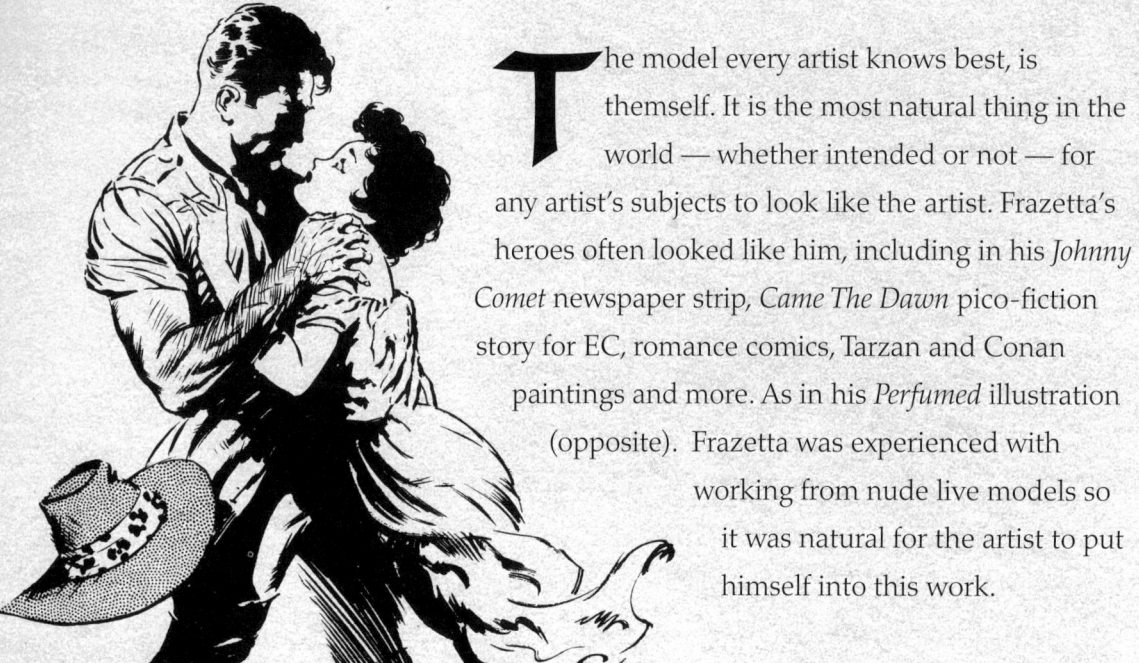

The model every artist knows best, is themself. It is the most natural thing in the world — whether intended or not — for any artist's subjects to look like the artist. Frazetta's heroes often looked like him, including in his *Johnny Comet* newspaper strip, *Came The Dawn* pico-fiction story for EC, romance comics, Tarzan and Conan paintings and more. As in his *Perfumed* illustration (opposite). Frazetta was experienced with working from nude live models so it was natural for the artist to put himself into this work.

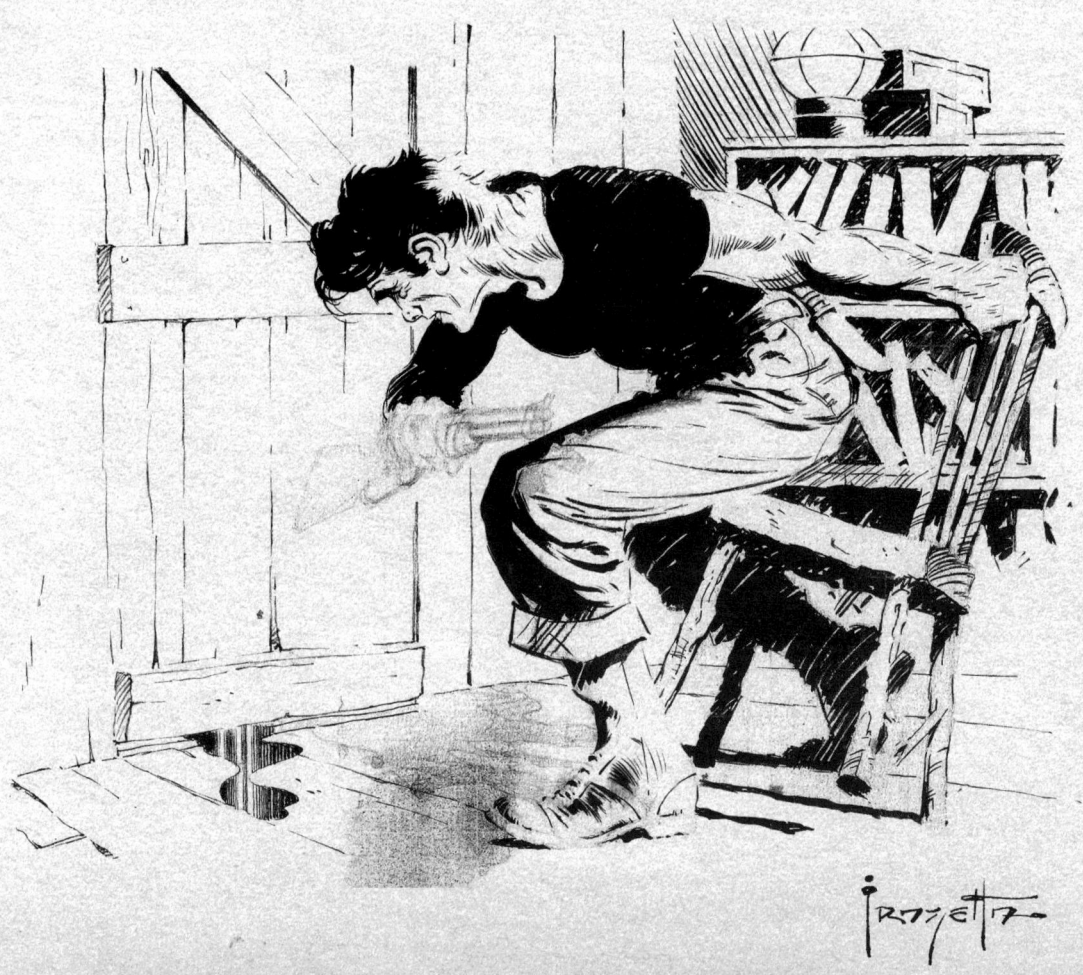

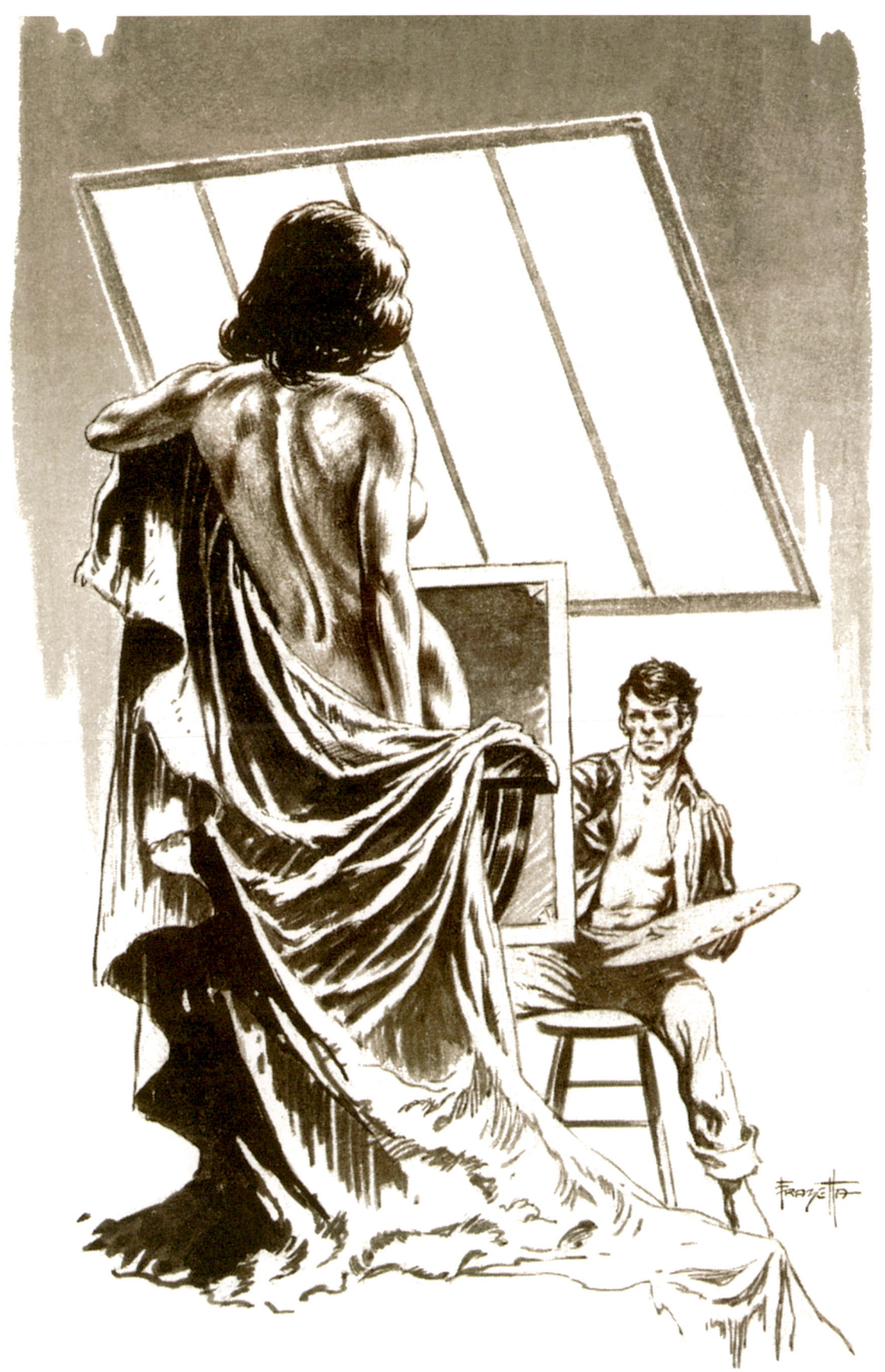

She struck the familiar pose with a knowing smile.
"What part of me would you like to work on today?" she asked throatily.

Perfumed,
Illustration #4

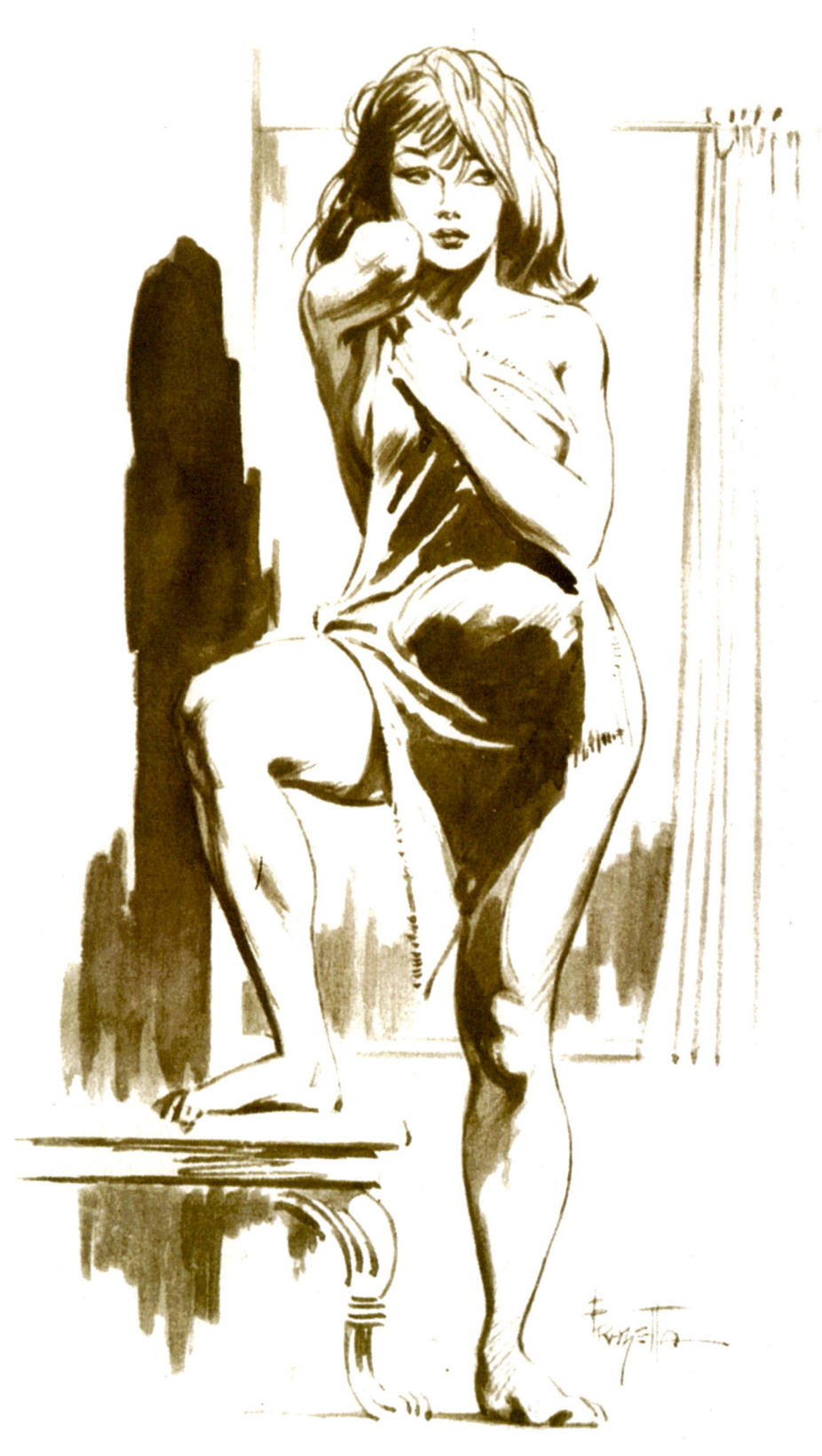

Imitation
Lovers,
Illustration #3.

*Nina came naked into the bathroom, a damp towel
hanging from her shoulders!*

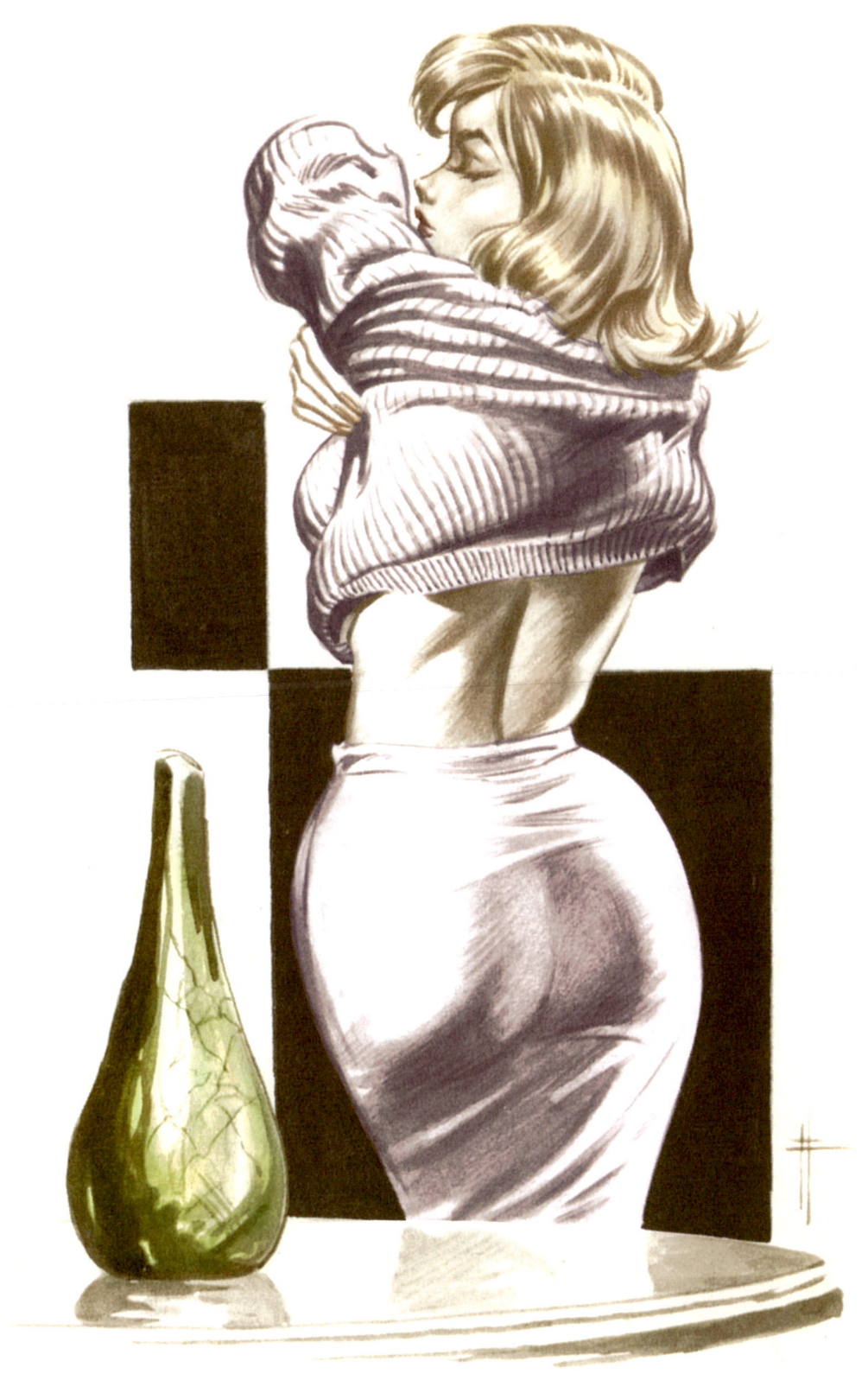

*Quietly in the darkness she undressed, fumbling
with buttons and zippers and hooks...*

Imitation
Lovers,
Illustration #2.

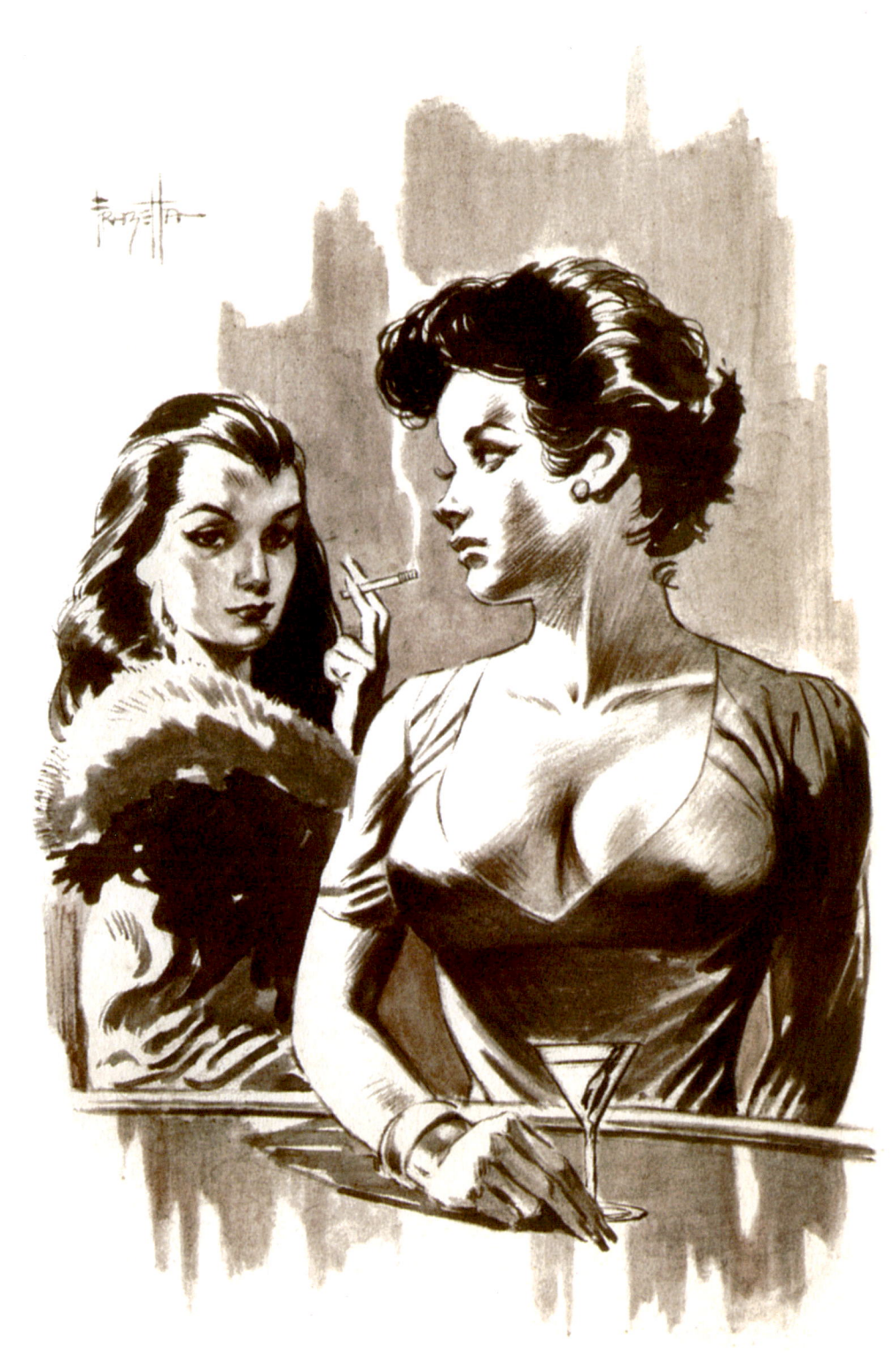

*She felt eyes looking up at her, curious eyes that
wanted to take her clothes off...*

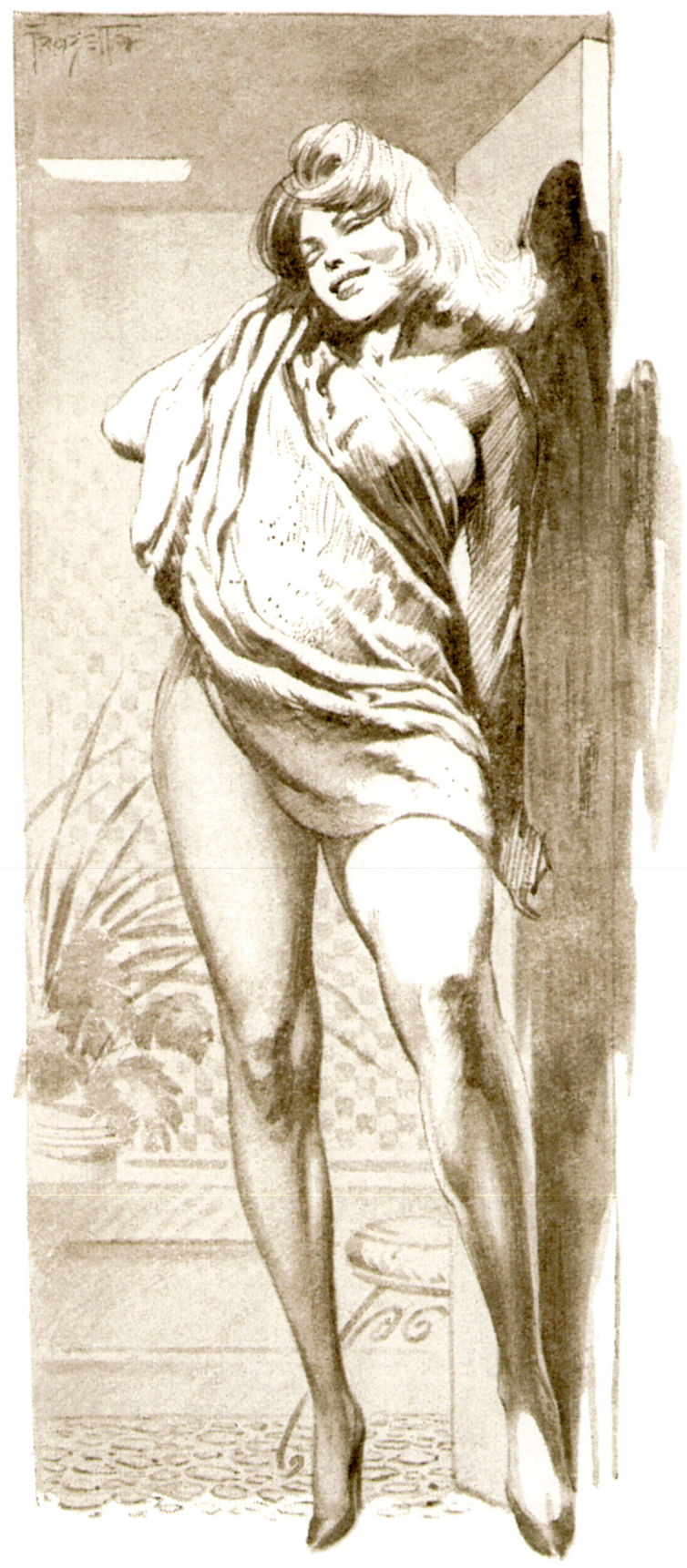

She strolled out of the bathroom with sensuous steps.

Dangerous Age,
Illustration #4.

Other than the previously mentioned *Sensuous Frazetta* fanzine on cheap newsprint, which printed only 21 of Frazetta's 26 Midwood men's paperback illustrations, and none of his men's magazine art; there was a similar collection called *Captain George's Comic World* #15 (Memory Lane Publications, 1970), which featured 22 of Frazetta's Midwood illustrations and a single Canaveral drawing. Some years later, in 1990, Eros Comics published a small, comic-book sized collection entitled, *Baby, You're Really Something!* which was titled after the illustration of the same name. The piece originally ran as the first illustration for *Dangerous Age* (Midwood, 1964).

Until the new, vastly expanded Vanguard Frazetta Classics edition of *The Sensuous Frazetta* which you now hold in your hands, *Baby, You're Really Something!* was the best most people could do to see samples of this rare, early 1960s sensuous work by Frazetta. *Baby, You're Really Something!* was reproduced with some production help by this author, J. David Spurlock, from the collection of artist-author-professor, Kenneth Smith, a friend of Frazetta's who, like Frazetta, was one of the cover painters for Warren Publishing's 1960s and '70s magazines, *Creepy* and *Eerie*. *Baby, You're Really Something!* included reprints of all 26 Midwood illustrations, one *Gent* magazine and one *Cavalcade* magazine illustration.

TWO NEW NOVELS UNDER ONE COVER
ILLUSTRATED

THE DANGEROUS AGE
Joan Ellis

BAD BY CHOICE
Jason Hytes

Baby, you're really something!

CLASSIC GOOD GIRL ART BY FRANK FRAZETTA

EROS comix

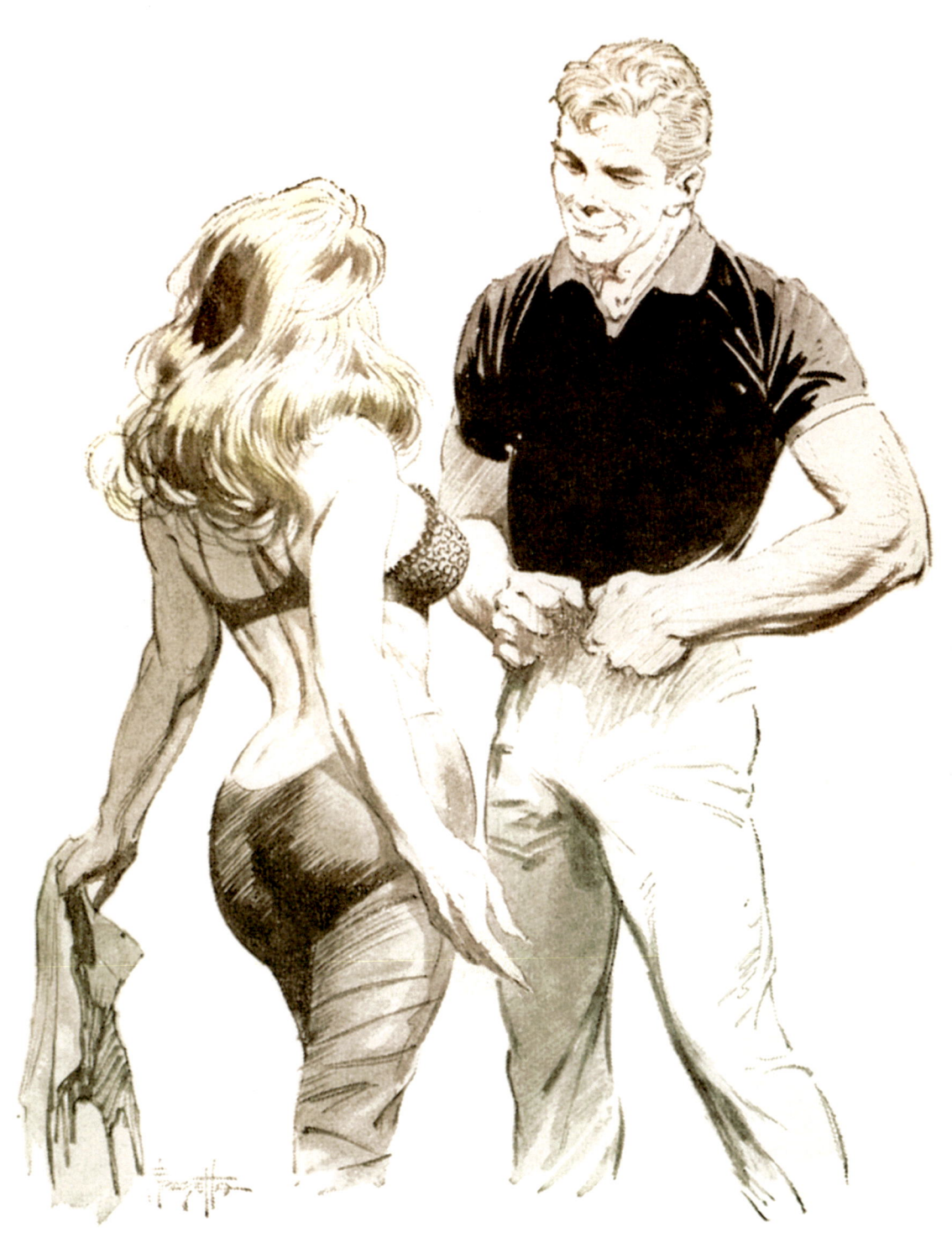

"Baby, you're really something!"

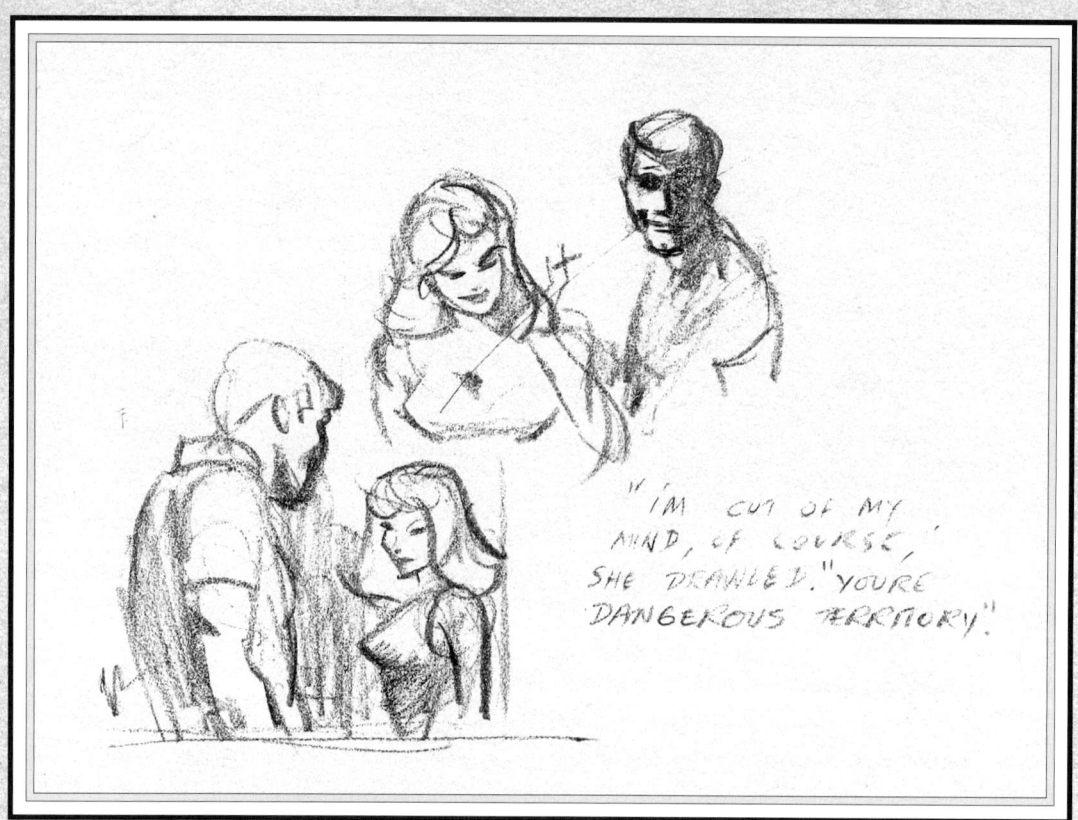

"I'M OUT OF MY MIND, OF COURSE," SHE DRAWLED. "YOU'RE DANGEROUS TERRITORY!"

Here, we show some of Frazetta's Midwood preliminary sketches. They are interesting when compared to the finished, published art, for both their contrasts and similarities. While the artist might experiment with the angle of view

Preliminary sketches to Illustration #2.

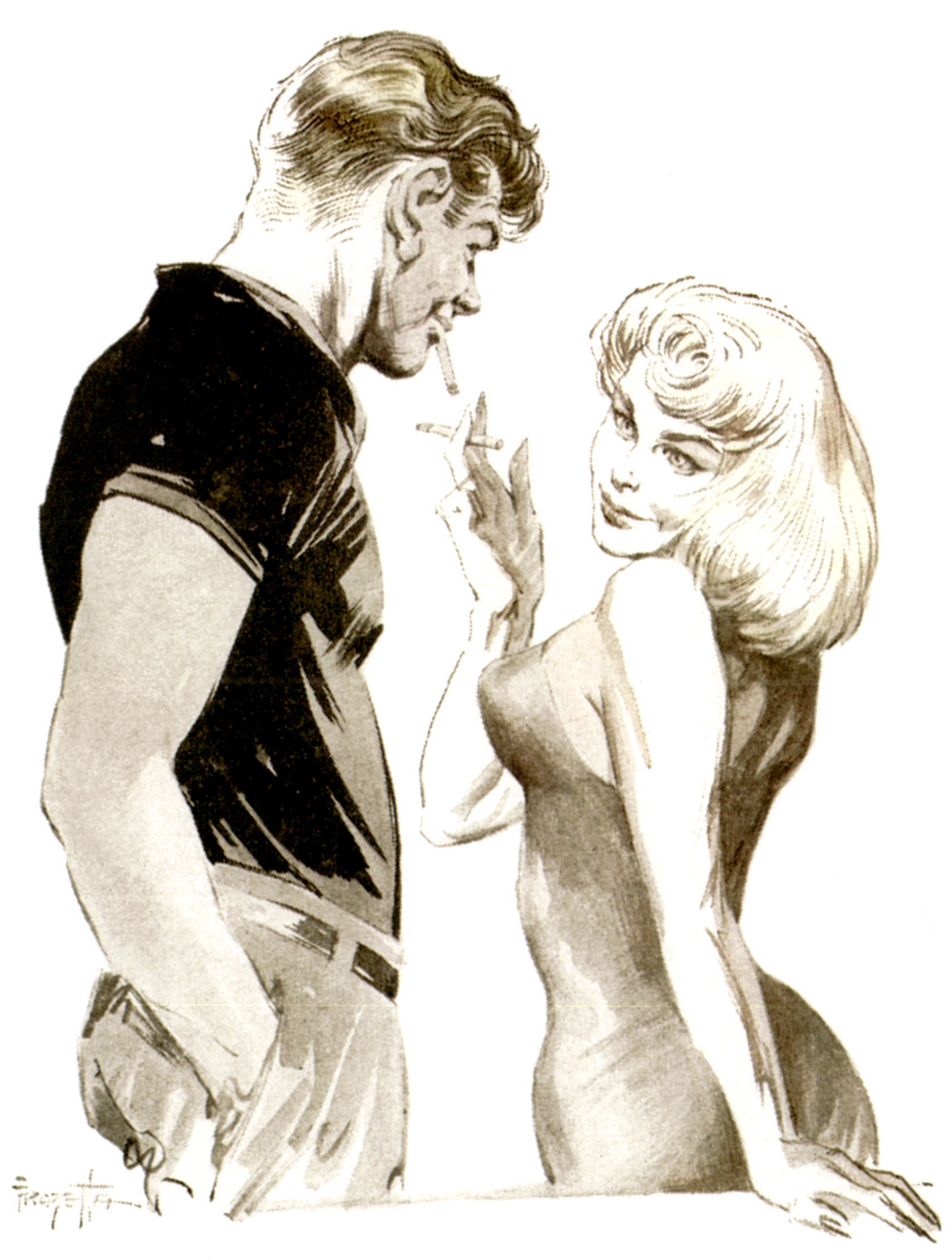

*"I must be out of my mind," she drawled.
"You're dangerous territory."*

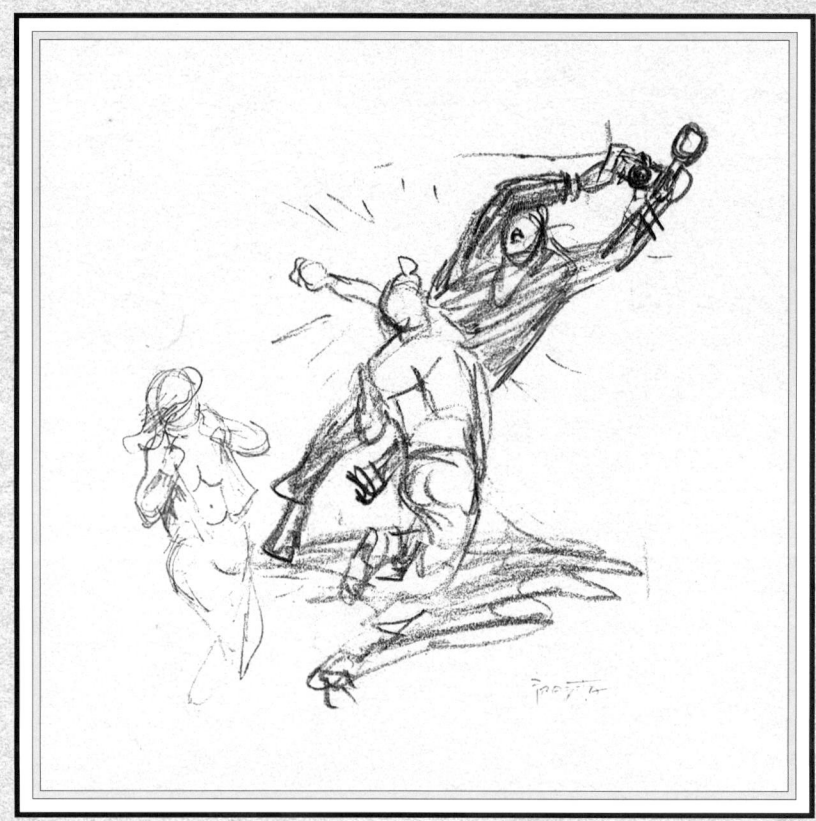

and/or composition, frequently, Frazetta's preliminaries are amazingly similar to his final compositions. Various factors come to play here, including his outstanding talent as well as a visual memory which borders

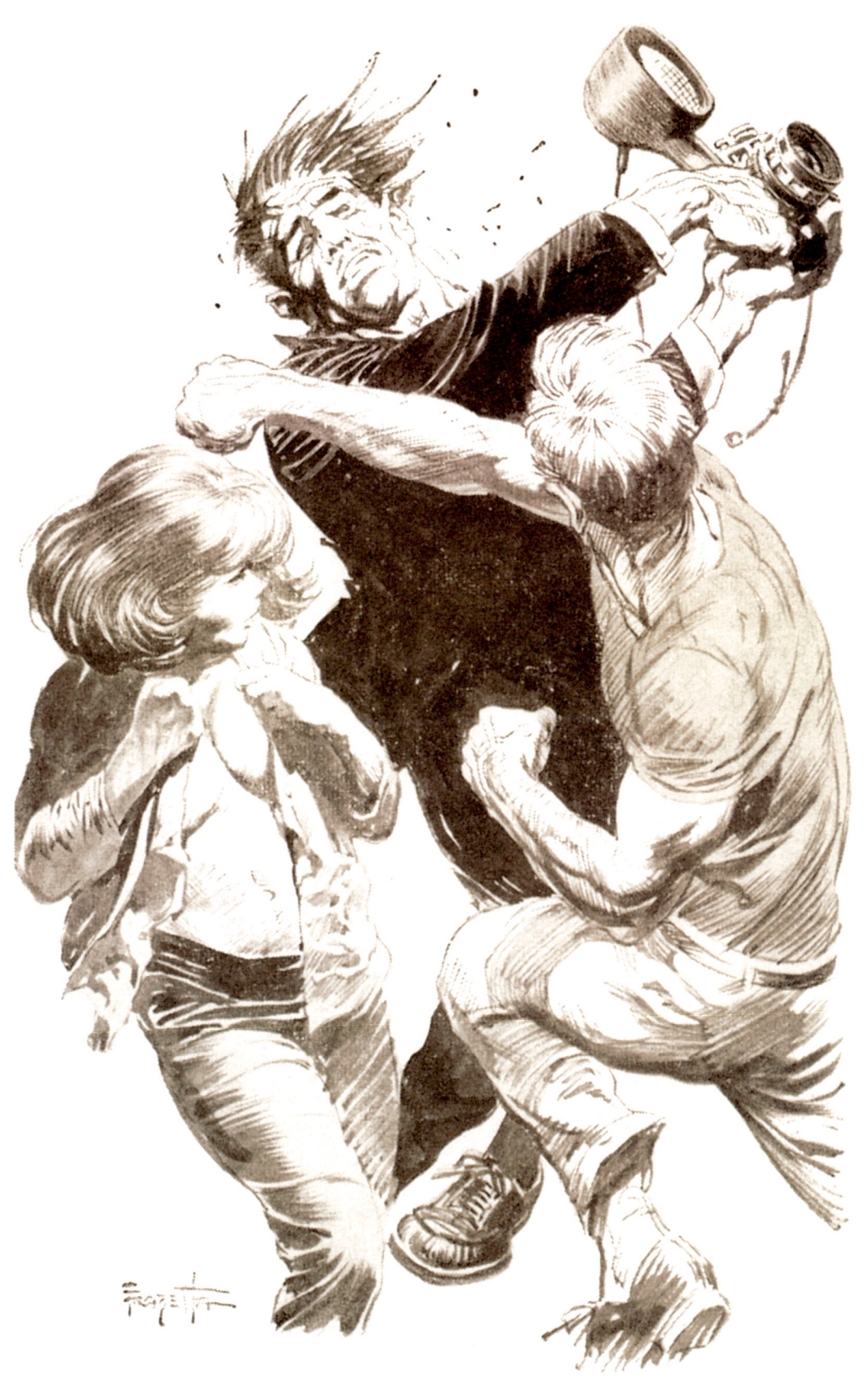

"What dirty sheet are you trying to make with this?"

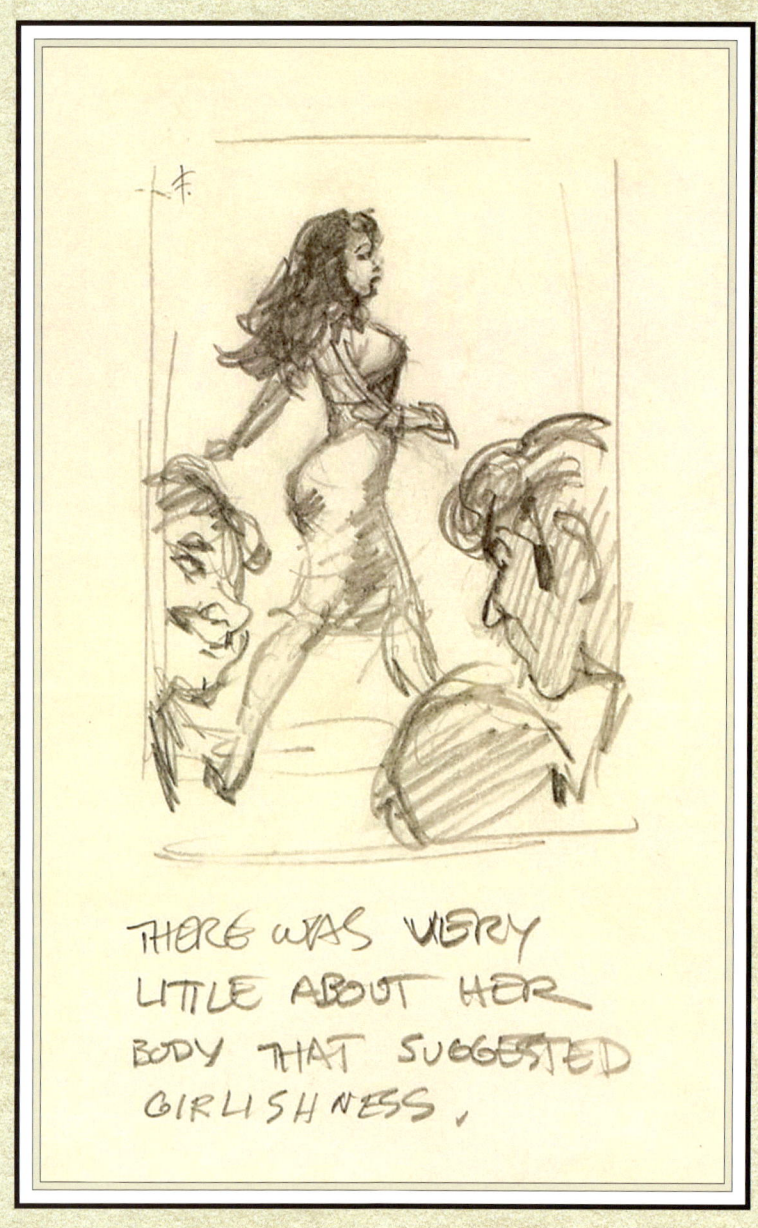

THERE WAS VERY
LITTLE ABOUT HER
BODY THAT SUGGESTED
GIRLISHNESS.

on the photographic. Also, unlike his friend and associate Roy Krenkel, who produced prodigious number of prelims for nearly every illustration, Frazetta felt that doing too many

Preliminary sketch to Illustration #1.

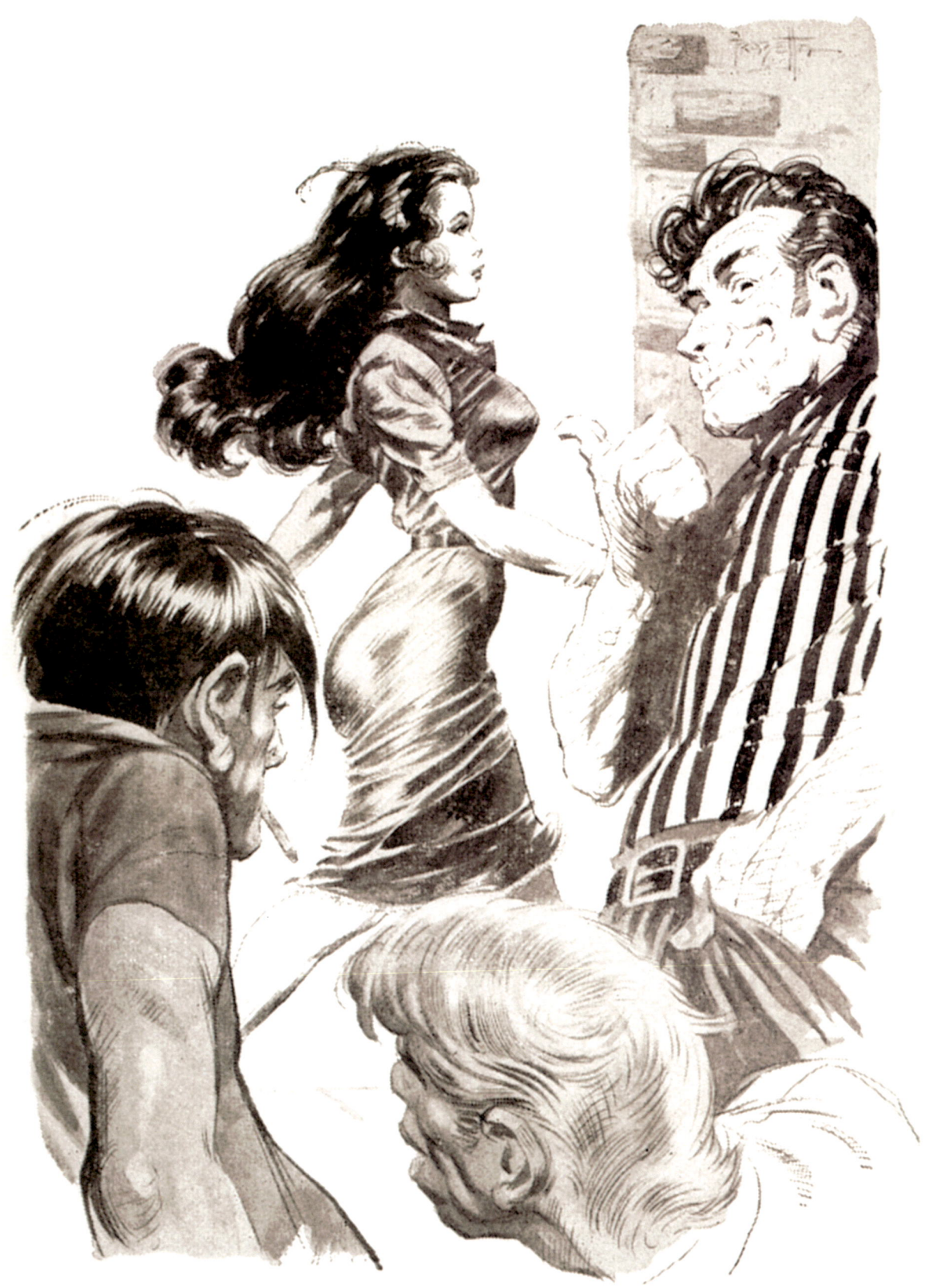

There was very little about her body that suggested girlishness.

Bad By Choice,
Illustration #1.

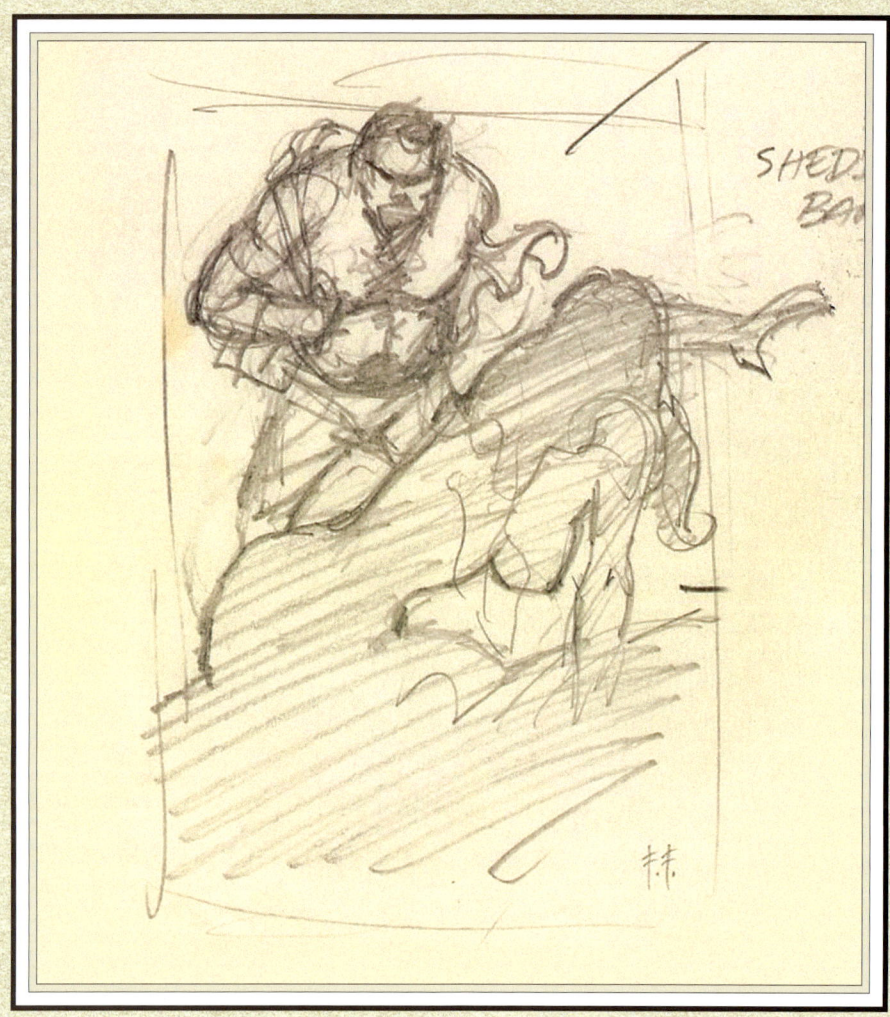

preliminaries would suck the vitality out of
the work; that if too many were done, the
artist would have nothing left to "say" in the
finished art.

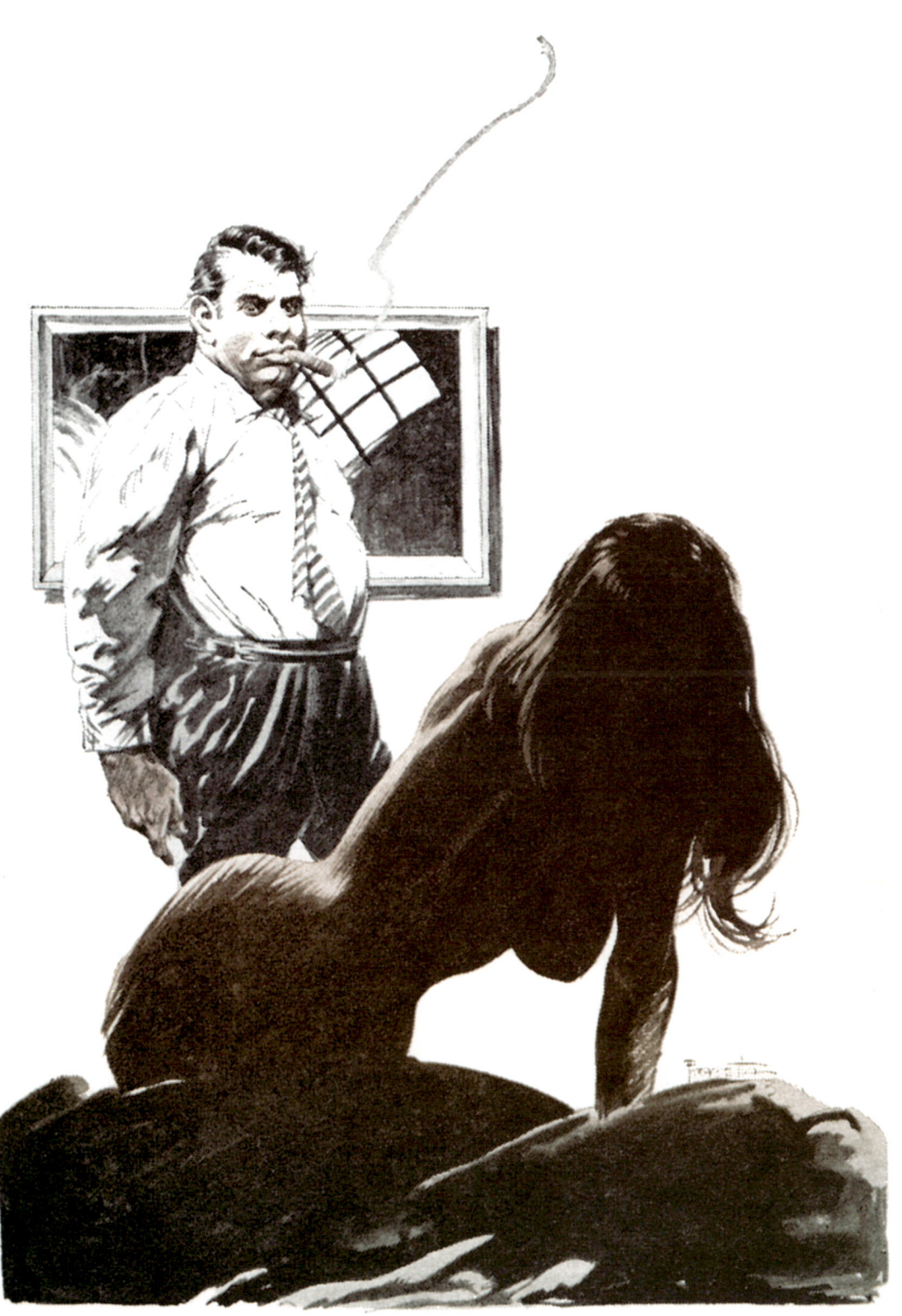

Snyder stood there, devouring her with his hungry eyes.

Bad By Choice,
Illustration #2.

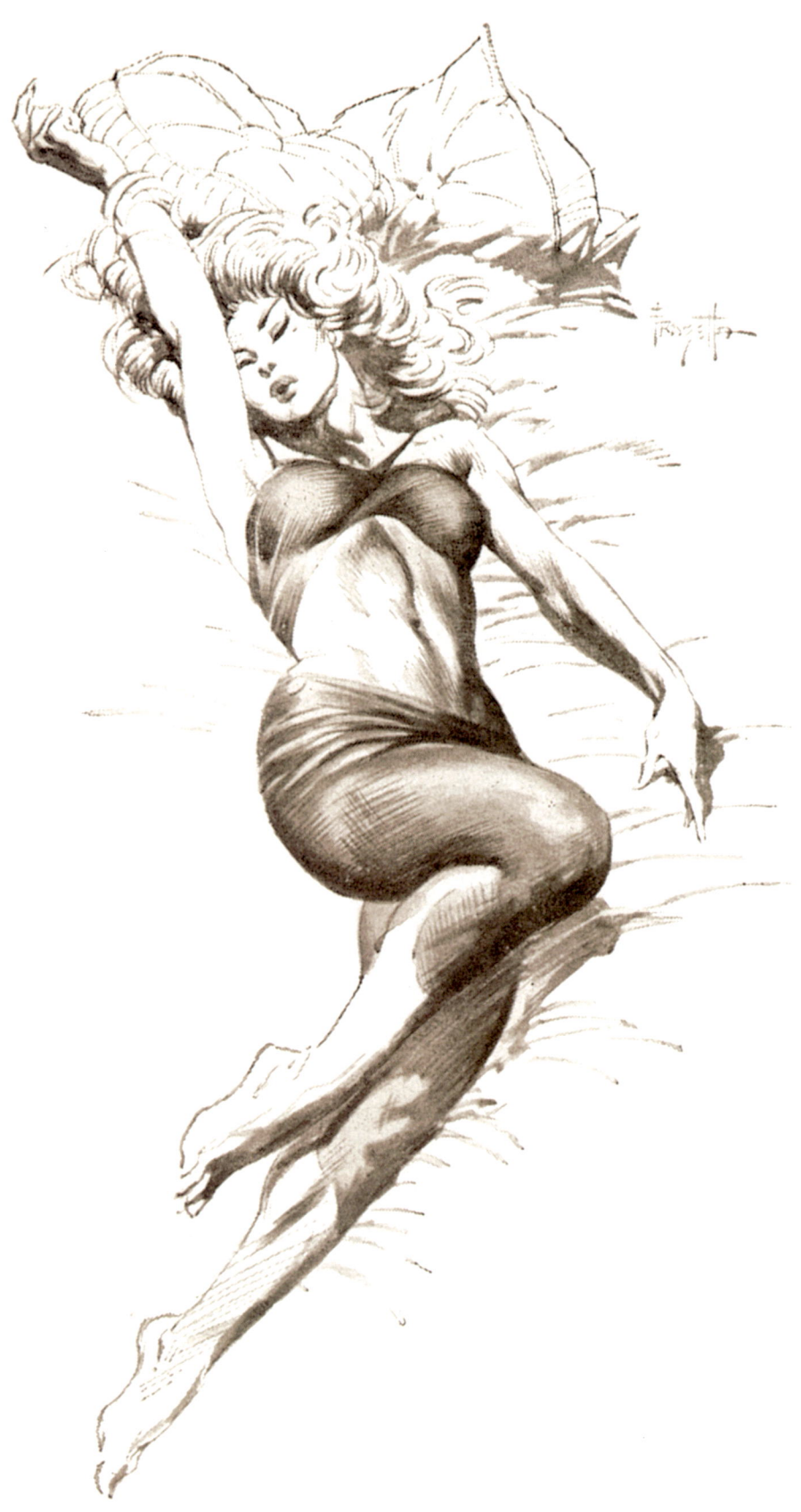

Terry stretched lazily, her superb figure uncurling with catlike grace.

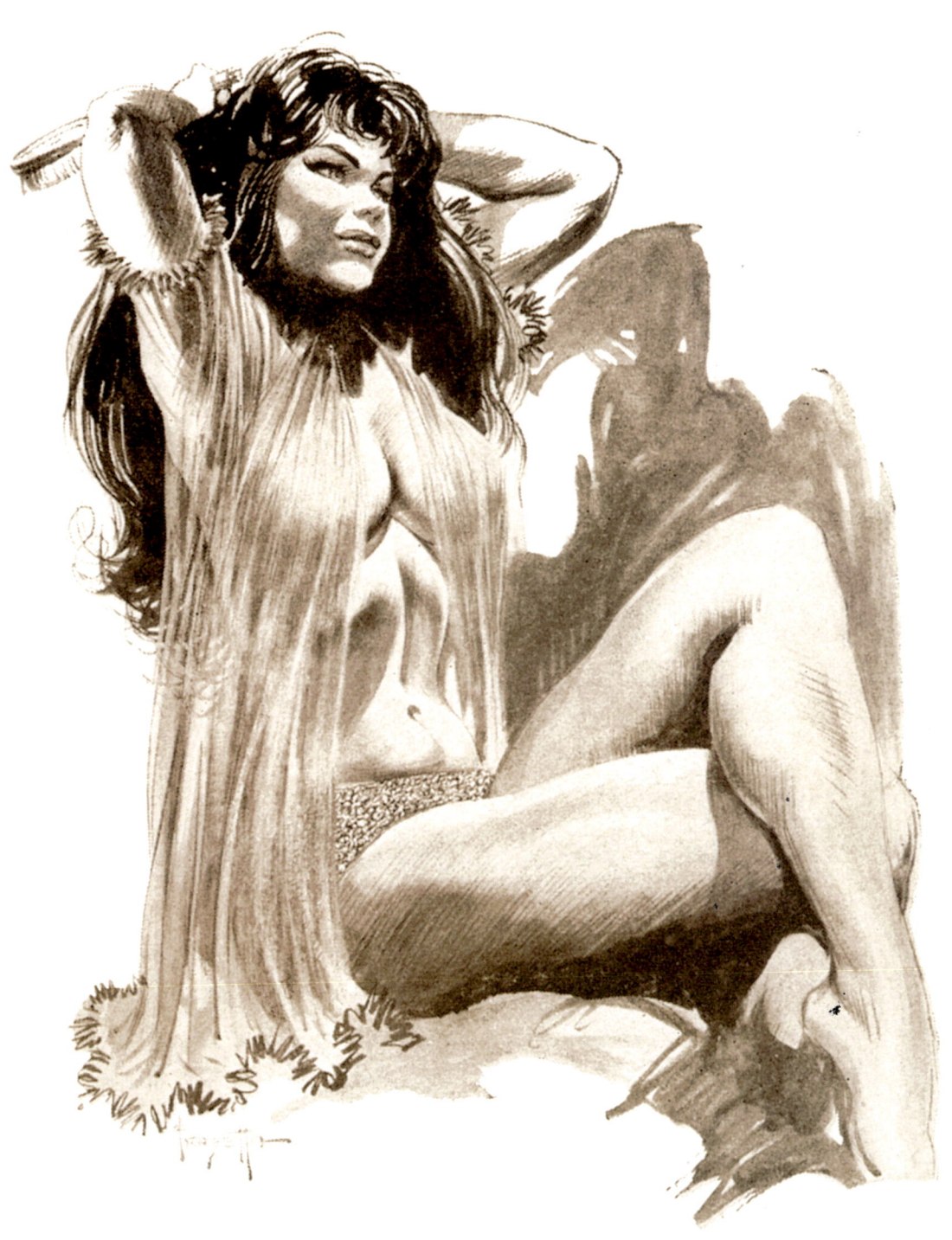

A flimsy pink negligee covered her firmly rounded body.

Bad By Choice,
Illustration #4.

SOMEBODY FELL! YEAH! HIM! HARRY! HE'D FALLEN, ALL RIGHT! RIGHT ON HIS FACE! SMACK INTO TROUBLE! THAT'S WHAT DAMES WERE! TROUBLE! THIS ONE! THIS CORA! HE'D HAVE TO MARRY HER UNLESS ... UNLESS ...
HARRY! WHAT ARE YOU STARING AT?
YOU, CORA!
CAU
DO NOT

IMPACT
NO. 13
MAR.
SHOCK
10¢
SUSPENSTORIES
JOLTING TALES OF TENSION IN THE EC TRADITION!

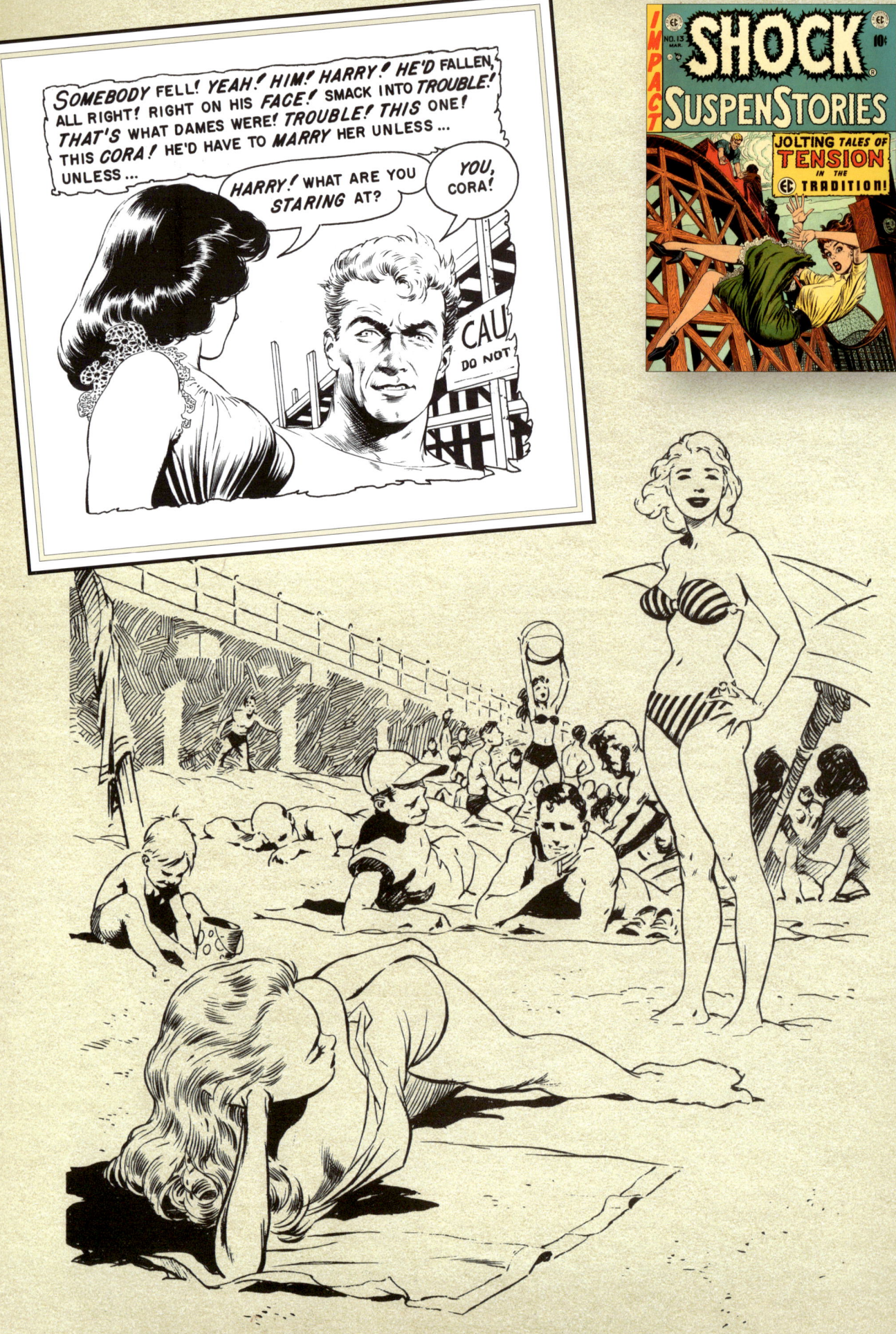

CHAPTER TWO
ROMANCE & CIGARETTES
SEQUENTIAL ART

Interviewed by Gary Groth in 1994 for *The Comics Journal*, Frazetta said, "I never heard about paperbacks in [the 1950s]. It just didn't occur to me that I could actually paint for a living. I dreamed about… making lots of money, doing my own [newspaper] strip." Frazetta did sample strips *Nina, Sweet Adeline, Buster Crabbe,* and *Tiga,* which Frazetta created in 1948, dialogued by Joe Greene, a scriptwriter for Standard Comics. The Tiga work was ultimately published as "Last Chance" in Wallace Wood's *WITZEND* magazine #3 in 1967 with new text by Wood and his associate, Bill Pearson.

Frazetta continued, "The handling of the pen — or brush — is very difficult. [For] comic books, about 90 percent of [the work] is brush. But it's just getting that control and the dexterity that goes with it. If you do it long enough, it becomes second nature. I did my love stories… I did the *Johnny Comet* strip for [two] years, drawing every single day, and I got better and better, and then right on into the *Buck Rogers* covers. It's like being an athlete — if you're out of shape, you can't fight, you can't run, you can't leap… Gotta get back in shape. And it holds true of art. Even if you can think and visualize the same, [if] that dexterity is gone, you have to get in there and start hacking away to warm up, and it begins to happen, gradually. My inking was at its all-time high [then]. I think [my] *Weird Science-Fantasy* cover is the ultimate in inking technique. Not that the drawing is all that perfect, or the concepts are all that great, but just the inking style itself was… I was just flying."

Some of Frazetta's comic book work seemed likewise, designed to attract attention from the newspaper strip syndicates including *Louie Lazybones, Thun'da,* and his romance comics, which are stunning. Each page — if not panel — is brimming with sensuality. From one story to the next, they seem to get better than the last — building to one of the greatest works in the history of comics, "Untamed Love."

From Dr. Dave Winiewicz' online blog, Frazetta said, "Not only do I want my line to form a figure, but I want the eye to have some fun along the way! So I add a lot of little subtleties for excitement. If I'm drawing a girl's face, I spend a lot of time on the eyes. It's not just the line that is important; it's everything around it and the thickness of the line, too. My world is real, not flat. I want it to look special."

IT WAS ALL THERE---WAITING FOR ME. A WAY OF LIFE THAT MEANT WEALTH, GRACIOUS LIVING, A CHANCE TO CRASH THE BLUE BOOK. BUT WHEN BILL KISSED ME, I KNEW I HAD FOUND---

A LOVE OF MY OWN

YOU COULDN'T LOVE A GUY LIKE ME. AFTER ALL, I'M ONLY A SHAVETAIL. YOU WON'T FIND MY NAME IN THE BLUE BOOK LIKE THE COLONEL. PICK YOURSELF A WINNER!

NO--(SOB)--I DON'T WANT ANYTHING--BUT YOU...(SOB)...BILL!

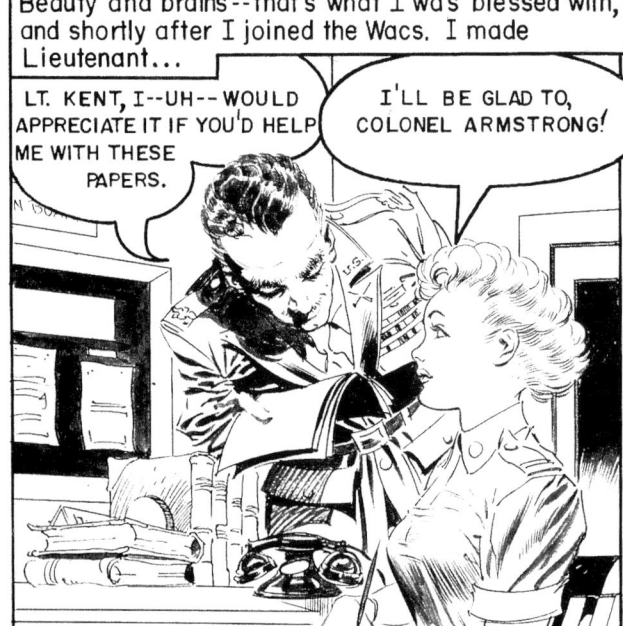

Beauty and brains--that's what I was blessed with, and shortly after I joined the Wacs. I made Lieutenant...

LT. KENT, I--UH--WOULD APPRECIATE IT IF YOU'D HELP ME WITH THESE PAPERS.

I'LL BE GLAD TO, COLONEL ARMSTRONG!

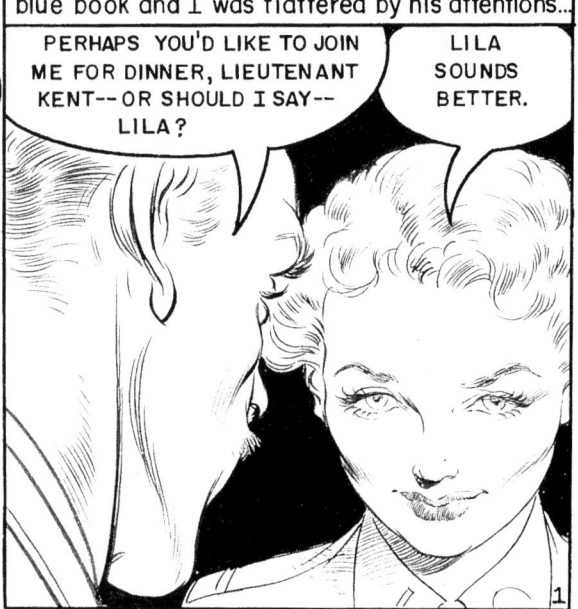

The Colonel's name had long been part of the blue book and I was flattered by his attentions...

PERHAPS YOU'D LIKE TO JOIN ME FOR DINNER, LIEUTENANT KENT--OR SHOULD I SAY-- LILA?

LILA SOUNDS BETTER.

It was all there---waiting for me. A way of life that meant wealth, gracious living, a chance to crash the blue book. But when Bill kissed me, I knew I had found---

A Love Of My Own

You couldn't love a guy like me. After all, I'm only a shavetail. You won't find my name in the blue book like the colonel. Pick yourself a winner!

No--(sob)--I don't want anything--but you...(sob)...Bill!

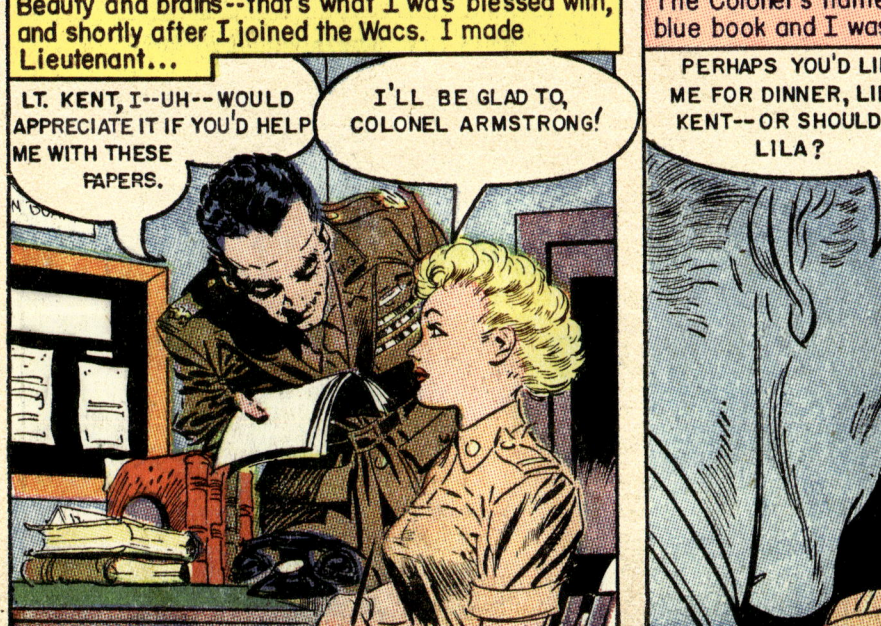

Beauty and brains--that's what I was blessed with, and shortly after I joined the Wacs. I made Lieutenant...

Lt. Kent, I--uh--would appreciate it if you'd help me with these papers.

I'll be glad to, Colonel Armstrong!

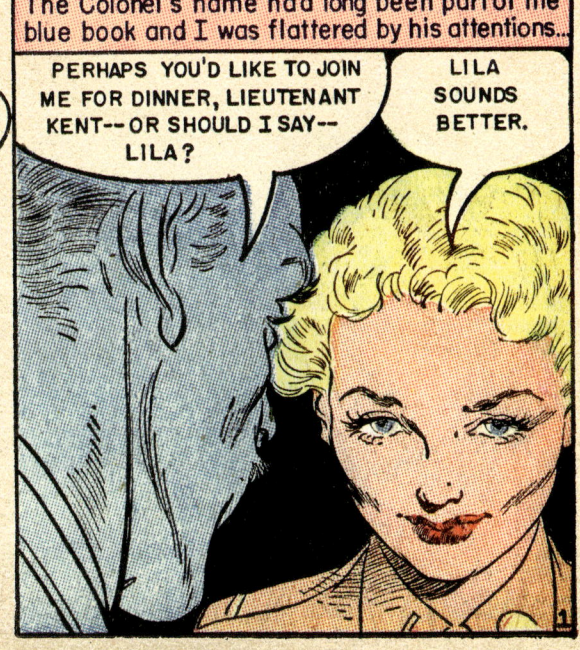

The Colonel's name had long been part of the blue book and I was flattered by his attentions...

Perhaps you'd like to join me for dinner, Lieutenant Kent--or should I say--Lila?

Lila sounds better.

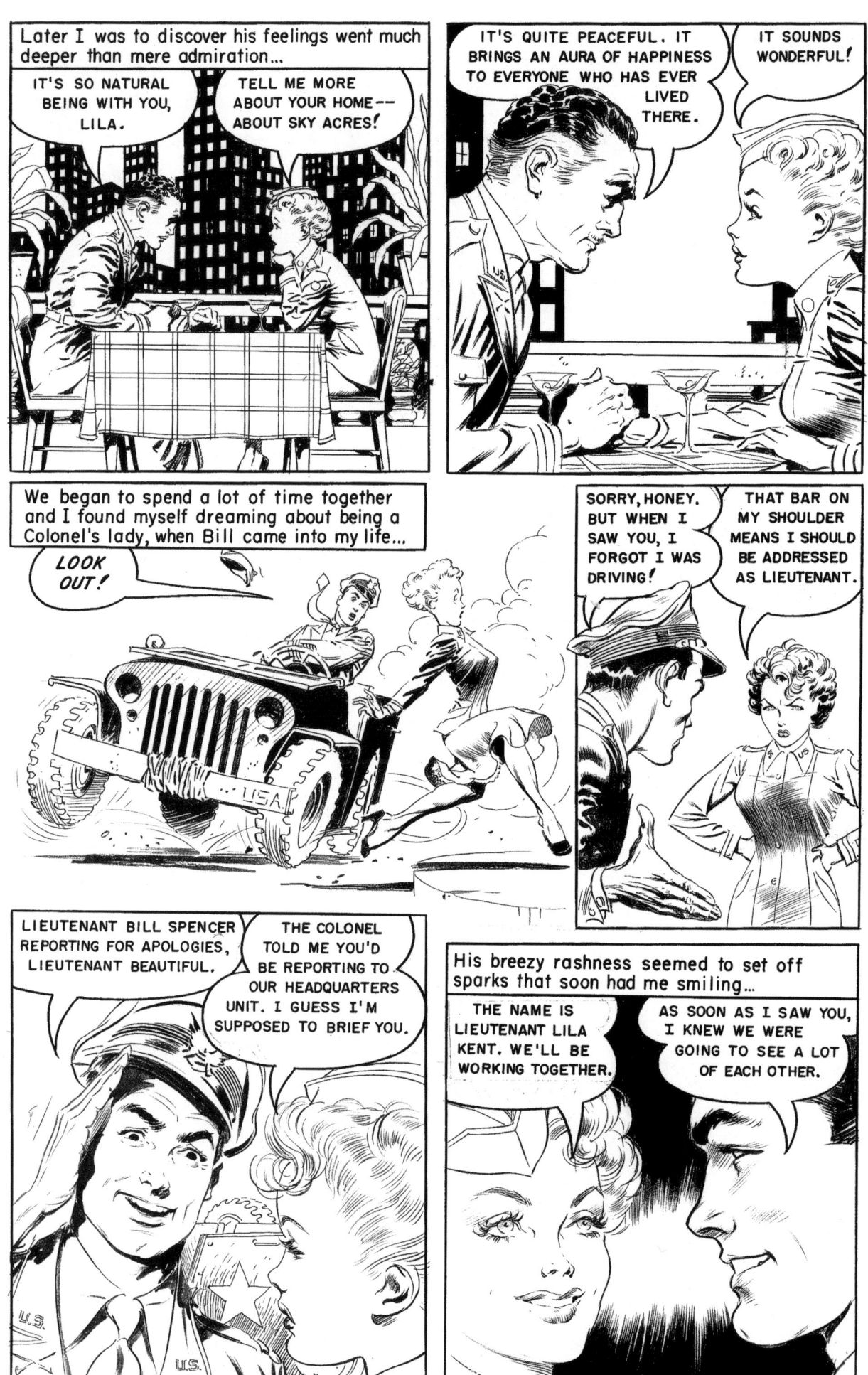

Personal Love #24 (Famous Funnies, November 1953)

Later I was to discover his feelings went much deeper than mere admiration...
IT'S SO NATURAL BEING WITH YOU, LILA.
TELL ME MORE ABOUT YOUR HOME--ABOUT SKY ACRES!
IT'S QUITE PEACEFUL. IT BRINGS AN AURA OF HAPPINESS TO EVERYONE WHO HAS EVER LIVED THERE.
IT SOUNDS WONDERFUL!
We began to spend a lot of time together and I found myself dreaming about being a Colonel's lady, when Bill came into my life...
LOOK OUT!
USA
SORRY, HONEY. BUT WHEN I SAW YOU, I FORGOT I WAS DRIVING!
THAT BAR ON MY SHOULDER MEANS I SHOULD BE ADDRESSED AS LIEUTENANT.
LIEUTENANT BILL SPENCER REPORTING FOR APOLOGIES, LIEUTENANT BEAUTIFUL.
THE COLONEL TOLD ME YOU'D BE REPORTING TO OUR HEADQUARTERS UNIT. I GUESS I'M SUPPOSED TO BRIEF YOU.
His breezy rashness seemed to set off sparks that soon had me smiling...
THE NAME IS LIEUTENANT LILA KENT. WE'LL BE WORKING TOGETHER.
AS SOON AS I SAW YOU, I KNEW WE WERE GOING TO SEE A LOT OF EACH OTHER.

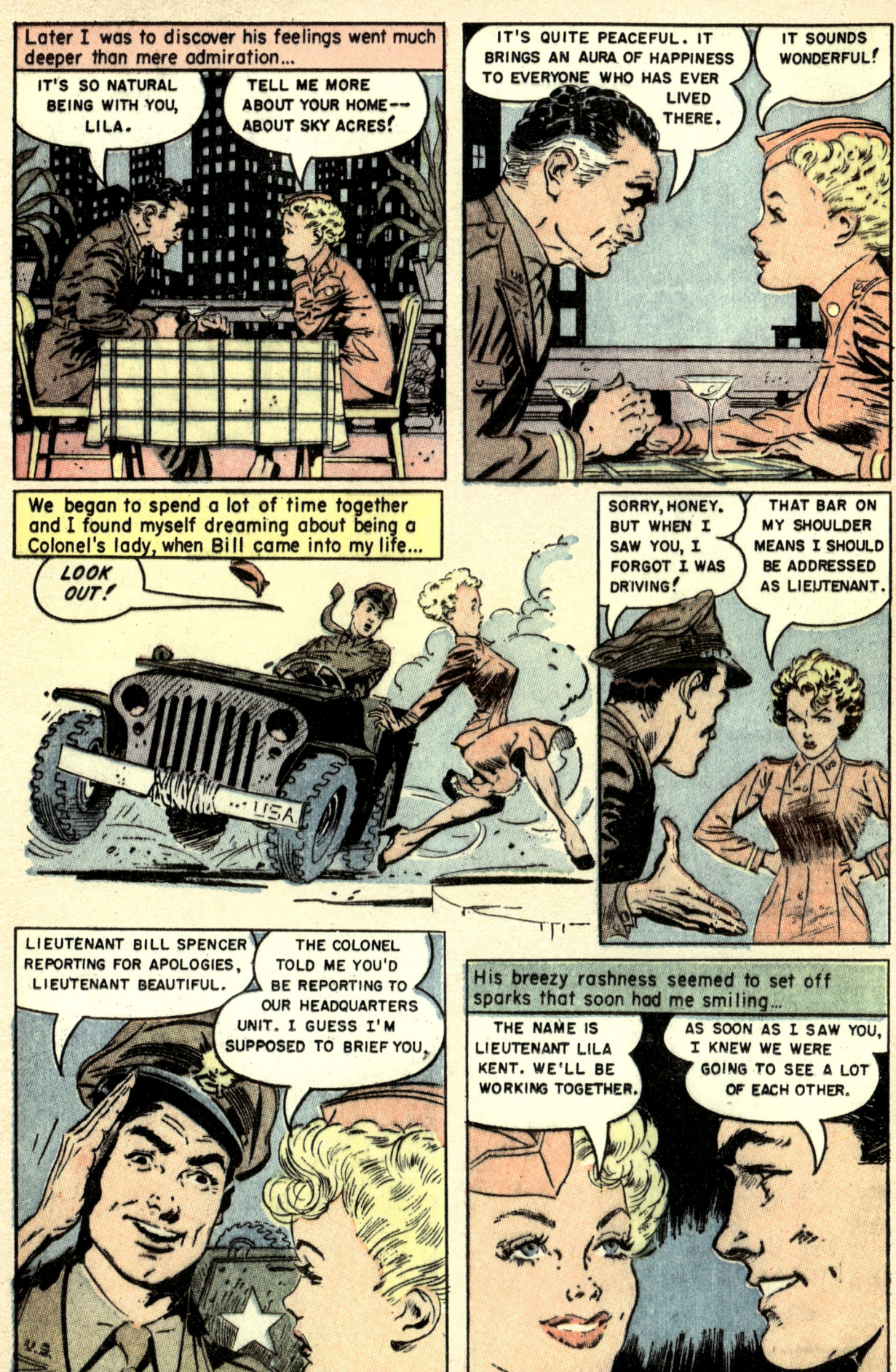

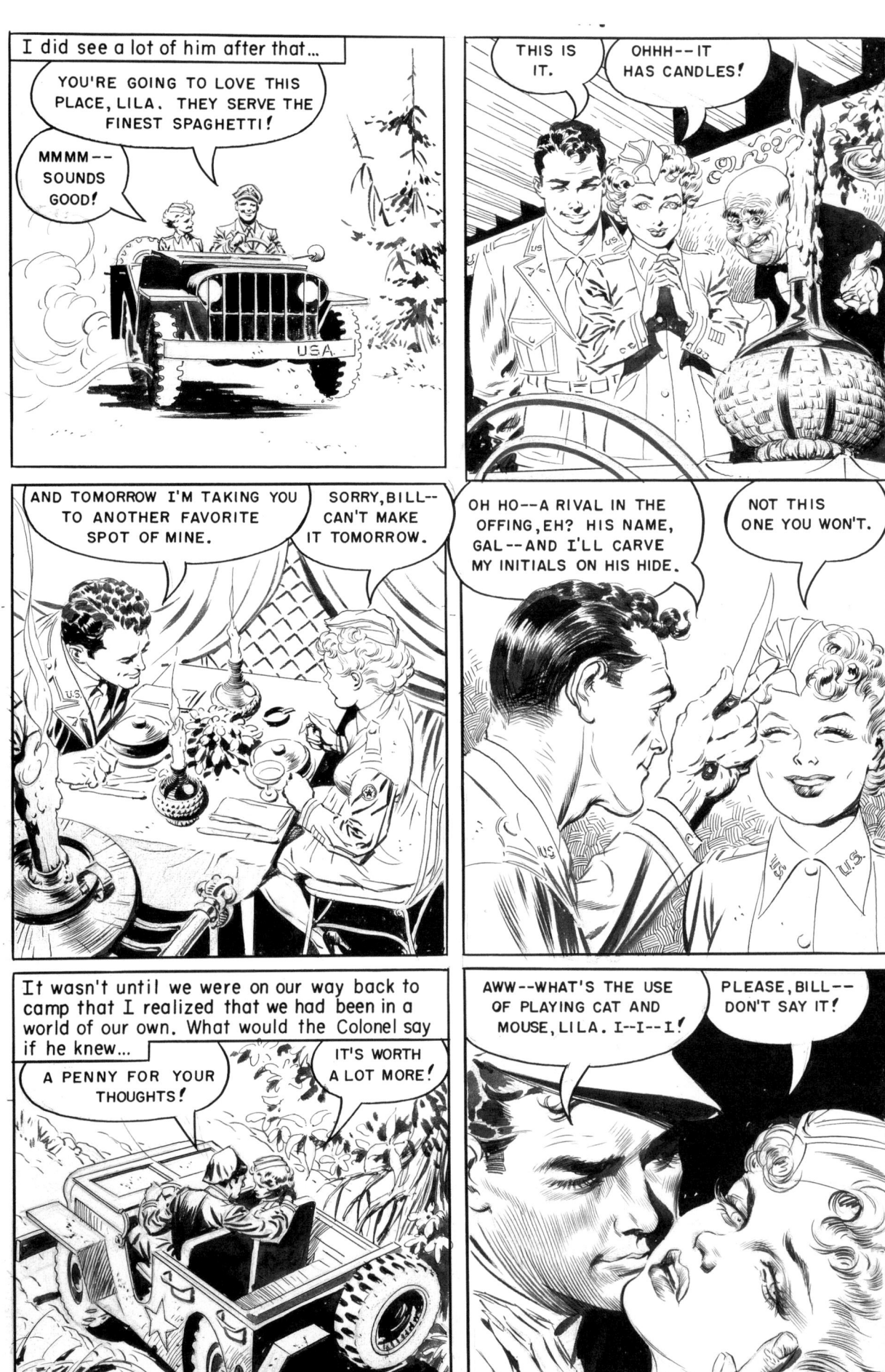

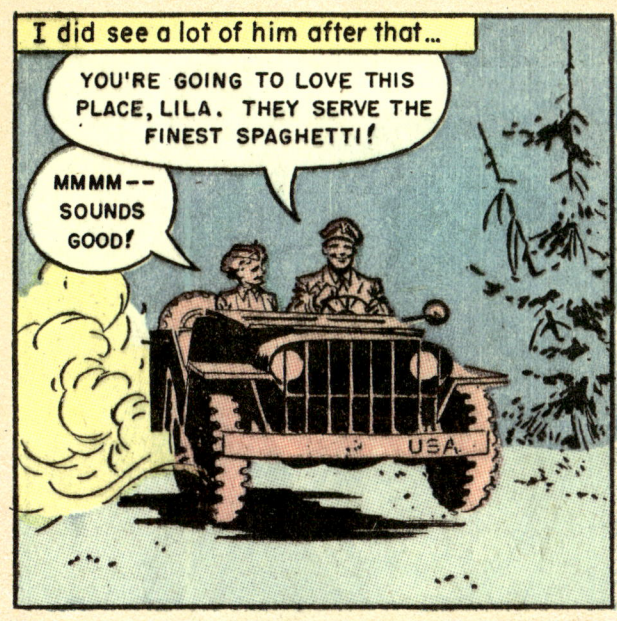

I did see a lot of him after that...

YOU'RE GOING TO LOVE THIS PLACE, LILA. THEY SERVE THE FINEST SPAGHETTI!

MMMM-- SOUNDS GOOD!

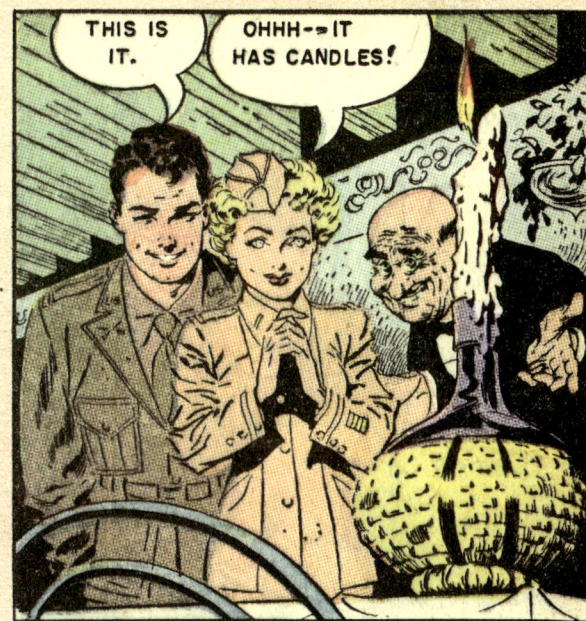

THIS IS IT.

OHHH--IT HAS CANDLES!

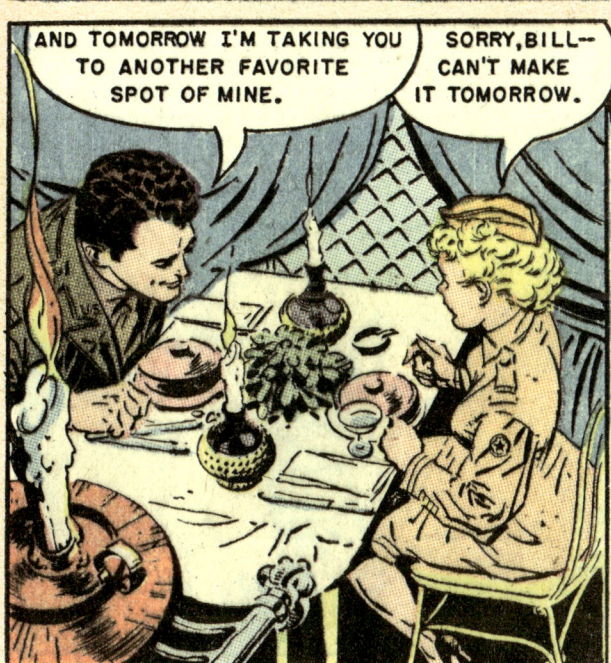

AND TOMORROW I'M TAKING YOU TO ANOTHER FAVORITE SPOT OF MINE.

SORRY, BILL-- CAN'T MAKE IT TOMORROW.

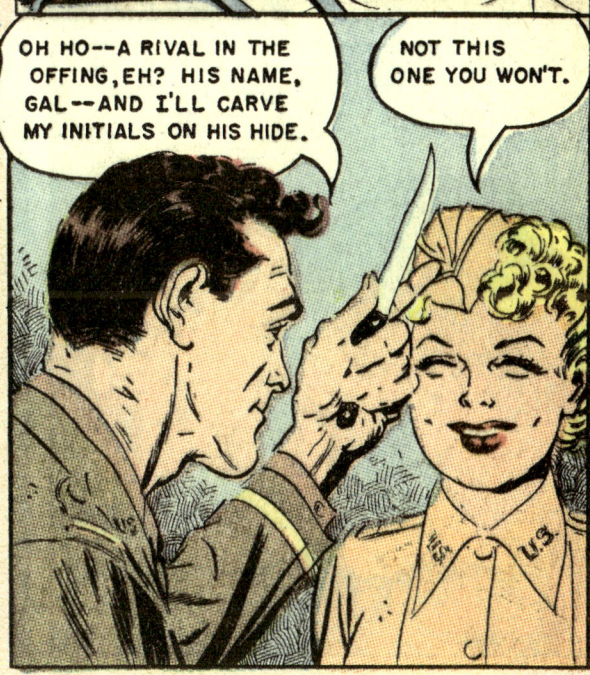

OH HO--A RIVAL IN THE OFFING, EH? HIS NAME, GAL--AND I'LL CARVE MY INITIALS ON HIS HIDE.

NOT THIS ONE YOU WON'T.

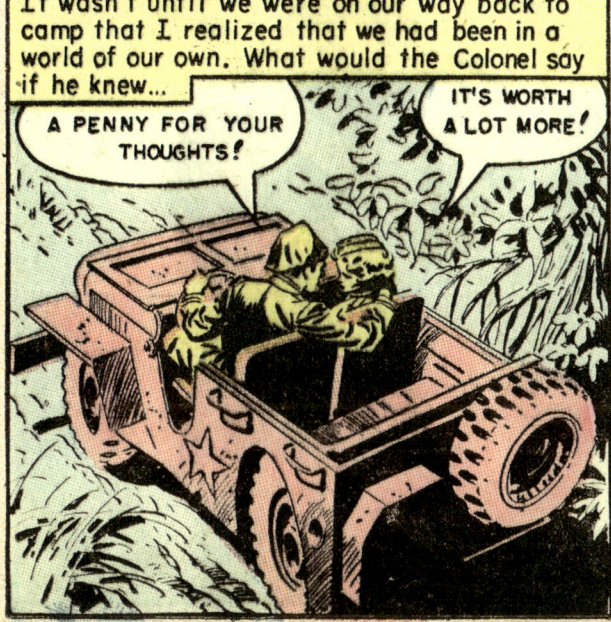

It wasn't until we were on our way back to camp that I realized that we had been in a world of our own. What would the Colonel say if he knew...

A PENNY FOR YOUR THOUGHTS!

IT'S WORTH A LOT MORE!

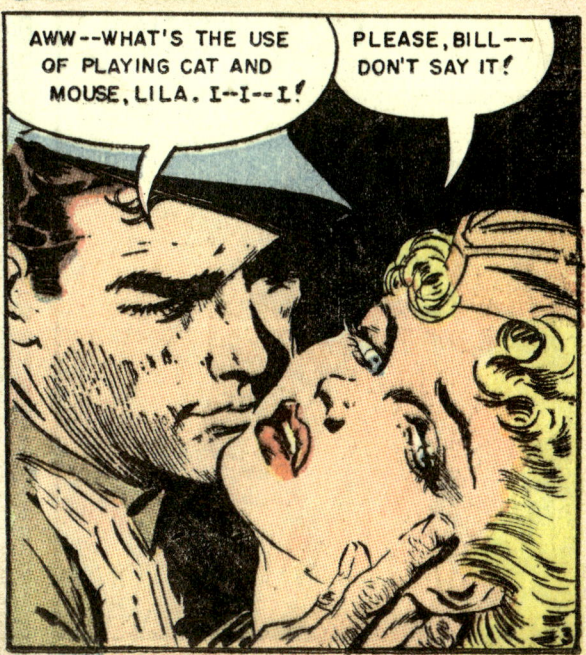

AWW--WHAT'S THE USE OF PLAYING CAT AND MOUSE, LILA. I--I--I!

PLEASE, BILL-- DON'T SAY IT!

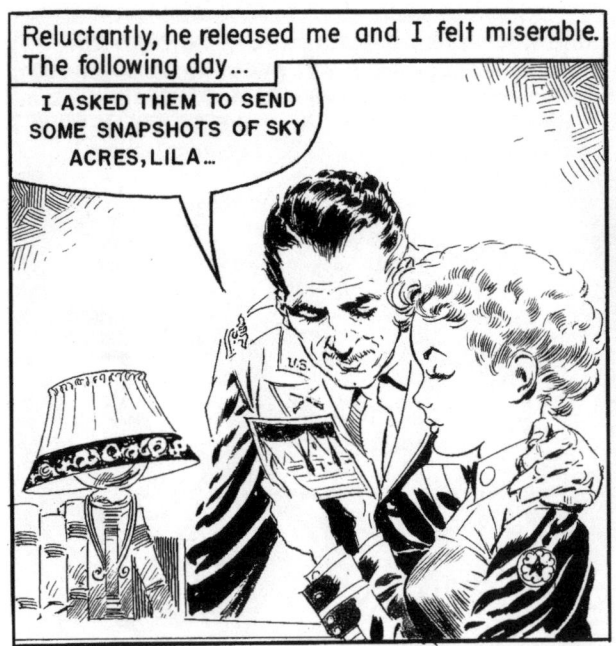

Reluctantly, he released me and I felt miserable. The following day...

I ASKED THEM TO SEND SOME SNAPSHOTS OF SKY ACRES, LILA...

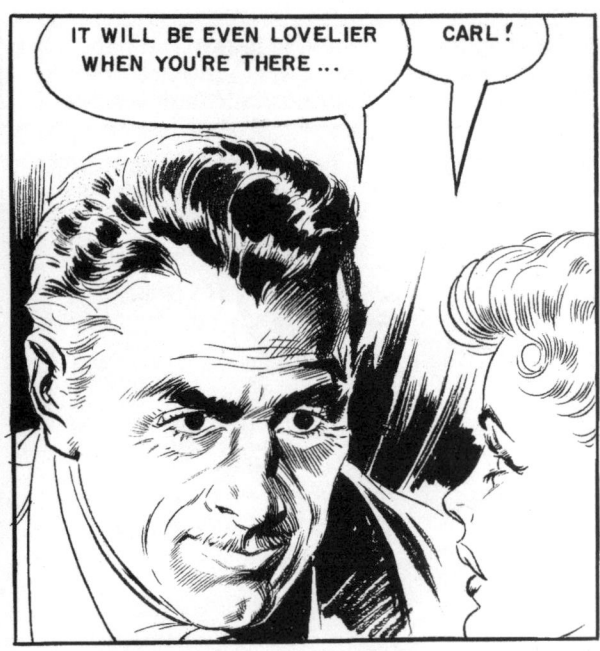

IT WILL BE EVEN LOVELIER WHEN YOU'RE THERE...

CARL!

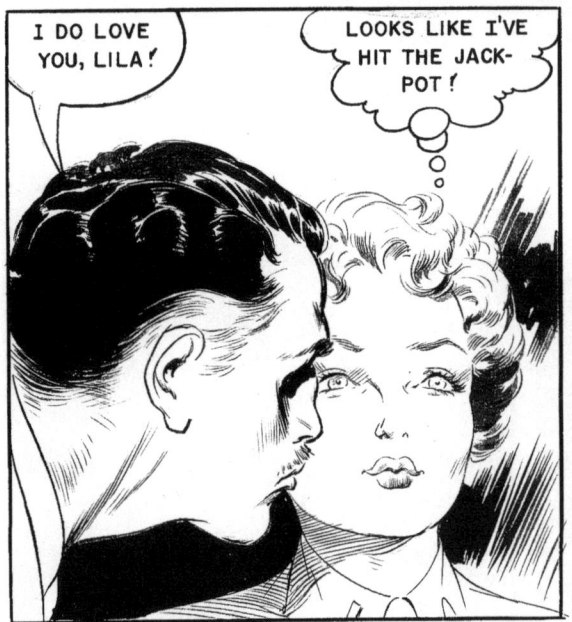

I DO LOVE YOU, LILA!

LOOKS LIKE I'VE HIT THE JACK-POT!

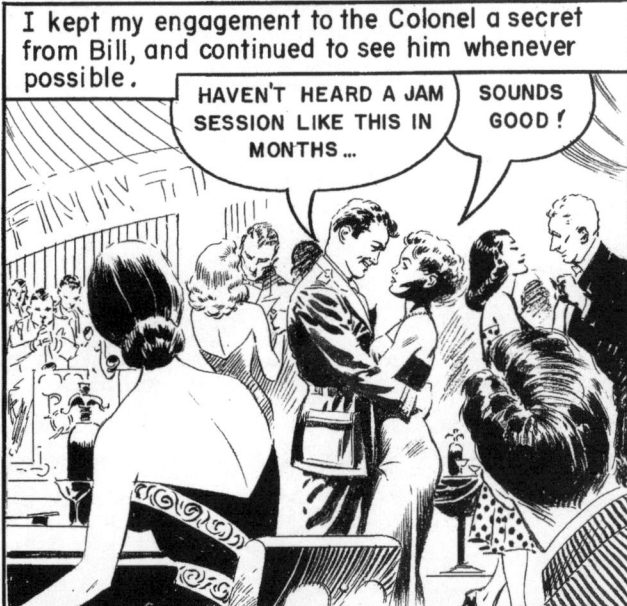

I kept my engagement to the Colonel a secret from Bill, and continued to see him whenever possible.

HAVEN'T HEARD A JAM SESSION LIKE THIS IN MONTHS...

SOUNDS GOOD!

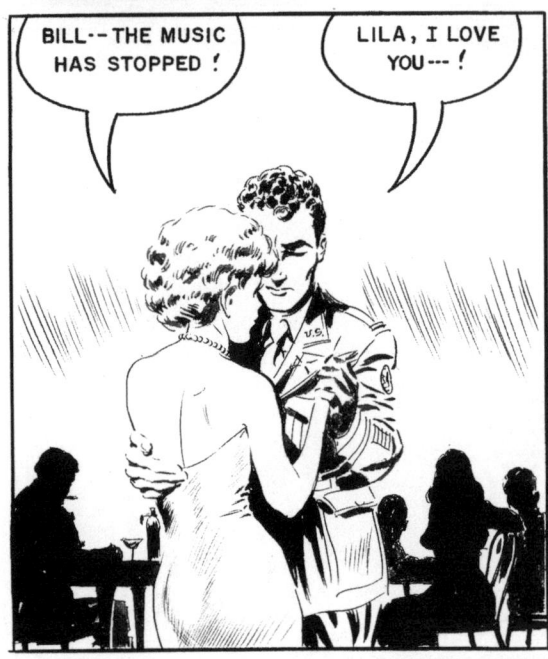

BILL -- THE MUSIC HAS STOPPED!

LILA, I LOVE YOU ---!

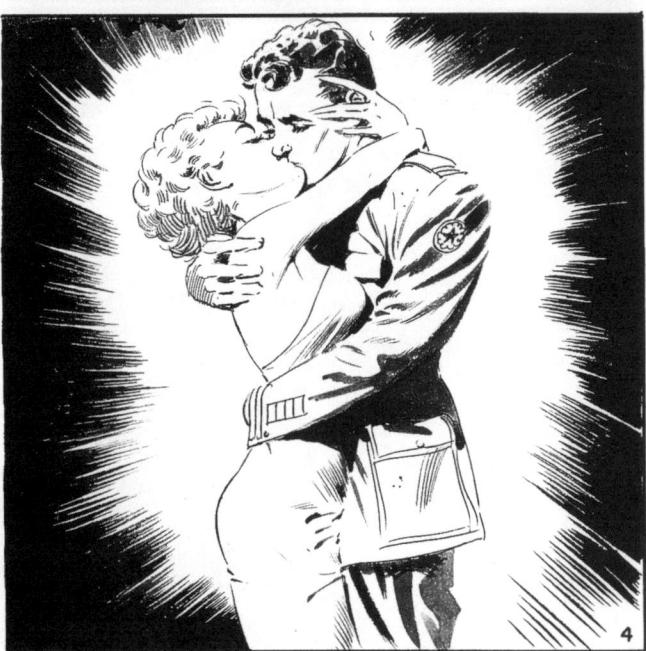

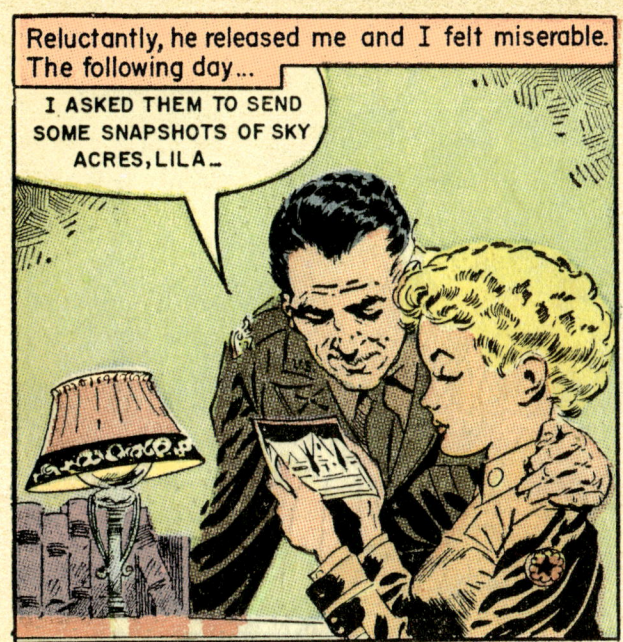

Reluctantly, he released me and I felt miserable. The following day...

I ASKED THEM TO SEND SOME SNAPSHOTS OF SKY ACRES, LILA...

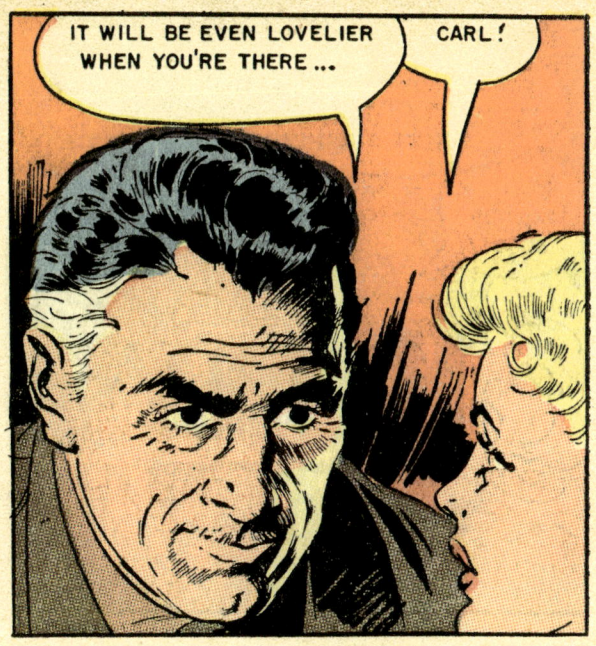

IT WILL BE EVEN LOVELIER WHEN YOU'RE THERE...

CARL!

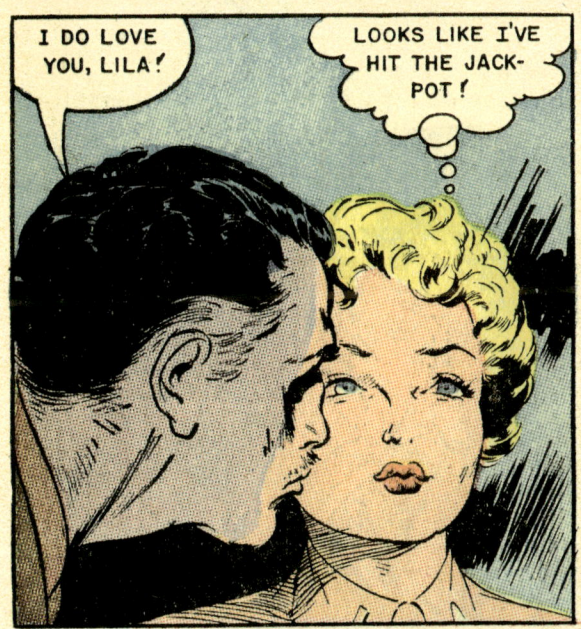

I DO LOVE YOU, LILA!

LOOKS LIKE I'VE HIT THE JACK-POT!

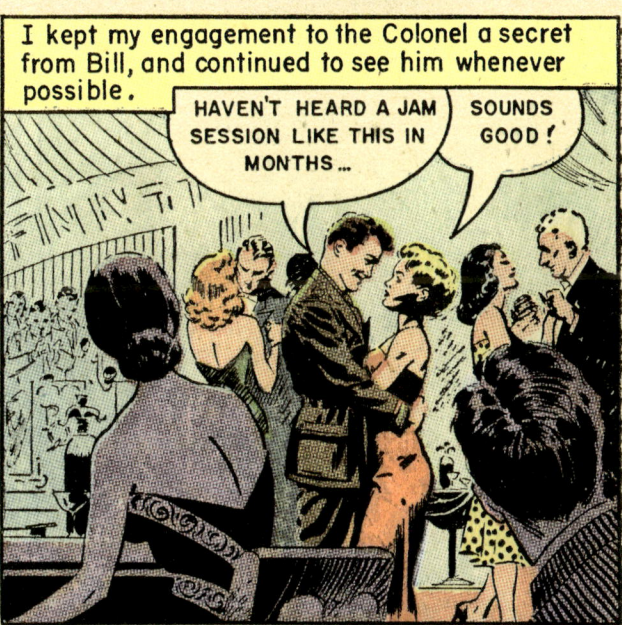

I kept my engagement to the Colonel a secret from Bill, and continued to see him whenever possible.

HAVEN'T HEARD A JAM SESSION LIKE THIS IN MONTHS...

SOUNDS GOOD!

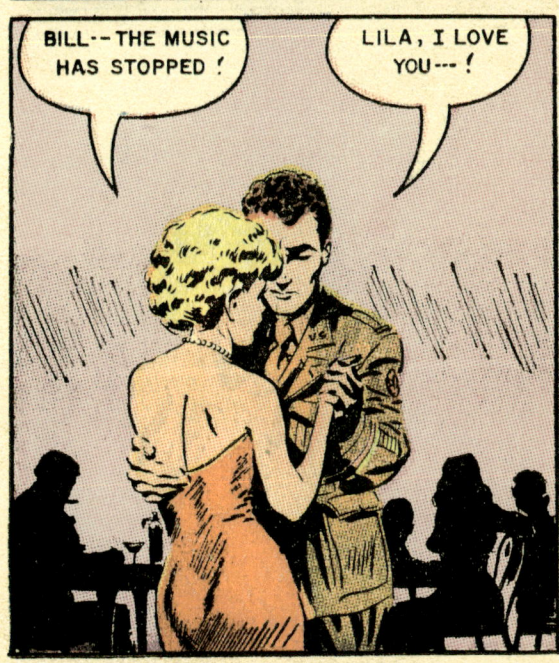

BILL -- THE MUSIC HAS STOPPED!

LILA, I LOVE YOU ---!

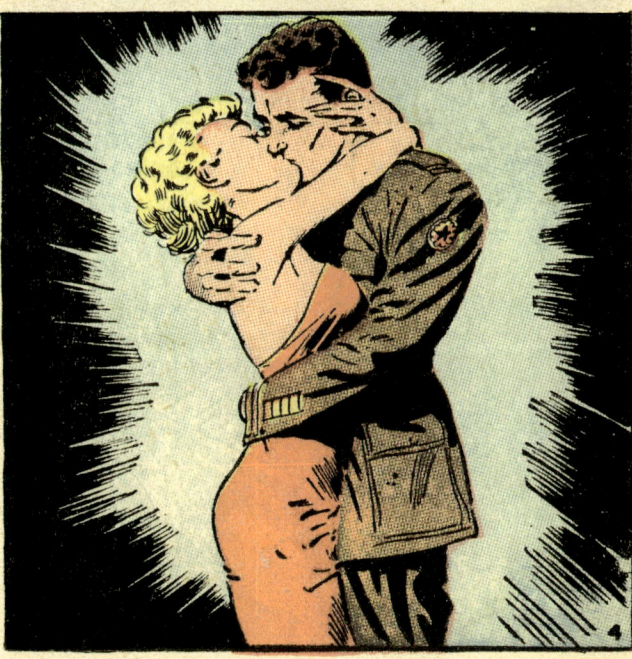

Conflicting forces seemed to tear at me in the days that followed. Suppose Carl found out. What if Bill found out about the Colonel? And then one night...

WHY SO SOBER-FACED TONIGHT, BILL?

I JUST HEARD ABOUT YOU AND COLONEL ARMSTRONG.

I SUPPOSE I SHOULD HAVE TOLD YOU!

BUT NOW THAT WE FEEL AS WE DO ABOUT EACH OTHER, YOU'LL HAVE TO BREAK YOUR ENGAGEMENT!

For a moment I stared at him--the full impact of what he was saying slowly sinking in...

NOW WAIT A MINUTE, BILL. WHAT WOULD I HAVE IF I MARRIED YOU.

WE'D HAVE EACH OTHER.

EXACTLY-- AREN'T YOU ASKING A LITTLE TOO MUCH?

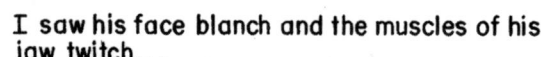

I saw his face blanch and the muscles of his jaw twitch...

DON'T SAY ANYMORE, LILA. SORRY I BROUGHT THE WHOLE THING UP.

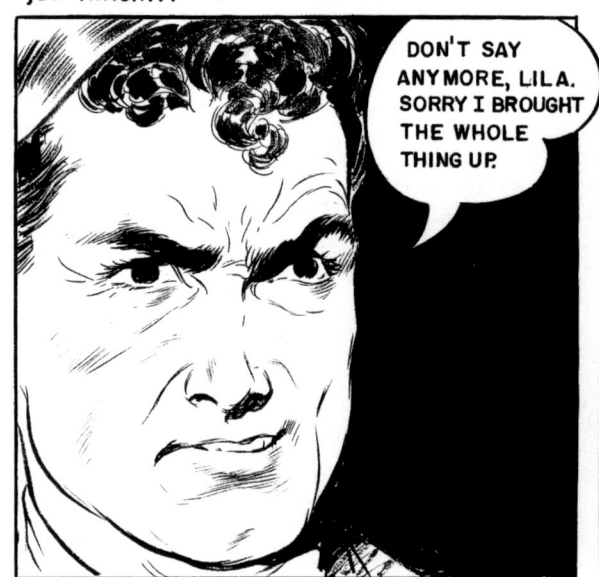

I WAS JUST NAIVE ENOUGH TO THINK THAT LOVE HAD SOME RELATIONSHIP TO MARRIAGE.

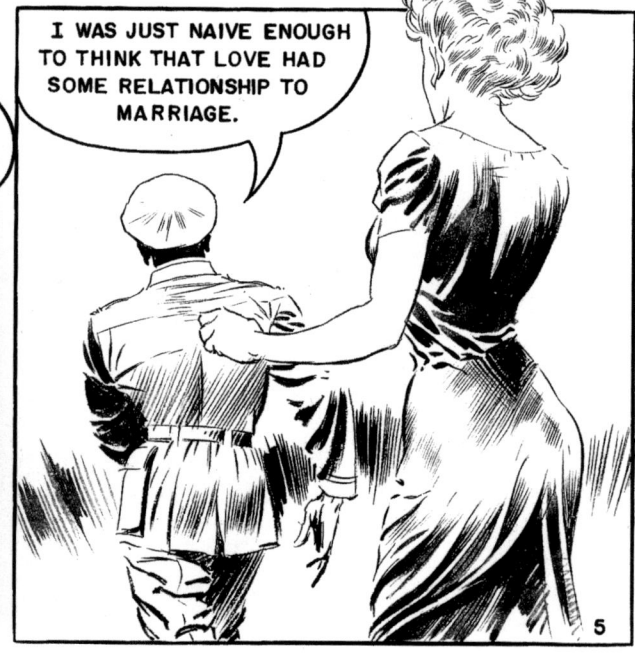

5

Personal Love #24 (Famous Funnies, November 1953)

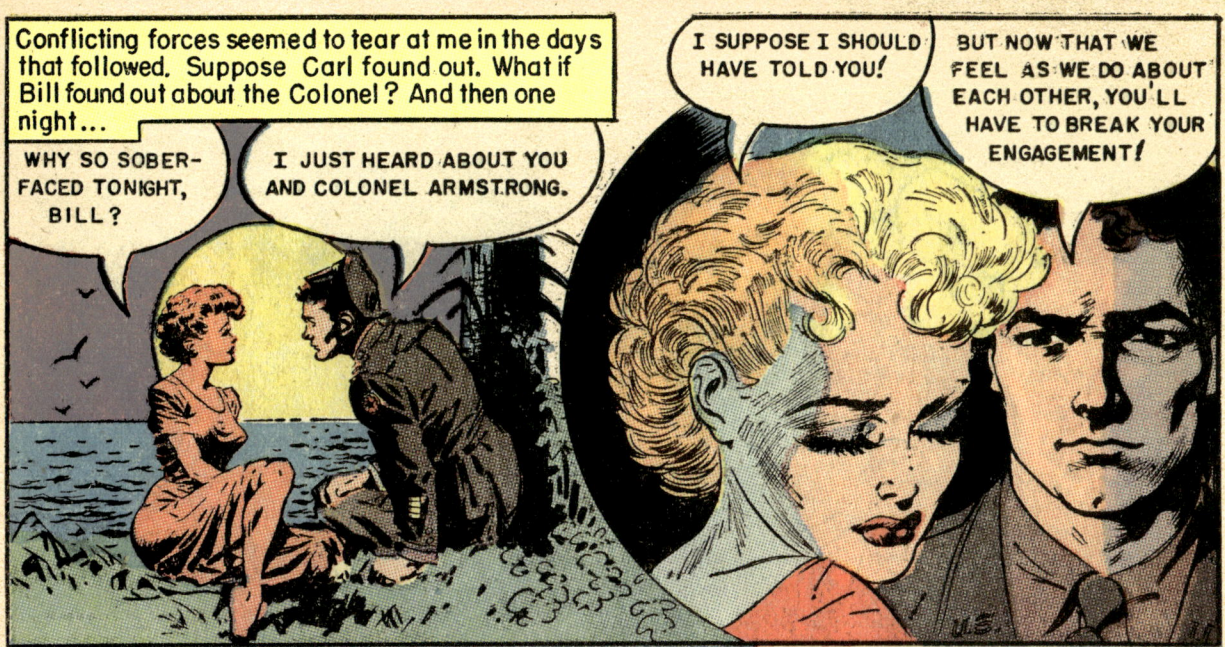

Conflicting forces seemed to tear at me in the days that followed. Suppose Carl found out. What if Bill found out about the Colonel? And then one night...

WHY SO SOBER-FACED TONIGHT, BILL?

I JUST HEARD ABOUT YOU AND COLONEL ARMSTRONG.

I SUPPOSE I SHOULD HAVE TOLD YOU!

BUT NOW THAT WE FEEL AS WE DO ABOUT EACH OTHER, YOU'LL HAVE TO BREAK YOUR ENGAGEMENT!

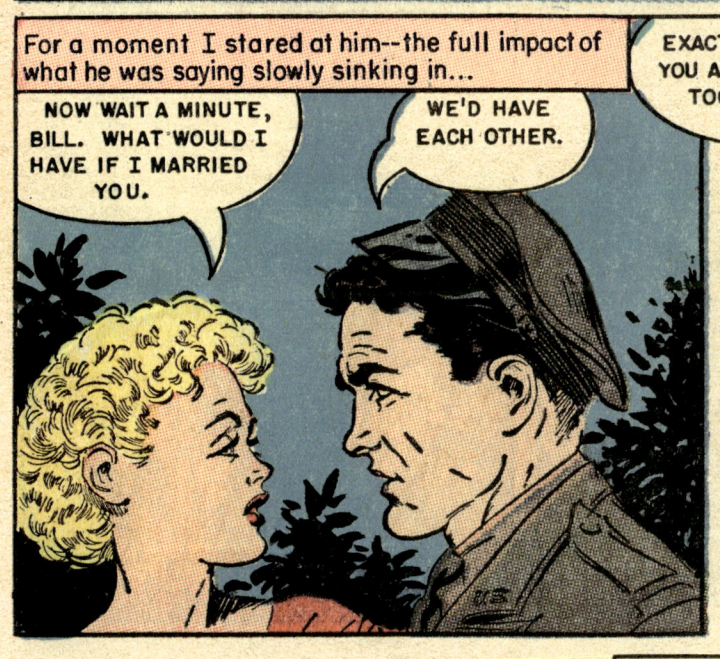

For a moment I stared at him--the full impact of what he was saying slowly sinking in...

NOW WAIT A MINUTE, BILL. WHAT WOULD I HAVE IF I MARRIED YOU.

WE'D HAVE EACH OTHER.

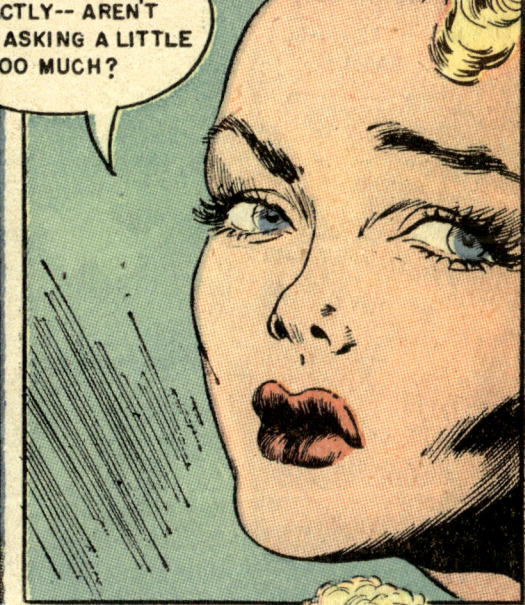

EXACTLY-- AREN'T YOU ASKING A LITTLE TOO MUCH?

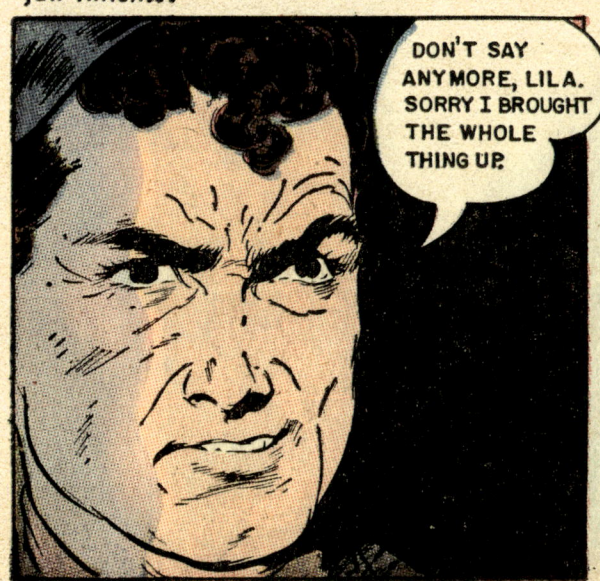

I saw his face blanch and the muscles of his jaw twitch...

DON'T SAY ANYMORE, LILA. SORRY I BROUGHT THE WHOLE THING UP.

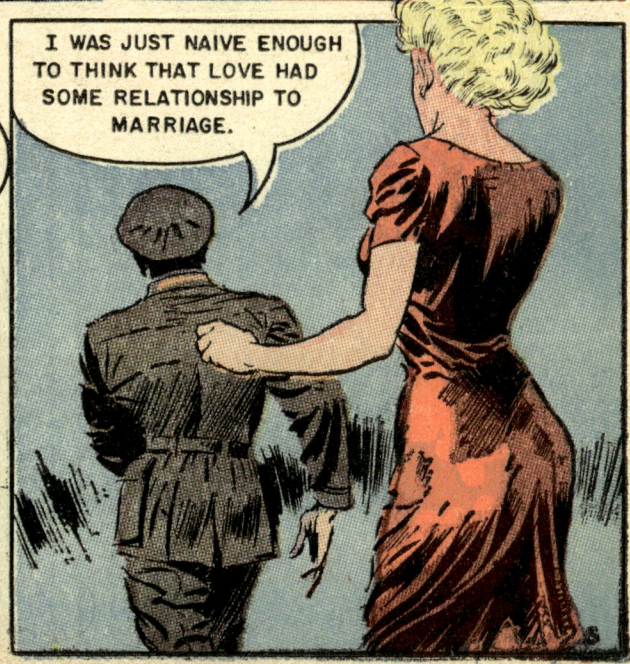

I WAS JUST NAIVE ENOUGH TO THINK THAT LOVE HAD SOME RELATIONSHIP TO MARRIAGE.

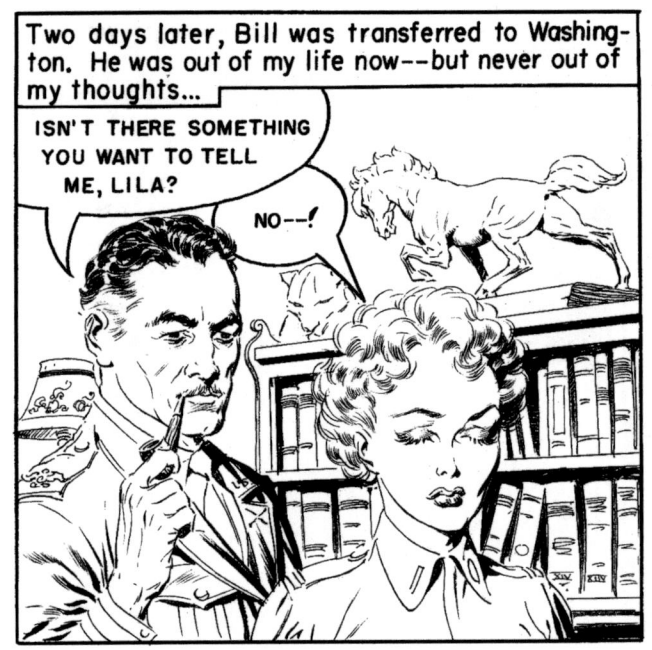

Two days later, Bill was transferred to Washington. He was out of my life now--but never out of my thoughts...

ISN'T THERE SOMETHING YOU WANT TO TELL ME, LILA?

NO--!

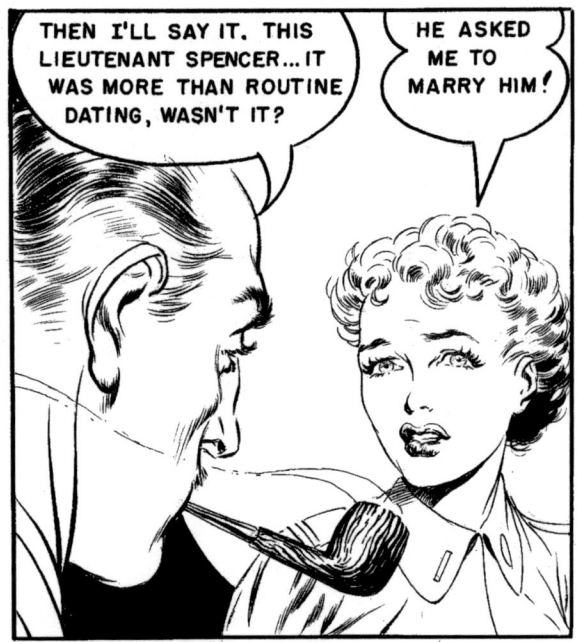

THEN I'LL SAY IT. THIS LIEUTENANT SPENCER...IT WAS MORE THAN ROUTINE DATING, WASN'T IT?

HE ASKED ME TO MARRY HIM!

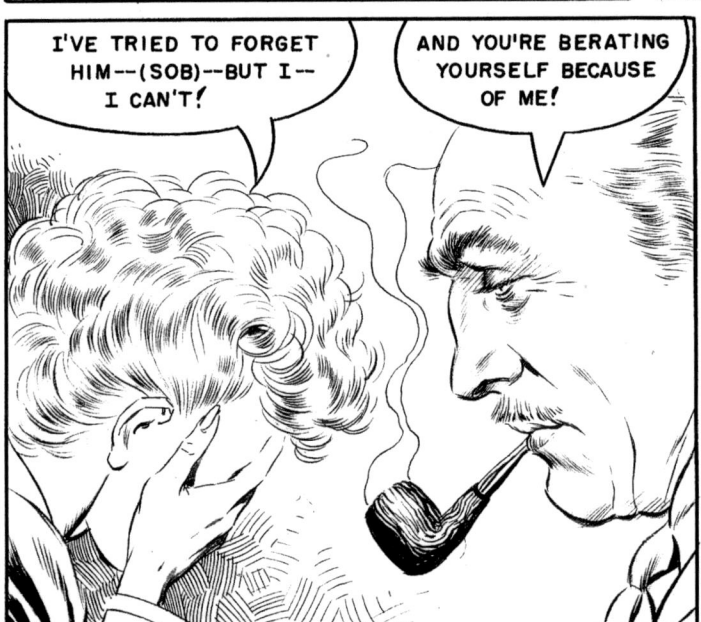

I'VE TRIED TO FORGET HIM--(SOB)--BUT I--I CAN'T!

AND YOU'RE BERATING YOURSELF BECAUSE OF ME!

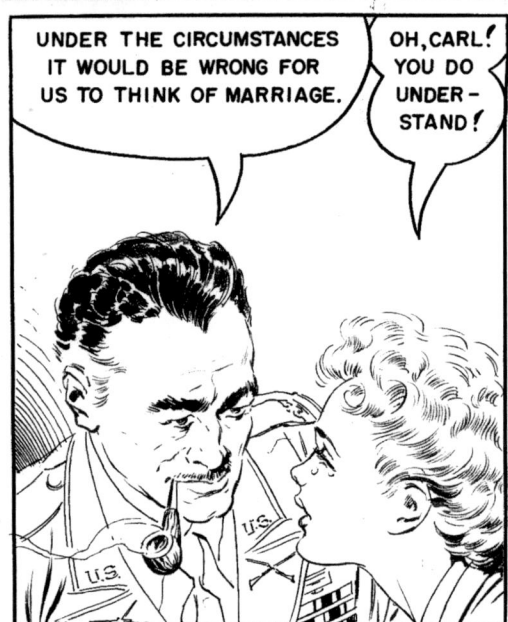

UNDER THE CIRCUMSTANCES IT WOULD BE WRONG FOR US TO THINK OF MARRIAGE.

OH, CARL! YOU DO UNDER-STAND!

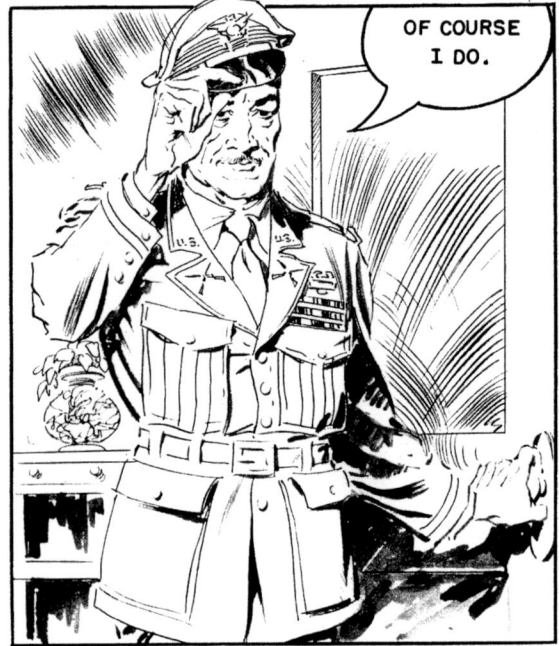

OF COURSE I DO.

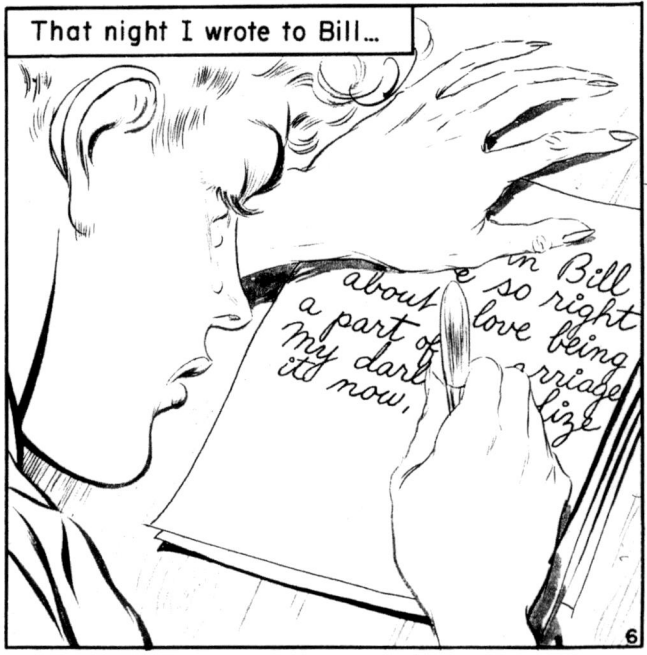

That night I wrote to Bill...

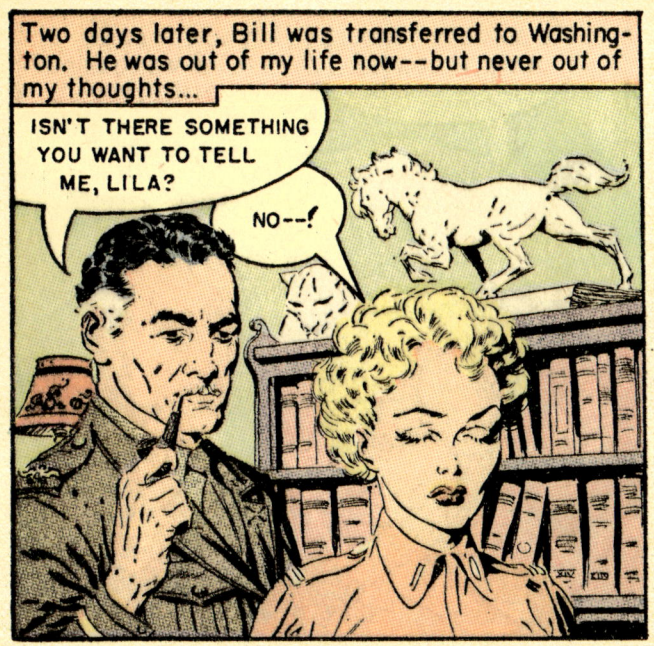

Two days later, Bill was transferred to Washington. He was out of my life now--but never out of my thoughts...

ISN'T THERE SOMETHING YOU WANT TO TELL ME, LILA?

NO--!

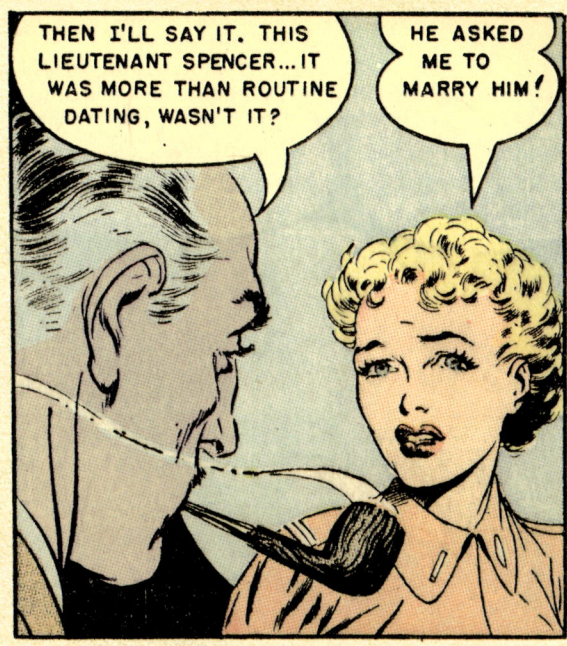

THEN I'LL SAY IT. THIS LIEUTENANT SPENCER...IT WAS MORE THAN ROUTINE DATING, WASN'T IT?

HE ASKED ME TO MARRY HIM!

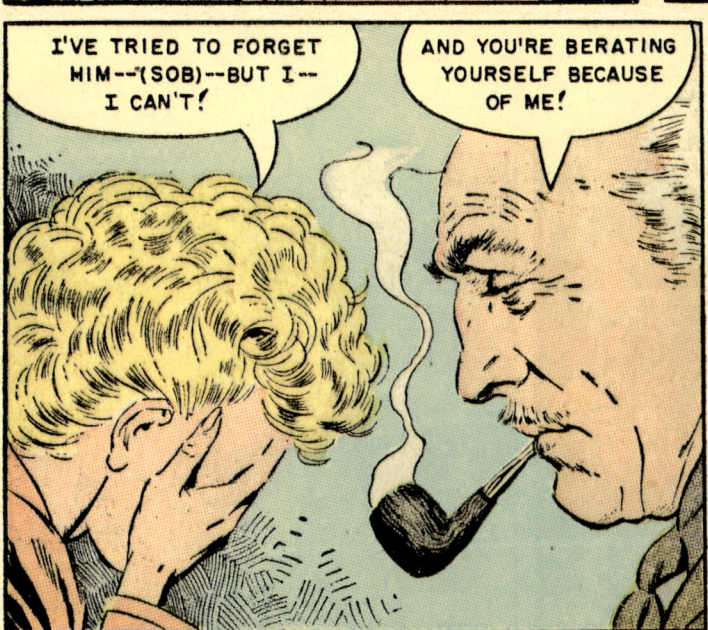

I'VE TRIED TO FORGET HIM--(SOB)--BUT I-- I CAN'T!

AND YOU'RE BERATING YOURSELF BECAUSE OF ME!

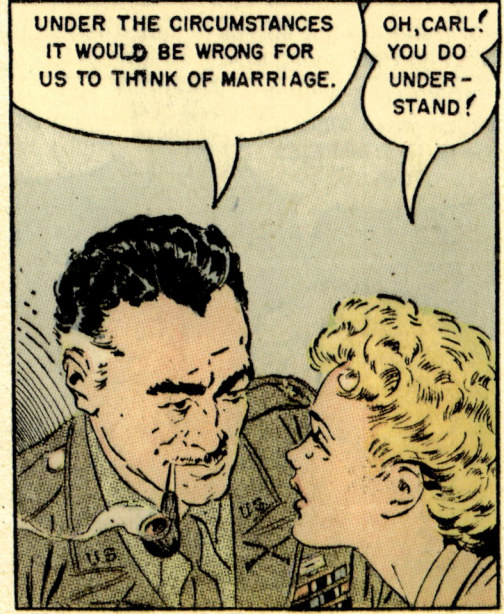

UNDER THE CIRCUMSTANCES IT WOULD BE WRONG FOR US TO THINK OF MARRIAGE.

OH, CARL! YOU DO UNDER- STAND!

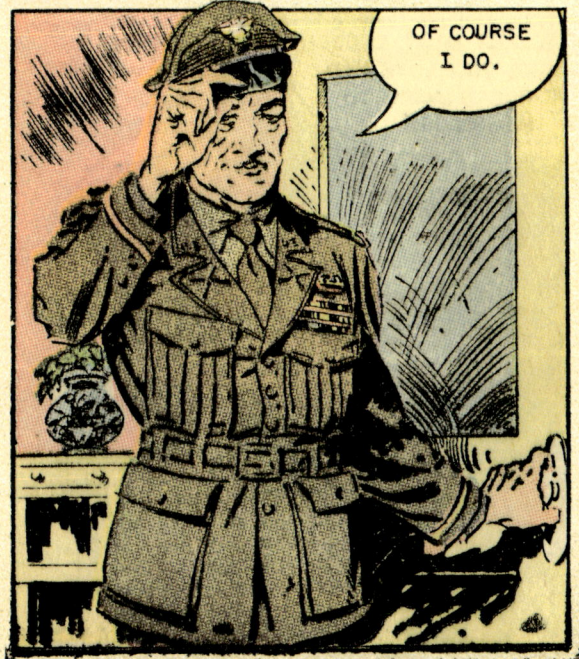

OF COURSE I DO.

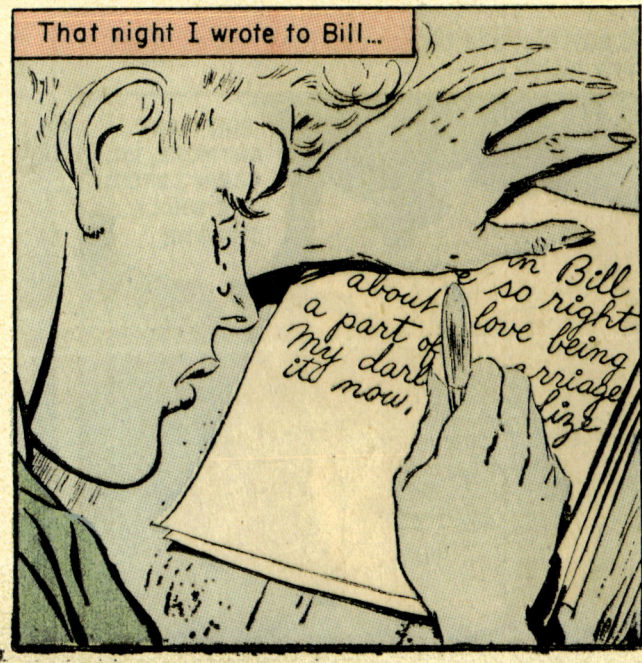

That night I wrote to Bill...

But two days after I mailed the letter, an item in the post newspaper caught my eye...

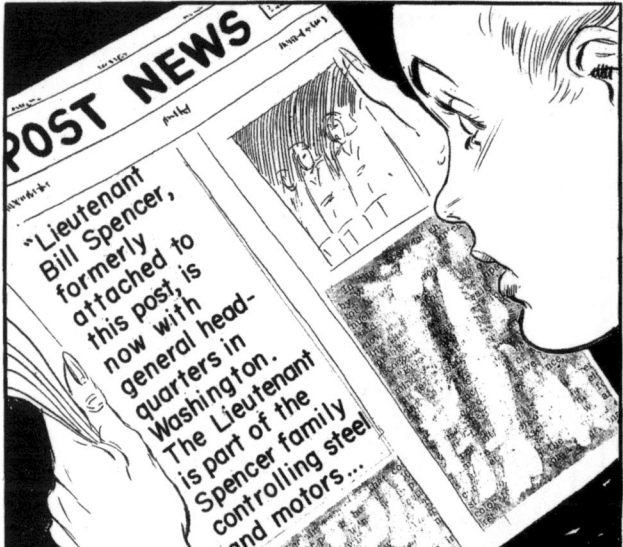

"Lieutenant Bill Spencer, formerly attached to this post, is now with general head-quarters in Washington. The Lieutenant is part of the Spencer family controlling steel and motors...

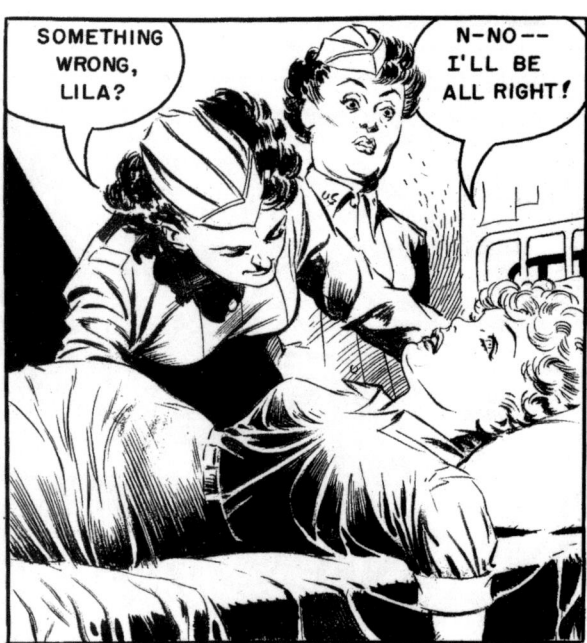

SOMETHING WRONG, LILA?

N-NO-- I'LL BE ALL RIGHT!

There was no sleep for me that night.

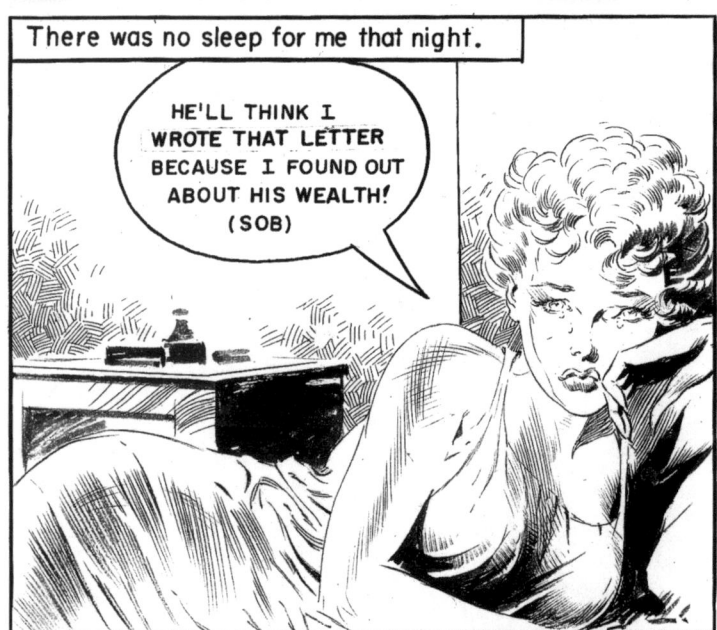

HE'LL THINK I WROTE THAT LETTER BECAUSE I FOUND OUT ABOUT HIS WEALTH! (SOB)

I went completely to pieces after that.

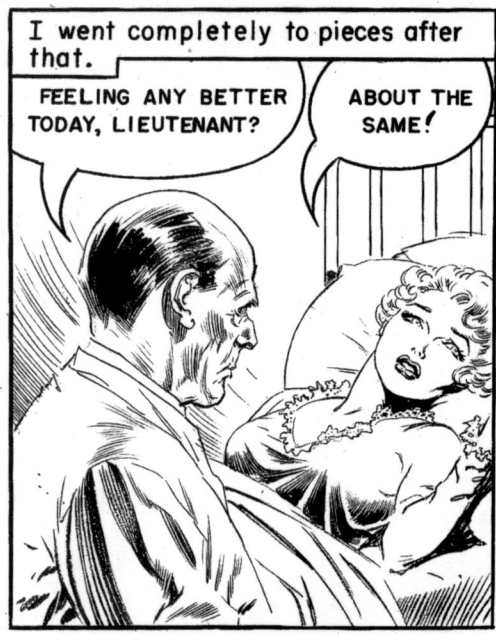

FEELING ANY BETTER TODAY, LIEUTENANT?

ABOUT THE SAME!

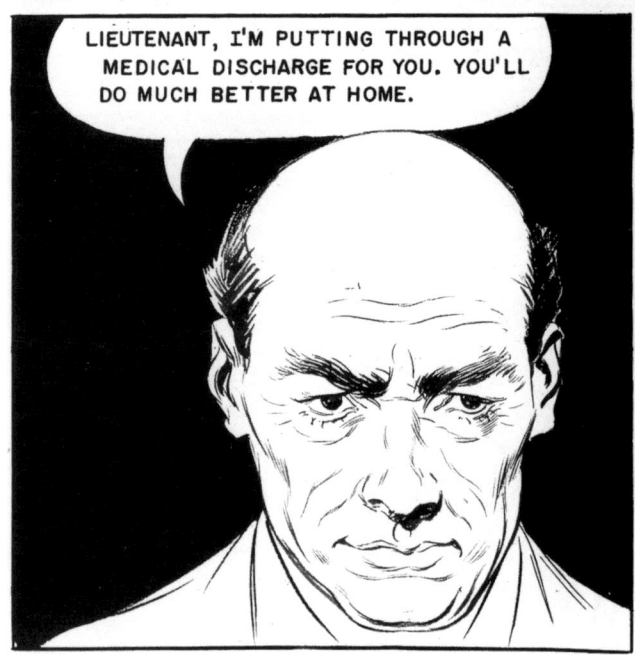

LIEUTENANT, I'M PUTTING THROUGH A MEDICAL DISCHARGE FOR YOU. YOU'LL DO MUCH BETTER AT HOME.

And a few weeks later found me on my way home...

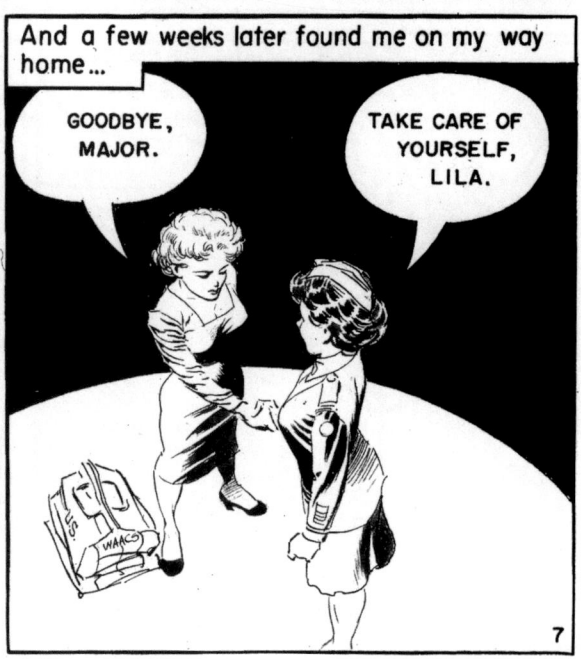

GOODBYE, MAJOR.

TAKE CARE OF YOURSELF, LILA.

7

Personal Love #24 (Famous Funnies, November 1953)

But two days after I mailed the letter, an item in the post newspaper caught my eye...

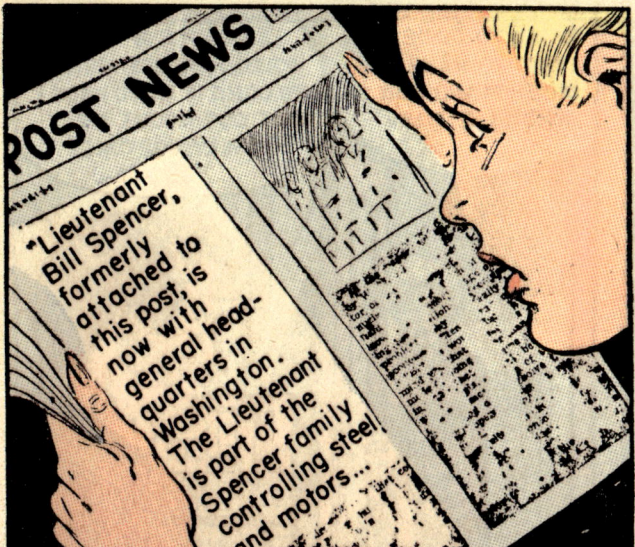

POST NEWS

"Lieutenant Bill Spencer, formerly attached to this post, is now with general headquarters in Washington. The Lieutenant is part of the Spencer family controlling steel and motors...

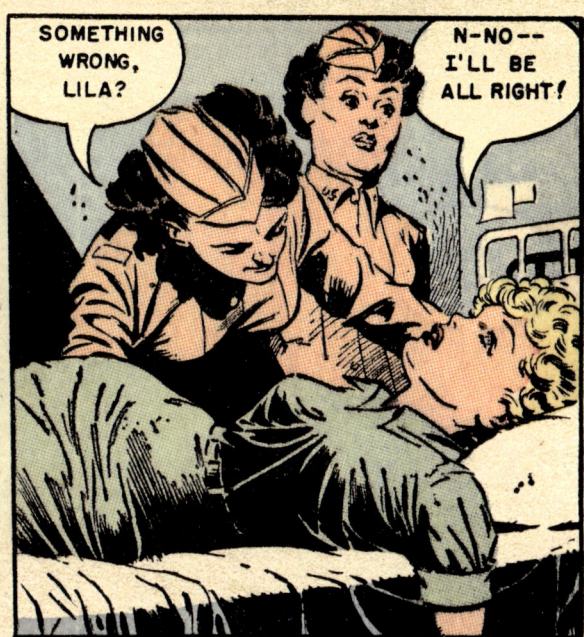

SOMETHING WRONG, LILA?

N-NO-- I'LL BE ALL RIGHT!

There was no sleep for me that night.

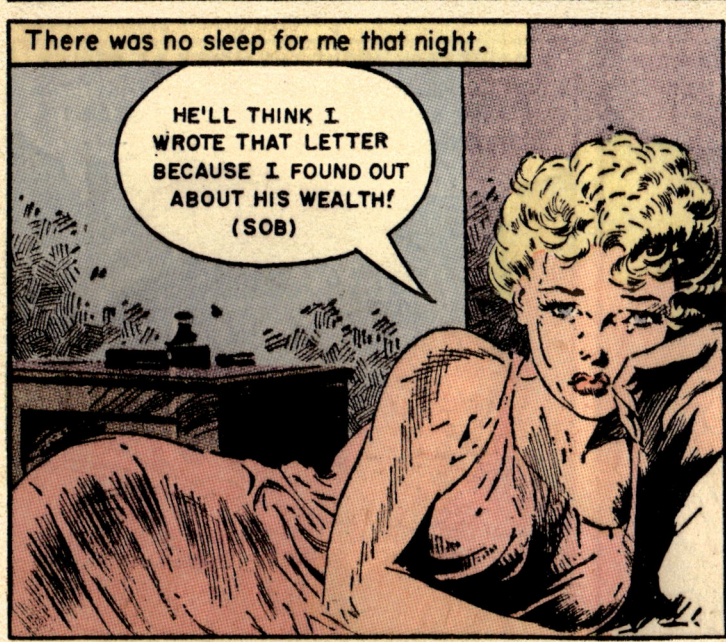

HE'LL THINK I WROTE THAT LETTER BECAUSE I FOUND OUT ABOUT HIS WEALTH! (SOB)

I went completely to pieces after that.

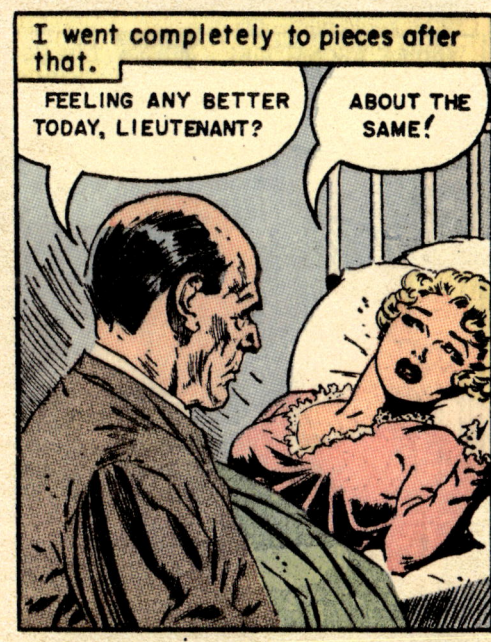

FEELING ANY BETTER TODAY, LIEUTENANT?

ABOUT THE SAME!

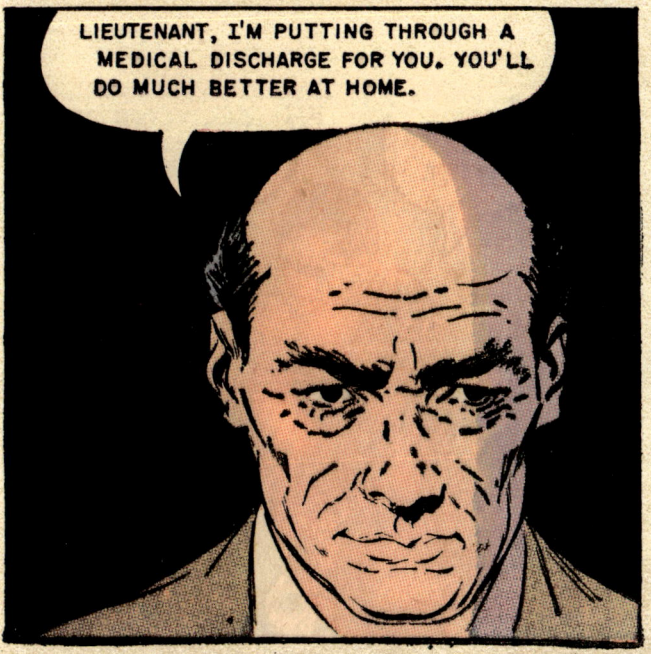

LIEUTENANT, I'M PUTTING THROUGH A MEDICAL DISCHARGE FOR YOU. YOU'LL DO MUCH BETTER AT HOME.

And a few weeks later found me on my way home...

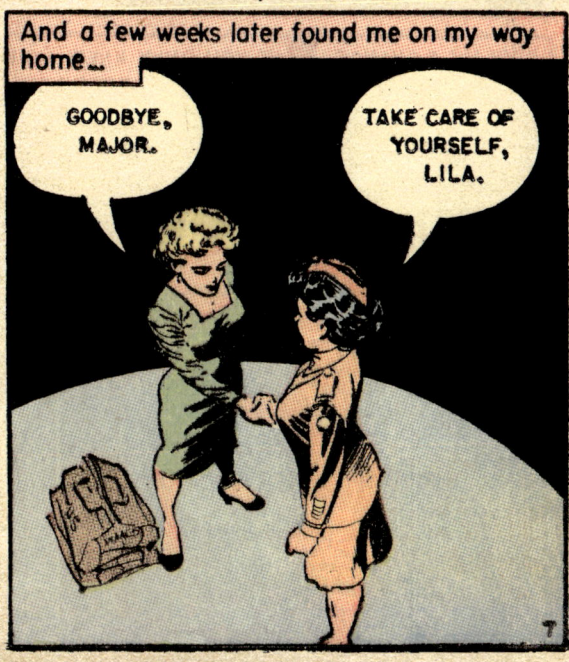

GOODBYE, MAJOR.

TAKE CARE OF YOURSELF, LILA.

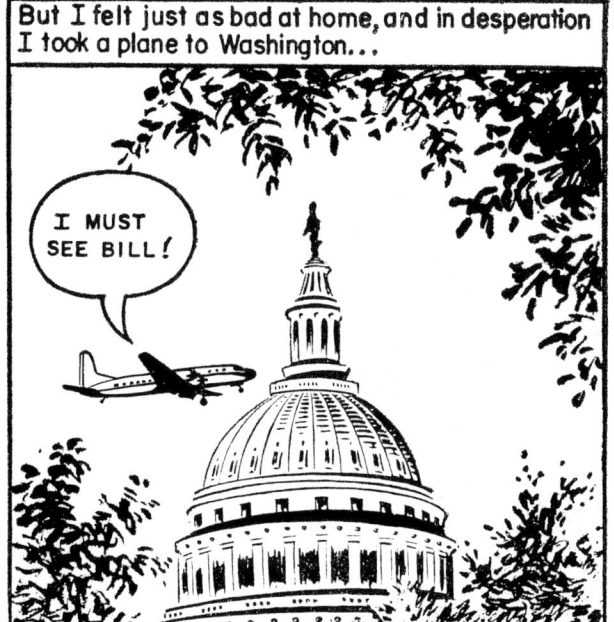

But I felt just as bad at home, and in desperation I took a plane to Washington...

I MUST SEE BILL!

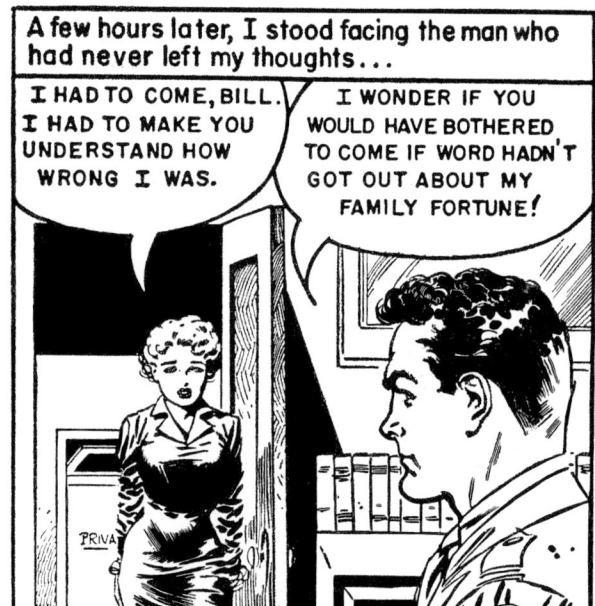

A few hours later, I stood facing the man who had never left my thoughts...

I HAD TO COME, BILL. I HAD TO MAKE YOU UNDERSTAND HOW WRONG I WAS.

I WONDER IF YOU WOULD HAVE BOTHERED TO COME IF WORD HADN'T GOT OUT ABOUT MY FAMILY FORTUNE!

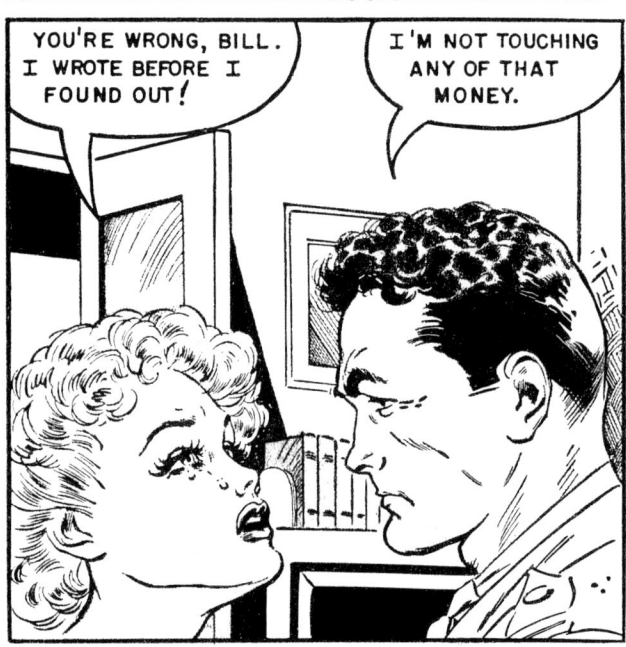

YOU'RE WRONG, BILL. I WROTE BEFORE I FOUND OUT!

I'M NOT TOUCHING ANY OF THAT MONEY.

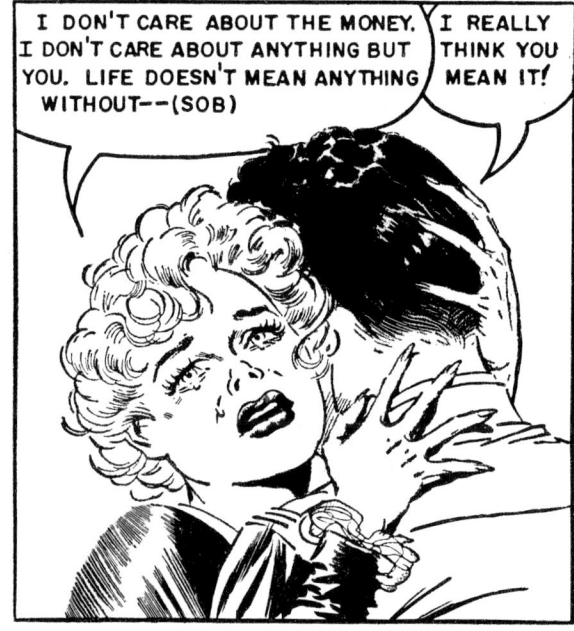

I DON'T CARE ABOUT THE MONEY. I DON'T CARE ABOUT ANYTHING BUT YOU. LIFE DOESN'T MEAN ANYTHING WITHOUT--(SOB)

I REALLY THINK YOU MEAN IT!

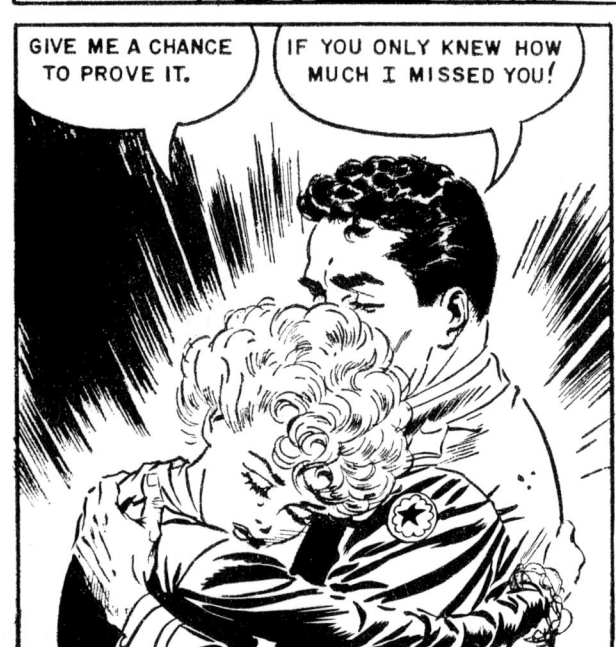

GIVE ME A CHANCE TO PROVE IT.

IF YOU ONLY KNEW HOW MUCH I MISSED YOU!

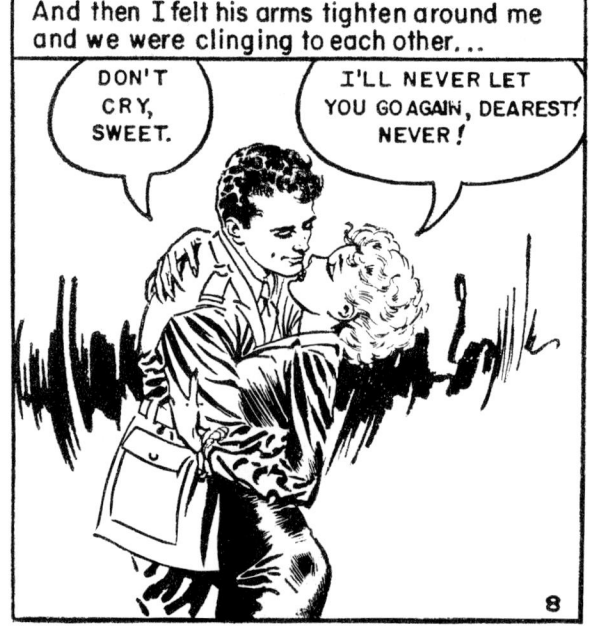

And then I felt his arms tighten around me and we were clinging to each other...

DON'T CRY, SWEET.

I'LL NEVER LET YOU GO AGAIN, DEAREST! NEVER!

8

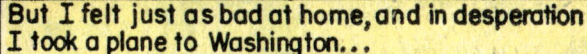
But I felt just as bad at home, and in desperation I took a plane to Washington...

I MUST SEE BILL!

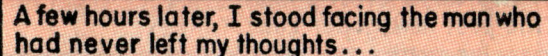
A few hours later, I stood facing the man who had never left my thoughts...

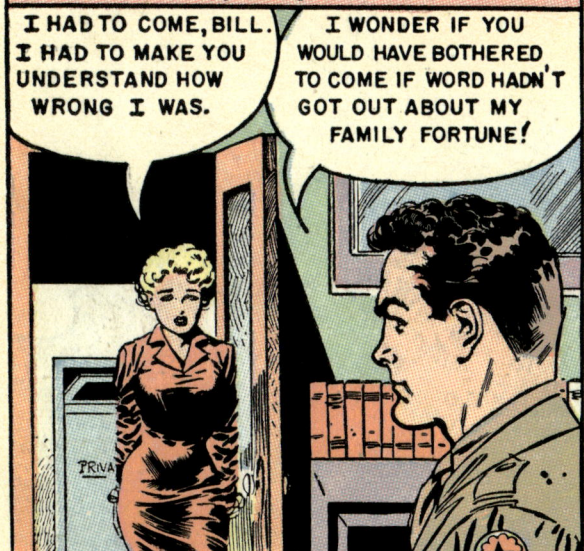
I HAD TO COME, BILL. I HAD TO MAKE YOU UNDERSTAND HOW WRONG I WAS.

I WONDER IF YOU WOULD HAVE BOTHERED TO COME IF WORD HADN'T GOT OUT ABOUT MY FAMILY FORTUNE!

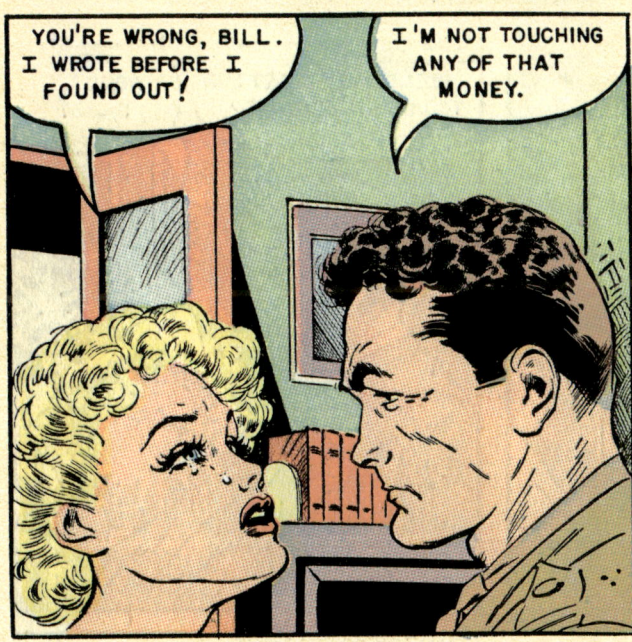
YOU'RE WRONG, BILL. I WROTE BEFORE I FOUND OUT!

I'M NOT TOUCHING ANY OF THAT MONEY.

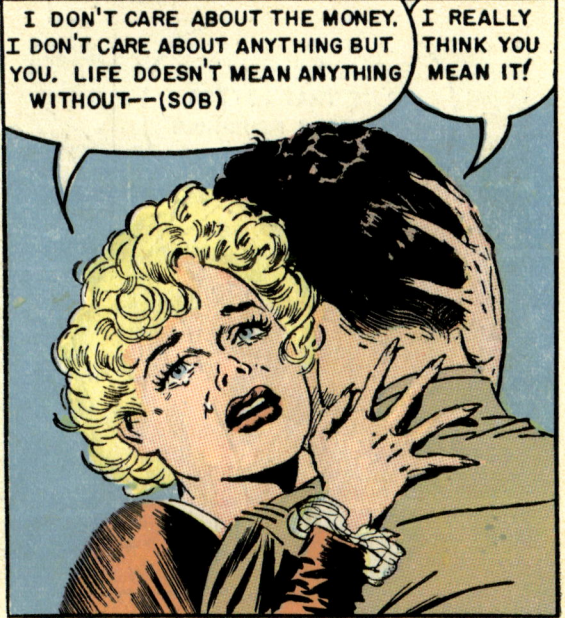
I DON'T CARE ABOUT THE MONEY. I DON'T CARE ABOUT ANYTHING BUT YOU. LIFE DOESN'T MEAN ANYTHING WITHOUT--(SOB)

I REALLY THINK YOU MEAN IT!

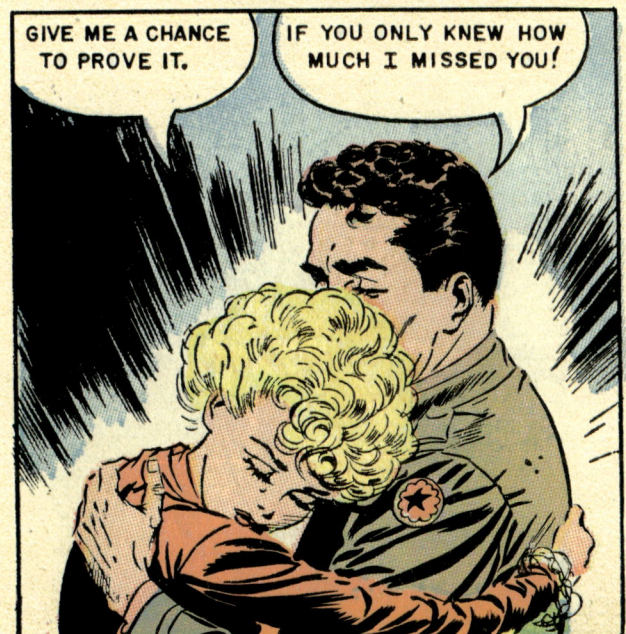
GIVE ME A CHANCE TO PROVE IT.

IF YOU ONLY KNEW HOW MUCH I MISSED YOU!

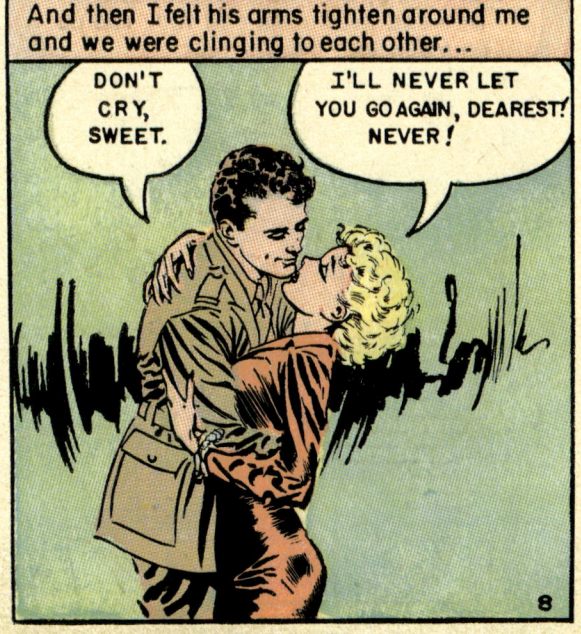
And then I felt his arms tighten around me and we were clinging to each other...

DON'T CRY, SWEET.

I'LL NEVER LET YOU GO AGAIN, DEAREST! NEVER!

8

TOO LATE FOR Love

HEY, LILA, I HAVE SOME NEWS FOR YOU. THEY SHIFTED YOU TO MY DEPARTMENT. FROM NOW ON, YOU'RE GOING TO BE MY PRIVATE SECRETARY!

NOW I'LL BE NEAR HIM ALL THE TIME! NOW IS MY CHANCE TO MAKE HIM FALL IN LOVE WITH ME!

FRANK FRAZETTA
53

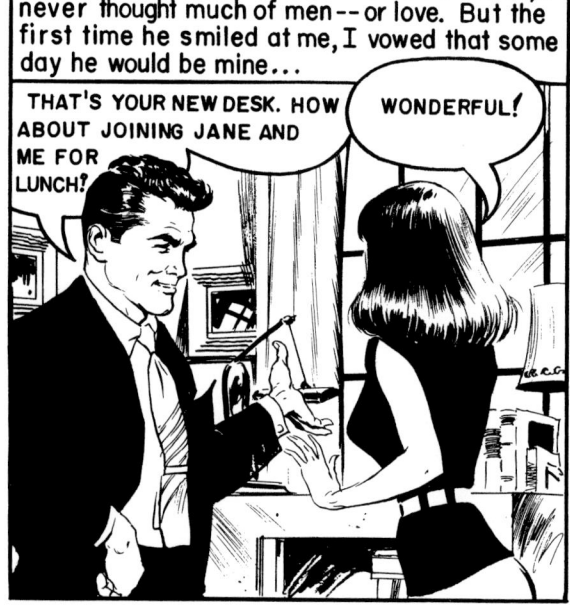

Until Tom came to work in the same office, I never thought much of men -- or love. But the first time he smiled at me, I vowed that some day he would be mine...

THAT'S YOUR NEW DESK. HOW ABOUT JOINING JANE AND ME FOR LUNCH?

WONDERFUL!

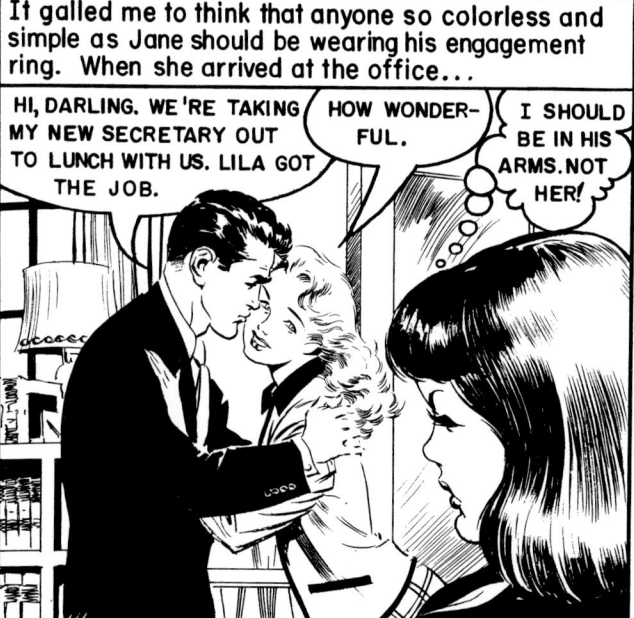

It galled me to think that anyone so colorless and simple as Jane should be wearing his engagement ring. When she arrived at the office...

HI, DARLING. WE'RE TAKING MY NEW SECRETARY OUT TO LUNCH WITH US. LILA GOT THE JOB.

HOW WONDERFUL.

I SHOULD BE IN HIS ARMS, NOT HER!

LILA ALWAYS BELIEVED THAT IF YOU WANTED SOMETHING BADLY ENOUGH -- TAKE IT! BUT WHEN SHE REACHED FOR A MAN THAT SOMEONE ELSE HAD CLAIM TO, THERE WAS ONLY PANGS OF REMORSE TO REMIND HER THAT IT WAS.......

TOO LATE FOR *Love*

HEY, LILA, I HAVE SOME NEWS FOR YOU. THEY SHIFTED YOU TO MY DEPARTMENT. FROM NOW ON, YOU'RE GOING TO BE MY PRIVATE SECRETARY!

NOW I'LL BE NEAR HIM ALL THE TIME! NOW IS MY CHANCE TO MAKE HIM FALL IN LOVE WITH ME!

FRANK FRAZETTA 53

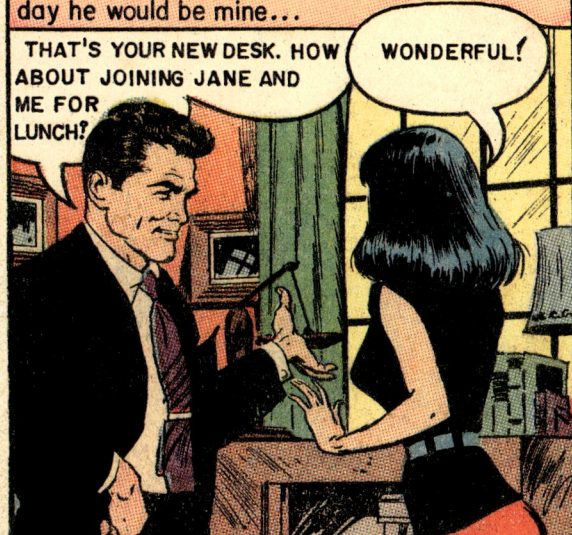

Until Tom came to work in the same office, I never thought much of men -- or love. But the first time he smiled at me, I vowed that some day he would be mine...

THAT'S YOUR NEW DESK. HOW ABOUT JOINING JANE AND ME FOR LUNCH?

WONDERFUL!

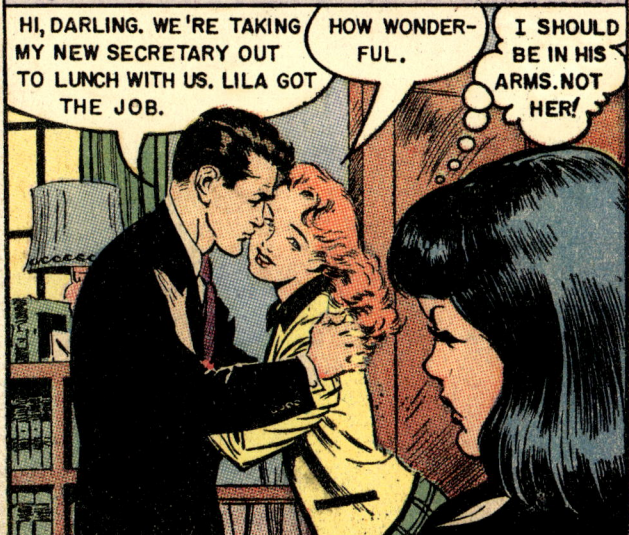

It galled me to think that anyone so colorless and simple as Jane should be wearing his engagement ring. When she arrived at the office...

HI, DARLING. WE'RE TAKING MY NEW SECRETARY OUT TO LUNCH WITH US. LILA GOT THE JOB.

HOW WONDERFUL.

I SHOULD BE IN HIS ARMS, NOT HER!

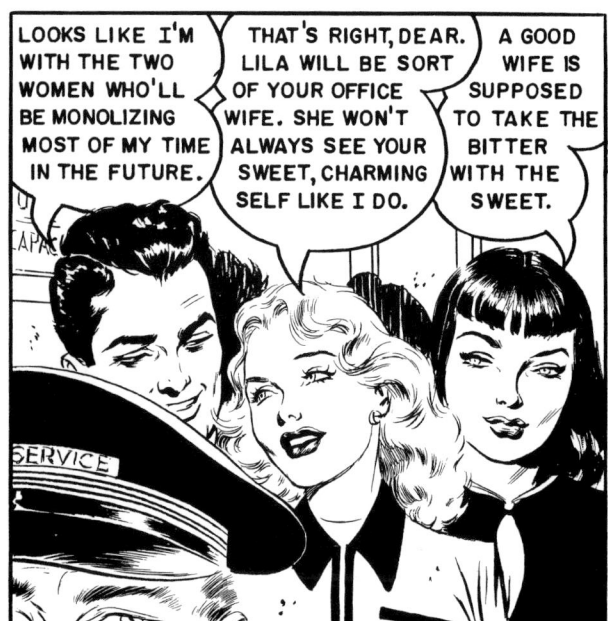

LOOKS LIKE I'M WITH THE TWO WOMEN WHO'LL BE MONOLIZING MOST OF MY TIME IN THE FUTURE.

THAT'S RIGHT, DEAR. LILA WILL BE SORT OF YOUR OFFICE WIFE. SHE WON'T ALWAYS SEE YOUR SWEET, CHARMING SELF LIKE I DO.

A GOOD WIFE IS SUPPOSED TO TAKE THE BITTER WITH THE SWEET.

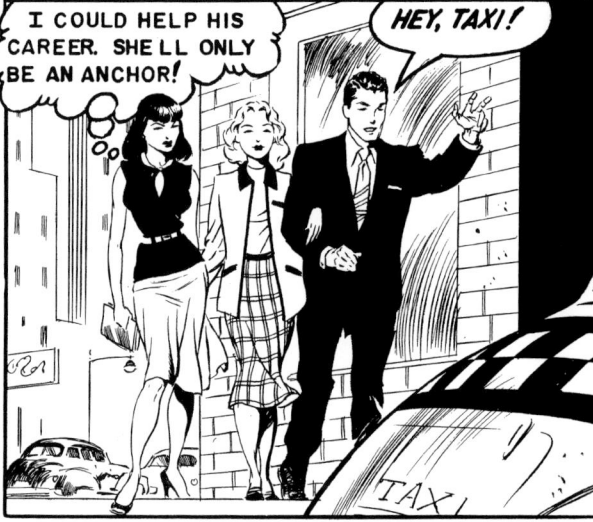

Jane saw no significance in my remark, but it infuriated me to think that a wish-washy person like her could attract a man like Tom...

I COULD HELP HIS CAREER. SHE'LL ONLY BE AN ANCHOR!

HEY, TAXI!

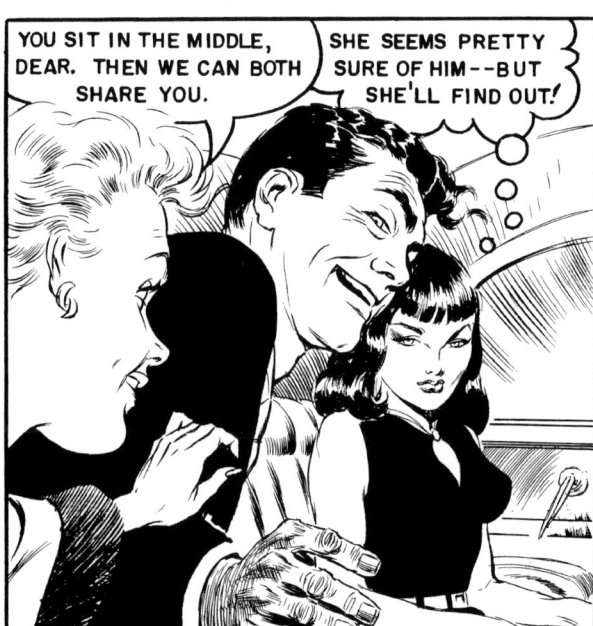

YOU SIT IN THE MIDDLE, DEAR. THEN WE CAN BOTH SHARE YOU.

SHE SEEMS PRETTY SURE OF HIM--BUT SHE'LL FIND OUT!

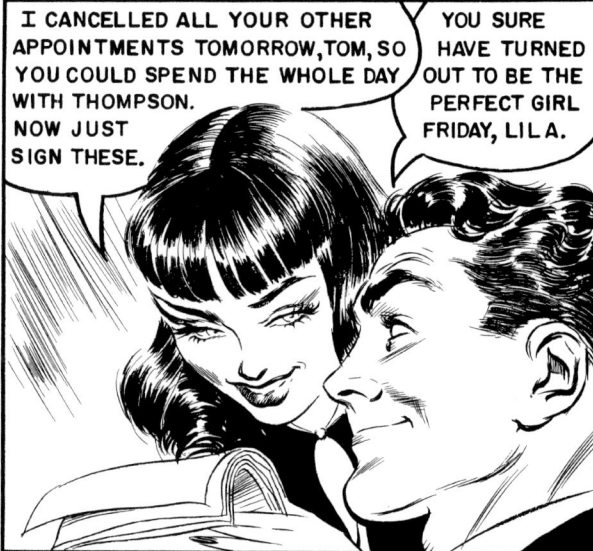

After that, I used every feminine trick I knew to make Tom conscious of me...

I CANCELLED ALL YOUR OTHER APPOINTMENTS TOMORROW, TOM, SO YOU COULD SPEND THE WHOLE DAY WITH THOMPSON. NOW JUST SIGN THESE.

YOU SURE HAVE TURNED OUT TO BE THE PERFECT GIRL FRIDAY, LILA.

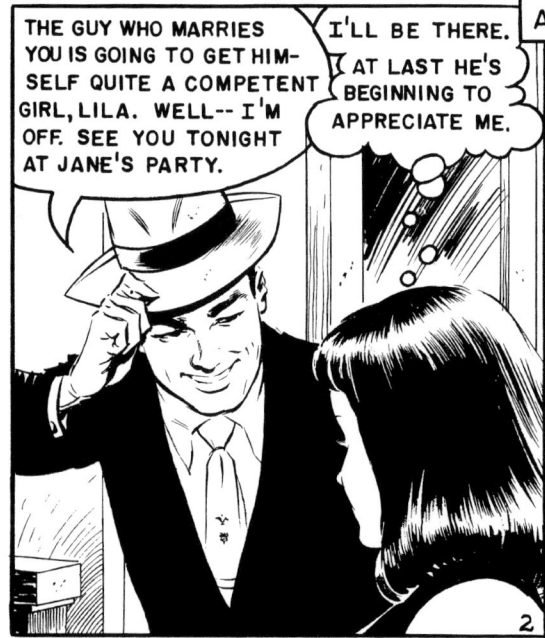

THE GUY WHO MARRIES YOU IS GOING TO GET HIM-SELF QUITE A COMPETENT GIRL, LILA. WELL-- I'M OFF. SEE YOU TONIGHT AT JANE'S PARTY.

I'LL BE THERE. AT LAST HE'S BEGINNING TO APPRECIATE ME.

2

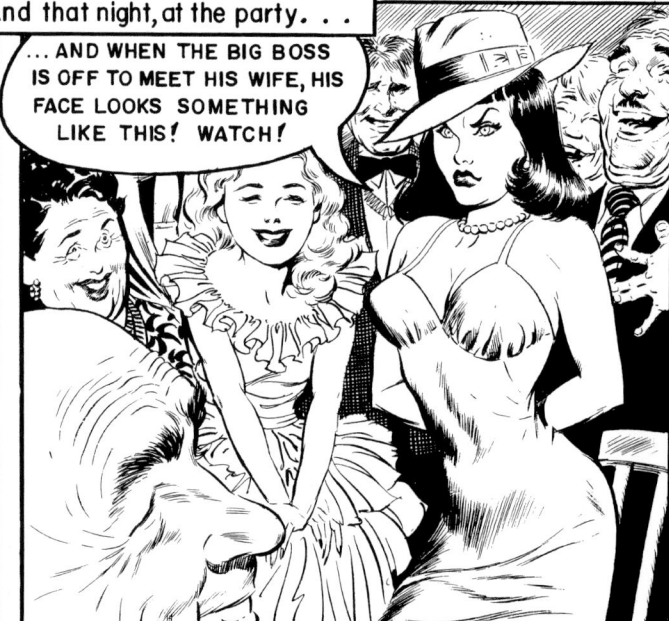

And that night, at the party...

...AND WHEN THE BIG BOSS IS OFF TO MEET HIS WIFE, HIS FACE LOOKS SOMETHING LIKE THIS! WATCH!

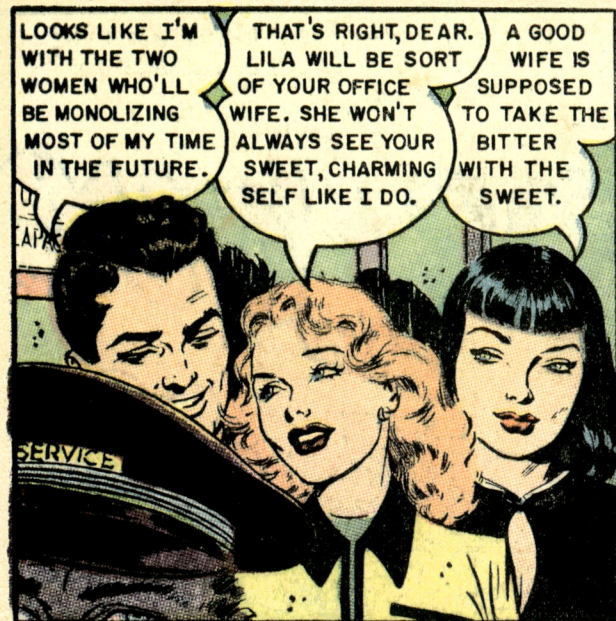

LOOKS LIKE I'M WITH THE TWO WOMEN WHO'LL BE MONOLIZING MOST OF MY TIME IN THE FUTURE.

THAT'S RIGHT, DEAR. LILA WILL BE SORT OF YOUR OFFICE WIFE. SHE WON'T ALWAYS SEE YOUR SWEET, CHARMING SELF LIKE I DO.

A GOOD WIFE IS SUPPOSED TO TAKE THE BITTER WITH THE SWEET.

Jane saw no significance in my remark, but it infuriated me to think that a wish-washy person like her could attract a man like Tom...

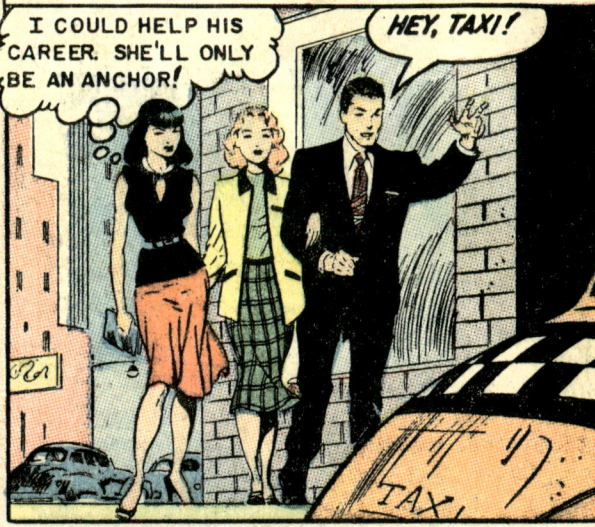

I COULD HELP HIS CAREER. SHE'LL ONLY BE AN ANCHOR!

HEY, TAXI!

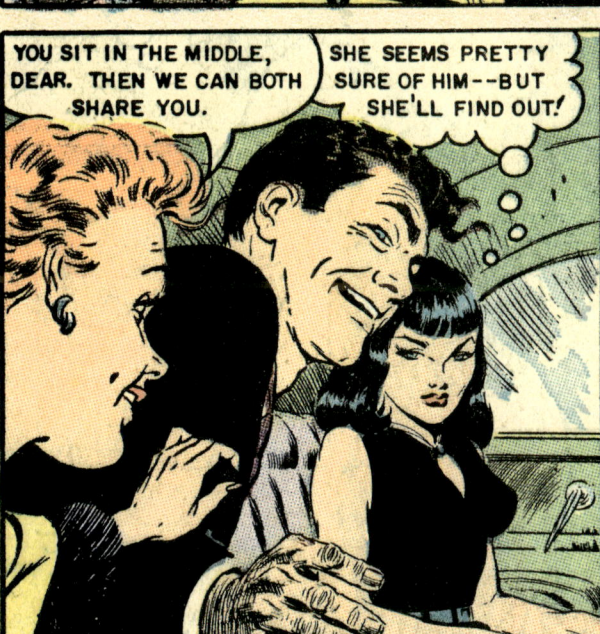

YOU SIT IN THE MIDDLE, DEAR. THEN WE CAN BOTH SHARE YOU.

SHE SEEMS PRETTY SURE OF HIM--BUT SHE'LL FIND OUT!

After that, I used every feminine trick I knew to make Tom conscious of me...

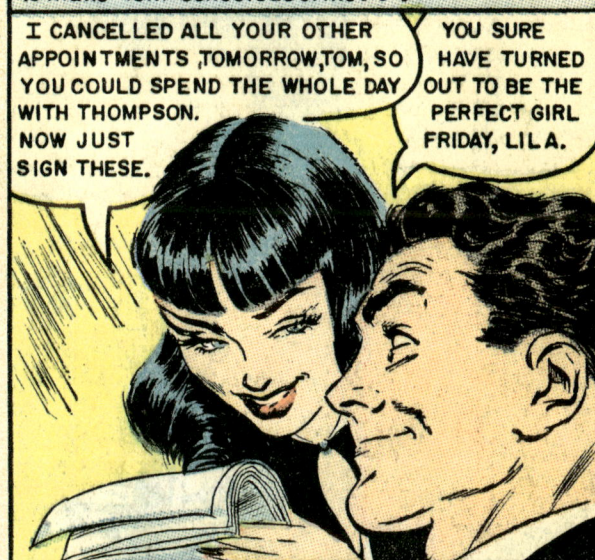

I CANCELLED ALL YOUR OTHER APPOINTMENTS, TOMORROW, TOM, SO YOU COULD SPEND THE WHOLE DAY WITH THOMPSON. NOW JUST SIGN THESE.

YOU SURE HAVE TURNED OUT TO BE THE PERFECT GIRL FRIDAY, LILA.

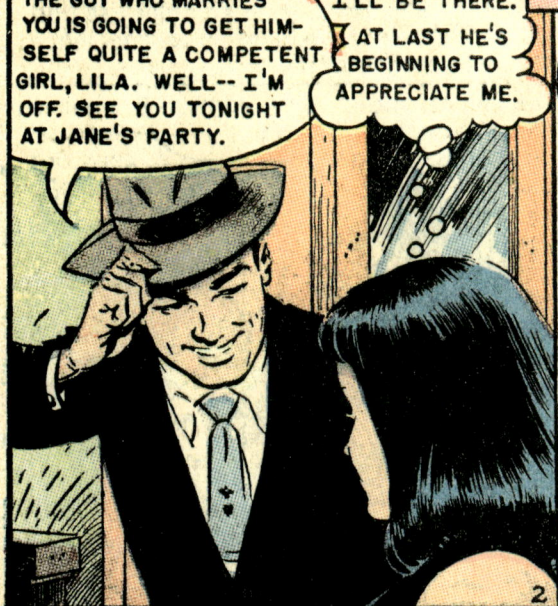

THE GUY WHO MARRIES YOU IS GOING TO GET HIM-SELF QUITE A COMPETENT GIRL, LILA. WELL-- I'M OFF. SEE YOU TONIGHT AT JANE'S PARTY.

I'LL BE THERE. AT LAST HE'S BEGINNING TO APPRECIATE ME.

And that night, at the party...

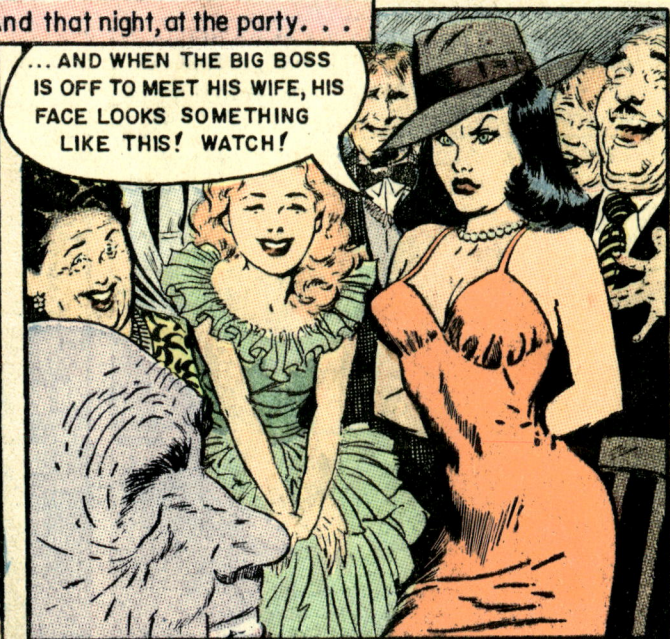

...AND WHEN THE BIG BOSS IS OFF TO MEET HIS WIFE, HIS FACE LOOKS SOMETHING LIKE THIS! WATCH!

2

Later, I saw Tom leave Jane and head toward me. Deftly, I guided him out to the porch...

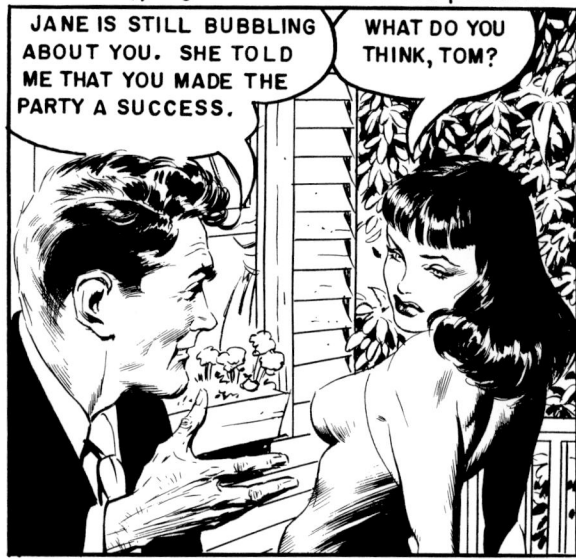

JANE IS STILL BUBBLING ABOUT YOU. SHE TOLD ME THAT YOU MADE THE PARTY A SUCCESS.

WHAT DO YOU THINK, TOM?

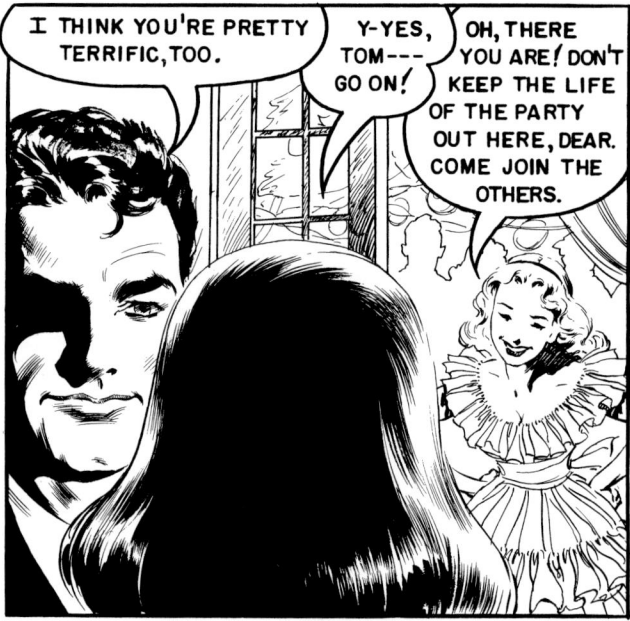

I THINK YOU'RE PRETTY TERRIFIC, TOO.

Y-YES, TOM--- GO ON!

OH, THERE YOU ARE! DON'T KEEP THE LIFE OF THE PARTY OUT HERE, DEAR. COME JOIN THE OTHERS.

I was wild with fury at Jane's sudden interruption. If only she hadn't shown up, Tom would have said what I yearned to hear...

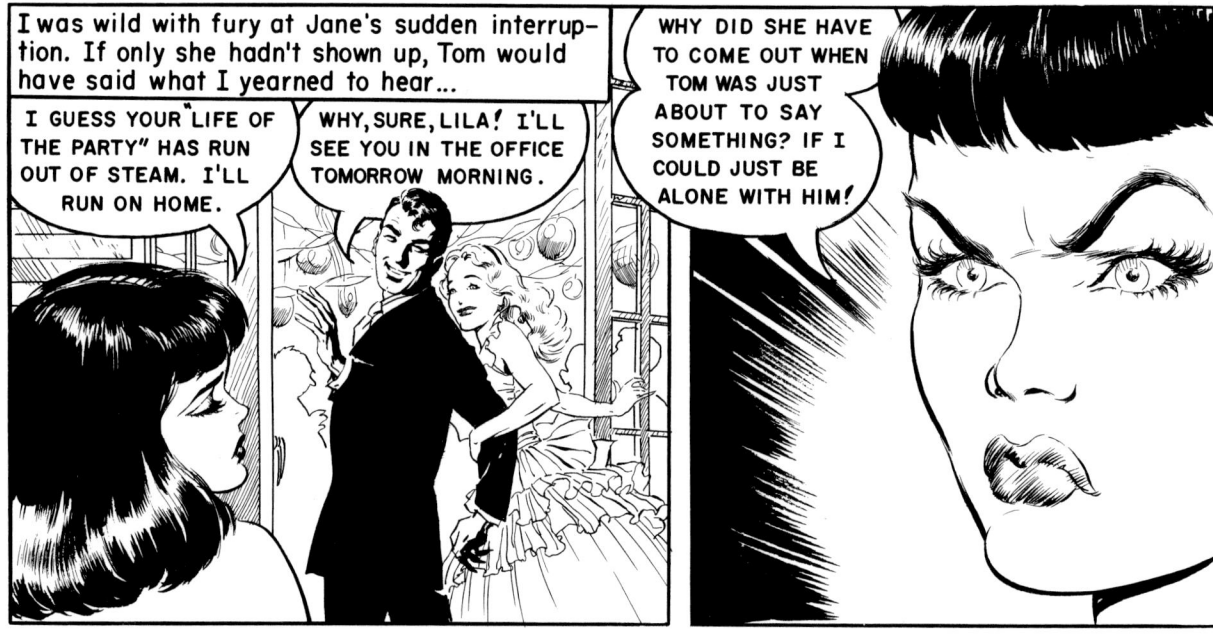

I GUESS YOUR "LIFE OF THE PARTY" HAS RUN OUT OF STEAM. I'LL RUN ON HOME.

WHY, SURE, LILA! I'LL SEE YOU IN THE OFFICE TOMORROW MORNING.

WHY DID SHE HAVE TO COME OUT WHEN TOM WAS JUST ABOUT TO SAY SOMETHING? IF I COULD JUST BE ALONE WITH HIM!

My chance came again when I persuaded Tom to take me along to see an important customer and on the way back...

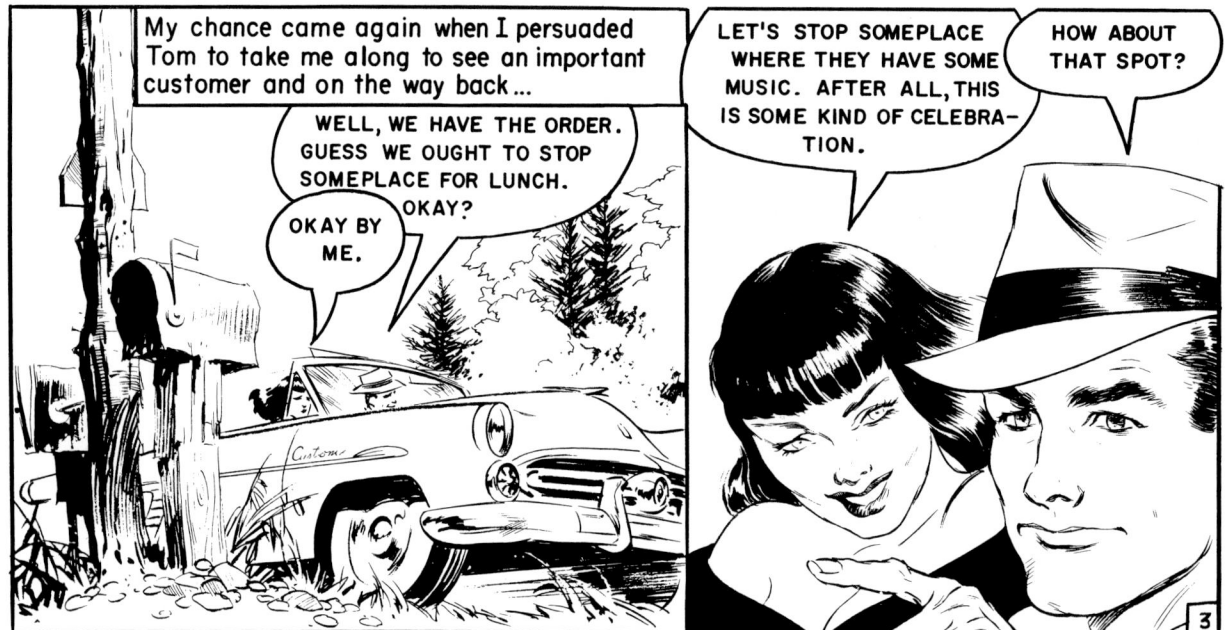

WELL, WE HAVE THE ORDER. GUESS WE OUGHT TO STOP SOMEPLACE FOR LUNCH. OKAY?

OKAY BY ME.

LET'S STOP SOMEPLACE WHERE THEY HAVE SOME MUSIC. AFTER ALL, THIS IS SOME KIND OF CELEBRATION.

HOW ABOUT THAT SPOT?

3

Later, I saw Tom leave Jane and head toward me. Deftly, I guided him out to the porch...

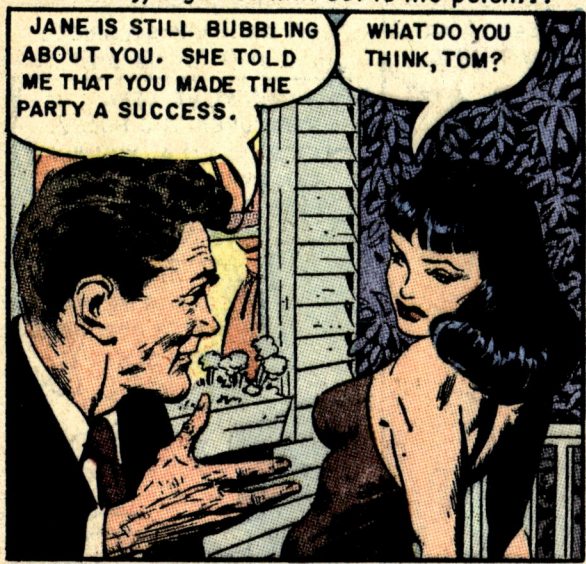

JANE IS STILL BUBBLING ABOUT YOU. SHE TOLD ME THAT YOU MADE THE PARTY A SUCCESS.

WHAT DO YOU THINK, TOM?

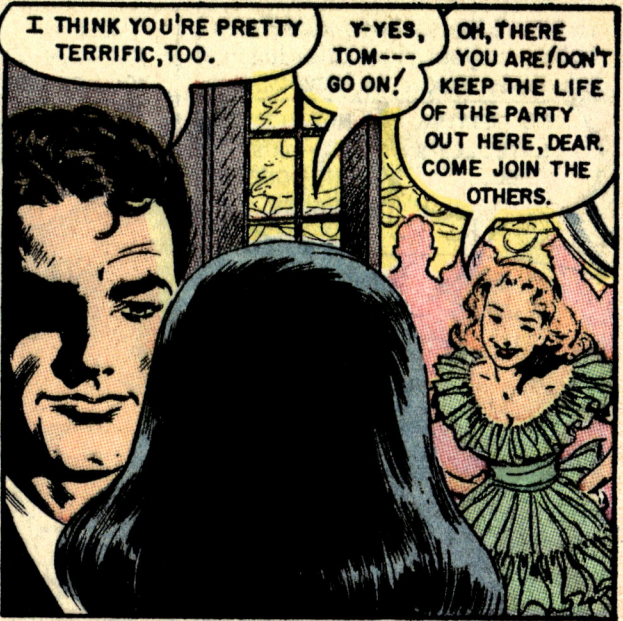

I THINK YOU'RE PRETTY TERRIFIC, TOO.

Y-YES, TOM--- GO ON!

OH, THERE YOU ARE! DON'T KEEP THE LIFE OF THE PARTY OUT HERE, DEAR. COME JOIN THE OTHERS.

I was wild with fury at Jane's sudden interruption. If only she hadn't shown up, Tom would have said what I yearned to hear...

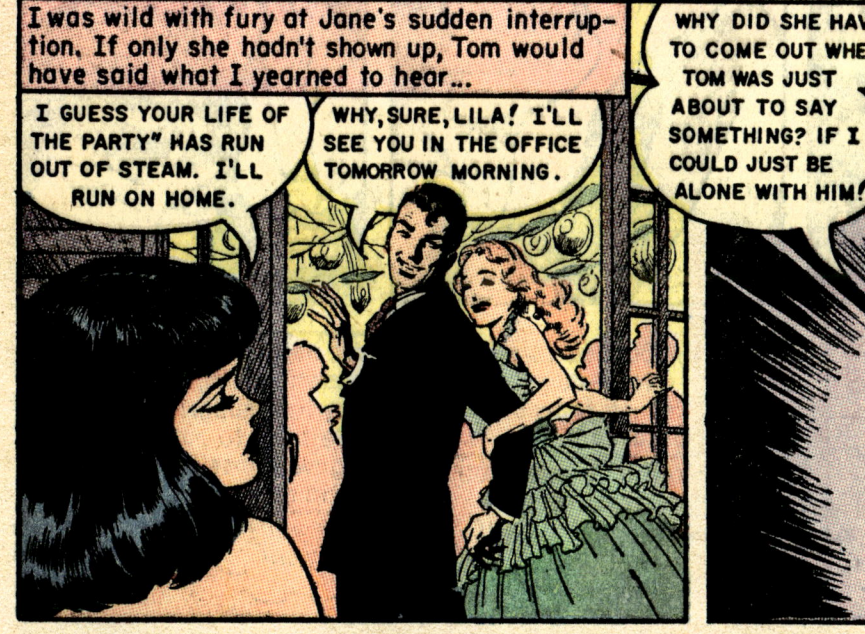

I GUESS YOUR LIFE OF THE PARTY" HAS RUN OUT OF STEAM. I'LL RUN ON HOME.

WHY, SURE, LILA! I'LL SEE YOU IN THE OFFICE TOMORROW MORNING.

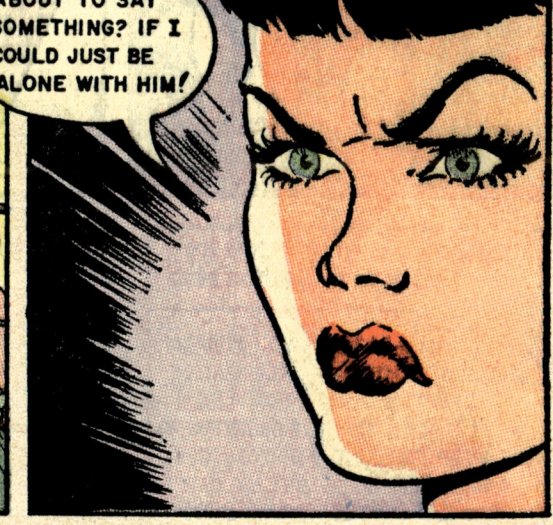

WHY DID SHE HAVE TO COME OUT WHEN TOM WAS JUST ABOUT TO SAY SOMETHING? IF I COULD JUST BE ALONE WITH HIM!

My chance came again when I persuaded Tom to take me along to see an important customer and on the way back...

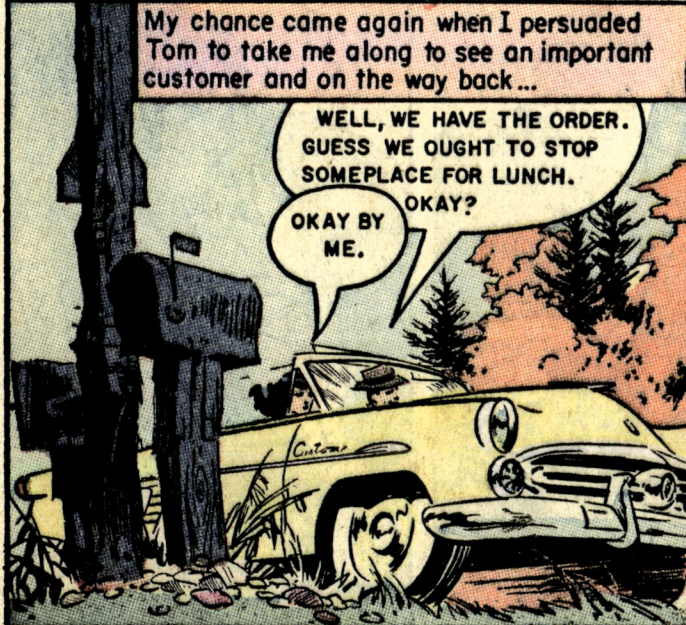

WELL, WE HAVE THE ORDER. GUESS WE OUGHT TO STOP SOMEPLACE FOR LUNCH. OKAY?

OKAY BY ME.

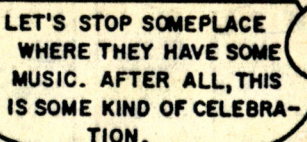

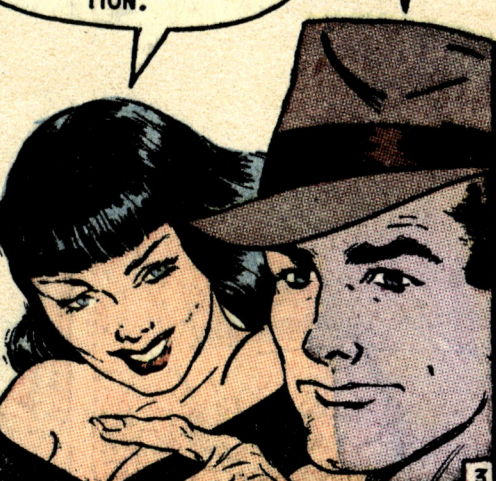

LET'S STOP SOMEPLACE WHERE THEY HAVE SOME MUSIC. AFTER ALL, THIS IS SOME KIND OF CELEBRATION.

HOW ABOUT THAT SPOT?

3

We found the sort of place I was looking for, but right after lunch Tom made a move to leave...

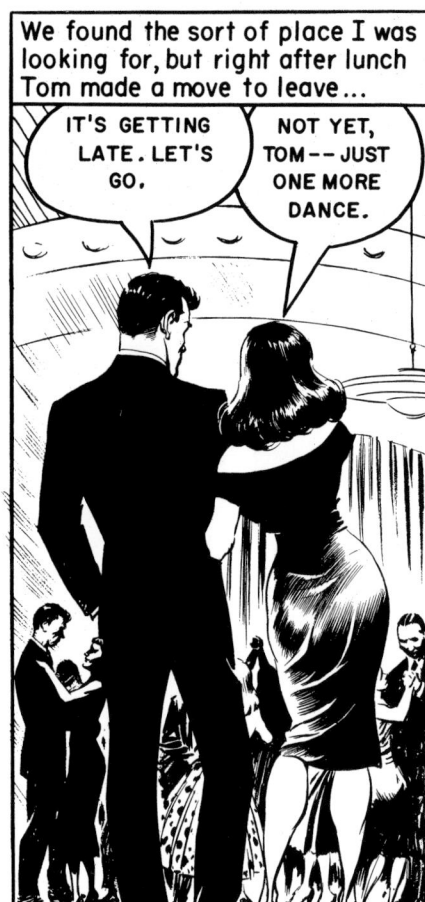

IT'S GETTING LATE. LET'S GO.

NOT YET, TOM-- JUST ONE MORE DANCE.

IT'S HARD TO SAY NO, WHEN YOU ASK LIKE THAT, LILA.

IT'S EASY TO ASK WHEN IT MEANS DANCING WITH YOU.

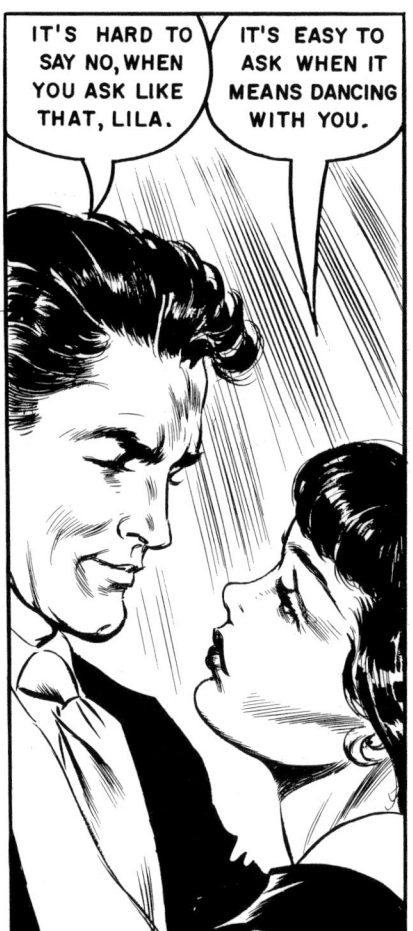

The music's beat matched the happy pounding of my heart and time seemed to stand still for us until ...

WOW! WE'VE BEEN HERE OVER TWO HOURS. LET'S GO, LILA. YOU SURE CAN MAKE A MAN FORGET EVERYTHING, WHEN YOU WANT TO.

HE'S FALLING FOR ME--AND HE'S BEGINNING TO SENSE IT.

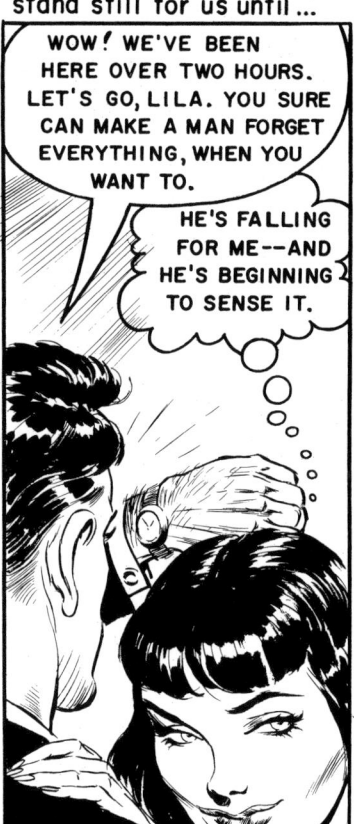

As we were driving I saw my opportunity to make him stop again...

OH, TOM -- I'VE ALWAYS WANTED TO SEE THE PLACE. CAN'T WE STOP FOR JUST A MINUTE?

YOU WOMEN ALL FALL FOR THE ROMANTIC SPOTS. O.K., BUT WE CAN'T STAY LONG.

See PARADISE HEIGHTS 1 MILE AHEAD

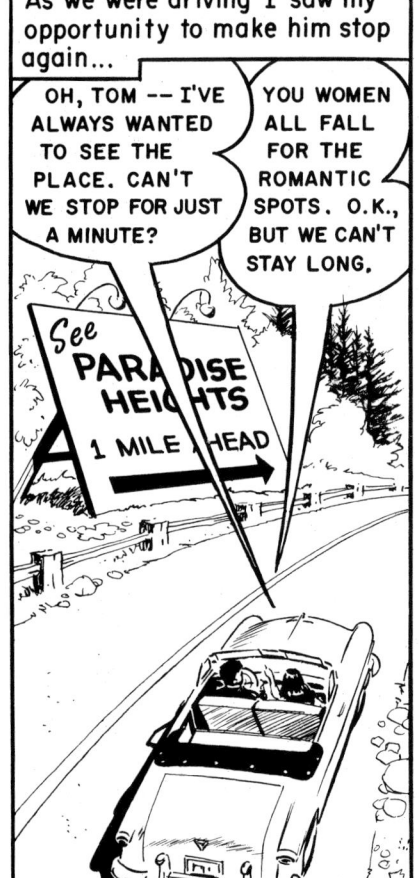

Nature surrounded us and we seemed to be alone in the world. I leaned provocatively toward Tom...

WOULDN'T YOU LIKE TO--KISS ME, TOM?

WHY--YOU LITTLE DEVIL!

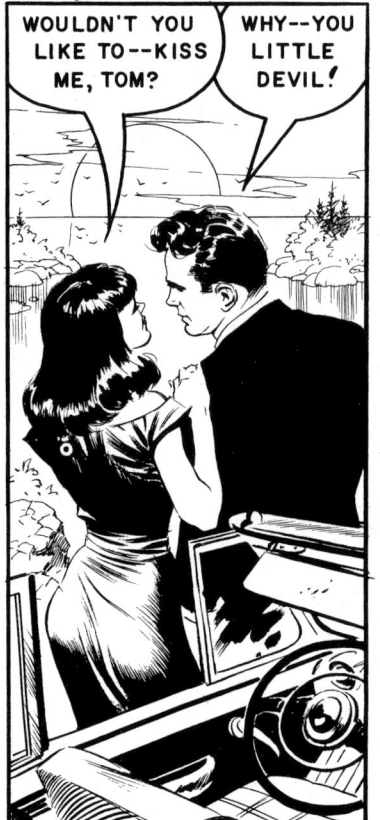

Before he could say anymore, I let myself go limp against him and my lips hungrily sought his. He tried to pull away and then gave himself up to that ecstatic moment...

I'VE WON! I'VE WON!

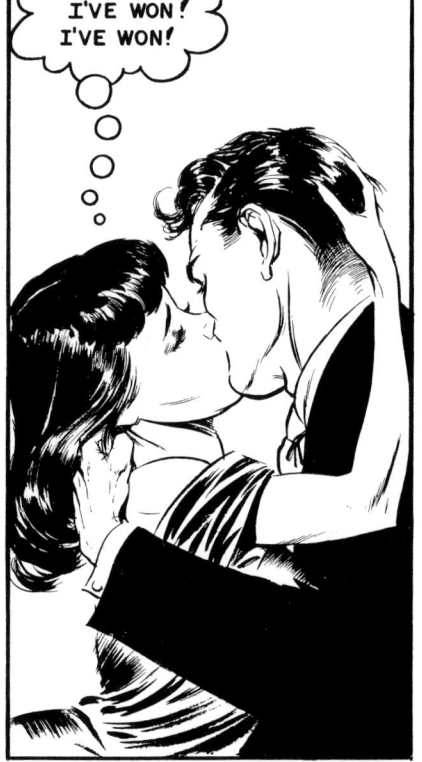

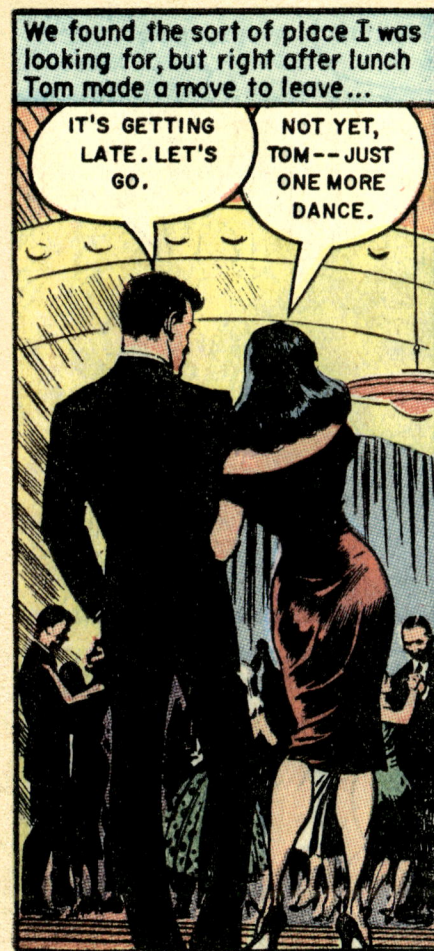

We found the sort of place I was looking for, but right after lunch Tom made a move to leave...

IT'S GETTING LATE. LET'S GO.

NOT YET, TOM -- JUST ONE MORE DANCE.

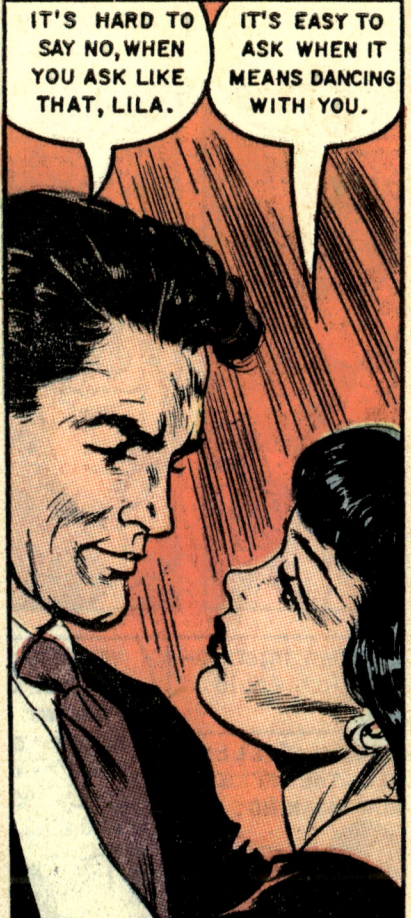

IT'S HARD TO SAY NO, WHEN YOU ASK LIKE THAT, LILA.

IT'S EASY TO ASK WHEN IT MEANS DANCING WITH YOU.

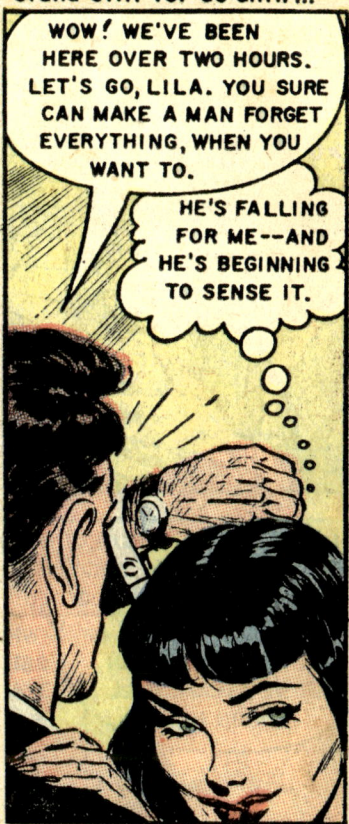

The music's beat matched the happy pounding of my heart and time seemed to stand still for us until...

WOW! WE'VE BEEN HERE OVER TWO HOURS. LET'S GO, LILA. YOU SURE CAN MAKE A MAN FORGET EVERYTHING, WHEN YOU WANT TO.

HE'S FALLING FOR ME--AND HE'S BEGINNING TO SENSE IT.

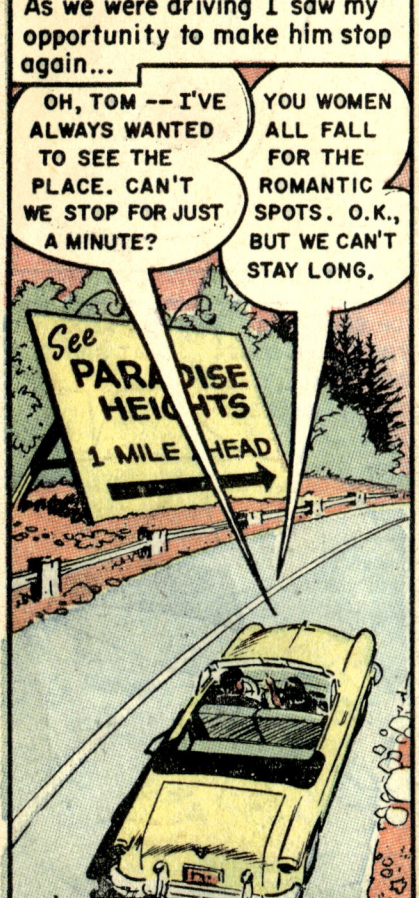

As we were driving I saw my opportunity to make him stop again...

OH, TOM -- I'VE ALWAYS WANTED TO SEE THE PLACE. CAN'T WE STOP FOR JUST A MINUTE?

YOU WOMEN ALL FALL FOR THE ROMANTIC SPOTS. O.K., BUT WE CAN'T STAY LONG.

See PARADISE HEIGHTS 1 MILE AHEAD

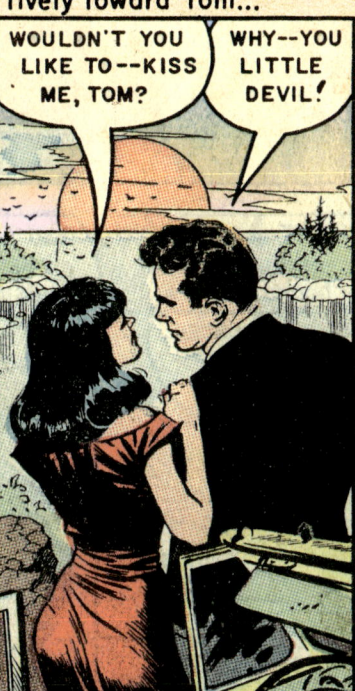

Nature surrounded us and we seemed to be alone in the world. I leaned provocatively toward Tom...

WOULDN'T YOU LIKE TO--KISS ME, TOM?

WHY--YOU LITTLE DEVIL!

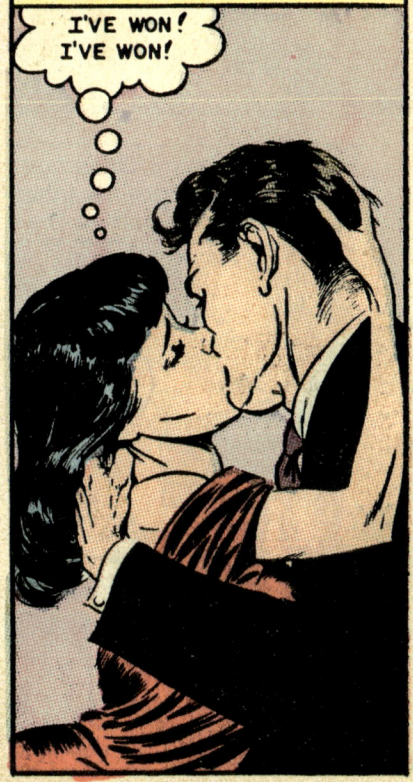

Before he could say anymore, I let myself go limp against him and my lips hungrily sought his. He tried to pull away and then gave himself up to that ecstatic moment...

I'VE WON! I'VE WON!

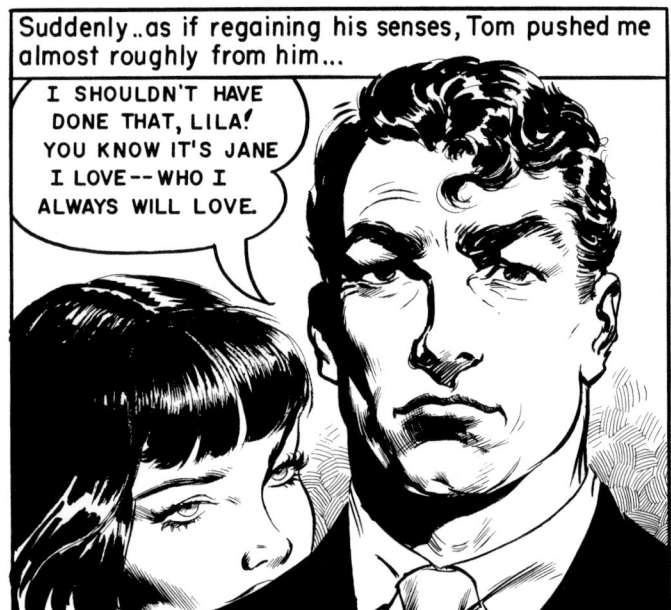

Suddenly..as if regaining his senses, Tom pushed me almost roughly from him...

I SHOULDN'T HAVE DONE THAT, LILA! YOU KNOW IT'S JANE I LOVE--WHO I ALWAYS WILL LOVE.

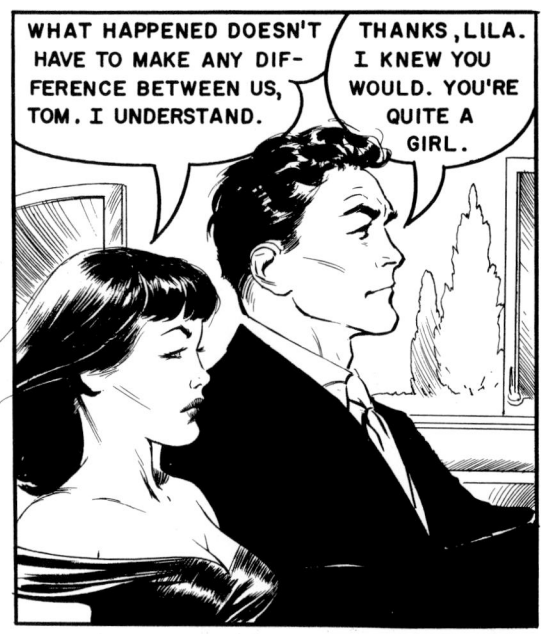

WHAT HAPPENED DOESN'T HAVE TO MAKE ANY DIFFERENCE BETWEEN US, TOM. I UNDERSTAND.

THANKS, LILA. I KNEW YOU WOULD. YOU'RE QUITE A GIRL.

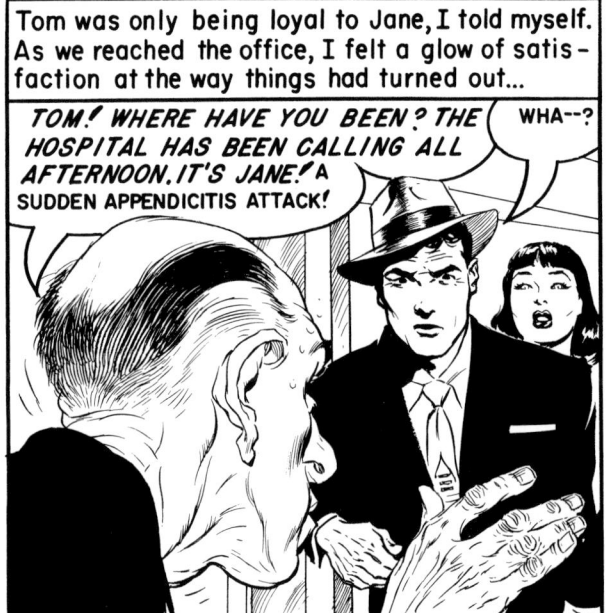

Tom was only being loyal to Jane, I told myself. As we reached the office, I felt a glow of satisfaction at the way things had turned out...

TOM! WHERE HAVE YOU BEEN? THE HOSPITAL HAS BEEN CALLING ALL AFTERNOON. IT'S JANE! A SUDDEN APPENDICITIS ATTACK!

WHA--?

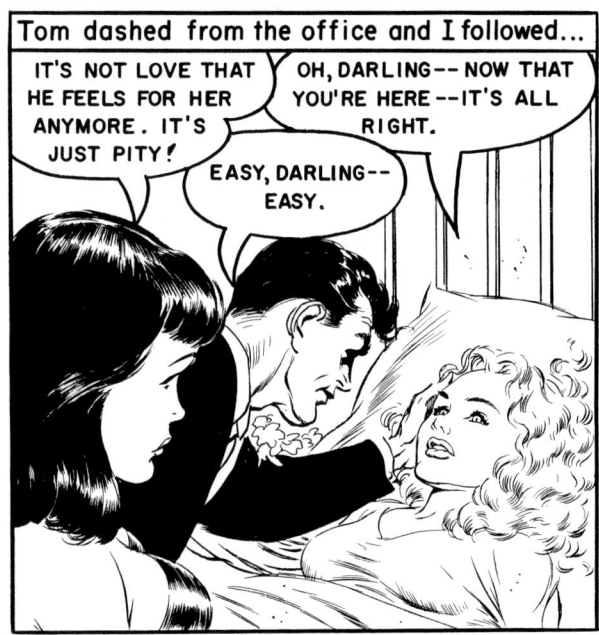

Tom dashed from the office and I followed...

IT'S NOT LOVE THAT HE FEELS FOR HER ANYMORE. IT'S JUST PITY!

EASY, DARLING-- EASY.

OH, DARLING-- NOW THAT YOU'RE HERE--IT'S ALL RIGHT.

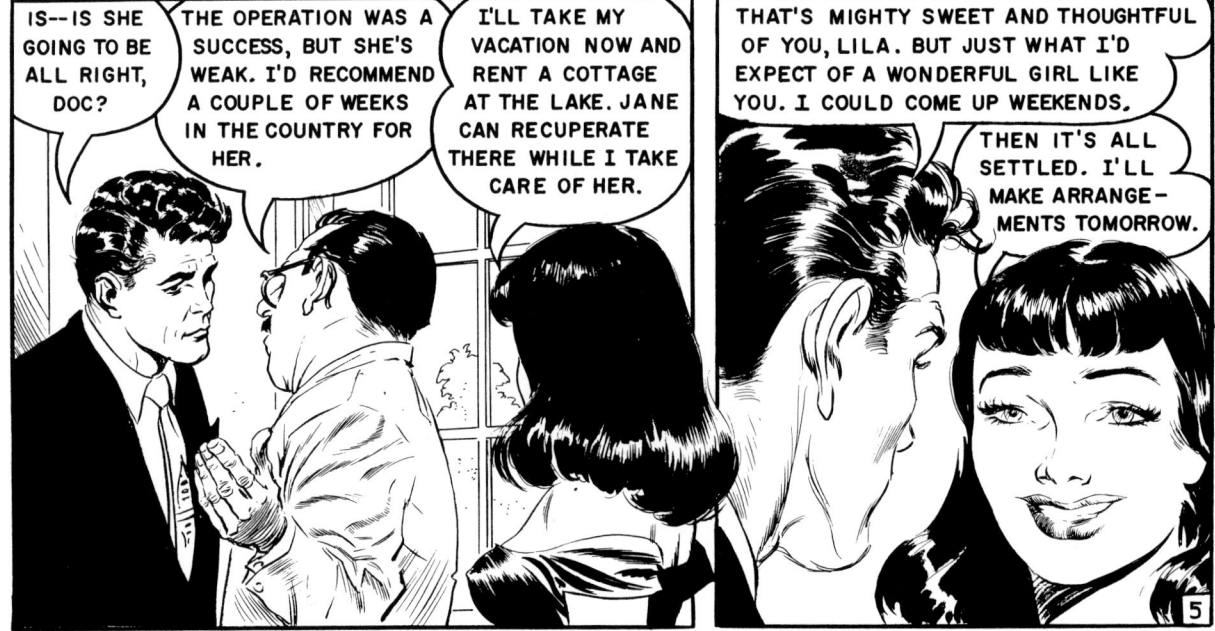

IS--IS SHE GOING TO BE ALL RIGHT, DOC?

THE OPERATION WAS A SUCCESS, BUT SHE'S WEAK. I'D RECOMMEND A COUPLE OF WEEKS IN THE COUNTRY FOR HER.

I'LL TAKE MY VACATION NOW AND RENT A COTTAGE AT THE LAKE. JANE CAN RECUPERATE THERE WHILE I TAKE CARE OF HER.

THAT'S MIGHTY SWEET AND THOUGHTFUL OF YOU, LILA. BUT JUST WHAT I'D EXPECT OF A WONDERFUL GIRL LIKE YOU. I COULD COME UP WEEKENDS.

THEN IT'S ALL SETTLED. I'LL MAKE ARRANGEMENTS TOMORROW.

5

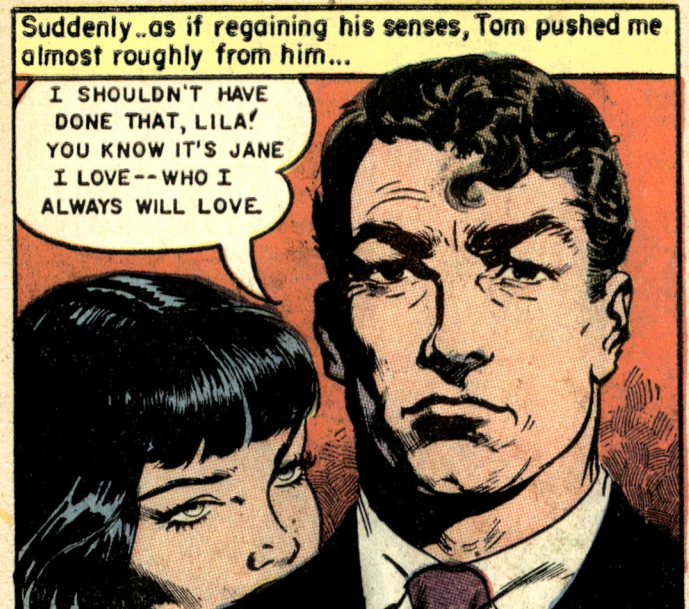

Suddenly...as if regaining his senses, Tom pushed me almost roughly from him...

I SHOULDN'T HAVE DONE THAT, LILA! YOU KNOW IT'S JANE I LOVE--WHO I ALWAYS WILL LOVE.

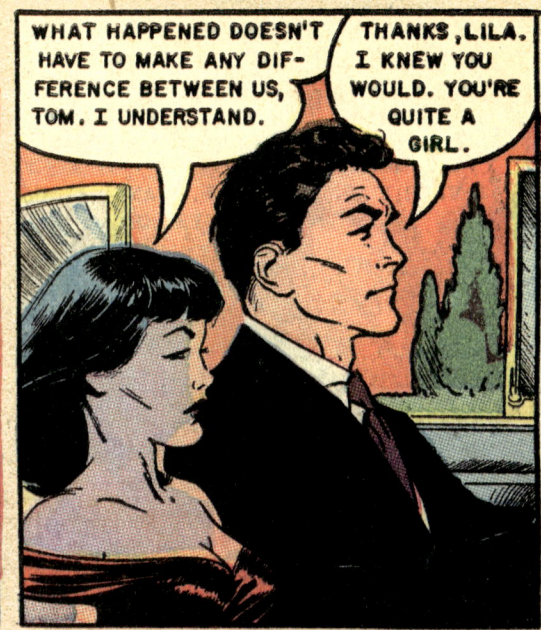

WHAT HAPPENED DOESN'T HAVE TO MAKE ANY DIFFERENCE BETWEEN US, TOM. I UNDERSTAND.

THANKS, LILA. I KNEW YOU WOULD. YOU'RE QUITE A GIRL.

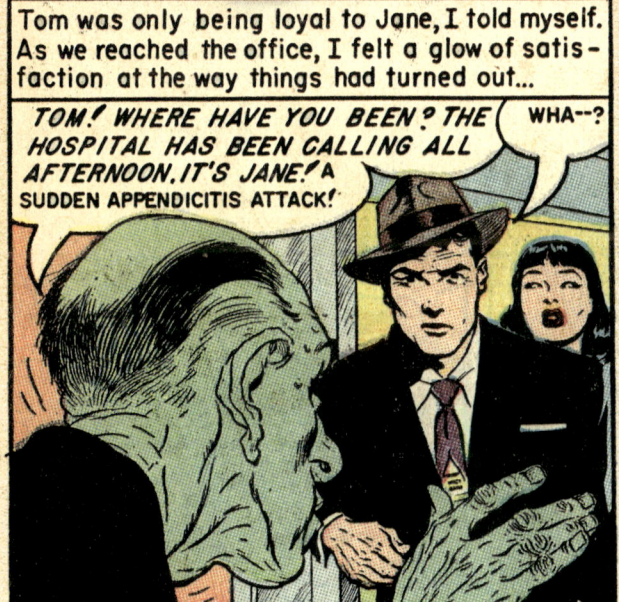

Tom was only being loyal to Jane, I told myself. As we reached the office, I felt a glow of satisfaction at the way things had turned out...

TOM! WHERE HAVE YOU BEEN? THE HOSPITAL HAS BEEN CALLING ALL AFTERNOON. IT'S JANE! A SUDDEN APPENDICITIS ATTACK!

WHA--?

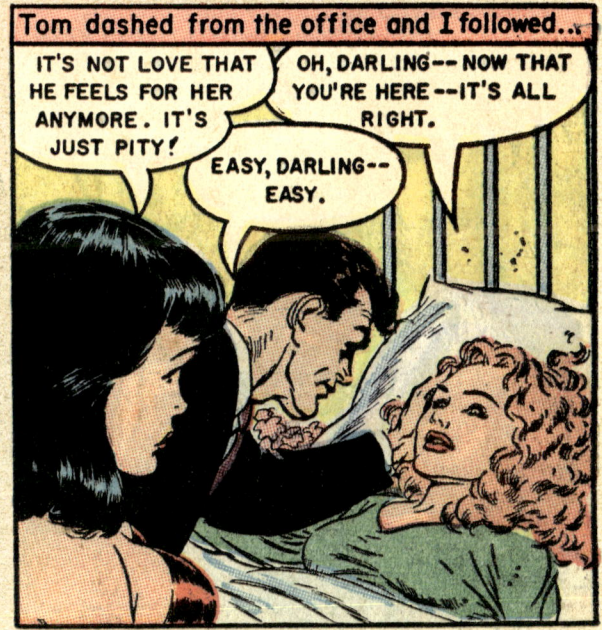

Tom dashed from the office and I followed...

IT'S NOT LOVE THAT HE FEELS FOR HER ANYMORE. IT'S JUST PITY!

OH, DARLING-- NOW THAT YOU'RE HERE--IT'S ALL RIGHT.

EASY, DARLING-- EASY.

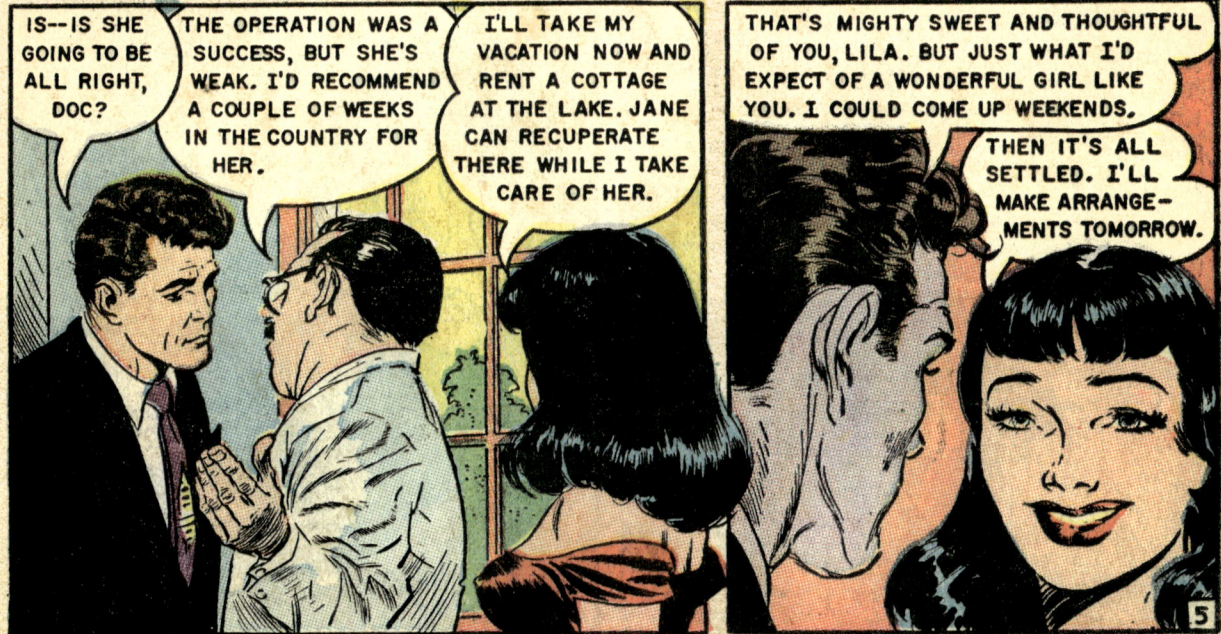

IS--IS SHE GOING TO BE ALL RIGHT, DOC?

THE OPERATION WAS A SUCCESS, BUT SHE'S WEAK. I'D RECOMMEND A COUPLE OF WEEKS IN THE COUNTRY FOR HER.

I'LL TAKE MY VACATION NOW AND RENT A COTTAGE AT THE LAKE. JANE CAN RECUPERATE THERE WHILE I TAKE CARE OF HER.

THAT'S MIGHTY SWEET AND THOUGHTFUL OF YOU, LILA. BUT JUST WHAT I'D EXPECT OF A WONDERFUL GIRL LIKE YOU. I COULD COME UP WEEKENDS.

THEN IT'S ALL SETTLED. I'LL MAKE ARRANGEMENTS TOMORROW.

5

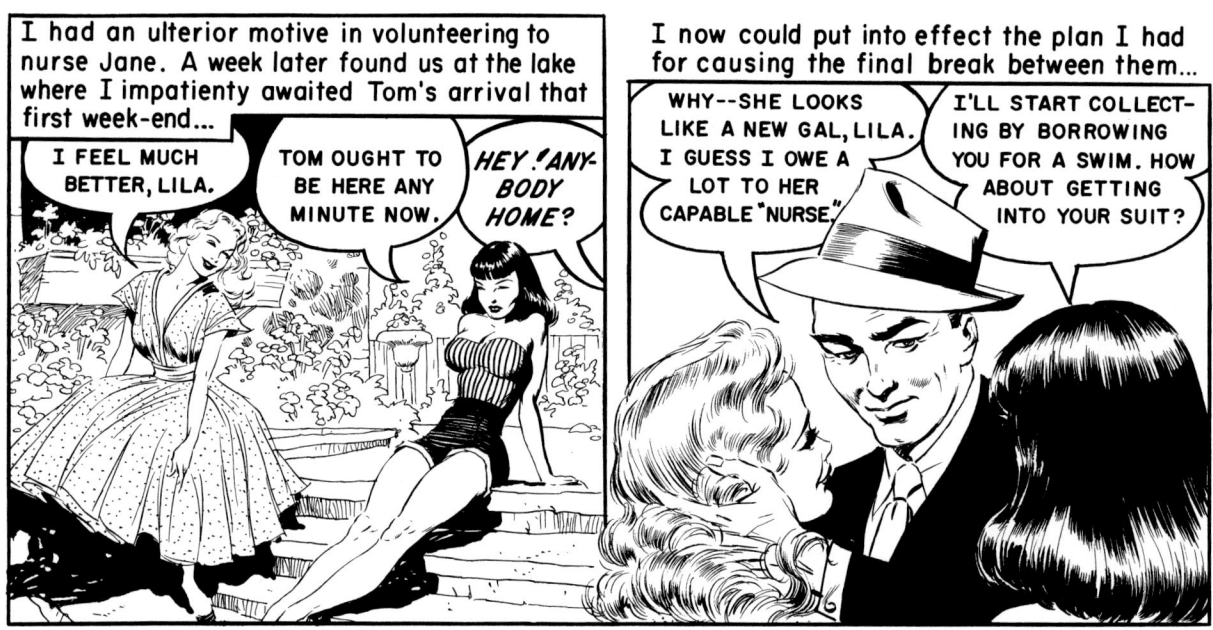

I had an ulterior motive in volunteering to nurse Jane. A week later found us at the lake where I impatiently awaited Tom's arrival that first week-end...

I FEEL MUCH BETTER, LILA.

TOM OUGHT TO BE HERE ANY MINUTE NOW.

HEY! ANY-BODY HOME?

I now could put into effect the plan I had for causing the final break between them...

WHY--SHE LOOKS LIKE A NEW GAL, LILA. I GUESS I OWE A LOT TO HER CAPABLE "NURSE."

I'LL START COLLECT-ING BY BORROWING YOU FOR A SWIM. HOW ABOUT GETTING INTO YOUR SUIT?

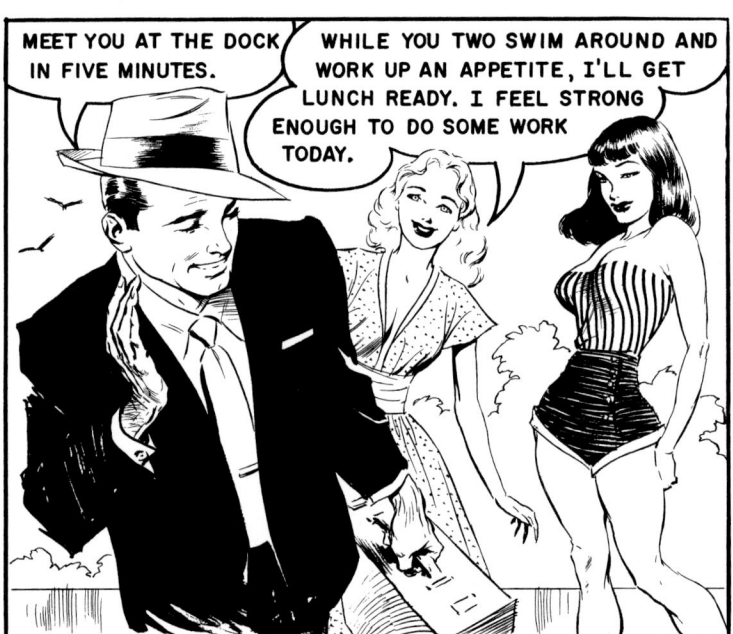

MEET YOU AT THE DOCK IN FIVE MINUTES.

WHILE YOU TWO SWIM AROUND AND WORK UP AN APPETITE, I'LL GET LUNCH READY. I FEEL STRONG ENOUGH TO DO SOME WORK TODAY.

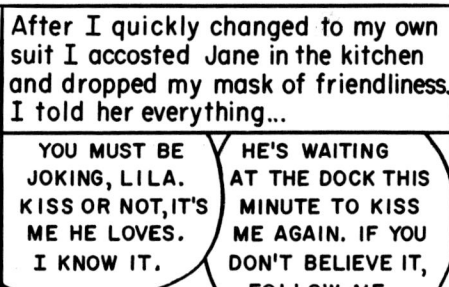

After I quickly changed to my own suit I accosted Jane in the kitchen and dropped my mask of friendliness. I told her everything...

YOU MUST BE JOKING, LILA. KISS OR NOT, IT'S ME HE LOVES. I KNOW IT.

HE'S WAITING AT THE DOCK THIS MINUTE TO KISS ME AGAIN. IF YOU DON'T BELIEVE IT, FOLLOW ME AND SEE.

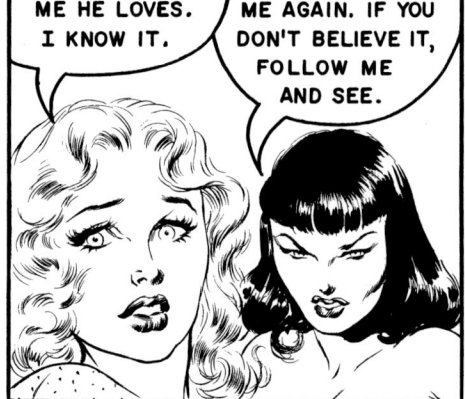

I dashed down to the dock and threw myself into Tom's arms--my lips yearningly seeking his. A heartbroken gasp told me that my plan was working...

WE'RE ALONE AT LAST, DARLING. KISS ME!

TOM---(GASP)--HOW--HOW COULD YOU?

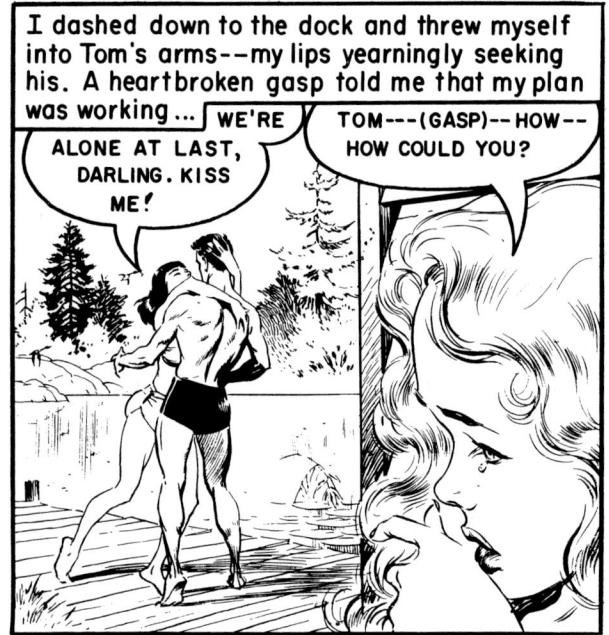

ARE YOU OUT OF YOUR MIND? JUST WHAT ARE YOU UP TO? JANE!

(SOB) (SOB)!

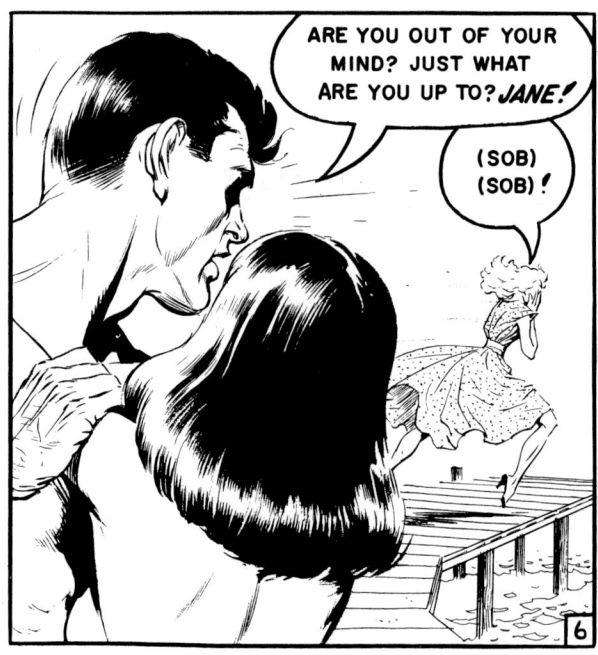

6

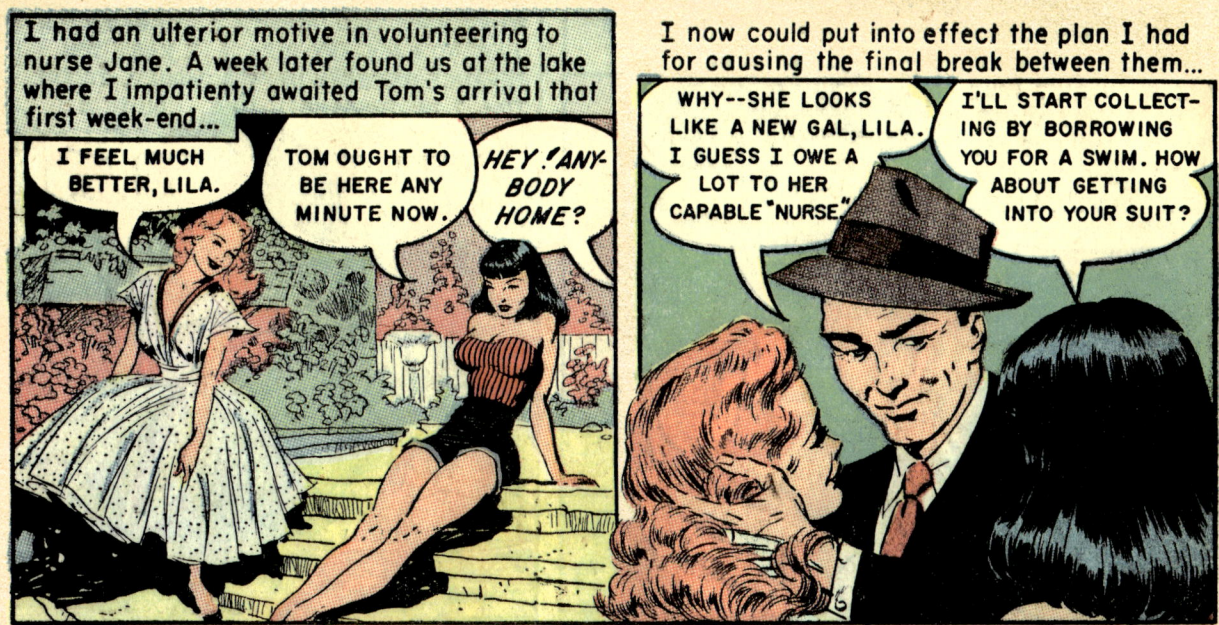

I had an ulterior motive in volunteering to nurse Jane. A week later found us at the lake where I impatiently awaited Tom's arrival that first week-end...

I FEEL MUCH BETTER, LILA.

TOM OUGHT TO BE HERE ANY MINUTE NOW.

HEY! ANYBODY HOME?

I now could put into effect the plan I had for causing the final break between them...

WHY--SHE LOOKS LIKE A NEW GAL, LILA. I GUESS I OWE A LOT TO HER CAPABLE "NURSE."

I'LL START COLLECTING BY BORROWING YOU FOR A SWIM. HOW ABOUT GETTING INTO YOUR SUIT?

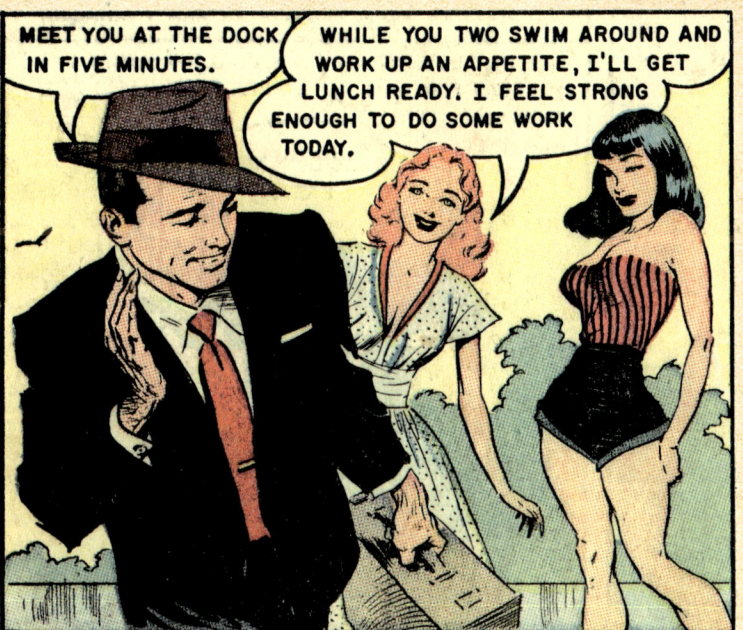

MEET YOU AT THE DOCK IN FIVE MINUTES.

WHILE YOU TWO SWIM AROUND AND WORK UP AN APPETITE, I'LL GET LUNCH READY. I FEEL STRONG ENOUGH TO DO SOME WORK TODAY.

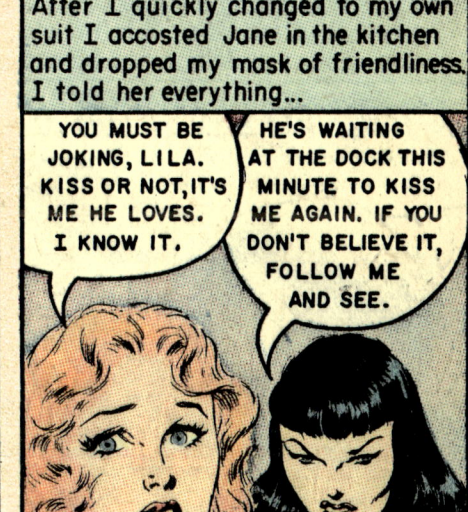

After I quickly changed to my own suit I accosted Jane in the kitchen and dropped my mask of friendliness. I told her everything...

YOU MUST BE JOKING, LILA. KISS OR NOT, IT'S ME HE LOVES. I KNOW IT.

HE'S WAITING AT THE DOCK THIS MINUTE TO KISS ME AGAIN. IF YOU DON'T BELIEVE IT, FOLLOW ME AND SEE.

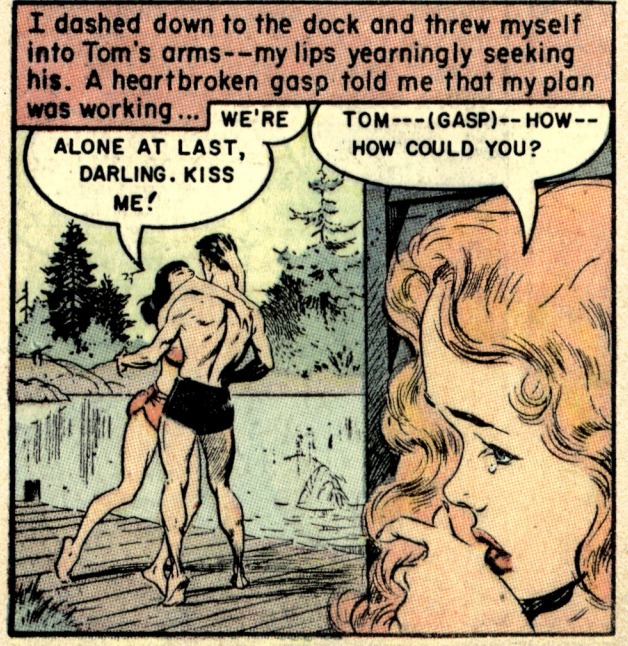

I dashed down to the dock and threw myself into Tom's arms--my lips yearningly seeking his. A heartbroken gasp told me that my plan was working...

WE'RE ALONE AT LAST, DARLING. KISS ME!

TOM---(GASP)--HOW-- HOW COULD YOU?

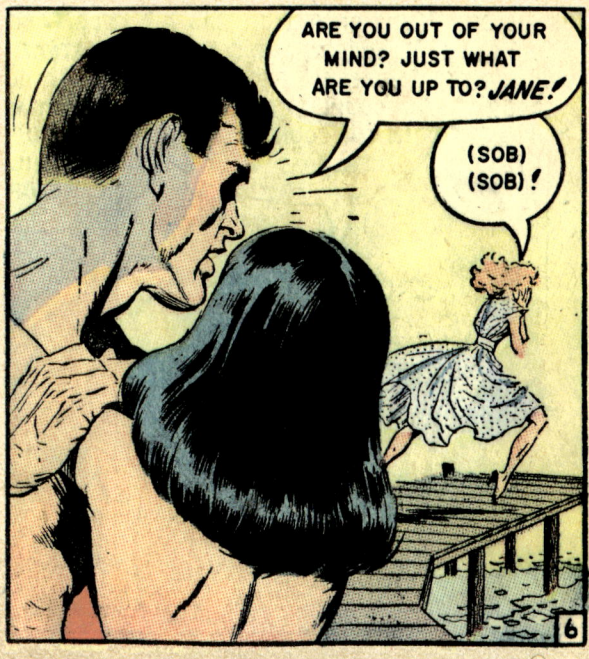

ARE YOU OUT OF YOUR MIND? JUST WHAT ARE YOU UP TO? JANE!

(SOB) (SOB)!

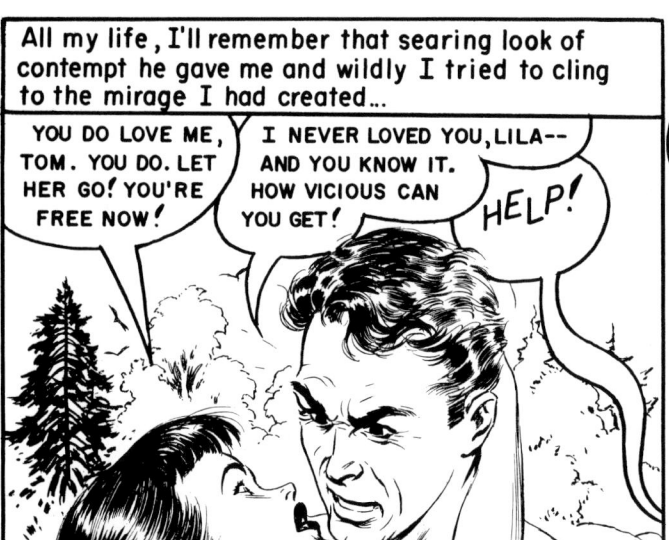

All my life, I'll remember that searing look of contempt he gave me and wildly I tried to cling to the mirage I had created...

YOU DO LOVE ME, TOM. YOU DO. LET HER GO! YOU'RE FREE NOW!

I NEVER LOVED YOU, LILA-- AND YOU KNOW IT. HOW VICIOUS CAN YOU GET!

HELP!

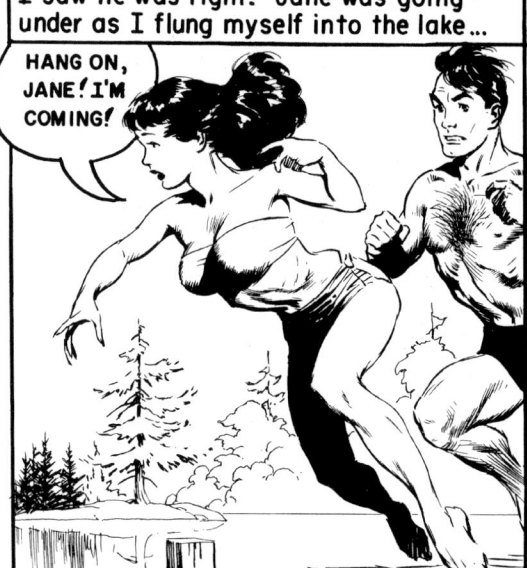

I saw he was right. Jane was going under as I flung myself into the lake...

HANG ON, JANE! I'M COMING!

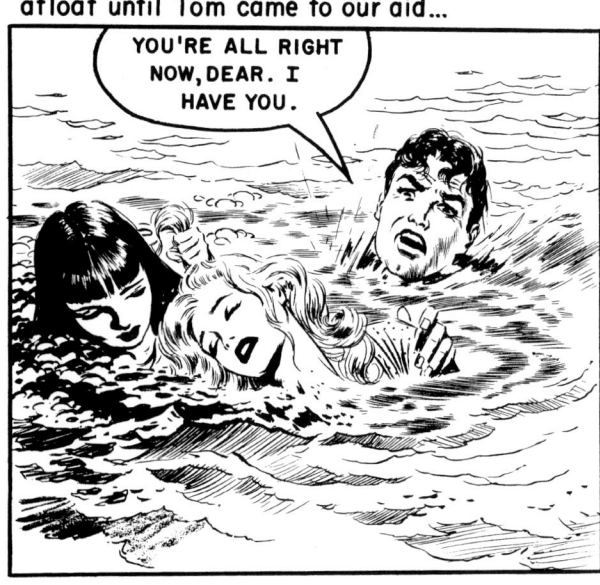

I managed to grasp her hair and keep her afloat until Tom came to our aid...

YOU'RE ALL RIGHT NOW, DEAR. I HAVE YOU.

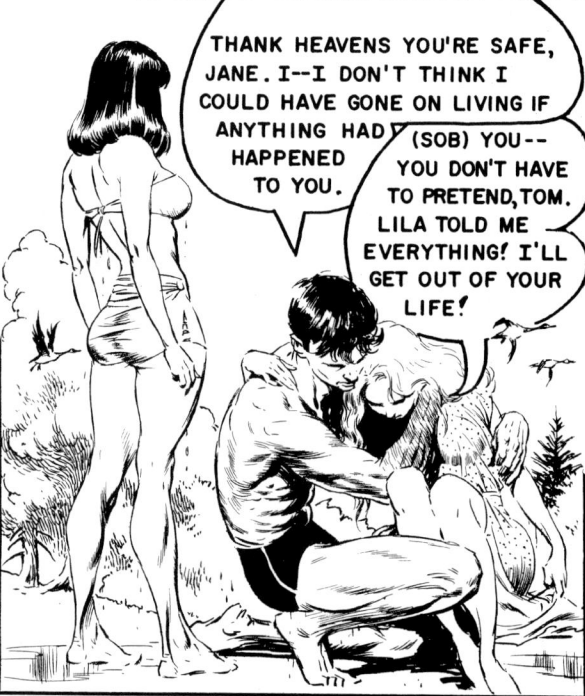

THANK HEAVENS YOU'RE SAFE, JANE. I--I DON'T THINK I COULD HAVE GONE ON LIVING IF ANYTHING HAD HAPPENED TO YOU.

(SOB) YOU-- YOU DON'T HAVE TO PRETEND, TOM. LILA TOLD ME EVERYTHING! I'LL GET OUT OF YOUR LIFE!

NO! YOU--YOU HAVE IT ALL WRONG. TOM NEVER LOVED ME. I KNOW THAT NOW. (SOB) I--I LIED TO YOU. I LIED! HE LOVES YOU!

IT'S TRUE, MY DARLING. THERE CAN NEVER BE ANYONE ELSE BUT YOU!

I started to walk off and looked back to find them clinging to each other. And somehow I felt an inner peace. My heart was no longer consumed with envy...

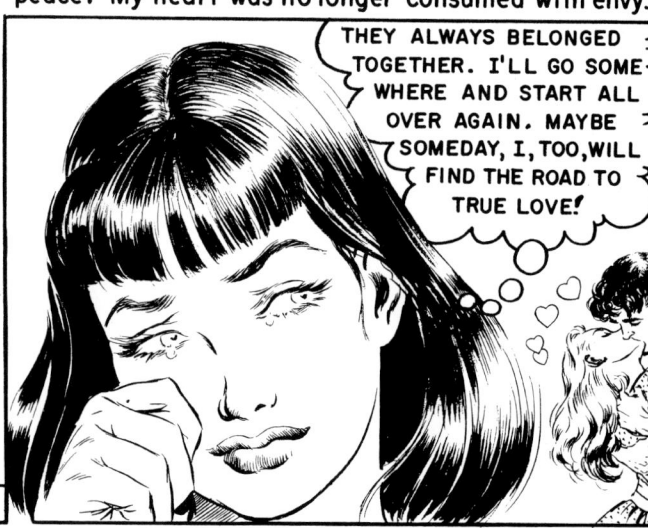

THEY ALWAYS BELONGED TOGETHER. I'LL GO SOME- WHERE AND START ALL OVER AGAIN. MAYBE SOMEDAY, I, TOO, WILL FIND THE ROAD TO TRUE LOVE!

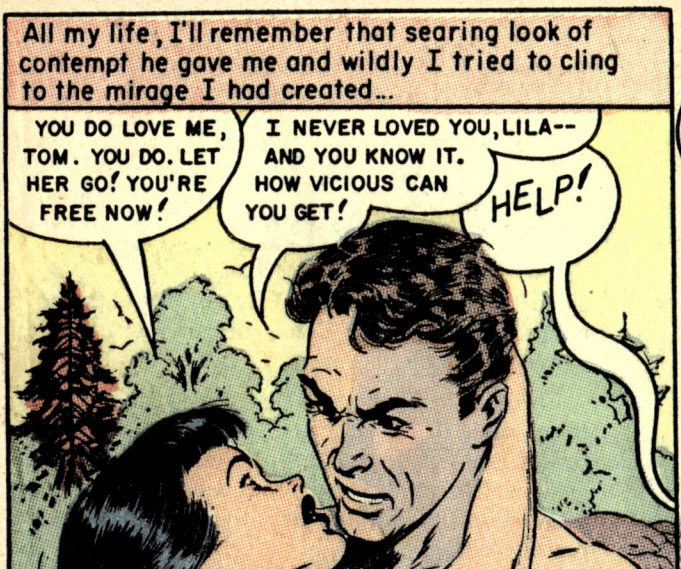

All my life, I'll remember that searing look of contempt he gave me and wildly I tried to cling to the mirage I had created...

YOU DO LOVE ME, TOM. YOU DO. LET HER GO! YOU'RE FREE NOW!

I NEVER LOVED YOU, LILA-- AND YOU KNOW IT. HOW VICIOUS CAN YOU GET!

HELP!

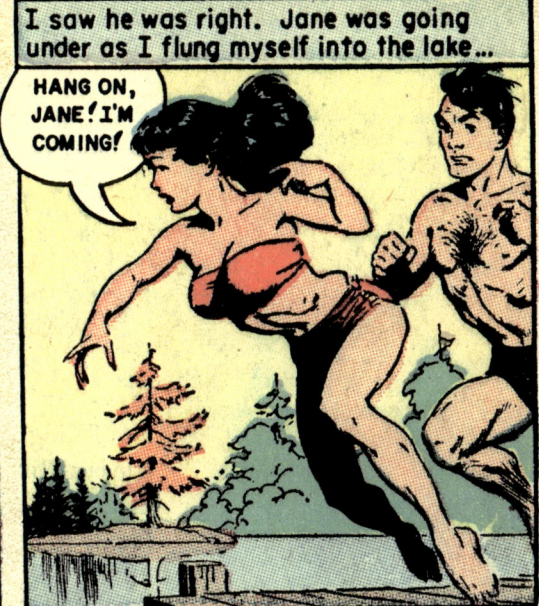

I saw he was right. Jane was going under as I flung myself into the lake...

HANG ON, JANE! I'M COMING!

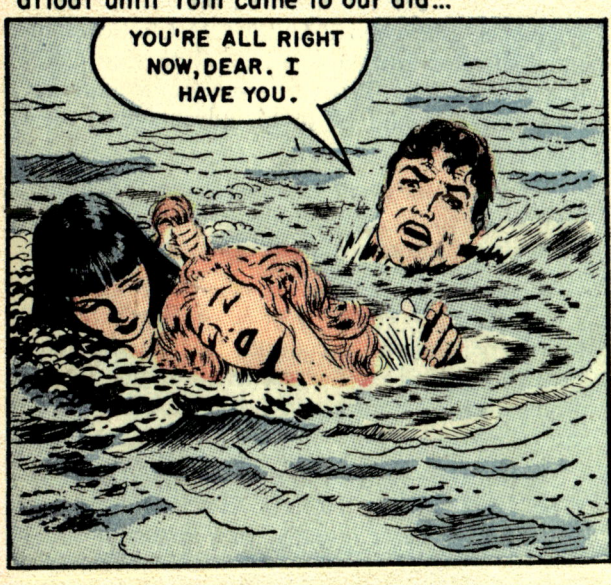

I managed to grasp her hair and keep her afloat until Tom came to our aid...

YOU'RE ALL RIGHT NOW, DEAR. I HAVE YOU.

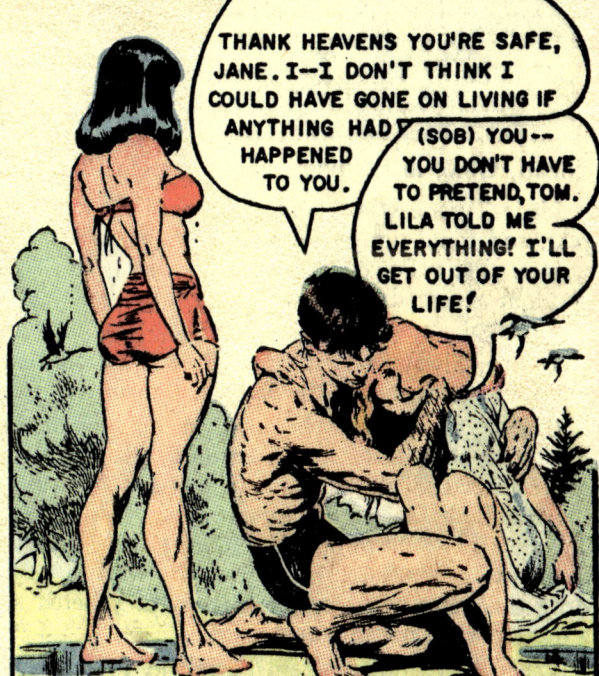

THANK HEAVENS YOU'RE SAFE, JANE. I--I DON'T THINK I COULD HAVE GONE ON LIVING IF ANYTHING HAD HAPPENED TO YOU.

(SOB) YOU-- YOU DON'T HAVE TO PRETEND, TOM. LILA TOLD ME EVERYTHING! I'LL GET OUT OF YOUR LIFE!

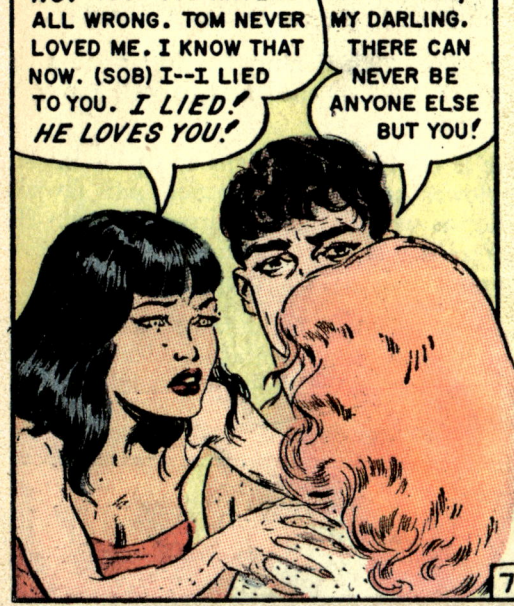

NO! YOU--YOU HAVE IT ALL WRONG. TOM NEVER LOVED ME. I KNOW THAT NOW. (SOB) I--I LIED TO YOU. I LIED! HE LOVES YOU!

IT'S TRUE, MY DARLING. THERE CAN NEVER BE ANYONE ELSE BUT YOU!

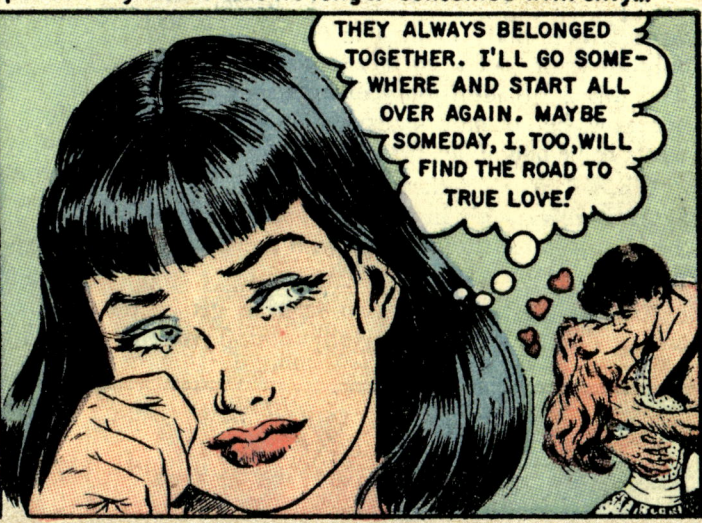

I started to walk off and looked back to find them clinging to each other. And somehow I felt an inner peace. My heart was no longer consumed with envy...

THEY ALWAYS BELONGED TOGETHER. I'LL GO SOME- WHERE AND START ALL OVER AGAIN. MAYBE SOMEDAY, I, TOO, WILL FIND THE ROAD TO TRUE LOVE!

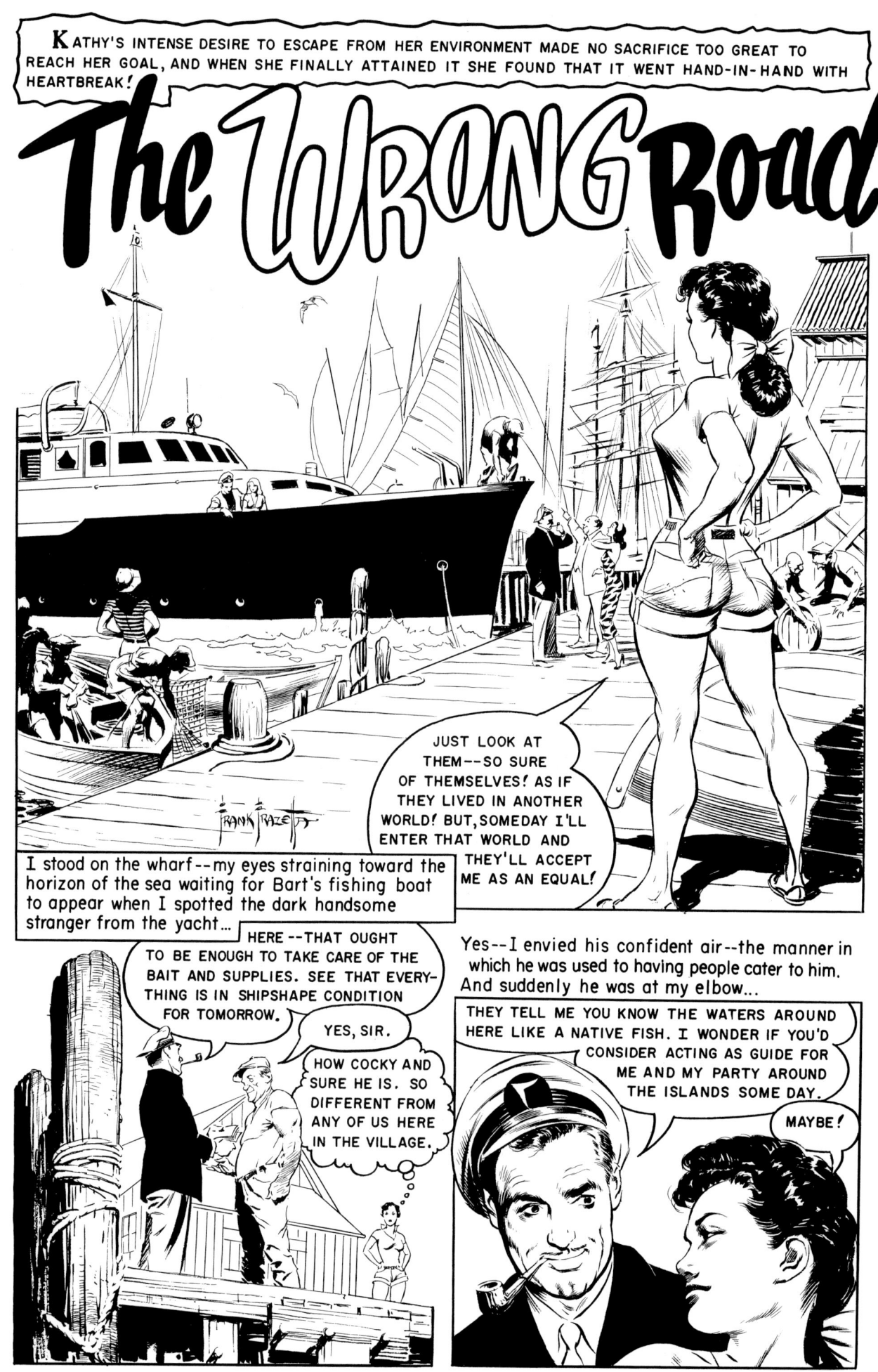

Personal Love #27 (Famous Funnies, June 1954)

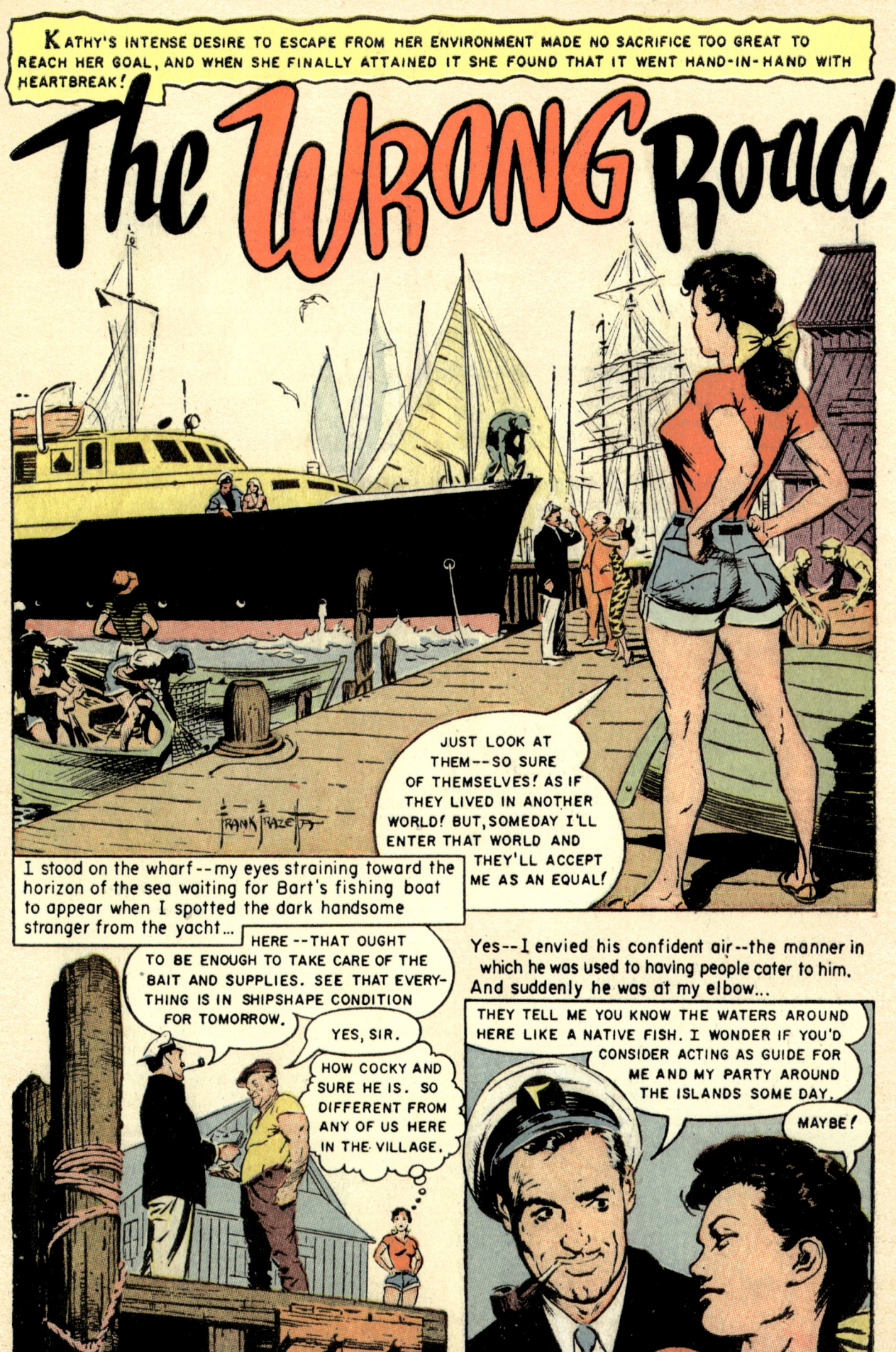

The Wrong Road

KATHY'S INTENSE DESIRE TO ESCAPE FROM HER ENVIRONMENT MADE NO SACRIFICE TOO GREAT TO REACH HER GOAL, AND WHEN SHE FINALLY ATTAINED IT SHE FOUND THAT IT WENT HAND-IN-HAND WITH HEARTBREAK!

JUST LOOK AT THEM--SO SURE OF THEMSELVES! AS IF THEY LIVED IN ANOTHER WORLD! BUT, SOMEDAY I'LL ENTER THAT WORLD AND THEY'LL ACCEPT ME AS AN EQUAL!

I stood on the wharf--my eyes straining toward the horizon of the sea waiting for Bart's fishing boat to appear when I spotted the dark handsome stranger from the yacht...

HERE--THAT OUGHT TO BE ENOUGH TO TAKE CARE OF THE BAIT AND SUPPLIES. SEE THAT EVERYTHING IS IN SHIPSHAPE CONDITION FOR TOMORROW.

YES, SIR.

HOW COCKY AND SURE HE IS. SO DIFFERENT FROM ANY OF US HERE IN THE VILLAGE.

Yes--I envied his confident air--the manner in which he was used to having people cater to him. And suddenly he was at my elbow...

THEY TELL ME YOU KNOW THE WATERS AROUND HERE LIKE A NATIVE FISH. I WONDER IF YOU'D CONSIDER ACTING AS GUIDE FOR ME AND MY PARTY AROUND THE ISLANDS SOME DAY.

MAYBE!

But just then I caught sight of Bart's fishing boat and I rushed happily to the water's edge waving happily at the man I loved...

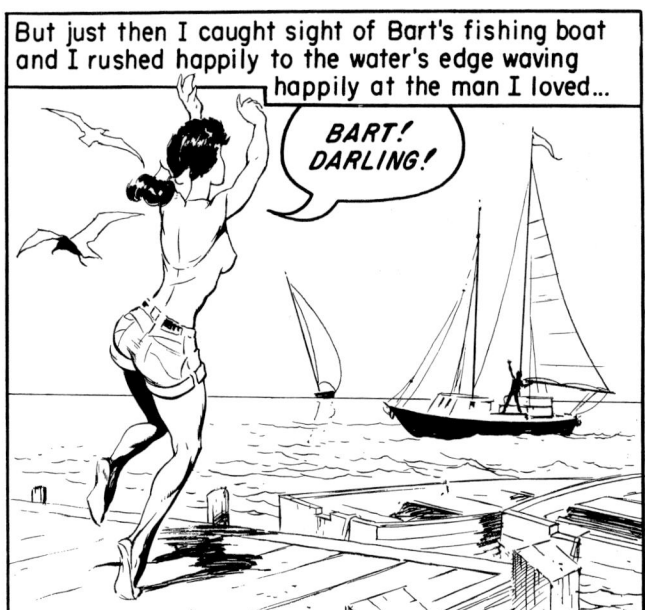

BART! DARLING!

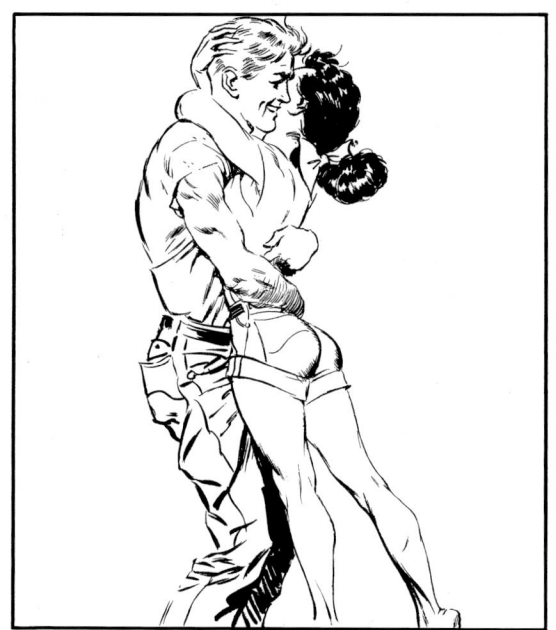

But my happiness was quickly dissipated as I saw the stranger enter a sleek convertible ...

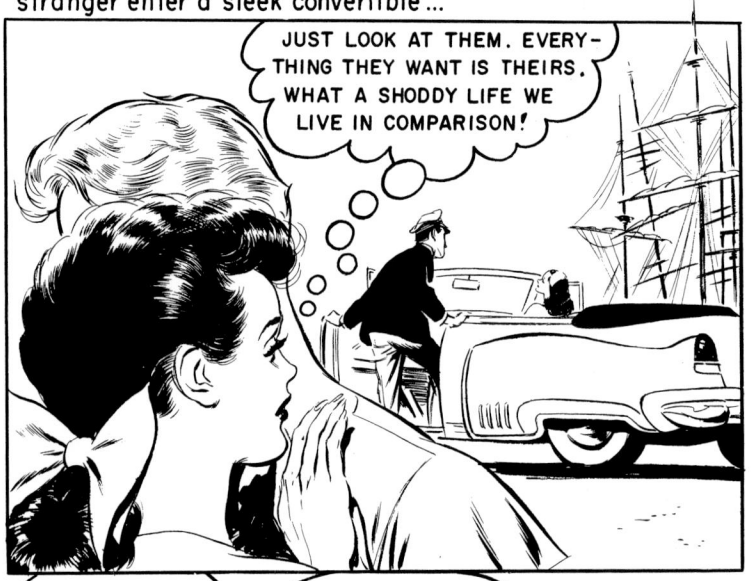

JUST LOOK AT THEM. EVERY-THING THEY WANT IS THEIRS. WHAT A SHODDY LIFE WE LIVE IN COMPARISON!

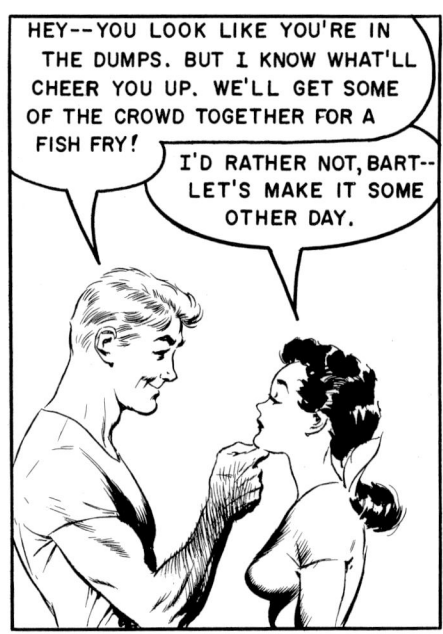

HEY--YOU LOOK LIKE YOU'RE IN THE DUMPS. BUT I KNOW WHAT'LL CHEER YOU UP. WE'LL GET SOME OF THE CROWD TOGETHER FOR A FISH FRY!

I'D RATHER NOT, BART-- LET'S MAKE IT SOME OTHER DAY.

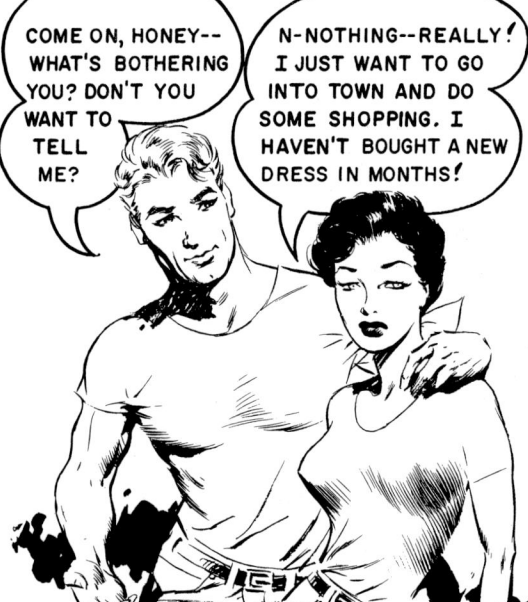

COME ON, HONEY-- WHAT'S BOTHERING YOU? DON'T YOU WANT TO TELL ME?

N-NOTHING--REALLY! I JUST WANT TO GO INTO TOWN AND DO SOME SHOPPING. I HAVEN'T BOUGHT A NEW DRESS IN MONTHS!

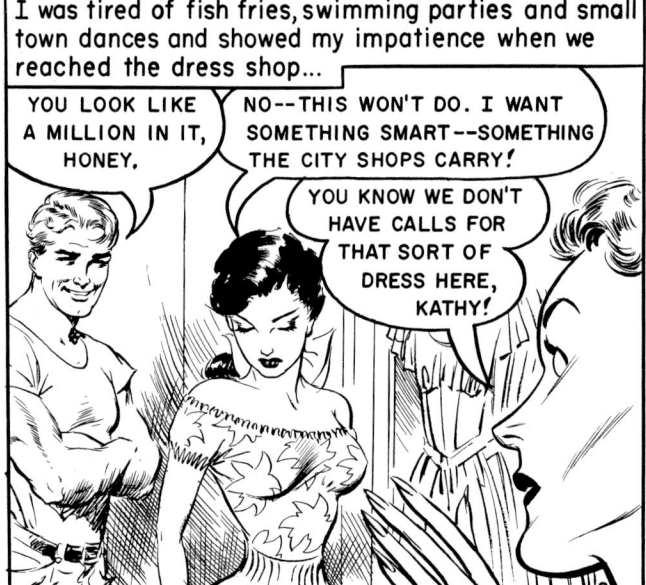

I was tired of fish fries, swimming parties and small town dances and showed my impatience when we reached the dress shop...

YOU LOOK LIKE A MILLION IN IT, HONEY.

NO--THIS WON'T DO. I WANT SOMETHING SMART--SOMETHING THE CITY SHOPS CARRY!

YOU KNOW WE DON'T HAVE CALLS FOR THAT SORT OF DRESS HERE, KATHY!

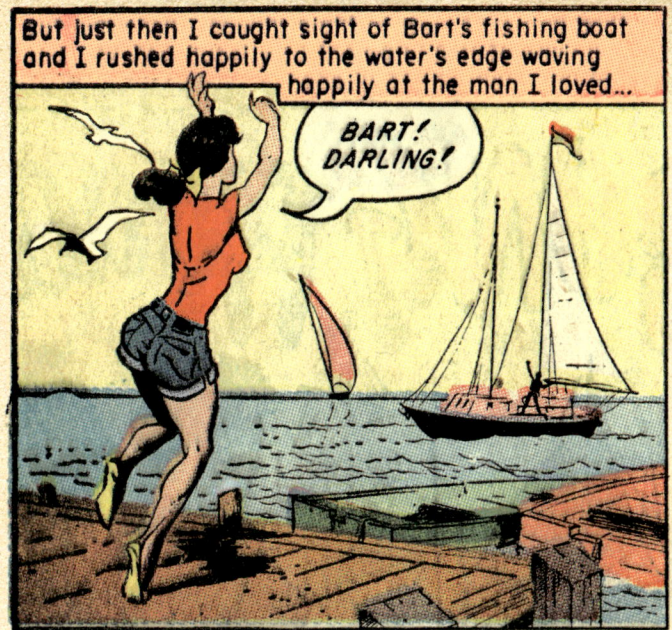

But just then I caught sight of Bart's fishing boat and I rushed happily to the water's edge waving happily at the man I loved...

BART! DARLING!

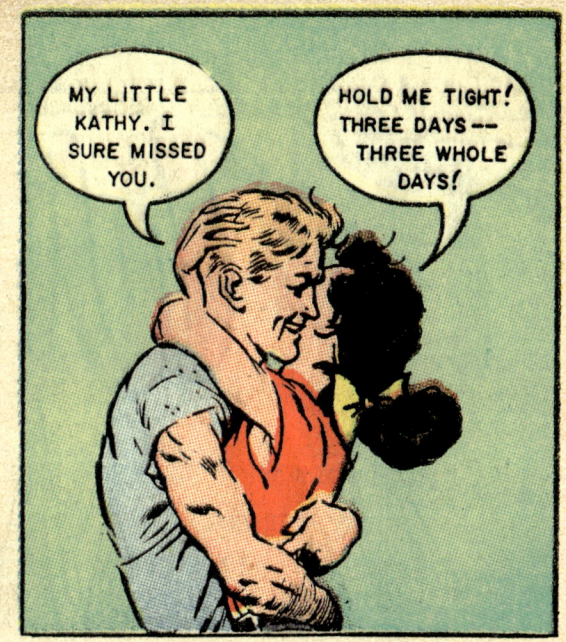

MY LITTLE KATHY. I SURE MISSED YOU.

HOLD ME TIGHT! THREE DAYS -- THREE WHOLE DAYS!

But my happiness was quickly dissipated as I saw the stranger enter a sleek convertible...

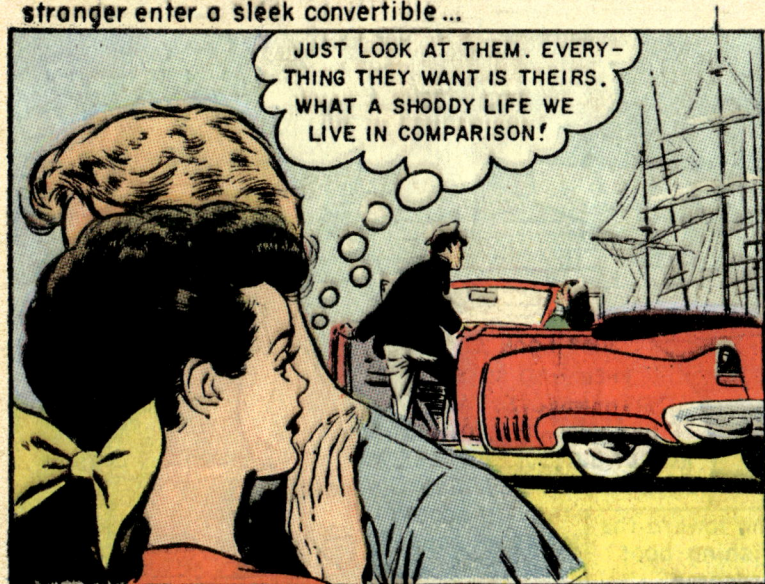

JUST LOOK AT THEM. EVERYTHING THEY WANT IS THEIRS. WHAT A SHODDY LIFE WE LIVE IN COMPARISON!

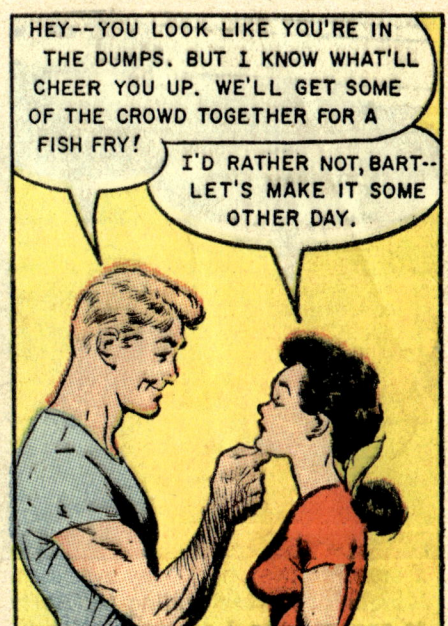

HEY--YOU LOOK LIKE YOU'RE IN THE DUMPS. BUT I KNOW WHAT'LL CHEER YOU UP. WE'LL GET SOME OF THE CROWD TOGETHER FOR A FISH FRY!

I'D RATHER NOT, BART-- LET'S MAKE IT SOME OTHER DAY.

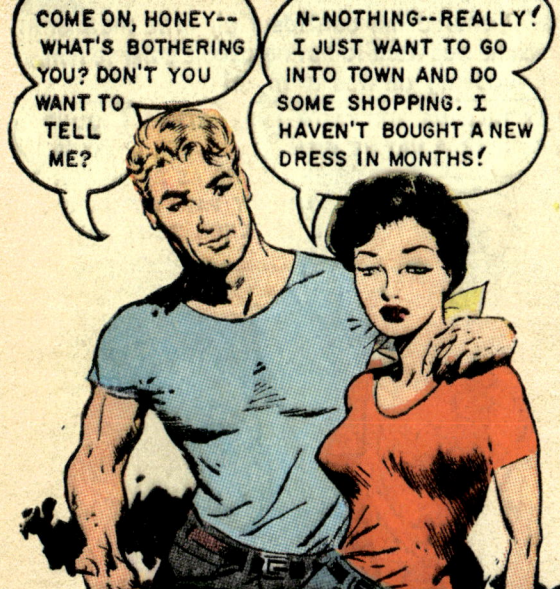

COME ON, HONEY-- WHAT'S BOTHERING YOU? DON'T YOU WANT TO TELL ME?

N-NOTHING--REALLY! I JUST WANT TO GO INTO TOWN AND DO SOME SHOPPING. I HAVEN'T BOUGHT A NEW DRESS IN MONTHS!

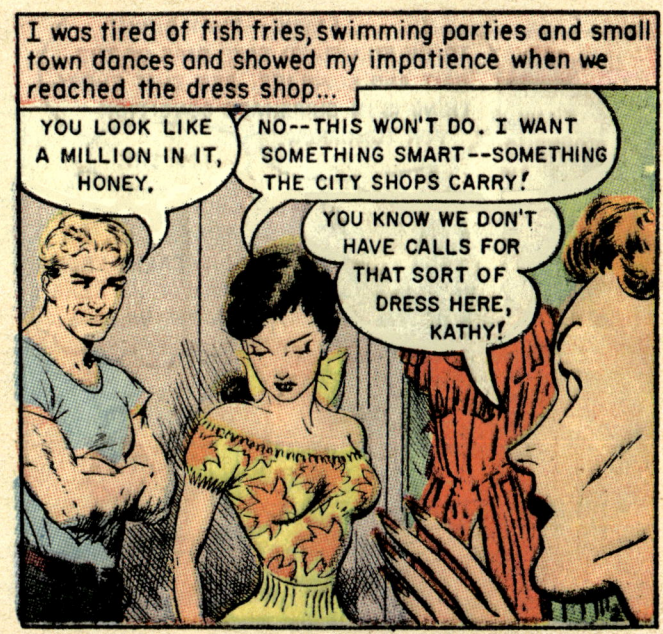

I was tired of fish fries, swimming parties and small town dances and showed my impatience when we reached the dress shop...

YOU LOOK LIKE A MILLION IN IT, HONEY.

NO--THIS WON'T DO. I WANT SOMETHING SMART--SOMETHING THE CITY SHOPS CARRY!

YOU KNOW WE DON'T HAVE CALLS FOR THAT SORT OF DRESS HERE, KATHY!

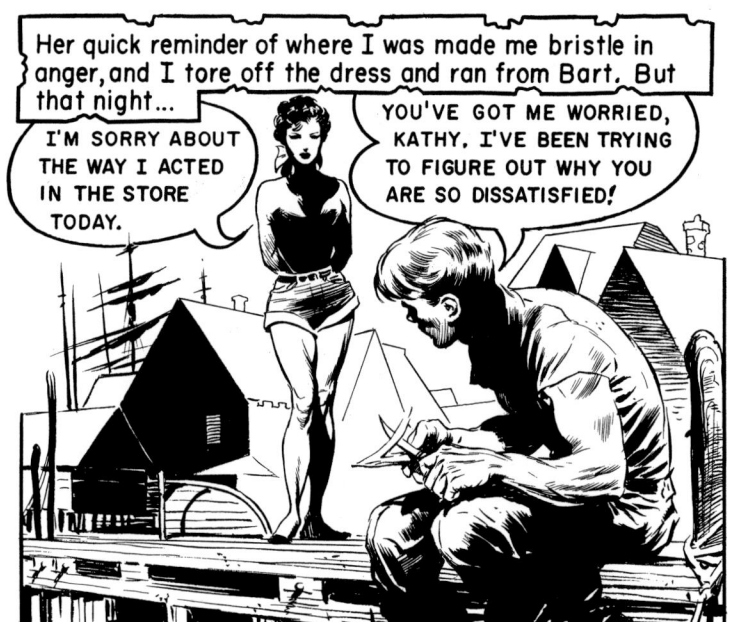

Her quick reminder of where I was made me bristle in anger, and I tore off the dress and ran from Bart. But that night...

I'M SORRY ABOUT THE WAY I ACTED IN THE STORE TODAY.

YOU'VE GOT ME WORRIED, KATHY. I'VE BEEN TRYING TO FIGURE OUT WHY YOU ARE SO DISSATISFIED!

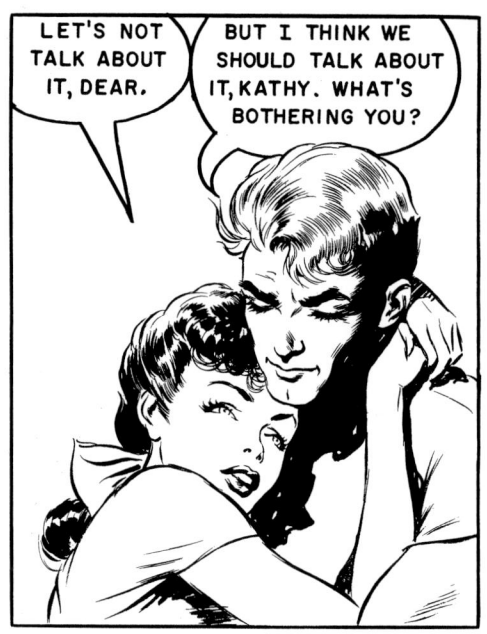

LET'S NOT TALK ABOUT IT, DEAR.

BUT I THINK WE SHOULD TALK ABOUT IT, KATHY. WHAT'S BOTHERING YOU?

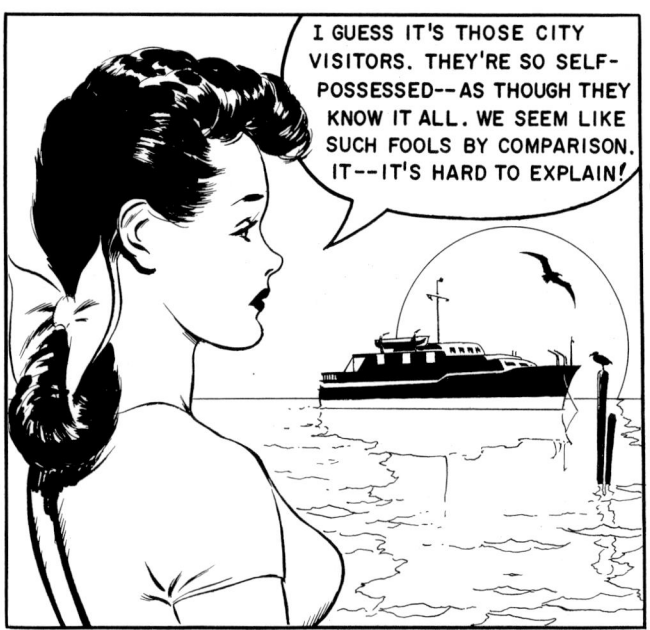

I GUESS IT'S THOSE CITY VISITORS. THEY'RE SO SELF-POSSESSED--AS THOUGH THEY KNOW IT ALL. WE SEEM LIKE SUCH FOOLS BY COMPARISON. IT--IT'S HARD TO EXPLAIN!

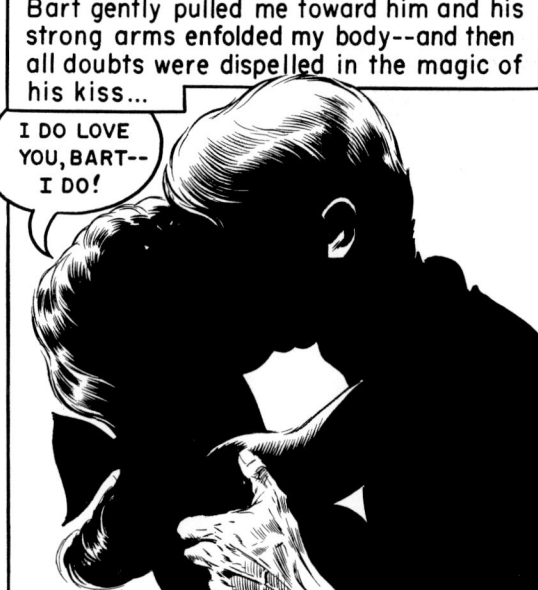

Bart gently pulled me toward him and his strong arms enfolded my body--and then all doubts were dispelled in the magic of his kiss...

I DO LOVE YOU, BART-- I DO!

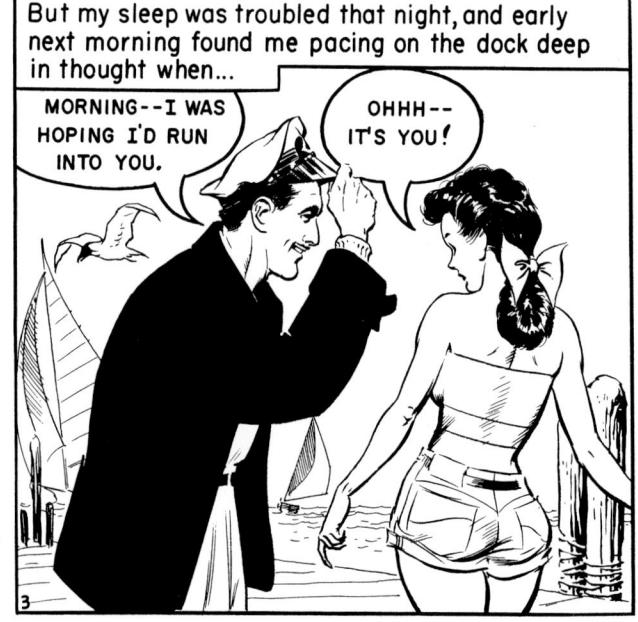

But my sleep was troubled that night, and early next morning found me pacing on the dock deep in thought when...

MORNING--I WAS HOPING I'D RUN INTO YOU.

OHHH-- IT'S YOU!

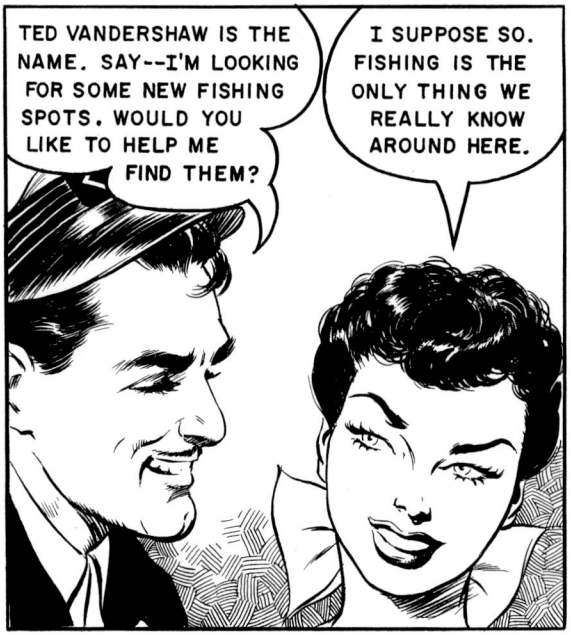

TED VANDERSHAW IS THE NAME. SAY--I'M LOOKING FOR SOME NEW FISHING SPOTS. WOULD YOU LIKE TO HELP ME FIND THEM?

I SUPPOSE SO. FISHING IS THE ONLY THING WE REALLY KNOW AROUND HERE.

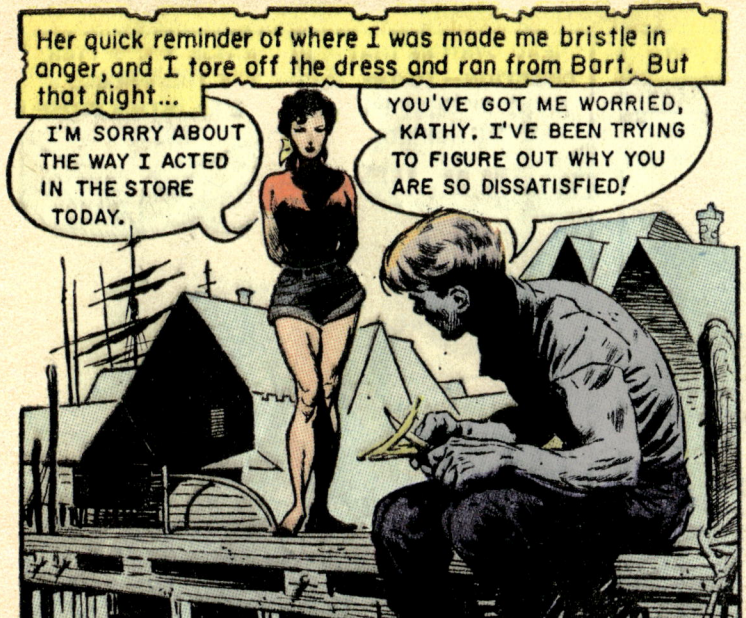

Her quick reminder of where I was made me bristle in anger, and I tore off the dress and ran from Bart. But that night...

I'M SORRY ABOUT THE WAY I ACTED IN THE STORE TODAY.

YOU'VE GOT ME WORRIED, KATHY. I'VE BEEN TRYING TO FIGURE OUT WHY YOU ARE SO DISSATISFIED!

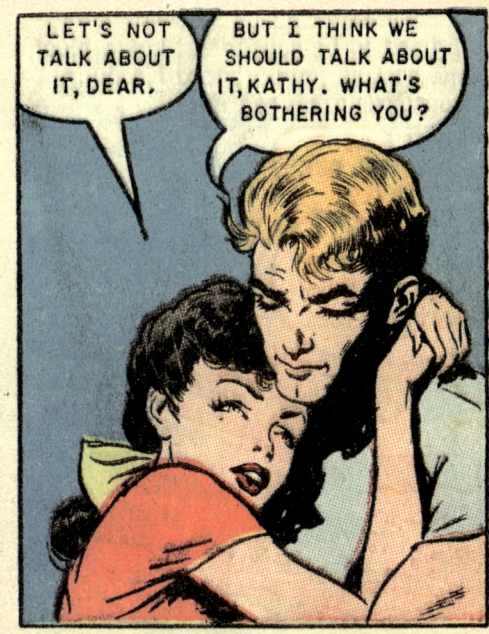

LET'S NOT TALK ABOUT IT, DEAR.

BUT I THINK WE SHOULD TALK ABOUT IT, KATHY. WHAT'S BOTHERING YOU?

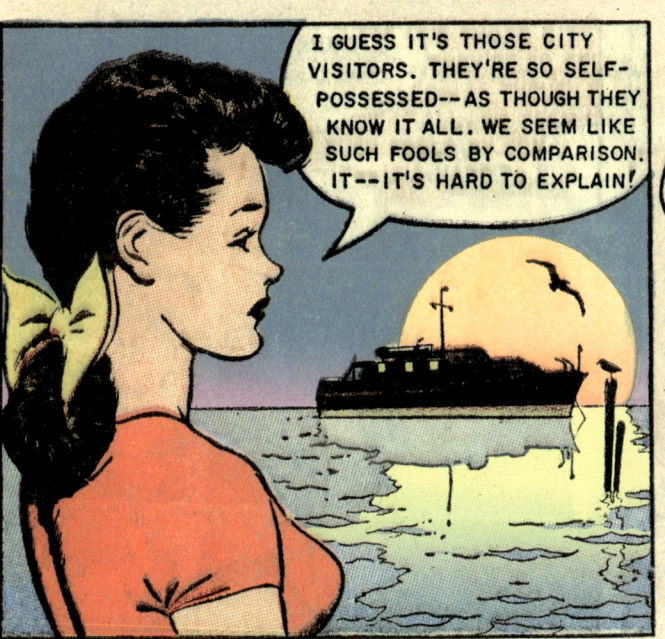

I GUESS IT'S THOSE CITY VISITORS. THEY'RE SO SELF-POSSESSED--AS THOUGH THEY KNOW IT ALL. WE SEEM LIKE SUCH FOOLS BY COMPARISON. IT--IT'S HARD TO EXPLAIN!

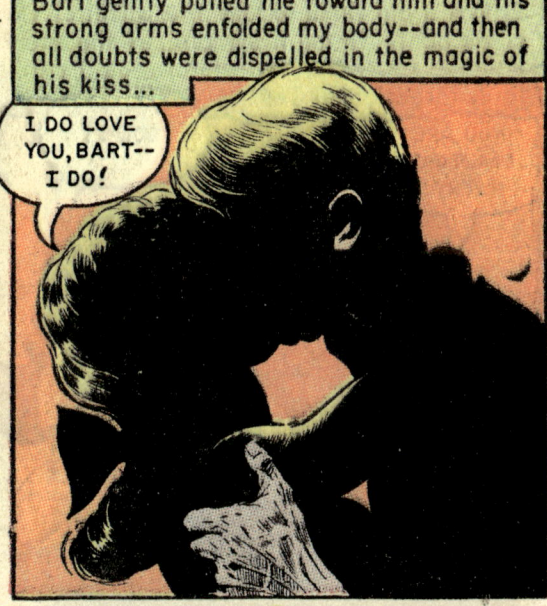

Bart gently pulled me toward him and his strong arms enfolded my body--and then all doubts were dispelled in the magic of his kiss...

I DO LOVE YOU, BART-- I DO!

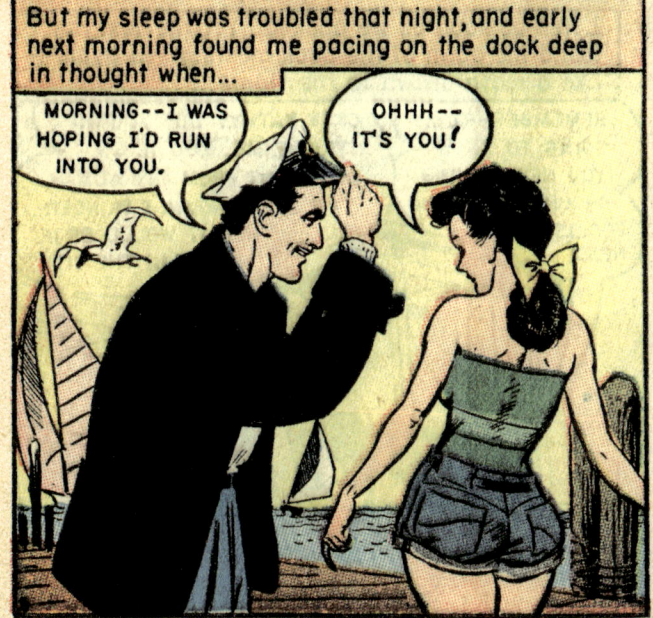

But my sleep was troubled that night, and early next morning found me pacing on the dock deep in thought when...

MORNING--I WAS HOPING I'D RUN INTO YOU.

OHHH-- IT'S YOU!

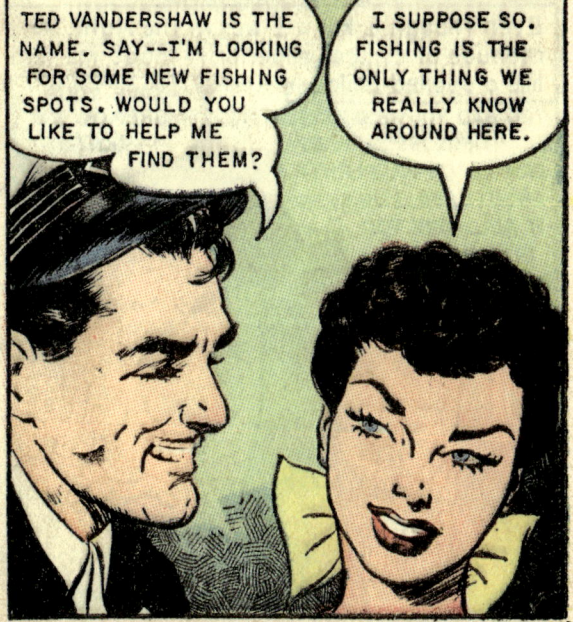

TED VANDERSHAW IS THE NAME. SAY--I'M LOOKING FOR SOME NEW FISHING SPOTS. WOULD YOU LIKE TO HELP ME FIND THEM?

I SUPPOSE SO. FISHING IS THE ONLY THING WE REALLY KNOW AROUND HERE.

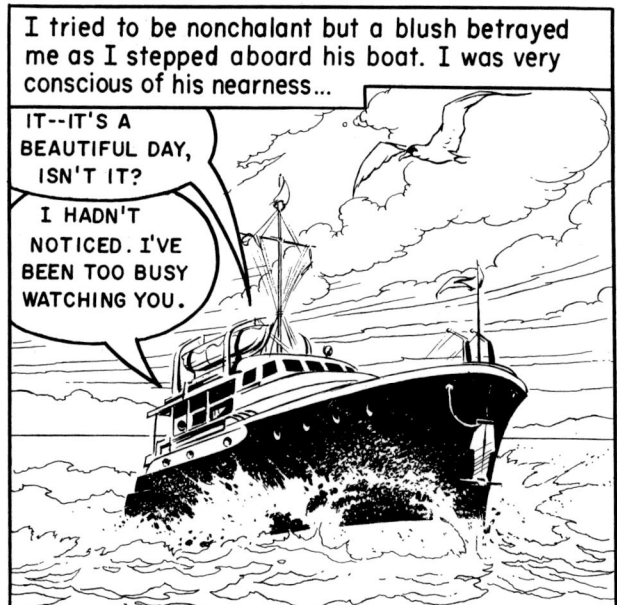

I tried to be nonchalant but a blush betrayed me as I stepped aboard his boat. I was very conscious of his nearness...

IT--IT'S A BEAUTIFUL DAY, ISN'T IT?

I HADN'T NOTICED. I'VE BEEN TOO BUSY WATCHING YOU.

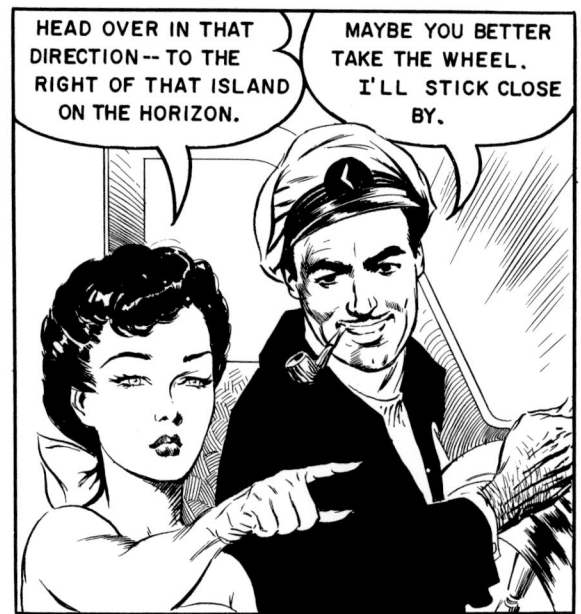

HEAD OVER IN THAT DIRECTION -- TO THE RIGHT OF THAT ISLAND ON THE HORIZON.

MAYBE YOU BETTER TAKE THE WHEEL. I'LL STICK CLOSE BY.

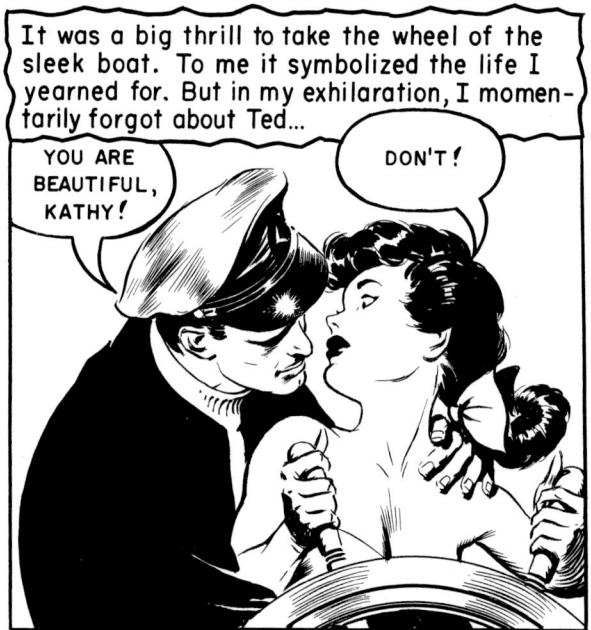

It was a big thrill to take the wheel of the sleek boat. To me it symbolized the life I yearned for. But in my exhilaration, I momentarily forgot about Ted...

YOU ARE BEAUTIFUL, KATHY!

DON'T!

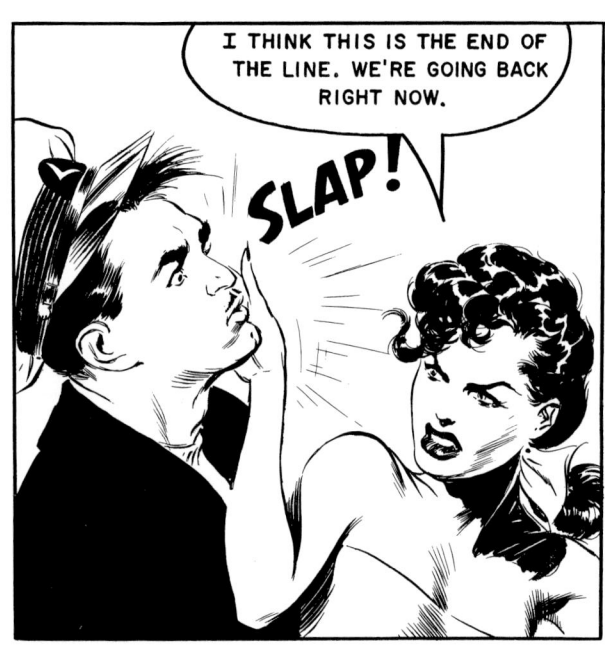

I THINK THIS IS THE END OF THE LINE. WE'RE GOING BACK RIGHT NOW.

SLAP!

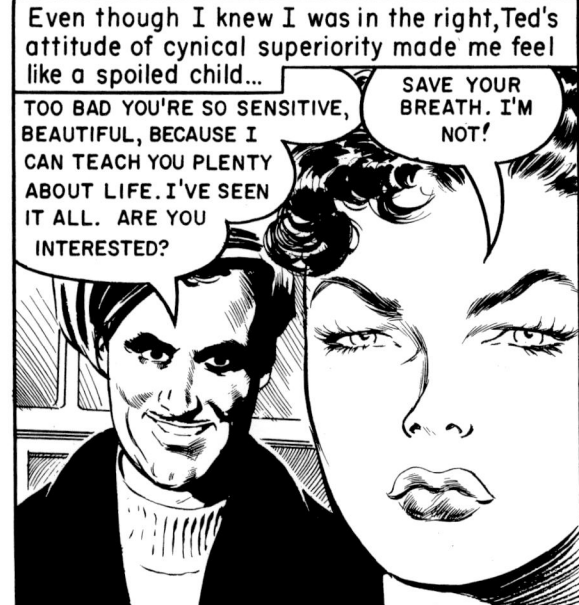

Even though I knew I was in the right, Ted's attitude of cynical superiority made me feel like a spoiled child...

TOO BAD YOU'RE SO SENSITIVE, BEAUTIFUL, BECAUSE I CAN TEACH YOU PLENTY ABOUT LIFE. I'VE SEEN IT ALL. ARE YOU INTERESTED?

SAVE YOUR BREATH. I'M NOT!

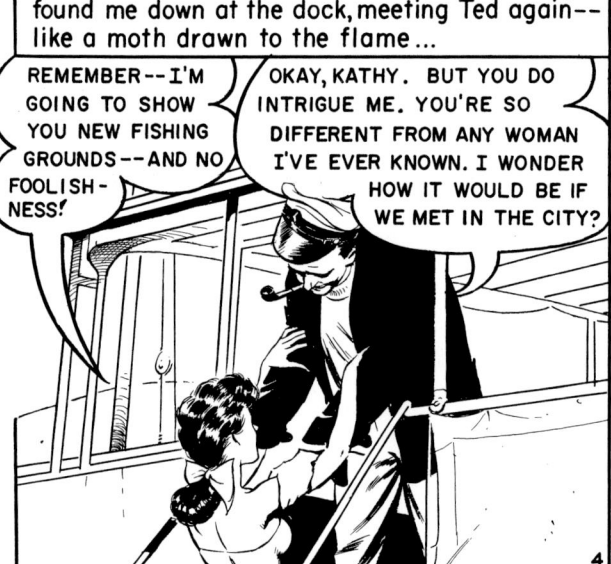

I fled as soon as we docked. Yet, the next day found me down at the dock, meeting Ted again -- like a moth drawn to the flame...

REMEMBER -- I'M GOING TO SHOW YOU NEW FISHING GROUNDS -- AND NO FOOLISH- NESS!

OKAY, KATHY. BUT YOU DO INTRIGUE ME. YOU'RE SO DIFFERENT FROM ANY WOMAN I'VE EVER KNOWN. I WONDER HOW IT WOULD BE IF WE MET IN THE CITY?

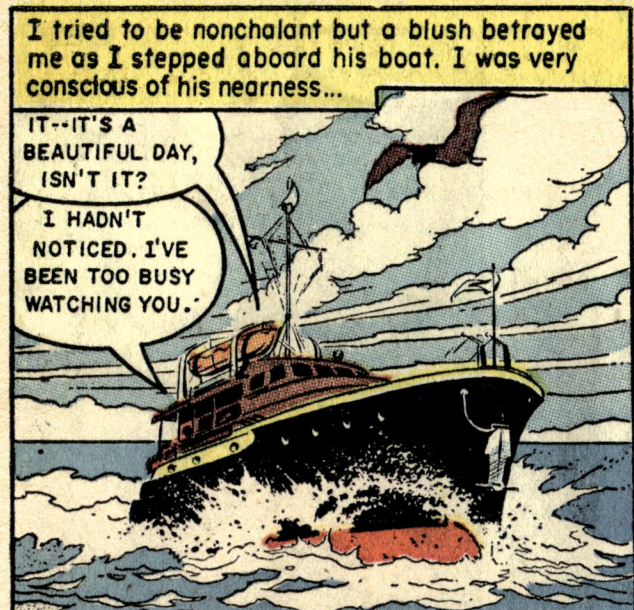

I tried to be nonchalant but a blush betrayed me as I stepped aboard his boat. I was very conscious of his nearness...

IT--IT'S A BEAUTIFUL DAY, ISN'T IT?

I HADN'T NOTICED. I'VE BEEN TOO BUSY WATCHING YOU.

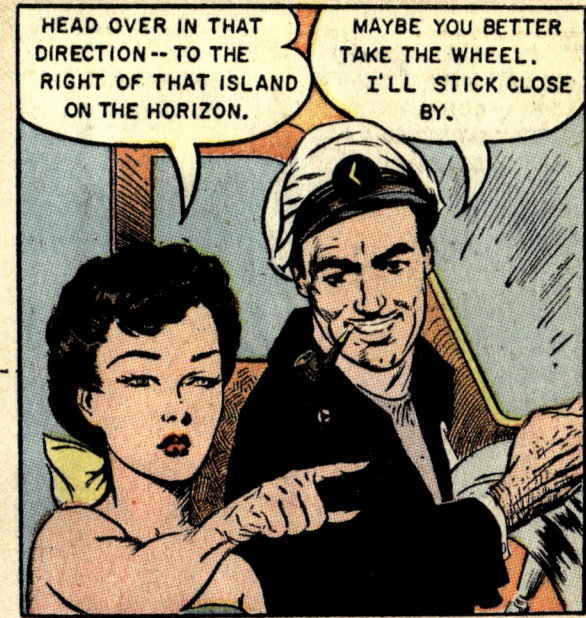

HEAD OVER IN THAT DIRECTION -- TO THE RIGHT OF THAT ISLAND ON THE HORIZON.

MAYBE YOU BETTER TAKE THE WHEEL. I'LL STICK CLOSE BY.

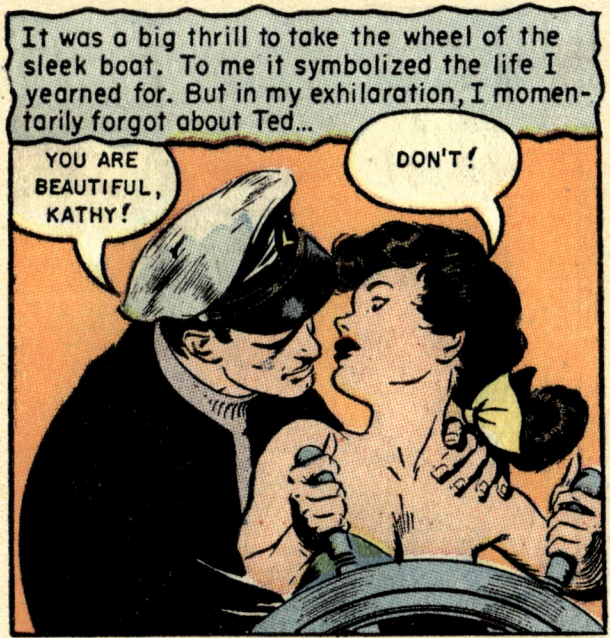

It was a big thrill to take the wheel of the sleek boat. To me it symbolized the life I yearned for. But in my exhilaration, I momentarily forgot about Ted...

YOU ARE BEAUTIFUL, KATHY!

DON'T!

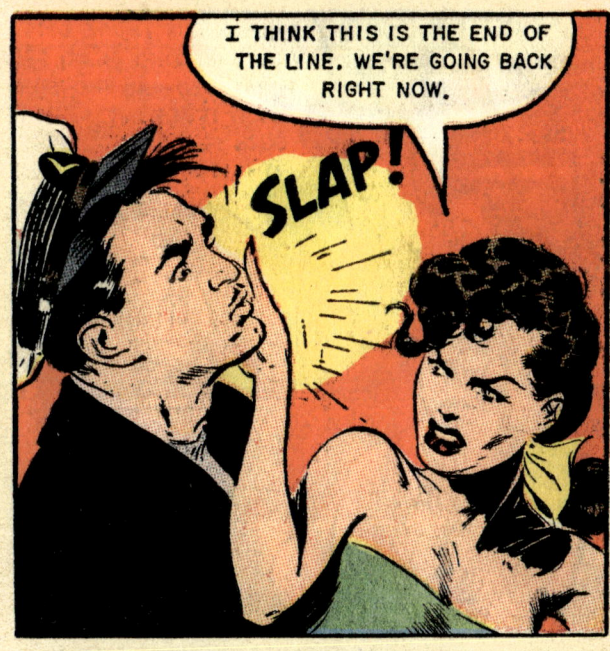

I THINK THIS IS THE END OF THE LINE. WE'RE GOING BACK RIGHT NOW.

SLAP!

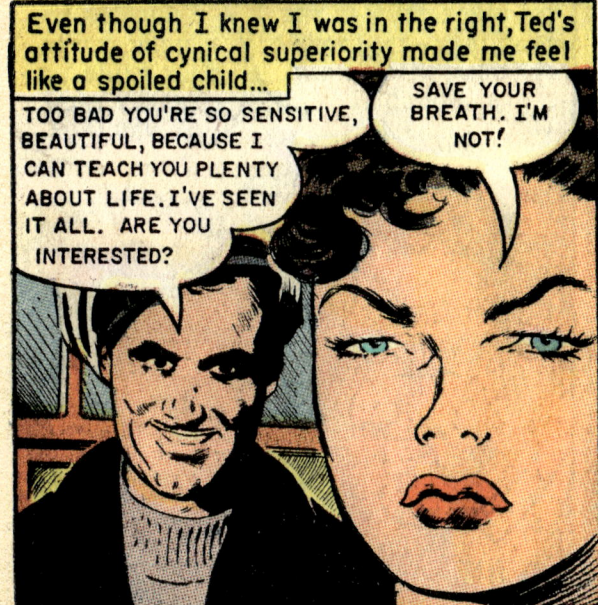

Even though I knew I was in the right, Ted's attitude of cynical superiority made me feel like a spoiled child...

TOO BAD YOU'RE SO SENSITIVE, BEAUTIFUL, BECAUSE I CAN TEACH YOU PLENTY ABOUT LIFE. I'VE SEEN IT ALL. ARE YOU INTERESTED?

SAVE YOUR BREATH. I'M NOT!

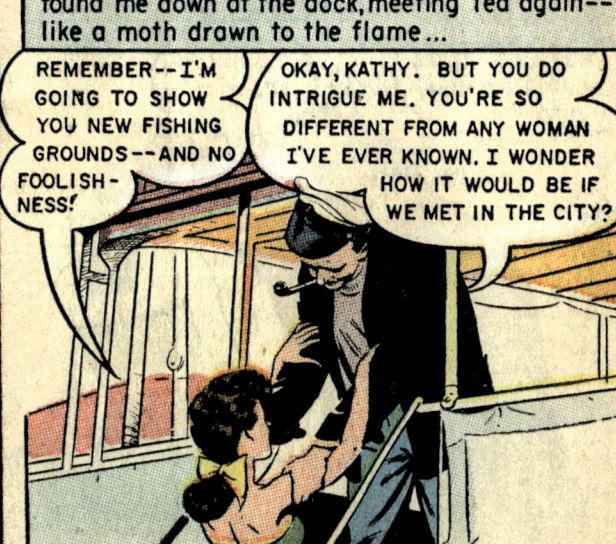

I fled as soon as we docked. Yet, the next day found me down at the dock, meeting Ted again-- like a moth drawn to the flame...

REMEMBER -- I'M GOING TO SHOW YOU NEW FISHING GROUNDS -- AND NO FOOLISH-NESS!

OKAY, KATHY. BUT YOU DO INTRIGUE ME. YOU'RE SO DIFFERENT FROM ANY WOMAN I'VE EVER KNOWN. I WONDER HOW IT WOULD BE IF WE MET IN THE CITY?

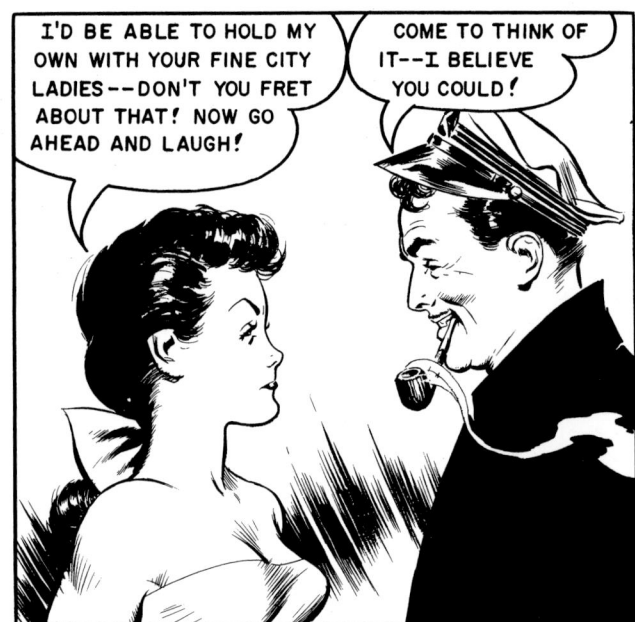

I'D BE ABLE TO HOLD MY OWN WITH YOUR FINE CITY LADIES--DON'T YOU FRET ABOUT THAT! NOW GO AHEAD AND LAUGH!

COME TO THINK OF IT--I BELIEVE YOU COULD!

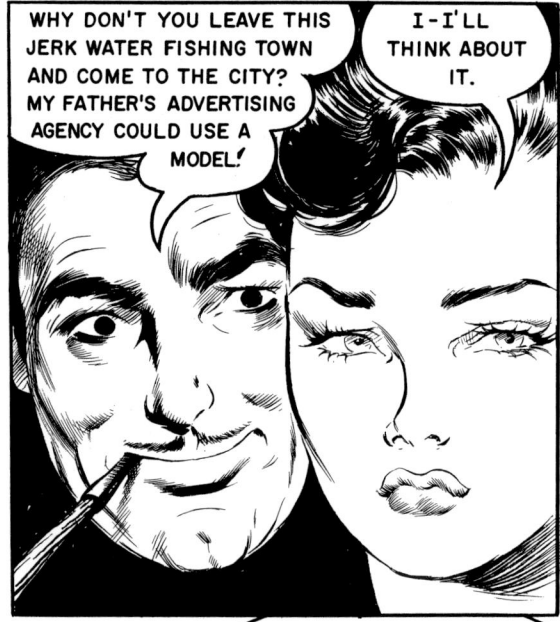

WHY DON'T YOU LEAVE THIS JERK WATER FISHING TOWN AND COME TO THE CITY? MY FATHER'S ADVERTISING AGENCY COULD USE A MODEL!

I-I'LL THINK ABOUT IT.

A new life beckoned to me and I glowed at the prospect. But that evening...

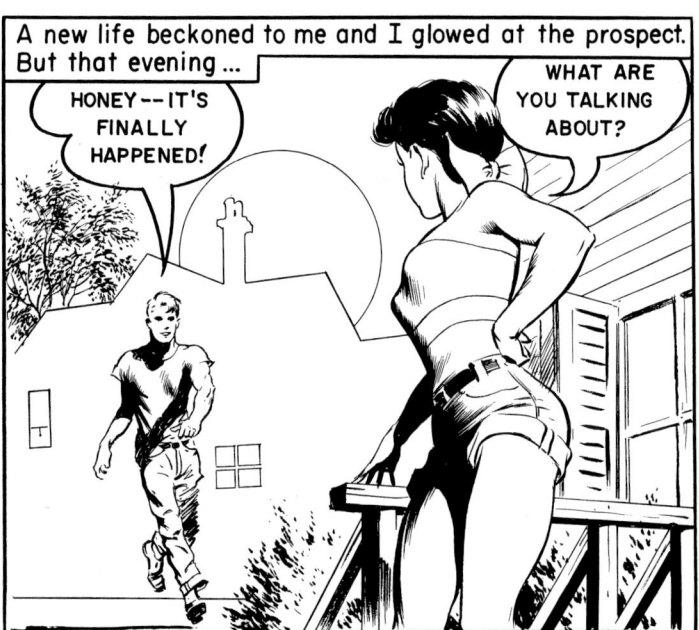

HONEY--IT'S FINALLY HAPPENED!

WHAT ARE YOU TALKING ABOUT?

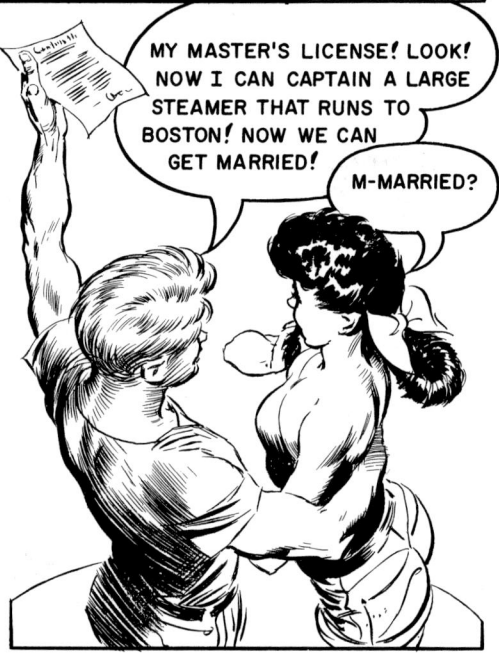

MY MASTER'S LICENSE! LOOK! NOW I CAN CAPTAIN A LARGE STEAMER THAT RUNS TO BOSTON! NOW WE CAN GET MARRIED!

M-MARRIED?

My heart pounded at the prospect. And yet some part of me was restraining my acceptance--a part willing to forego love for the glamour of the city...

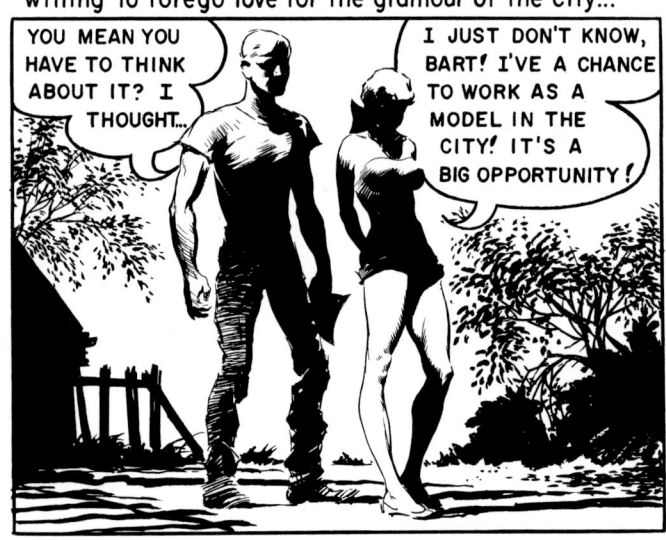

YOU MEAN YOU HAVE TO THINK ABOUT IT? I THOUGHT...

I JUST DON'T KNOW, BART! I'VE A CHANCE TO WORK AS A MODEL IN THE CITY! IT'S A BIG OPPORTUNITY!

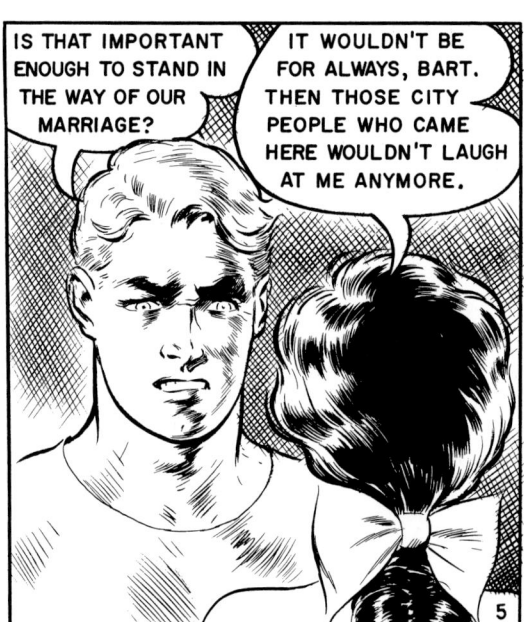

IS THAT IMPORTANT ENOUGH TO STAND IN THE WAY OF OUR MARRIAGE?

IT WOULDN'T BE FOR ALWAYS, BART. THEN THOSE CITY PEOPLE WHO CAME HERE WOULDN'T LAUGH AT ME ANYMORE.

5

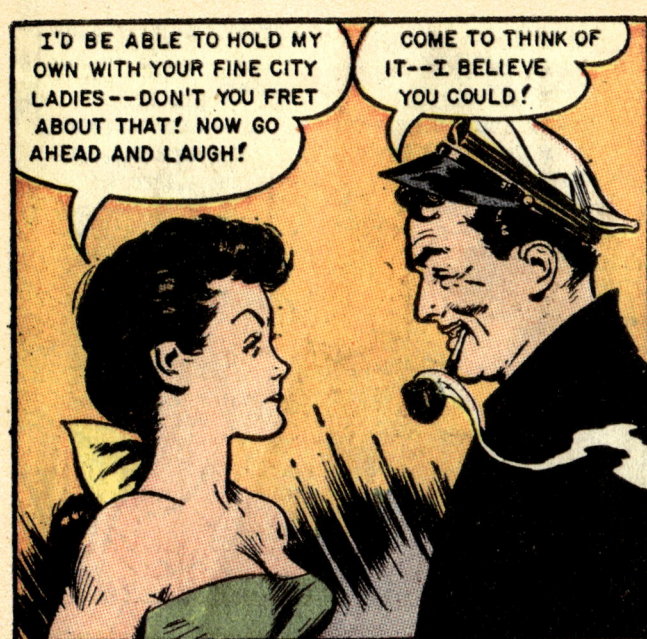

I'D BE ABLE TO HOLD MY OWN WITH YOUR FINE CITY LADIES--DON'T YOU FRET ABOUT THAT! NOW GO AHEAD AND LAUGH!

COME TO THINK OF IT--I BELIEVE YOU COULD!

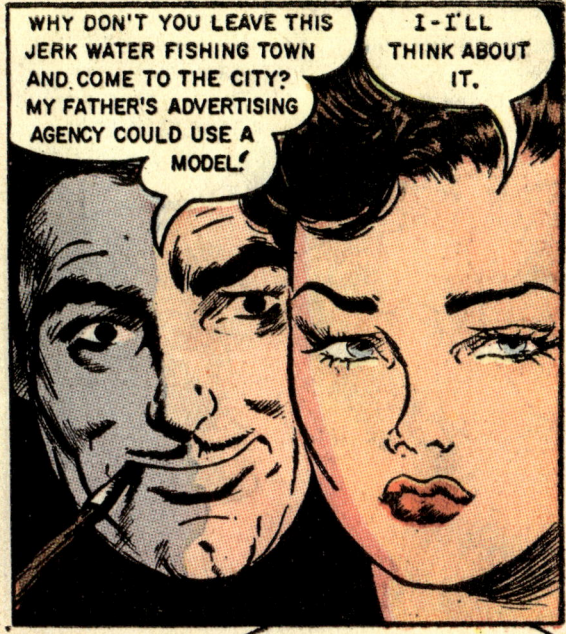

WHY DON'T YOU LEAVE THIS JERK WATER FISHING TOWN AND COME TO THE CITY? MY FATHER'S ADVERTISING AGENCY COULD USE A MODEL!

I-I'LL THINK ABOUT IT.

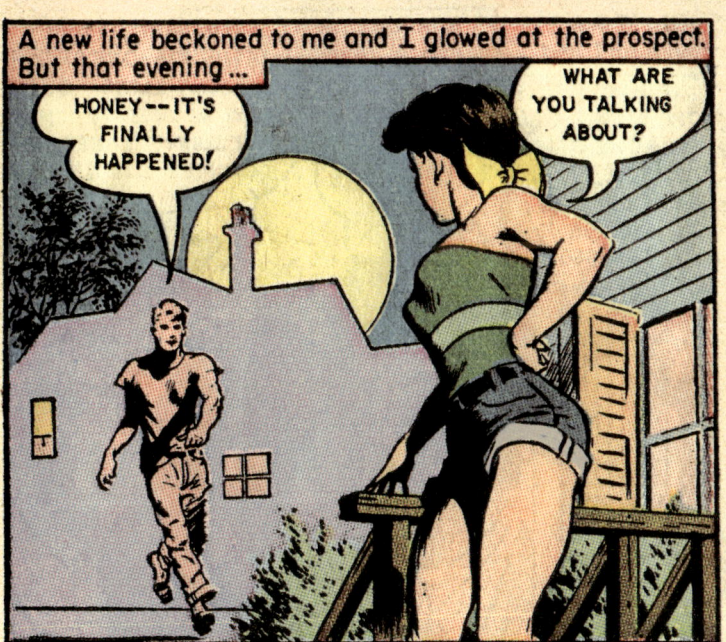

A new life beckoned to me and I glowed at the prospect. But that evening...

HONEY--IT'S FINALLY HAPPENED!

WHAT ARE YOU TALKING ABOUT?

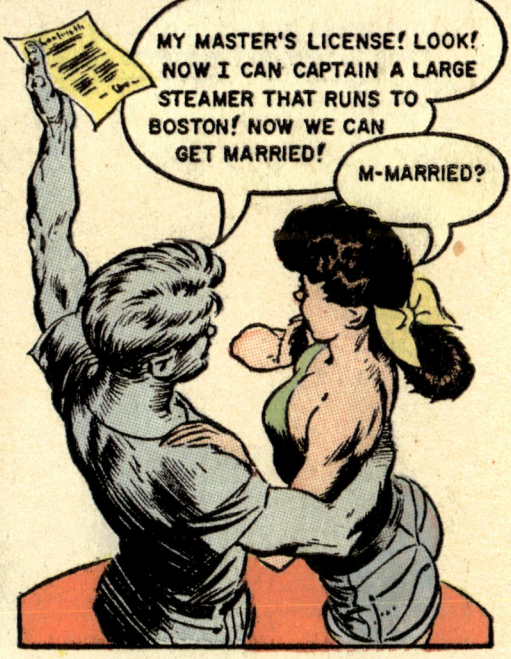

MY MASTER'S LICENSE! LOOK! NOW I CAN CAPTAIN A LARGE STEAMER THAT RUNS TO BOSTON! NOW WE CAN GET MARRIED!

M-MARRIED?

My heart pounded at the prospect. And yet some part of me was restraining my acceptance--a part willing to forego love for the glamour of the city...

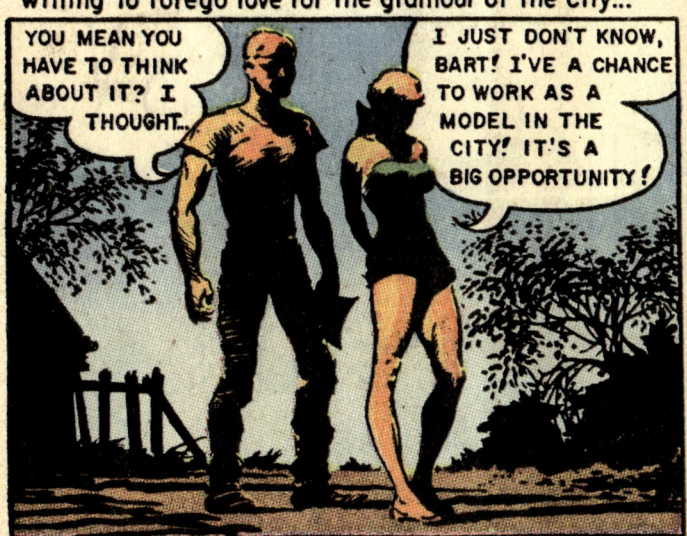

YOU MEAN YOU HAVE TO THINK ABOUT IT? I THOUGHT...

I JUST DON'T KNOW, BART! I'VE A CHANCE TO WORK AS A MODEL IN THE CITY! IT'S A BIG OPPORTUNITY!

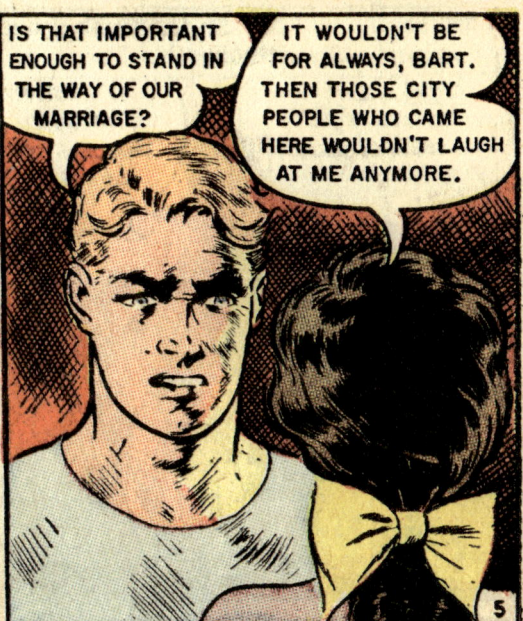

IS THAT IMPORTANT ENOUGH TO STAND IN THE WAY OF OUR MARRIAGE?

IT WOULDN'T BE FOR ALWAYS, BART. THEN THOSE CITY PEOPLE WHO CAME HERE WOULDN'T LAUGH AT ME ANYMORE.

5

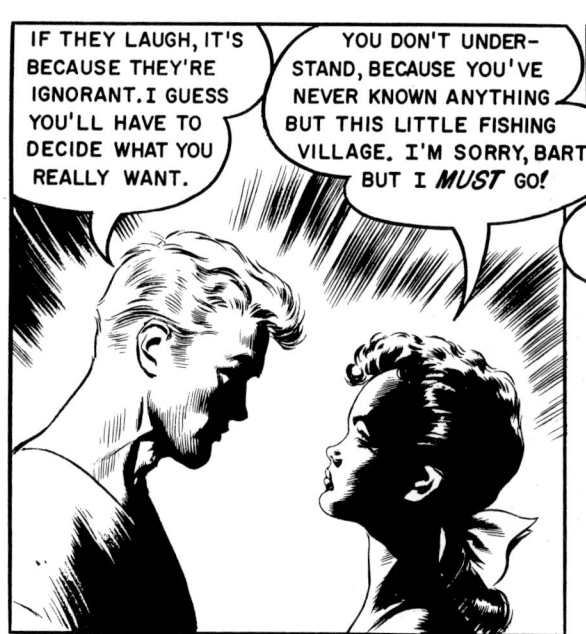

IF THEY LAUGH, IT'S BECAUSE THEY'RE IGNORANT. I GUESS YOU'LL HAVE TO DECIDE WHAT YOU REALLY WANT.

YOU DON'T UNDERSTAND, BECAUSE YOU'VE NEVER KNOWN ANYTHING BUT THIS LITTLE FISHING VILLAGE. I'M SORRY, BART-- BUT I *MUST* GO!

Without another word, he turned and walked away. I left for the city the following week with my hopes high and my determination strong...

OUR AGENCY IS INTERESTED IN THIS YOUNG LADY, CLAIRE. PUT HER THROUGH THE MODELLING TRAINING COURSE.

I'LL PERSONALLY SEE TO HER TRAINING, MR. VANDERSHAW!

The first weeks passed in a flurry of excitement. I was beginning to take on the pseudo-sophistication that I had envied in the others...

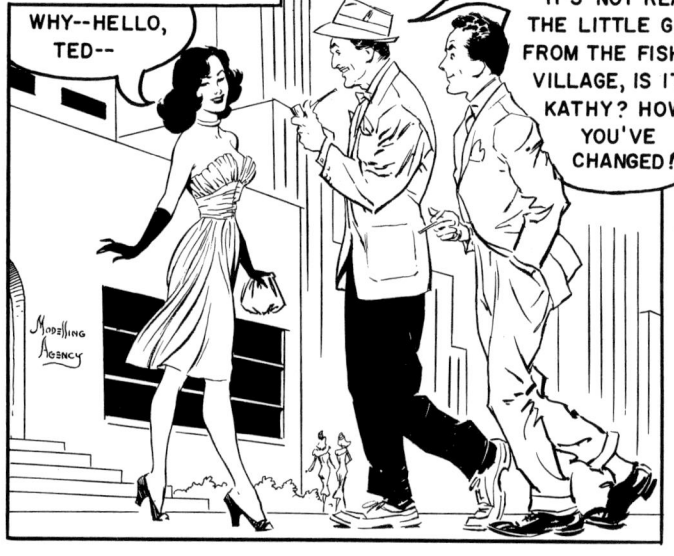

WHY--HELLO, TED--

IT'S NOT REALLY THE LITTLE GIRL FROM THE FISHING VILLAGE, IS IT, KATHY? HOW YOU'VE CHANGED!

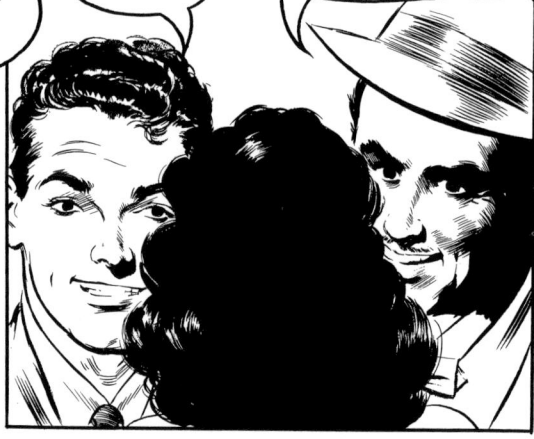

HOW ABOUT A KNOCK-DOWN, TED? YOU'VE BEEN KEEPING HER IN THE DARK, YOU ROGUE!

KATHY, THIS IS ROD DESMOND--ONE OF OUR ACCOUNT EXECS--BUT PAY NO HEED TO HIM. I'M GOING TO KEEP YOU OCCUPIED MYSELF!

In the months that passed, I suppose I became more superficially attractive, but I began to lose my gaiety...

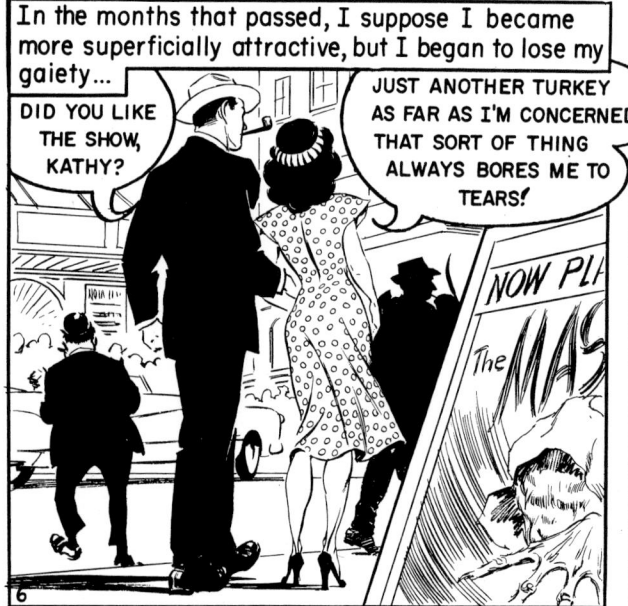

DID YOU LIKE THE SHOW, KATHY?

JUST ANOTHER TURKEY AS FAR AS I'M CONCERNED. THAT SORT OF THING ALWAYS BORES ME TO TEARS!

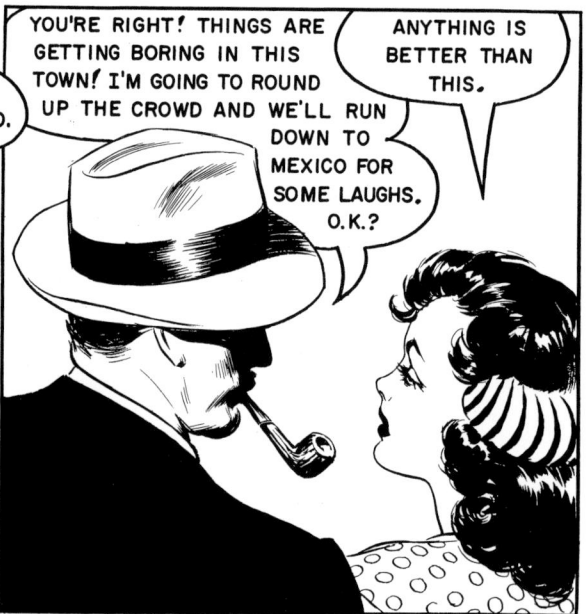

YOU'RE RIGHT! THINGS ARE GETTING BORING IN THIS TOWN! I'M GOING TO ROUND UP THE CROWD AND WE'LL RUN DOWN TO MEXICO FOR SOME LAUGHS. O.K.?

ANYTHING IS BETTER THAN THIS.

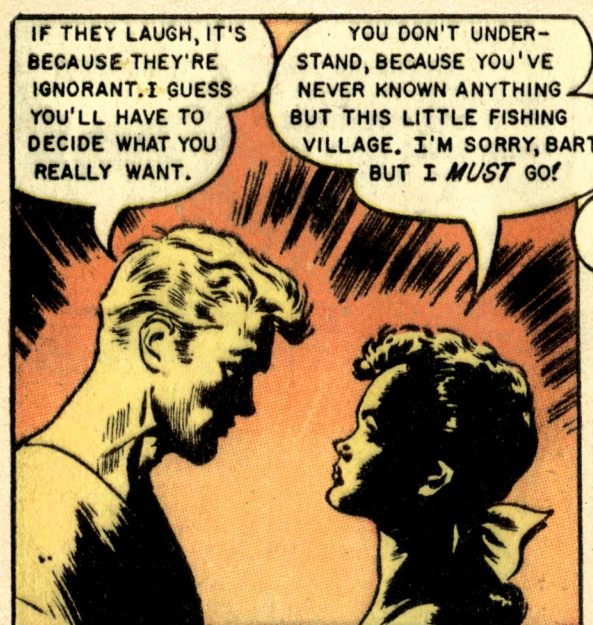

IF THEY LAUGH, IT'S BECAUSE THEY'RE IGNORANT. I GUESS YOU'LL HAVE TO DECIDE WHAT YOU REALLY WANT.

YOU DON'T UNDERSTAND, BECAUSE YOU'VE NEVER KNOWN ANYTHING BUT THIS LITTLE FISHING VILLAGE. I'M SORRY, BART-- BUT I *MUST* GO!

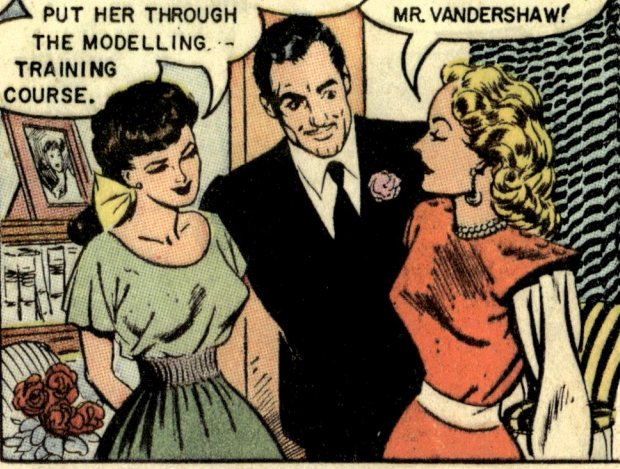

Without another word, he turned and walked away. I left for the city the following week with my hopes high and my determination strong...

OUR AGENCY IS INTERESTED IN THIS YOUNG LADY, CLAIRE. PUT HER THROUGH THE MODELLING TRAINING COURSE.

I'LL PERSONALLY SEE TO HER TRAINING, MR. VANDERSHAW!

The first weeks passed in a flurry of excitement. I was beginning to take on the pseudo-sophistication that I had envied in the others...

WHY--HELLO, TED--

IT'S NOT REALLY THE LITTLE GIRL FROM THE FISHING VILLAGE, IS IT, KATHY? HOW YOU'VE CHANGED!

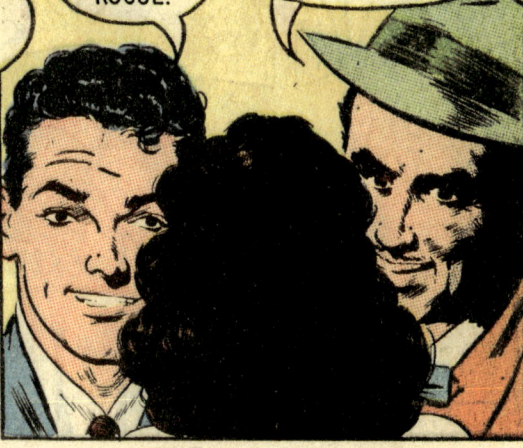

HOW ABOUT A KNOCK-DOWN, TED? YOU'VE BEEN KEEPING HER IN THE DARK, YOU ROGUE!

KATHY, THIS IS ROD DESMOND--ONE OF OUR ACCOUNT EXECS--BUT PAY NO HEED TO HIM. I'M GOING TO KEEP YOU OCCUPIED MYSELF!

In the months that passed, I suppose I became more superficially attractive, but I began to lose my gaiety...

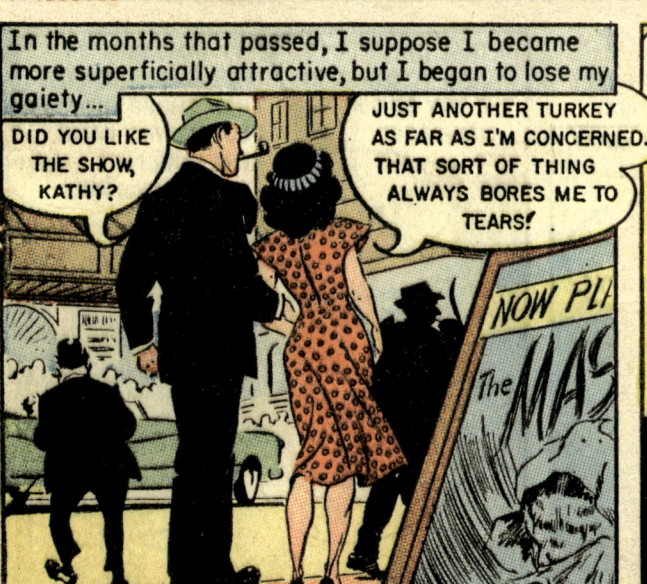

DID YOU LIKE THE SHOW, KATHY?

JUST ANOTHER TURKEY AS FAR AS I'M CONCERNED. THAT SORT OF THING ALWAYS BORES ME TO TEARS!

NOW PL THE MA

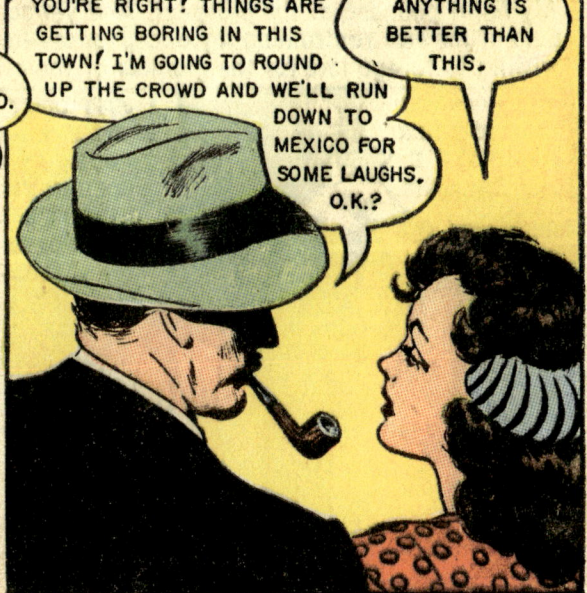

YOU'RE RIGHT! THINGS ARE GETTING BORING IN THIS TOWN! I'M GOING TO ROUND UP THE CROWD AND WE'LL RUN DOWN TO MEXICO FOR SOME LAUGHS. O.K.?

ANYTHING IS BETTER THAN THIS.

But as time passed the laughter became hollow--the gaiety affected--and I was getting thoroughly fed up with Ted and his crowd...

STOP IT, TED. YOU'RE ACTING LIKE A SILLY GOOP!

BUT CHARLOTTE SAID SHE WON'T MARRY ME! (SNIFF, SNIFF) HOW ABOUT YOU MARRYING ME TONIGHT? WE'LL SHOW HER.

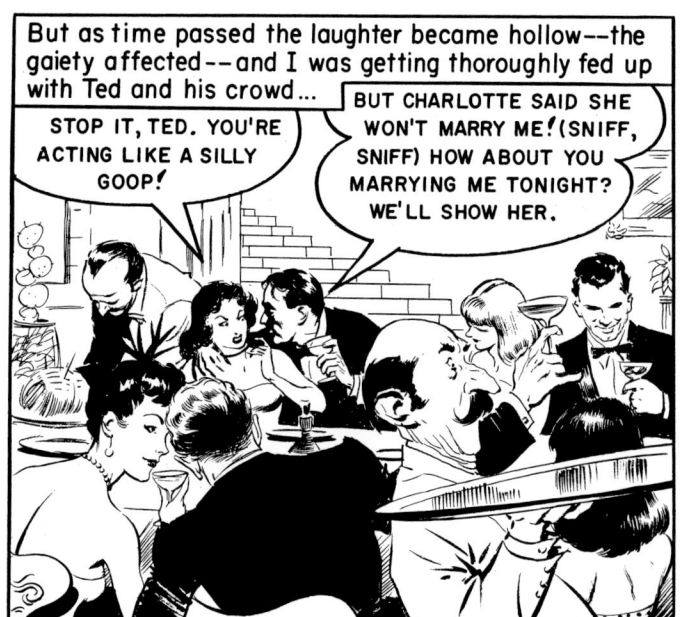

MARRY YOU? JUST AS SIMPLE AS THAT, EH? BUT I GUESS YOU AND YOUR KIND FIND MARRIAGE ONLY A GAME, AFTER ALL. IN FACT, ALL OF LIFE IS A GAME THAT YOU'LL GO ON PLAYING WITH.

THERE YOU GO! ALL I DID WAS ASK YOU TO MARRY ME AND YOU GIVE ME A SERMON.

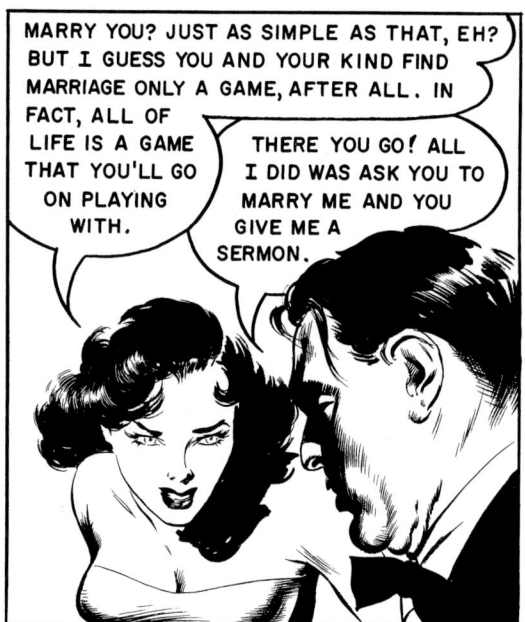

Suddenly I was overwhelmed with disgust at Ted and his kind. The longing for Bart's strong arms--the sincerity of his love became an unappeasable hunger, and I found myself running...

HEY--WHERE ARE YOU GOING?

HOME--AND BACK TO BART'S ARM'S!

WAIT HERE FOR ME. I WANT YOU TO DRIVE ME TO THE AIRPORT!

SI, SI, SENORITA!

BART WAS RIGHT. THE LIFE HERE IS NATURAL AND REAL--NOT PRE-TENTIOUS LIKE TED'S LIFE. OH BART, DARLING-- I WANT YOUR ARMS AROUND ME.

PSSST--AIN'T THAT KATHY OVER THERE? HEARD SHE WENT TO THE CITY. THE GAL SURE LOOKS DIFFERENT.

•7

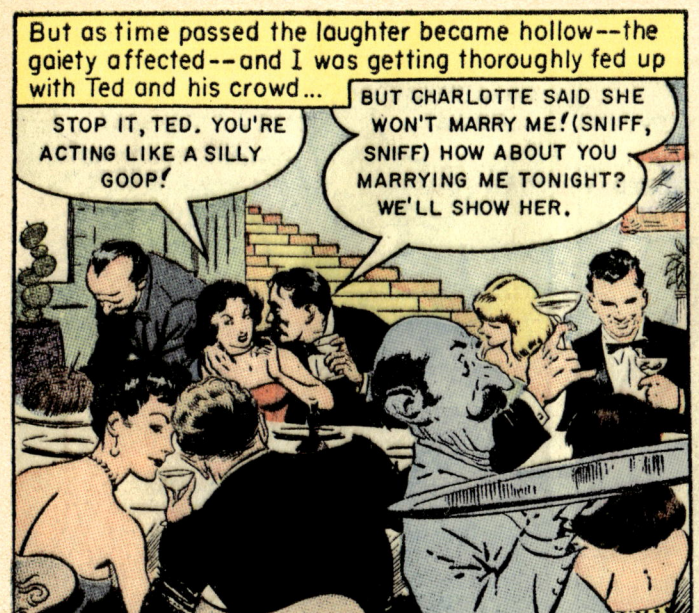

But as time passed the laughter became hollow—the gaiety affected—and I was getting thoroughly fed up with Ted and his crowd...

STOP IT, TED. YOU'RE ACTING LIKE A SILLY GOOP!

BUT CHARLOTTE SAID SHE WON'T MARRY ME! (SNIFF, SNIFF) HOW ABOUT YOU MARRYING ME TONIGHT? WE'LL SHOW HER.

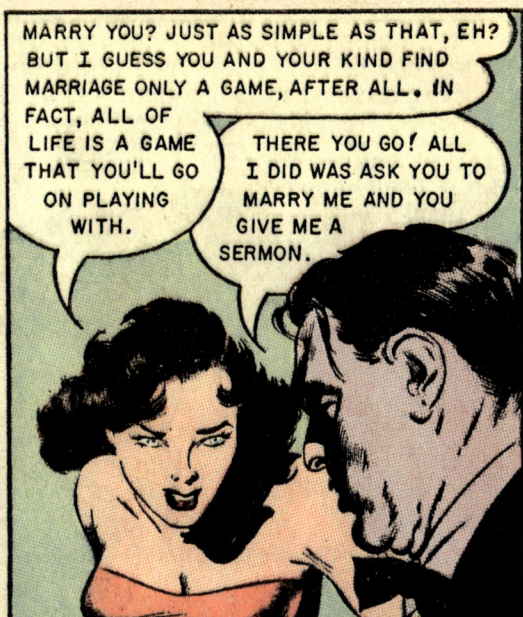

MARRY YOU? JUST AS SIMPLE AS THAT, EH? BUT I GUESS YOU AND YOUR KIND FIND MARRIAGE ONLY A GAME, AFTER ALL. IN FACT, ALL OF LIFE IS A GAME THAT YOU'LL GO ON PLAYING WITH.

THERE YOU GO! ALL I DID WAS ASK YOU TO MARRY ME AND YOU GIVE ME A SERMON.

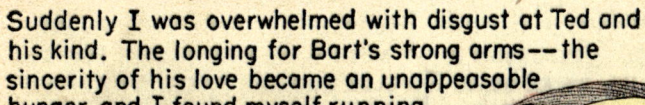

Suddenly I was overwhelmed with disgust at Ted and his kind. The longing for Bart's strong arms—the sincerity of his love became an unappeasable hunger, and I found myself running...

HEY—WHERE ARE YOU GOING?

HOME—AND BACK TO BART'S ARM'S!

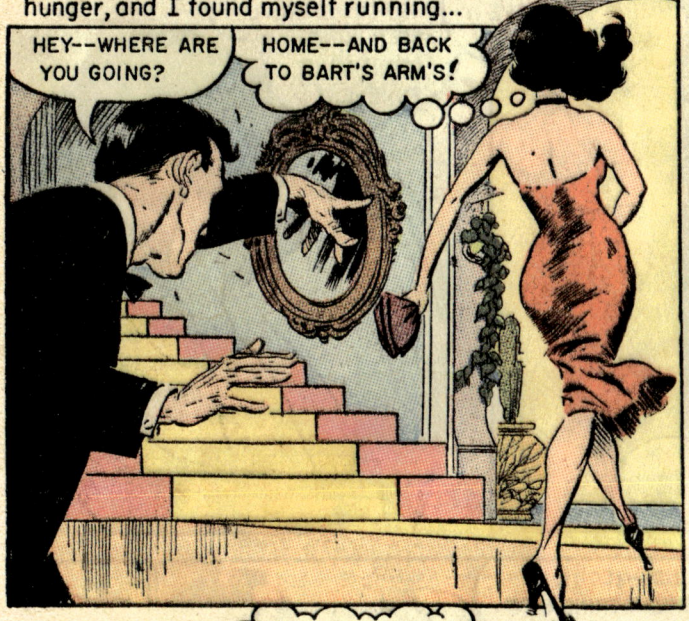

WAIT HERE FOR ME. I WANT YOU TO DRIVE ME TO THE AIRPORT!

SI, SI, SENORITA!

PSSST—AIN'T THAT KATHY OVER THERE? HEARD SHE WENT TO THE CITY. THE GAL SURE LOOKS DIFFERENT.

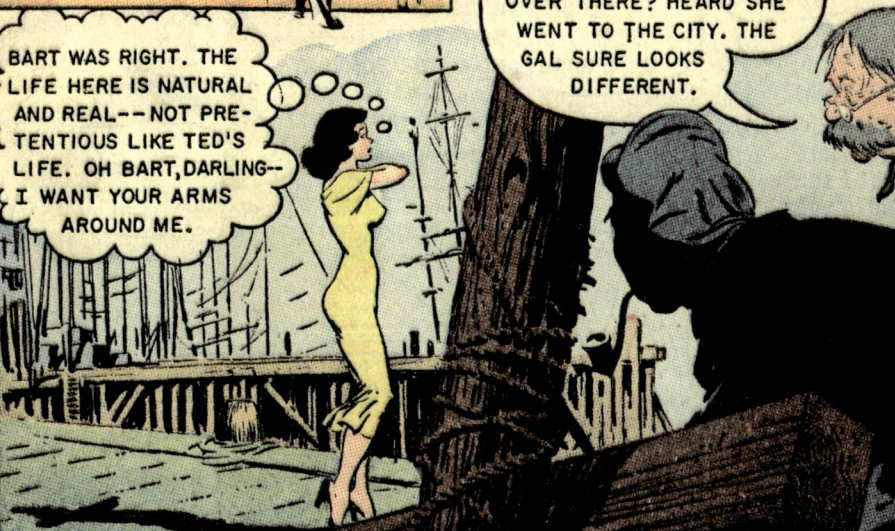

Many anxious hours later found me back home where I learned Bart was out to sea. The day he was to return, I donned my finest clothes and with singing heart went down to meet him...

BART WAS RIGHT. THE LIFE HERE IS NATURAL AND REAL—NOT PRETENTIOUS LIKE TED'S LIFE. OH BART, DARLING— I WANT YOUR ARMS AROUND ME.

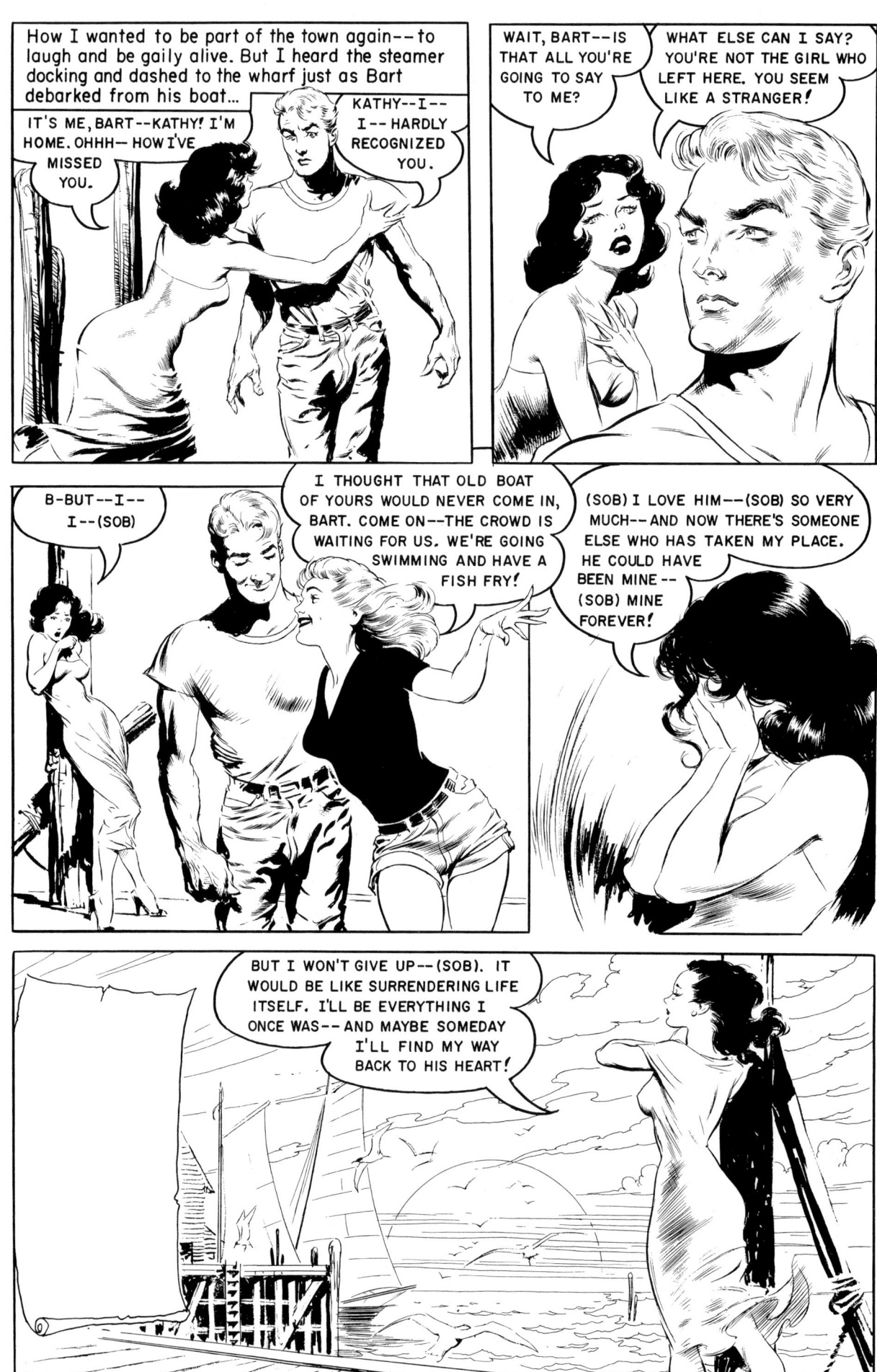

How I wanted to be part of the town again-- to laugh and be gaily alive. But I heard the steamer docking and dashed to the wharf just as Bart debarked from his boat...

IT'S ME, BART--KATHY! I'M HOME. OHHH-- HOW I'VE MISSED YOU.

KATHY--I-- I-- HARDLY RECOGNIZED YOU.

WAIT, BART--IS THAT ALL YOU'RE GOING TO SAY TO ME?

WHAT ELSE CAN I SAY? YOU'RE NOT THE GIRL WHO LEFT HERE. YOU SEEM LIKE A STRANGER!

B-BUT--I-- I--(SOB)

I THOUGHT THAT OLD BOAT OF YOURS WOULD NEVER COME IN, BART. COME ON--THE CROWD IS WAITING FOR US. WE'RE GOING SWIMMING AND HAVE A FISH FRY!

(SOB) I LOVE HIM--(SOB) SO VERY MUCH-- AND NOW THERE'S SOMEONE ELSE WHO HAS TAKEN MY PLACE. HE COULD HAVE BEEN MINE-- (SOB) MINE FOREVER!

BUT I WON'T GIVE UP--(SOB). IT WOULD BE LIKE SURRENDERING LIFE ITSELF. I'LL BE EVERYTHING I ONCE WAS-- AND MAYBE SOMEDAY I'LL FIND MY WAY BACK TO HIS HEART!

8

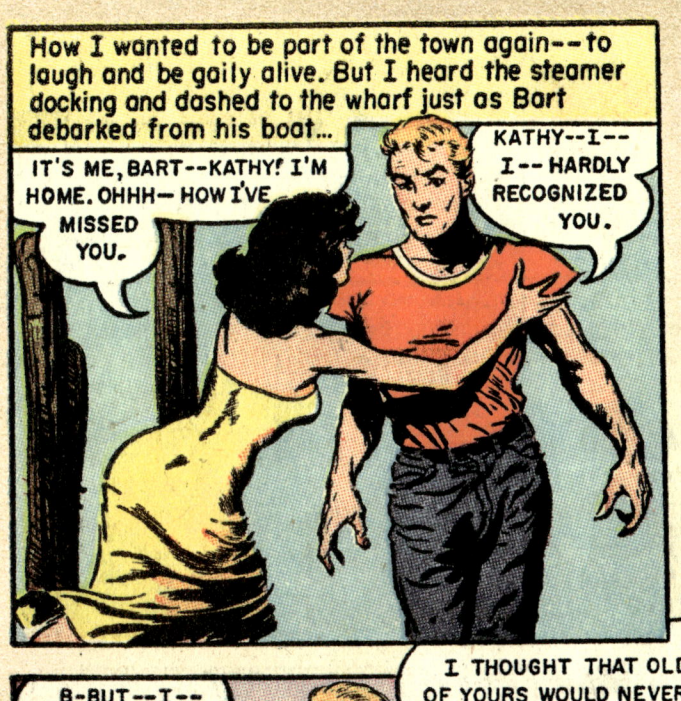

How I wanted to be part of the town again--to laugh and be gaily alive. But I heard the steamer docking and dashed to the wharf just as Bart debarked from his boat...

IT'S ME, BART--KATHY! I'M HOME. OHHH-- HOW I'VE MISSED YOU.

KATHY--I-- I-- HARDLY RECOGNIZED YOU.

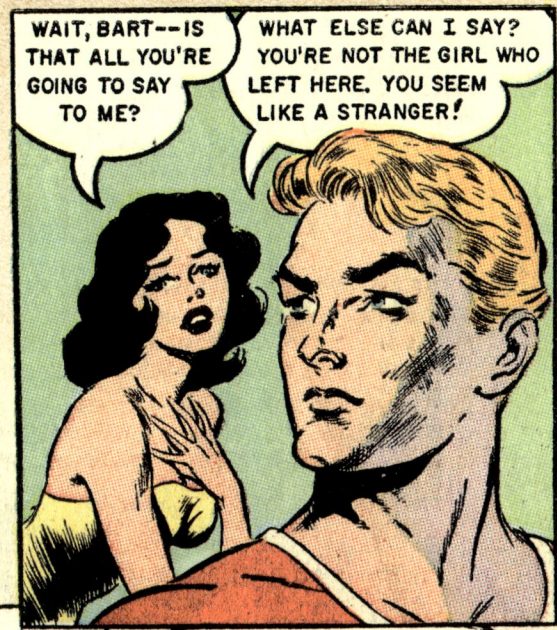

WAIT, BART--IS THAT ALL YOU'RE GOING TO SAY TO ME?

WHAT ELSE CAN I SAY? YOU'RE NOT THE GIRL WHO LEFT HERE. YOU SEEM LIKE A STRANGER!

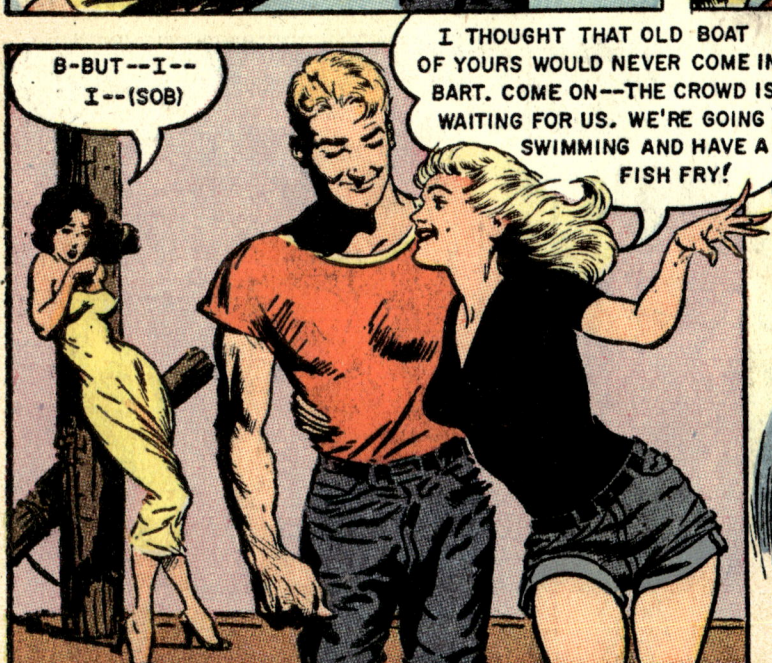

B-BUT--I-- I--(SOB)

I THOUGHT THAT OLD BOAT OF YOURS WOULD NEVER COME IN, BART. COME ON--THE CROWD IS WAITING FOR US. WE'RE GOING SWIMMING AND HAVE A FISH FRY!

(SOB) I LOVE HIM--(SOB) SO VERY MUCH--AND NOW THERE'S SOMEONE ELSE WHO HAS TAKEN MY PLACE. HE COULD HAVE BEEN MINE-- (SOB) MINE FOREVER!

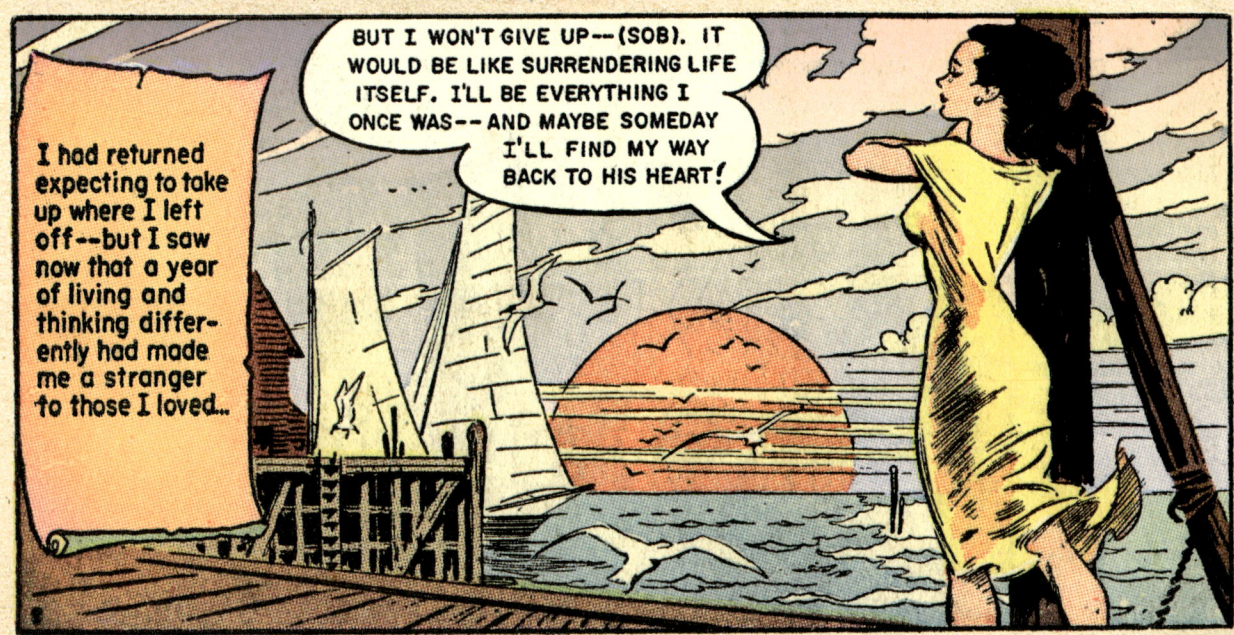

I had returned expecting to take up where I left off--but I saw now that a year of living and thinking differently had made me a stranger to those I loved...

BUT I WON'T GIVE UP--(SOB). IT WOULD BE LIKE SURRENDERING LIFE ITSELF. I'LL BE EVERYTHING I ONCE WAS--AND MAYBE SOMEDAY I'LL FIND MY WAY BACK TO HIS HEART!

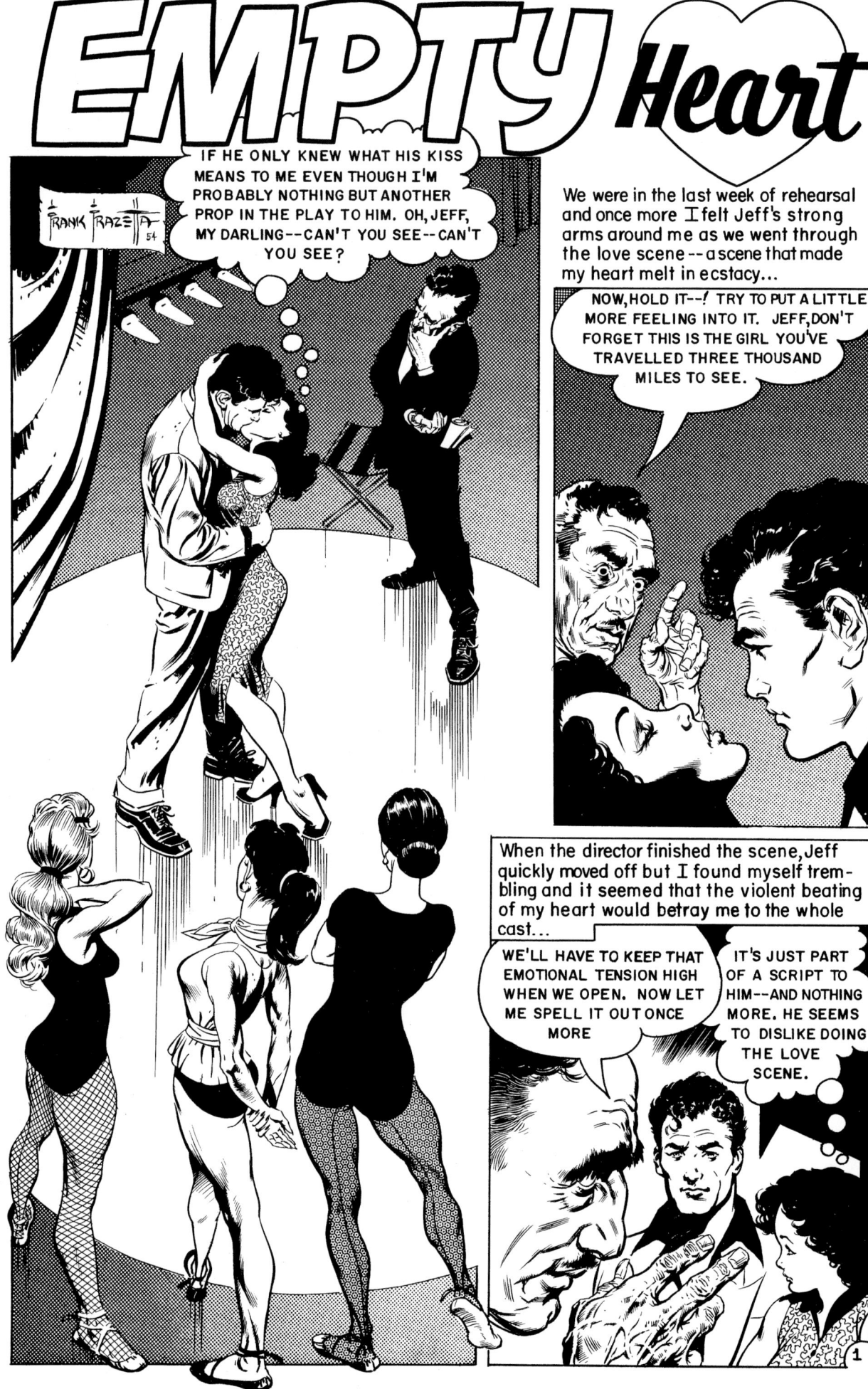

EMPTY Heart

IF HE ONLY KNEW WHAT HIS KISS MEANS TO ME EVEN THOUGH I'M PROBABLY NOTHING BUT ANOTHER PROP IN THE PLAY TO HIM. OH, JEFF, MY DARLING--CAN'T YOU SEE--CAN'T YOU SEE?

FRANK FRAZETTA 54

We were in the last week of rehearsal and once more I felt Jeff's strong arms around me as we went through the love scene -- a scene that made my heart melt in ecstacy...

NOW, HOLD IT--! TRY TO PUT A LITTLE MORE FEELING INTO IT. JEFF, DON'T FORGET THIS IS THE GIRL YOU'VE TRAVELLED THREE THOUSAND MILES TO SEE.

When the director finished the scene, Jeff quickly moved off but I found myself trembling and it seemed that the violent beating of my heart would betray me to the whole cast...

WE'LL HAVE TO KEEP THAT EMOTIONAL TENSION HIGH WHEN WE OPEN. NOW LET ME SPELL IT OUT ONCE MORE

IT'S JUST PART OF A SCRIPT TO HIM--AND NOTHING MORE. HE SEEMS TO DISLIKE DOING THE LOVE SCENE.

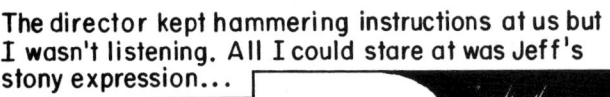

The director kept hammering instructions at us but I wasn't listening. All I could stare at was Jeff's stony expression...

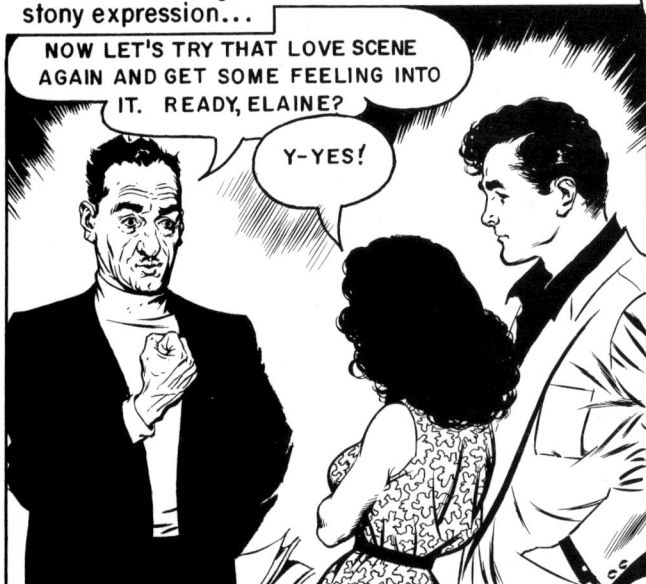

NOW LET'S TRY THAT LOVE SCENE AGAIN AND GET SOME FEELING INTO IT. READY, ELAINE?

Y-YES!

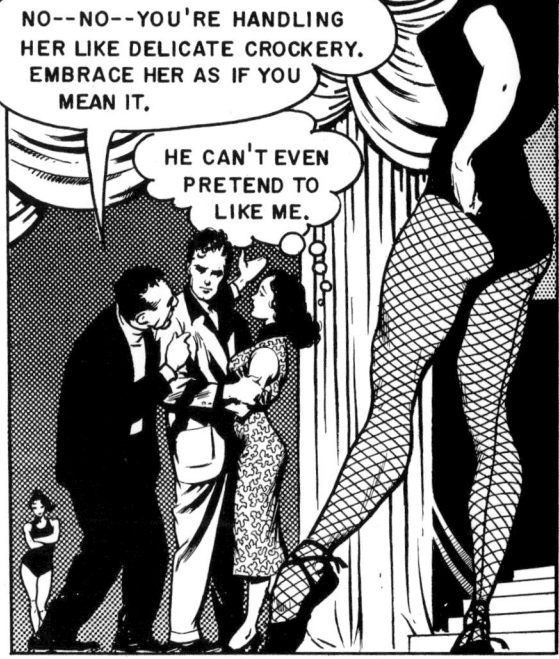

NO--NO--YOU'RE HANDLING HER LIKE DELICATE CROCKERY. EMBRACE HER AS IF YOU MEAN IT.

HE CAN'T EVEN PRETEND TO LIKE ME.

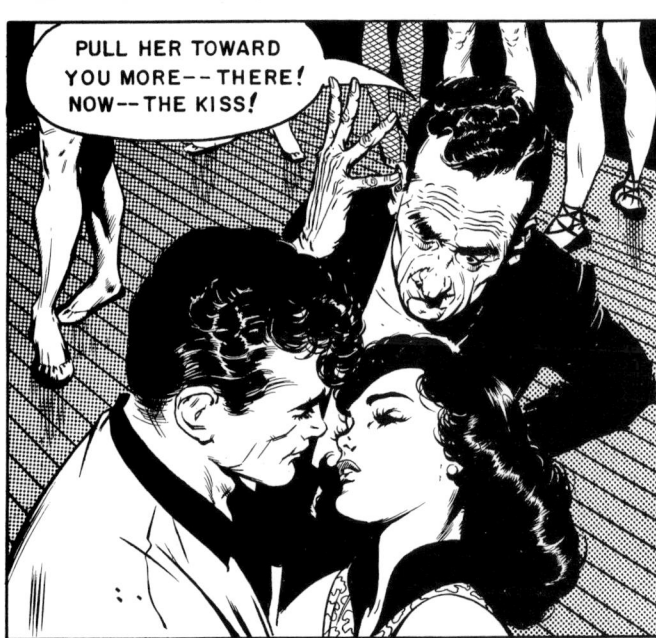

PULL HER TOWARD YOU MORE--THERE! NOW--THE KISS!

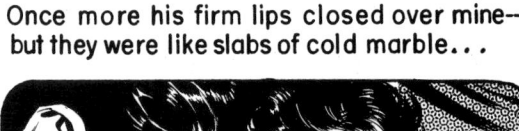

Once more his firm lips closed over mine-- but they were like slabs of cold marble...

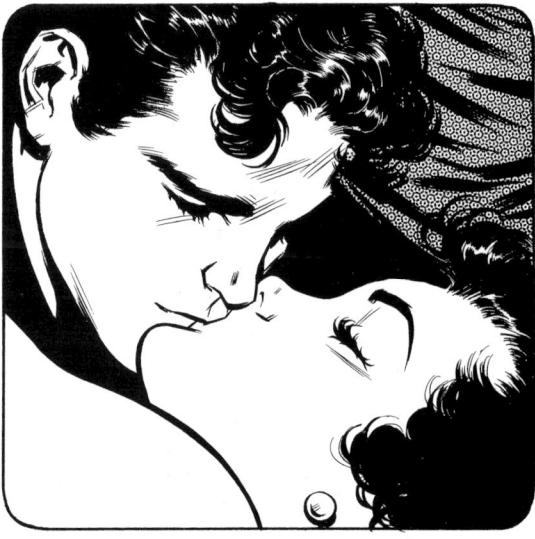

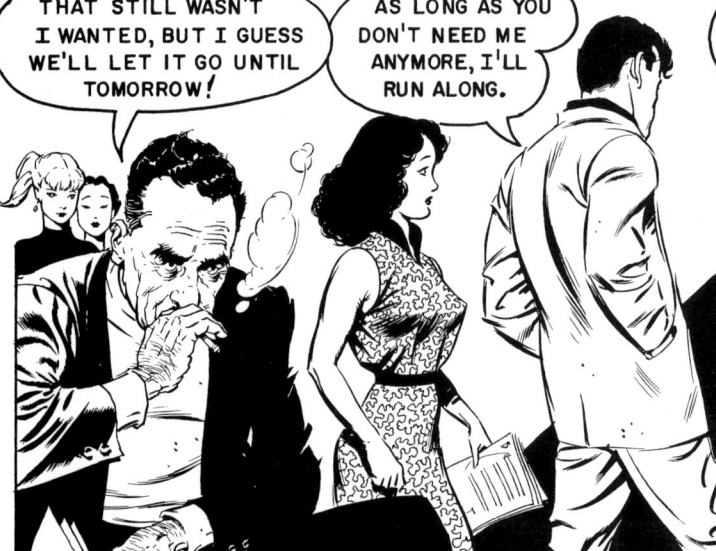

THAT STILL WASN'T I WANTED, BUT I GUESS WE'LL LET IT GO UNTIL TOMORROW!

AS LONG AS YOU DON'T NEED ME ANYMORE, I'LL RUN ALONG.

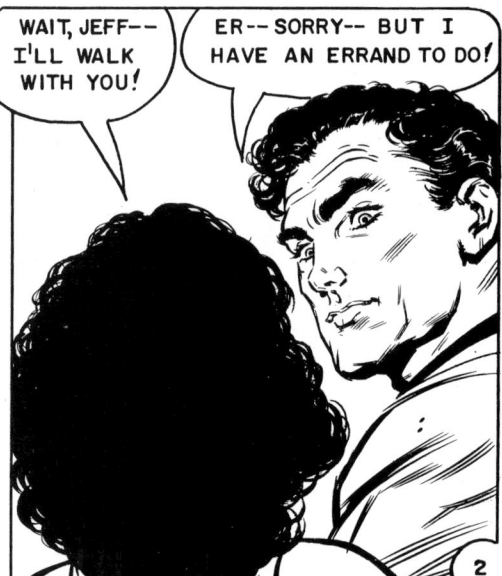

WAIT, JEFF-- I'LL WALK WITH YOU!

ER-- SORRY-- BUT I HAVE AN ERRAND TO DO!

2

The director kept hammering instructions at us but I wasn't listening. All I could stare at was Jeff's stony expression...

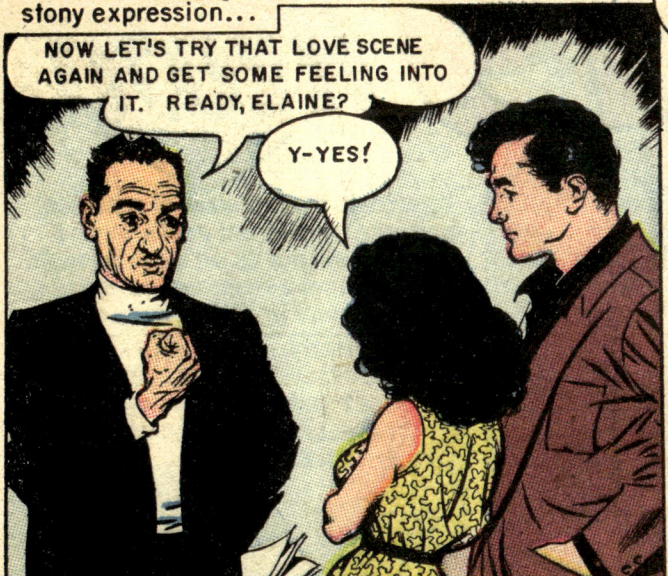

NOW LET'S TRY THAT LOVE SCENE AGAIN AND GET SOME FEELING INTO IT. READY, ELAINE?

Y-YES!

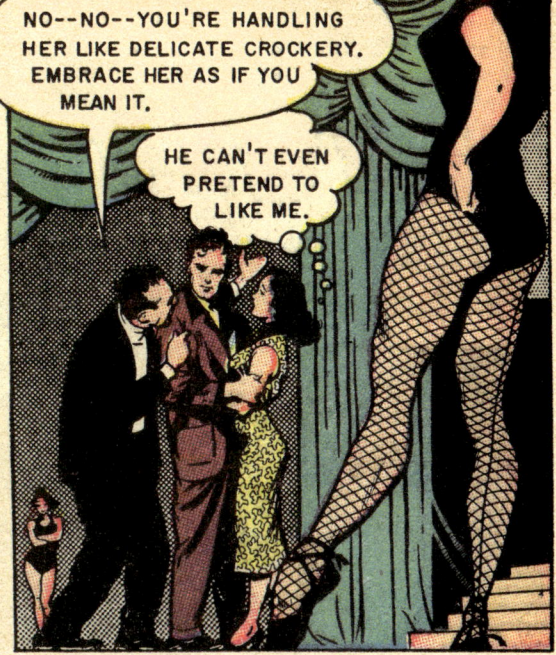

NO--NO--YOU'RE HANDLING HER LIKE DELICATE CROCKERY. EMBRACE HER AS IF YOU MEAN IT.

HE CAN'T EVEN PRETEND TO LIKE ME.

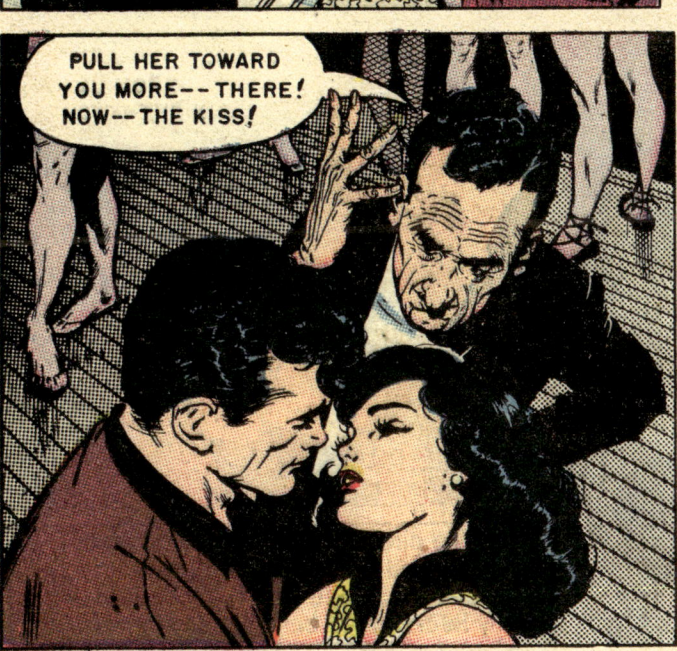

PULL HER TOWARD YOU MORE--THERE! NOW--THE KISS!

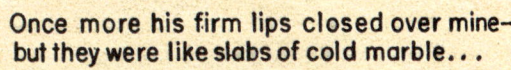

Once more his firm lips closed over mine-- but they were like slabs of cold marble...

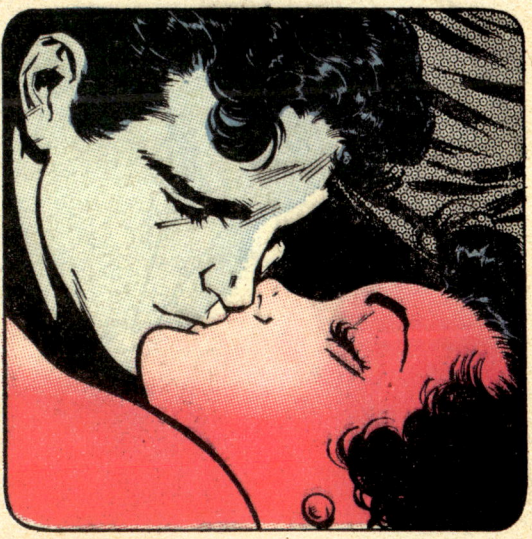

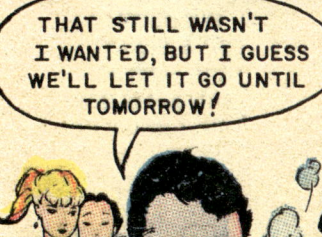

THAT STILL WASN'T I WANTED, BUT I GUESS WE'LL LET IT GO UNTIL TOMORROW!

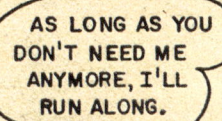

AS LONG AS YOU DON'T NEED ME ANYMORE, I'LL RUN ALONG.

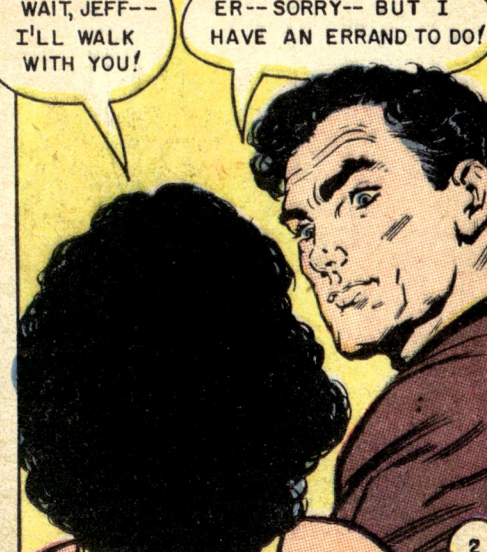

WAIT, JEFF-- I'LL WALK WITH YOU!

ER--SORRY--BUT I HAVE AN ERRAND TO DO!

2

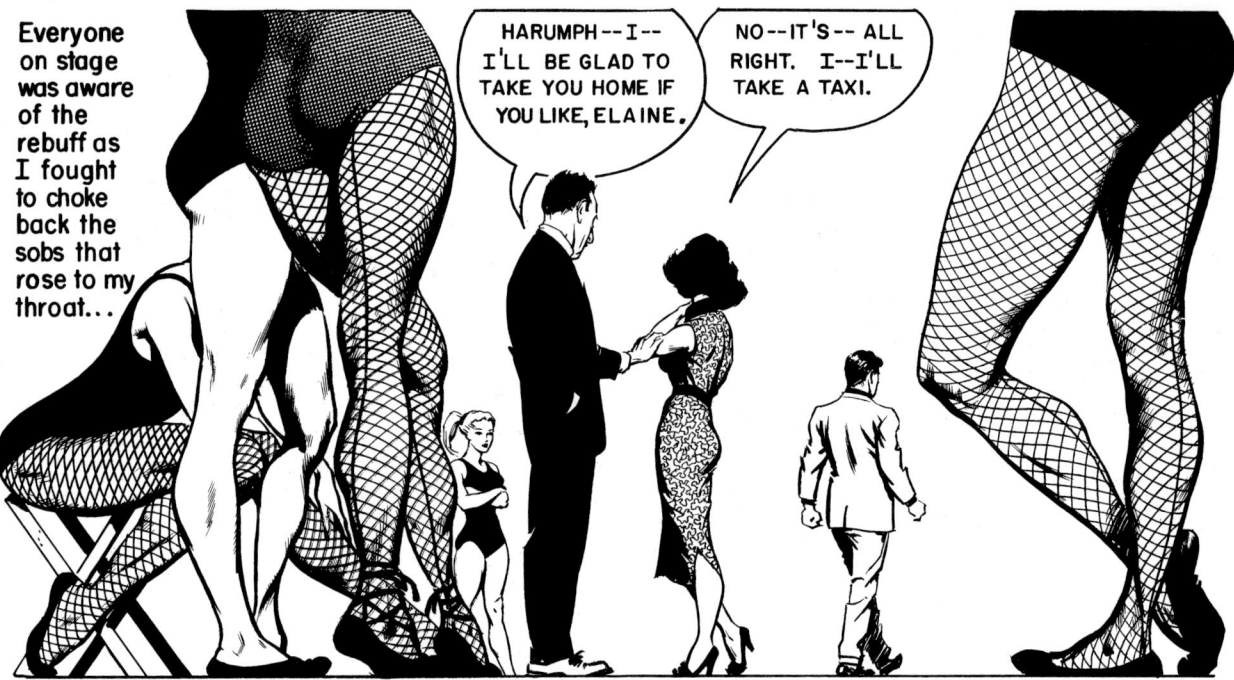

Everyone on stage was aware of the rebuff as I fought to choke back the sobs that rose to my throat...

HARUMPH--I--I'LL BE GLAD TO TAKE YOU HOME IF YOU LIKE, ELAINE.

NO--IT'S-- ALL RIGHT. I--I'LL TAKE A TAXI.

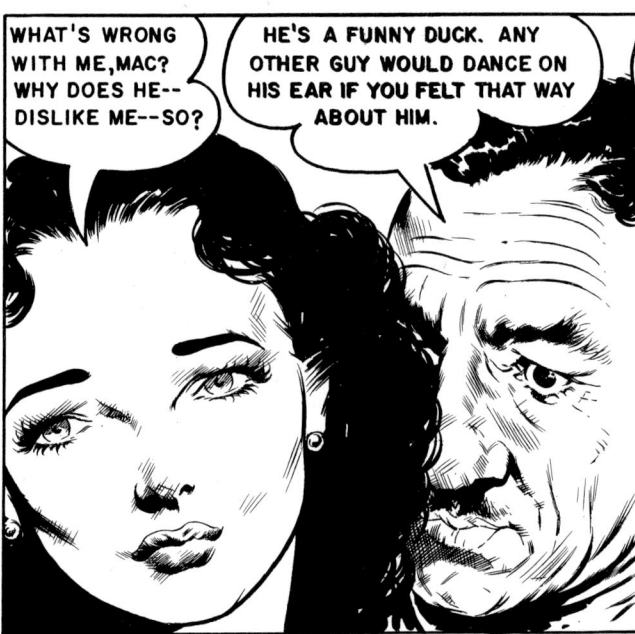

WHAT'S WRONG WITH ME, MAC? WHY DOES HE-- DISLIKE ME--SO?

HE'S A FUNNY DUCK. ANY OTHER GUY WOULD DANCE ON HIS EAR IF YOU FELT THAT WAY ABOUT HIM.

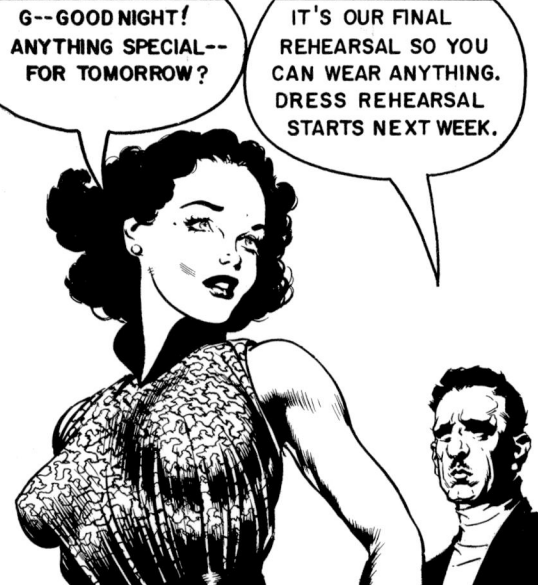

G--GOOD NIGHT! ANYTHING SPECIAL-- FOR TOMORROW?

IT'S OUR FINAL REHEARSAL SO YOU CAN WEAR ANYTHING. DRESS REHEARSAL STARTS NEXT WEEK.

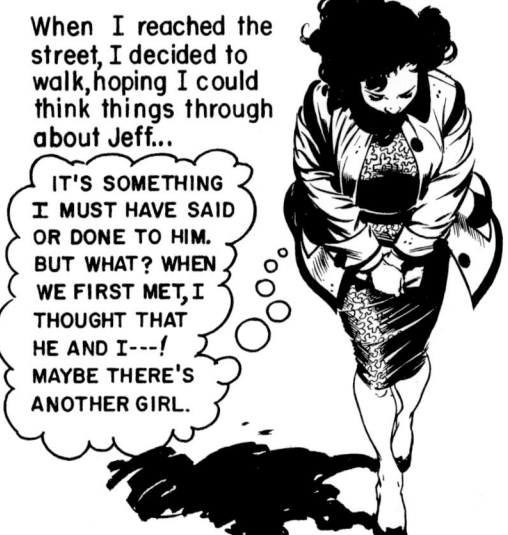

When I reached the street, I decided to walk, hoping I could think things through about Jeff...

IT'S SOMETHING I MUST HAVE SAID OR DONE TO HIM. BUT WHAT? WHEN WE FIRST MET, I THOUGHT THAT HE AND I---! MAYBE THERE'S ANOTHER GIRL.

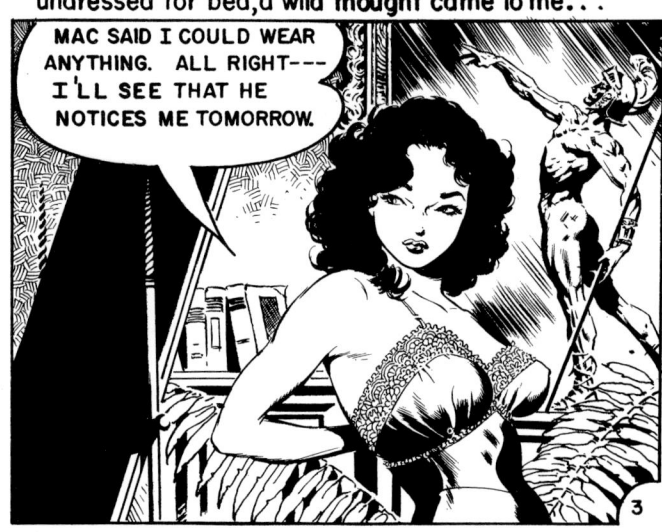

That thought took hold and I couldn't shake it. As I undressed for bed, a wild thought came to me...

MAC SAID I COULD WEAR ANYTHING. ALL RIGHT--- I'LL SEE THAT HE NOTICES ME TOMORROW.

3

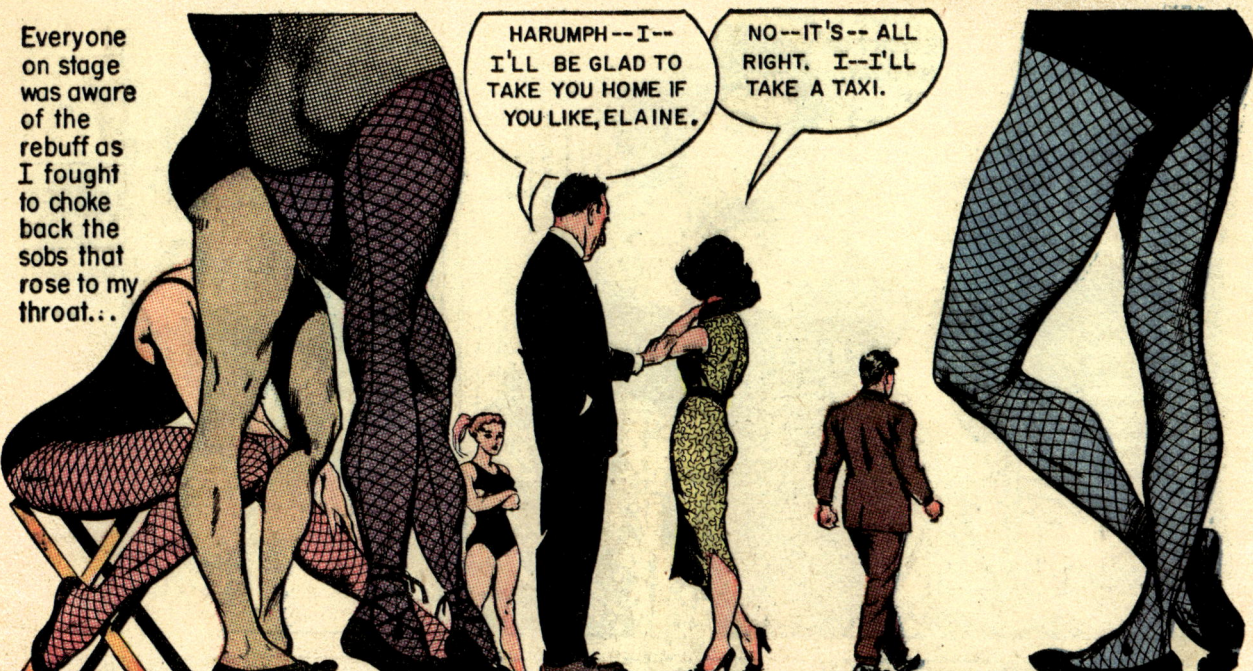

Everyone on stage was aware of the rebuff as I fought to choke back the sobs that rose to my throat...

HARUMPH--I--I'LL BE GLAD TO TAKE YOU HOME IF YOU LIKE, ELAINE.

NO--IT'S--ALL RIGHT. I--I'LL TAKE A TAXI.

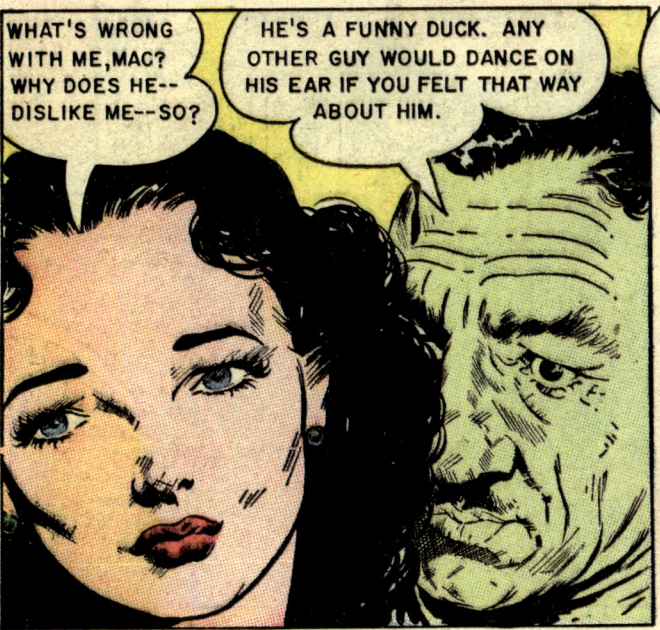

WHAT'S WRONG WITH ME, MAC? WHY DOES HE--DISLIKE ME--SO?

HE'S A FUNNY DUCK. ANY OTHER GUY WOULD DANCE ON HIS EAR IF YOU FELT THAT WAY ABOUT HIM.

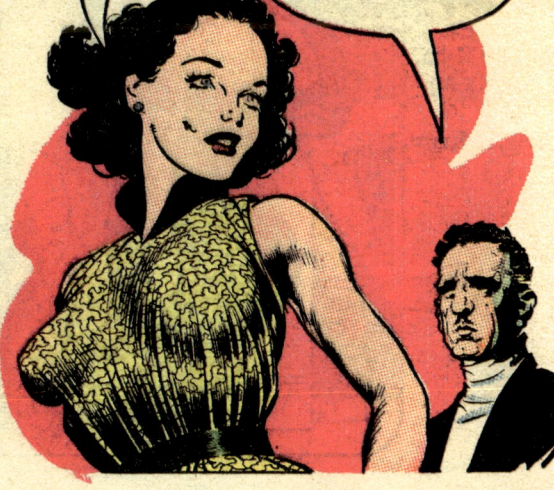

G--GOOD NIGHT! ANYTHING SPECIAL--FOR TOMORROW?

IT'S OUR FINAL REHEARSAL SO YOU CAN WEAR ANYTHING. DRESS REHEARSAL STARTS NEXT WEEK.

When I reached the street, I decided to walk, hoping I could think things through about Jeff...

IT'S SOMETHING I MUST HAVE SAID OR DONE TO HIM. BUT WHAT? WHEN WE FIRST MET, I THOUGHT THAT HE AND I---! MAYBE THERE'S ANOTHER GIRL.

That thought took hold and I couldn't shake it. As I undressed for bed, a wild thought came to me...

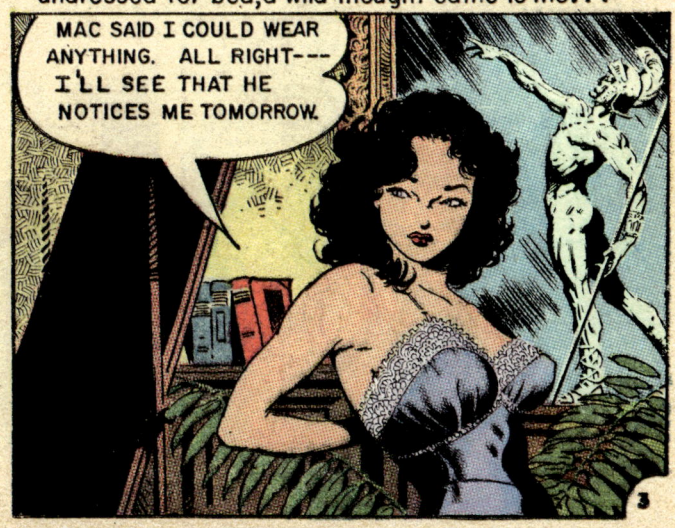

MAC SAID I COULD WEAR ANYTHING. ALL RIGHT---I'LL SEE THAT HE NOTICES ME TOMORROW.

Just before rehearsal the following day, I raided my wardrobe for the best, and dressed with deliberate care...

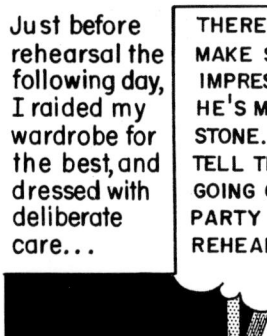

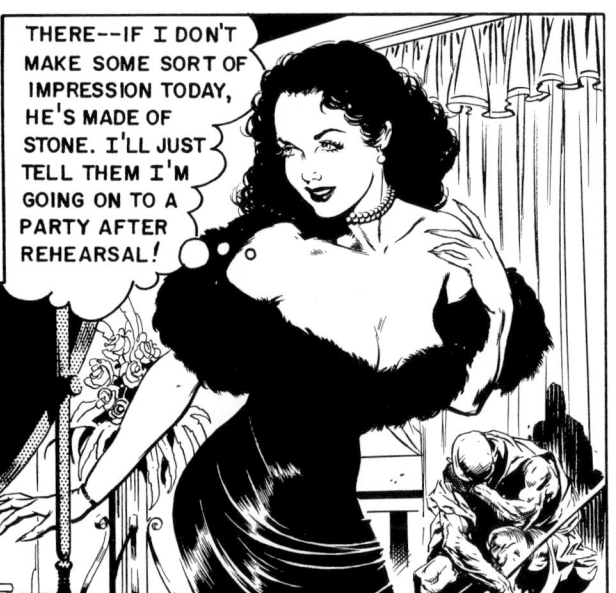

THERE--IF I DON'T MAKE SOME SORT OF IMPRESSION TODAY, HE'S MADE OF STONE. I'LL JUST TELL THEM I'M GOING ON TO A PARTY AFTER REHEARSAL!

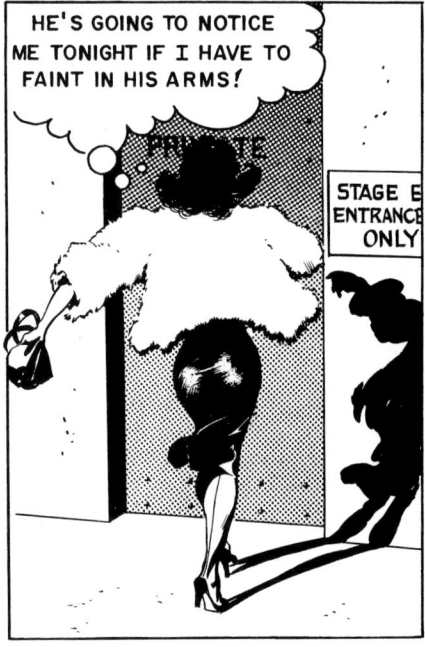

HE'S GOING TO NOTICE ME TONIGHT IF I HAVE TO FAINT IN HIS ARMS!

STAGE ENTRANCE ONLY

A chorus of whistles greeted me as I entered the theatre, but I only had eyes for Jeff who was talking to the director...

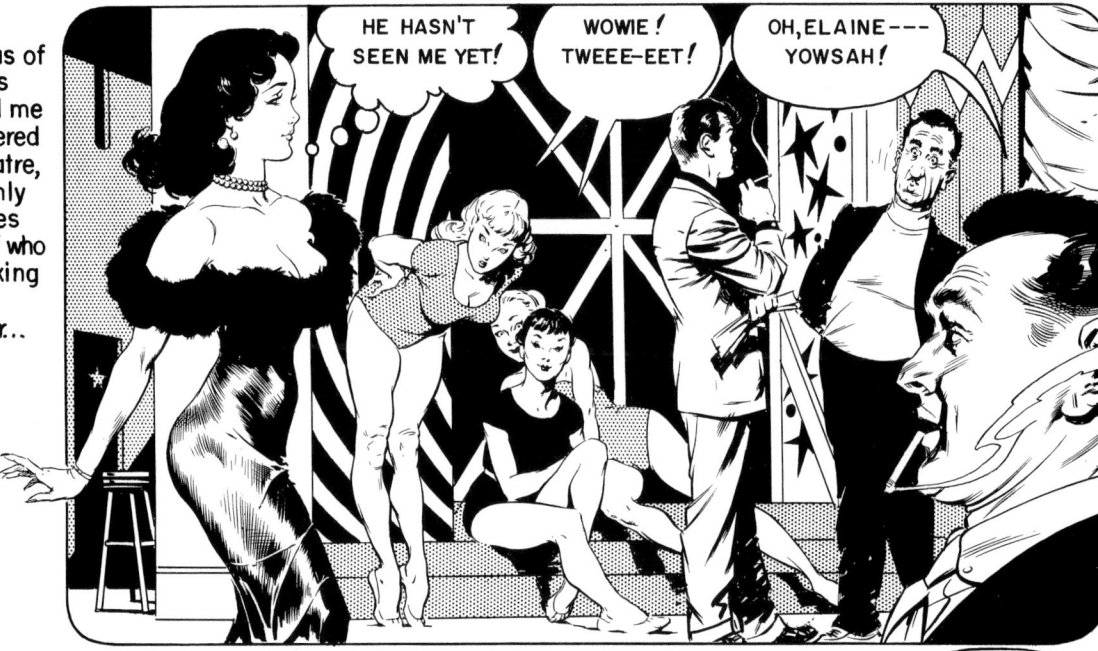

HE HASN'T SEEN ME YET!

WOWIE! TWEEE-EET!

OH, ELAINE--- YOWSAH!

The commotion caused Jeff to turn and when he saw me, his eyes widened and he paled...

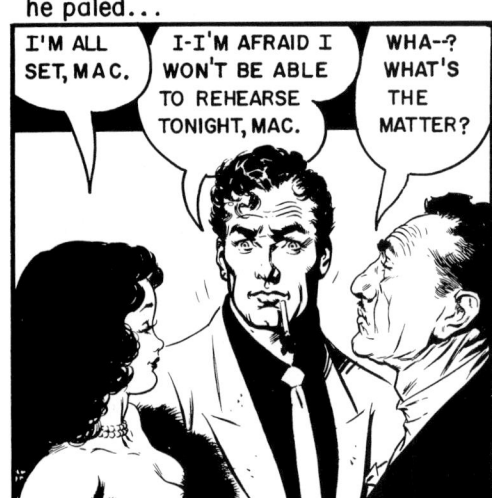

I'M ALL SET, MAC.

I-I'M AFRAID I WON'T BE ABLE TO REHEARSE TONIGHT, MAC.

WHA--? WHAT'S THE MATTER?

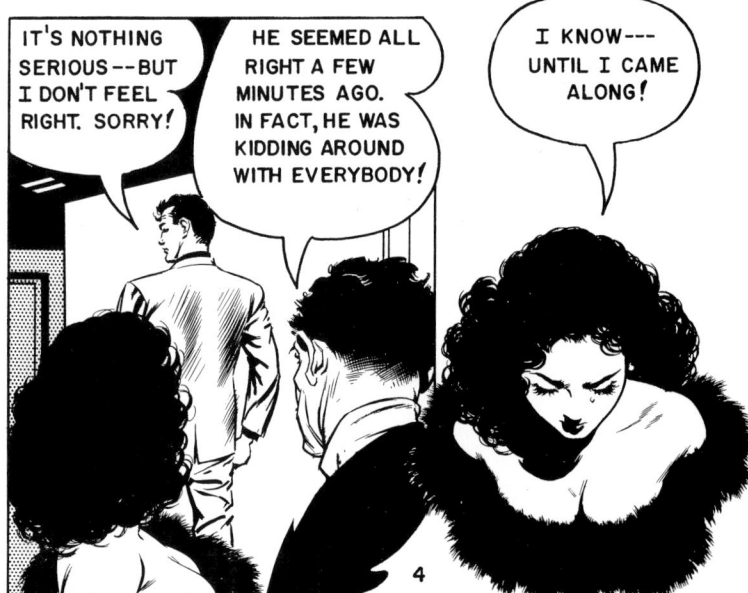

IT'S NOTHING SERIOUS--BUT I DON'T FEEL RIGHT. SORRY!

HE SEEMED ALL RIGHT A FEW MINUTES AGO. IN FACT, HE WAS KIDDING AROUND WITH EVERYBODY!

I KNOW--- UNTIL I CAME ALONG!

4

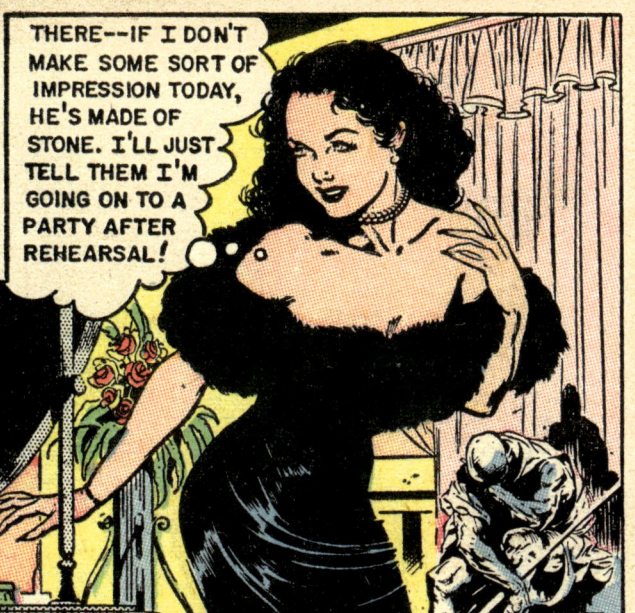

Just before rehearsal the following day, I raided my wardrobe for the best, and dressed with deliberate care...

THERE--IF I DON'T MAKE SOME SORT OF IMPRESSION TODAY, HE'S MADE OF STONE. I'LL JUST TELL THEM I'M GOING ON TO A PARTY AFTER REHEARSAL!

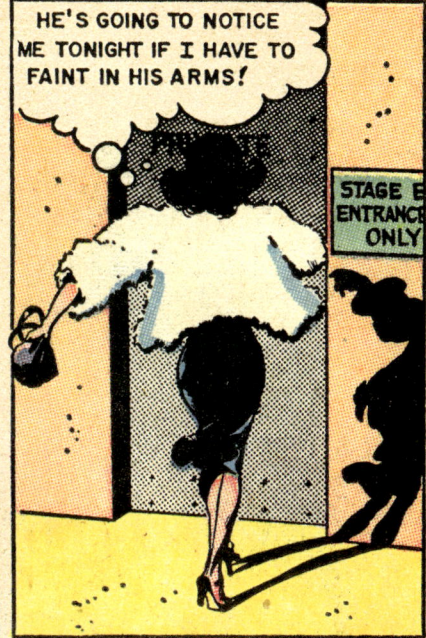

HE'S GOING TO NOTICE ME TONIGHT IF I HAVE TO FAINT IN HIS ARMS!

STAGE E ENTRANCE ONLY

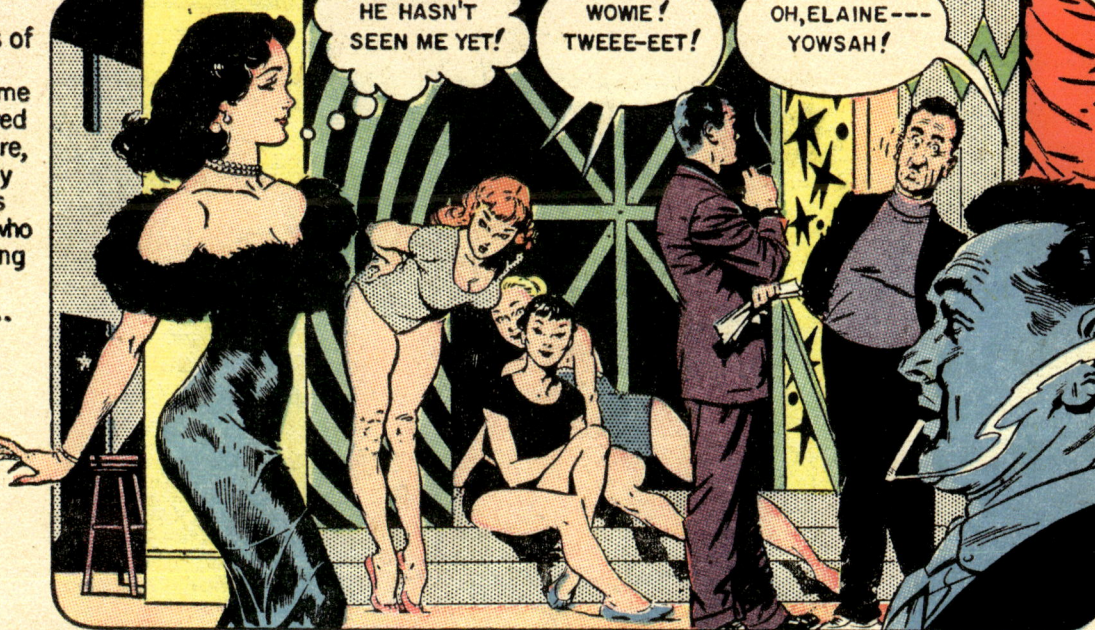

A chorus of whistles greeted me as I entered the theatre, but I only had eyes for Jeff who was talking to the director..

HE HASN'T SEEN ME YET!

WOWIE! TWEEE-EET!

OH, ELAINE--- YOWSAH!

The commotion caused Jeff to turn and when he saw me, his eyes widened and he paled...

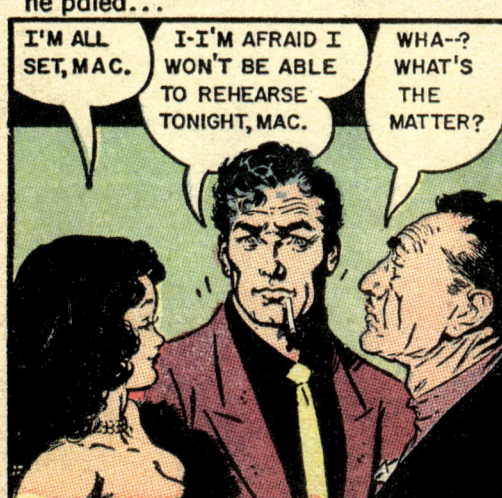

I'M ALL SET, MAC.

I-I'M AFRAID I WON'T BE ABLE TO REHEARSE TONIGHT, MAC.

WHA--? WHAT'S THE MATTER?

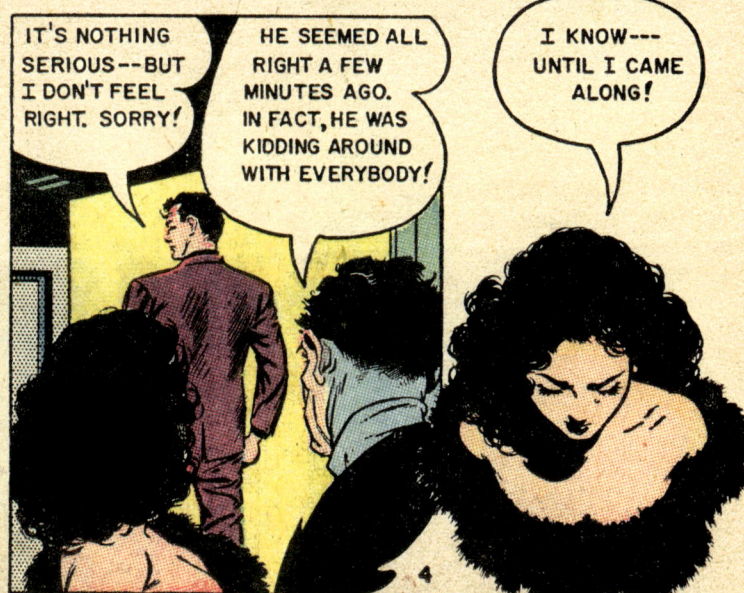

IT'S NOTHING SERIOUS--BUT I DON'T FEEL RIGHT. SORRY!

HE SEEMED ALL RIGHT A FEW MINUTES AGO. IN FACT, HE WAS KIDDING AROUND WITH EVERYBODY!

I KNOW--- UNTIL I CAME ALONG!

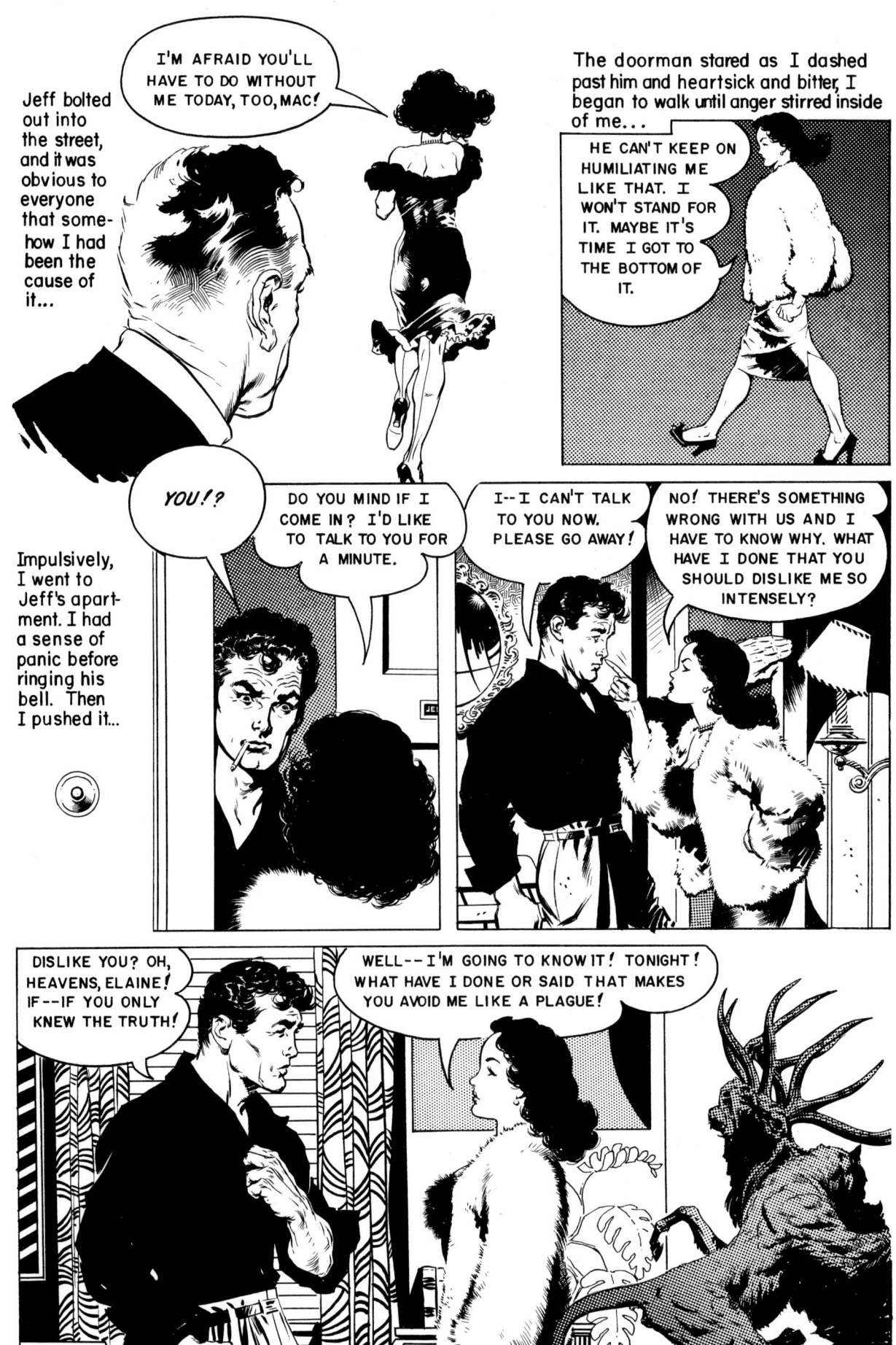

Jeff bolted out into the street, and it was obvious to everyone that somehow I had been the cause of it...

I'M AFRAID YOU'LL HAVE TO DO WITHOUT ME TODAY, TOO, MAC!

The doorman stared as I dashed past him and heartsick and bitter, I began to walk until anger stirred inside of me...

HE CAN'T KEEP ON HUMILIATING ME LIKE THAT. I WON'T STAND FOR IT. MAYBE IT'S TIME I GOT TO THE BOTTOM OF IT.

Impulsively, I went to Jeff's apartment. I had a sense of panic before ringing his bell. Then I pushed it...

YOU!?

DO YOU MIND IF I COME IN? I'D LIKE TO TALK TO YOU FOR A MINUTE.

I--I CAN'T TALK TO YOU NOW. PLEASE GO AWAY!

NO! THERE'S SOMETHING WRONG WITH US AND I HAVE TO KNOW WHY. WHAT HAVE I DONE THAT YOU SHOULD DISLIKE ME SO INTENSELY?

DISLIKE YOU? OH, HEAVENS, ELAINE! IF--IF YOU ONLY KNEW THE TRUTH!

WELL-- I'M GOING TO KNOW IT! TONIGHT! WHAT HAVE I DONE OR SAID THAT MAKES YOU AVOID ME LIKE A PLAGUE!

5

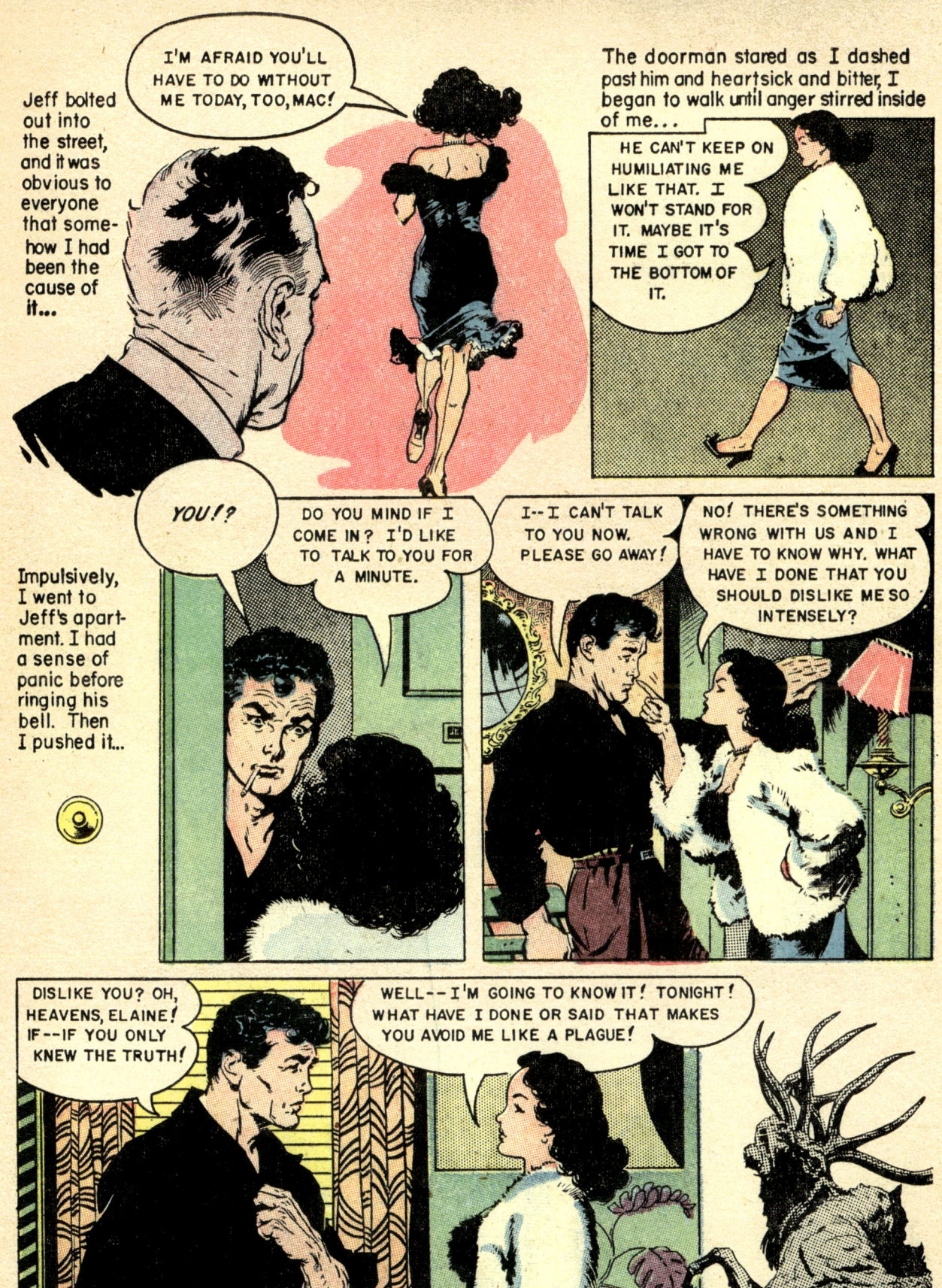

Jeff bolted out into the street, and it was obvious to everyone that somehow I had been the cause of it...

I'M AFRAID YOU'LL HAVE TO DO WITHOUT ME TODAY, TOO, MAC!

The doorman stared as I dashed past him and heartsick and bitter, I began to walk until anger stirred inside of me...

HE CAN'T KEEP ON HUMILIATING ME LIKE THAT. I WON'T STAND FOR IT. MAYBE IT'S TIME I GOT TO THE BOTTOM OF IT.

Impulsively, I went to Jeff's apartment. I had a sense of panic before ringing his bell. Then I pushed it...

YOU!?

DO YOU MIND IF I COME IN? I'D LIKE TO TALK TO YOU FOR A MINUTE.

I--I CAN'T TALK TO YOU NOW. PLEASE GO AWAY!

NO! THERE'S SOMETHING WRONG WITH US AND I HAVE TO KNOW WHY. WHAT HAVE I DONE THAT YOU SHOULD DISLIKE ME SO INTENSELY?

DISLIKE YOU? OH, HEAVENS, ELAINE! IF--IF YOU ONLY KNEW THE TRUTH!

WELL-- I'M GOING TO KNOW IT! TONIGHT! WHAT HAVE I DONE OR SAID THAT MAKES YOU AVOID ME LIKE A PLAGUE!

He nervously wet his lips and just stared at me wordlessly. Once more, the wild yearning to feel his lips on mine assailed me.
FOR THREE WEEKS YOU'VE HELD ME IN YOUR ARMS AT REHEARSALS, AND IT'S OBVIOUS TO EVERYONE HOW YOU DISLIKE ME. WHAT HAVE I DONE TO YOU?
YOU--- YOU JUST DON'T UNDERSTAND!
I--(SOB) SHOULD SAY I DON'T UNDERSTAND!
YOU LITTLE FOOL! YOU DRIVE ME HALF MAD EACH NIGHT WHEN YOU STEP INTO MY ARMS. I KNOW IT'S ONLY PART OF A SCRIPT SOMEBODY WITH A TYPEWRITER DREAMED UP. BUT WHEN I KISS YOU---!
JEFF--WH--WHAT ARE YOU TRYING TO SAY?
IT'S WHAT I'VE BEEN TRYING NOT TO SAY! I LOVE YOU! LOVE YOU!
I'M SO WILDLY IN LOVE WITH YOU THAT I CAN'T GO ON RECITING LOVE LINES AND TAKING YOU IN MY ARMS WHEN IT'S ALL A MOCKERY AND A SHAM!
I wanted to laugh. I wanted to cry. So I began to do both slightly hysterical with joy...
WHY--WHY DIDN'T YOU SAY SO, YOU BIG GOOP! (SOB) I--I'M SUFFERING FROM THE SAME DISEASE.
And then our lips hungrily sought each other and this time his lips ignited a flame of love inside of me that would never be extinguished...
OH, MY DARLING. WHAT RIGHT HAD I TO THINK THAT ANYONE SO LOVELY-- COULD LOVE ME?
I DON'T WANT YOU AT MY FEET, SWEETHEART. I JUST WANT TO BE IN YOUR ARMS--FOR ALWAYS!
The END

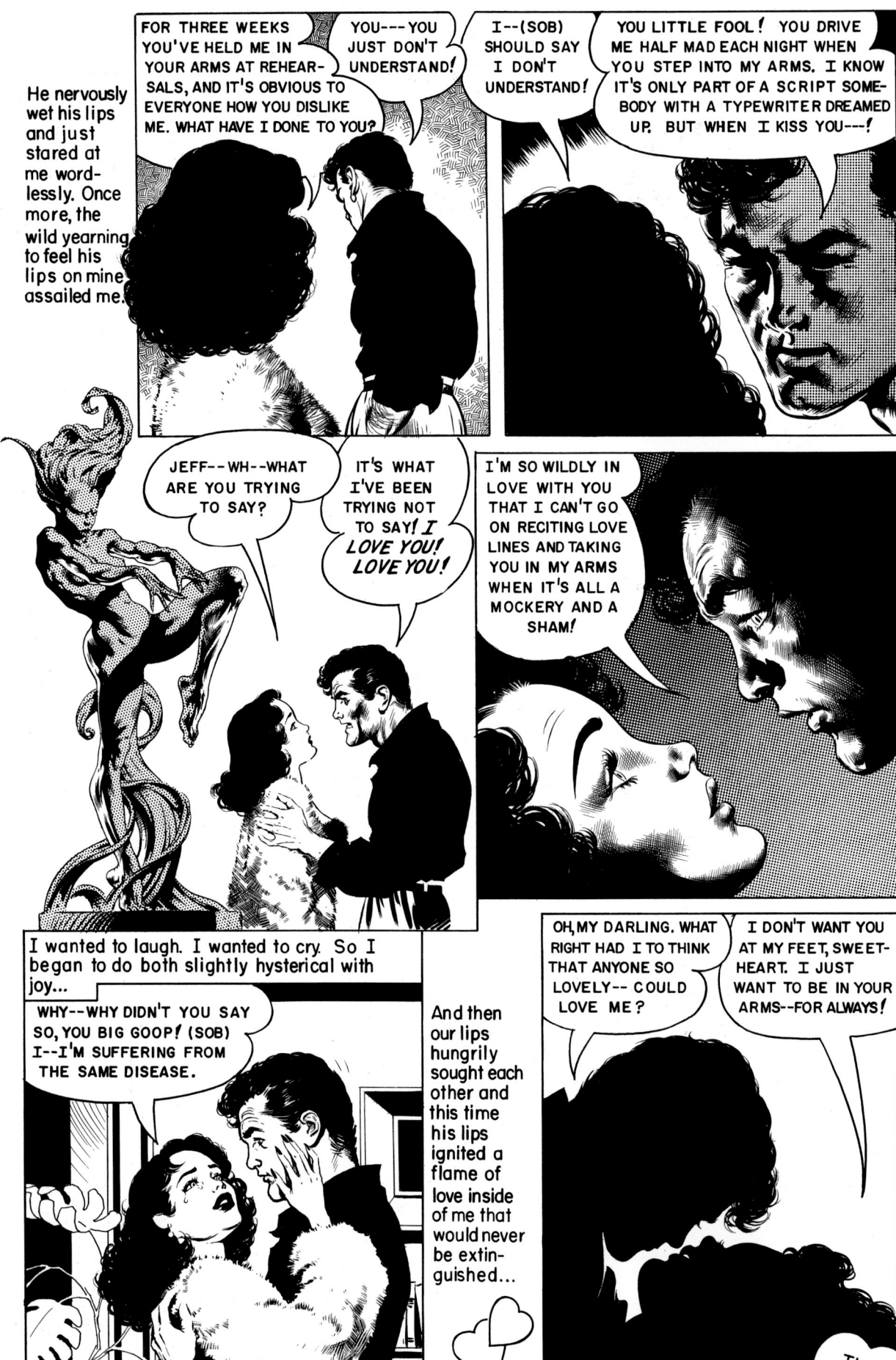

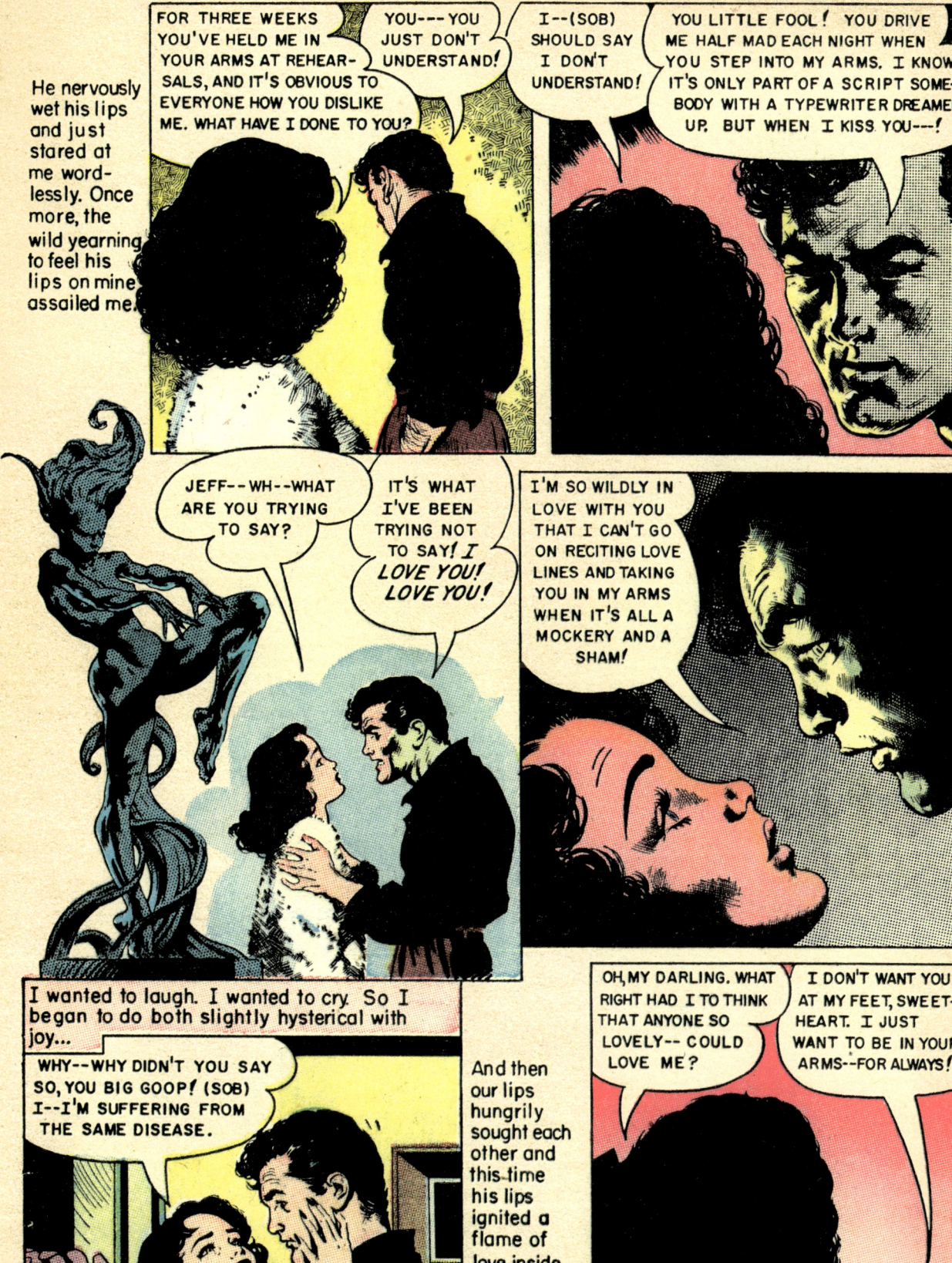

AGAINST THE BACKGROUND OF THE UNTAMED JUNGLE, MONA SAW THE THIN VENEER OF HER LOVE EXPOSED TO FORCES SHE COULDN'T CONTROL! HER MIND KEPT TELLING HER THAT SHE WAS PLEDGED TO DON BUT HER HEART KEPT YEARNING FOR THE STRANGER WHO TAUGHT HER THE MEANING OF...

UNTAMED Love

FRANK FRAZETTA 54

When Don first suggested I accompany him on a hunting safari in Africa, I was luke warm to the idea, but now that we had reached the dark continent, I felt a mounting excitement engulf me...

I KNEW YOU'D LOVE IT ONCE WE ARRIVED HERE. YOU'RE IN FOR THE ADVENTURE OF YOUR LIFE, DARLING.

I ALWAYS CONSIDERED MYSELF A HOT HOUSE FLOWER, DON. BUT THIS -- IT SEEMS SO MYSTERIOUS AND EXCITING...

YOU'RE JUST A BEAUTIFUL ANIMAL AT HEART, MY DARLING. THAT'S WHY I WANT YOU FOR MY VERY OWN.

IS THAT WHY YOU WANT TO MARRY ME, DON? BECAUSE I'M JUST ANOTHER ANIMAL YOU'VE CAPTURED?

Personal Love #32 (Famous Funnies, April 1955)

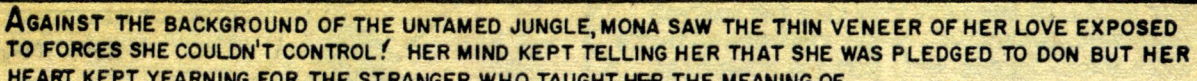

AGAINST THE BACKGROUND OF THE UNTAMED JUNGLE, MONA SAW THE THIN VENEER OF HER LOVE EXPOSED TO FORCES SHE COULDN'T CONTROL! HER MIND KEPT TELLING HER THAT SHE WAS PLEDGED TO DON BUT HER HEART KEPT YEARNING FOR THE STRANGER WHO TAUGHT HER THE MEANING OF. . .

UNTAMED Love

FRANK FRAZETTA 54

When Don first suggested my brother and I accompany him on a hunting safari in Africa, I was cool to the idea, but now that we had reached the dark continent, I felt a mounting excitement engulf me...

I KNEW YOU'D LOVE IT ONCE WE ARRIVED HERE. YOU'RE IN FOR THE ADVENTURE OF YOUR LIFE, DARLING.

I ALWAYS CONSIDERED MYSELF A HOT HOUSE FLOWER, DON. BUT THIS—IT SEEMS SO MYSTERIOUS AND EXCITING...

YOU'RE JUST A BEAUTIFUL THING AT HEART, MY DARLING. THAT'S WHY I WANT YOU FOR MY VERY OWN.

IS THAT WHY YOU WANT TO MARRY ME, DON? BECAUSE I'M JUST ANOTHER ANIMAL YOU'VE CAPTURED?

1

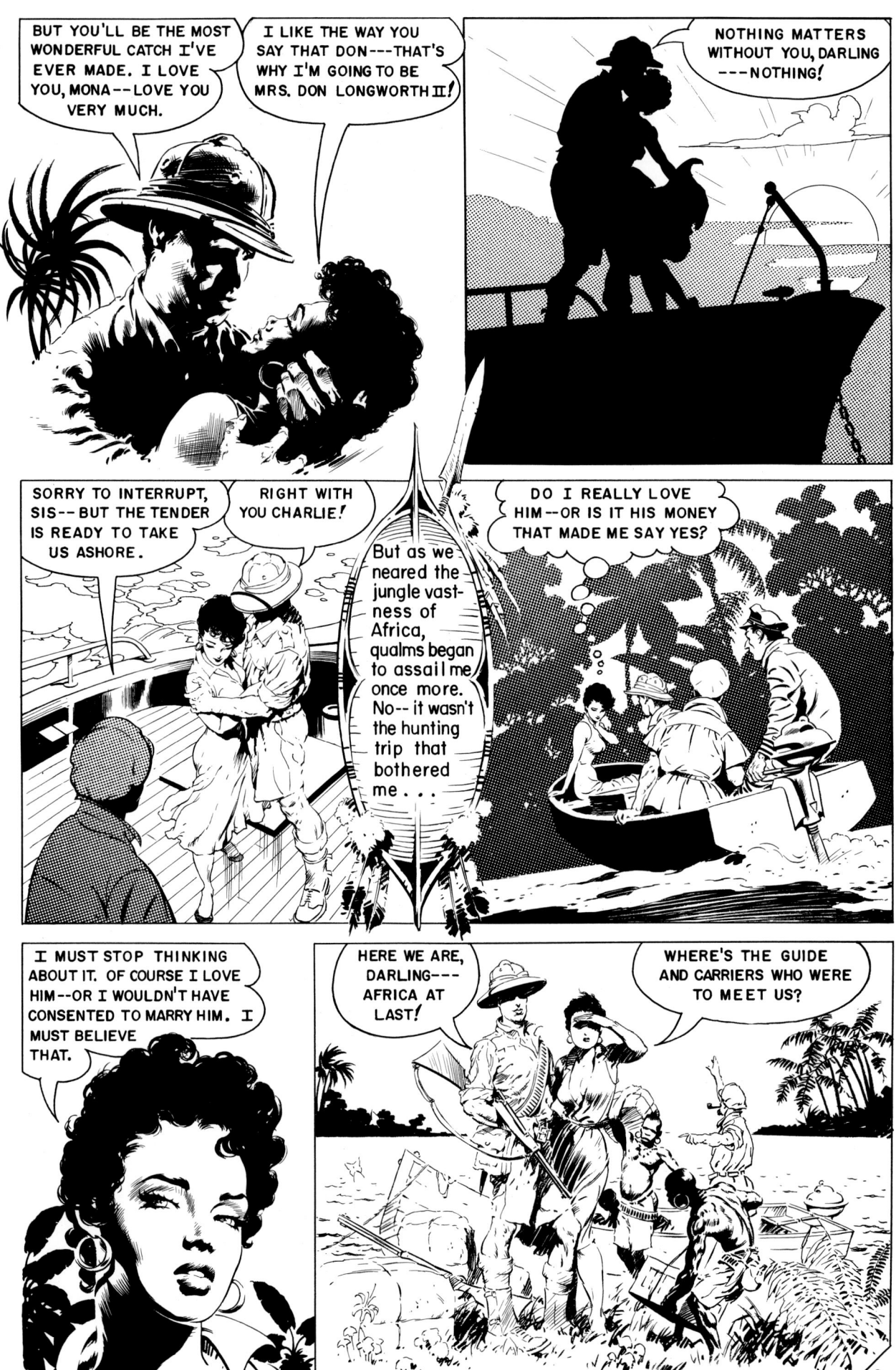

 Personal Love #32 (Famous Funnies, April 1955)

BUT YOU'LL BE THE MOST WONDERFUL CATCH I'VE EVER MADE. I LOVE YOU, MONA--LOVE YOU VERY MUCH.
I LIKE THE WAY YOU SAY THAT DON---THAT'S WHY I'M GOING TO BE MRS. DON LONGWORTH II!
NOTHING MATTERS WITHOUT YOU, DARLING ---NOTHING!
SORRY TO INTERRUPT, SIS--BUT THE TENDER IS READY TO TAKE US ASHORE.
RIGHT WITH YOU CHARLIE!
But as we neared the jungle vastness of Africa, qualms began to assail me once more. No-- it wasn't the hunting trip that bothered me . . .
DO I REALLY LOVE HIM--OR IS IT HIS MONEY THAT MADE ME SAY YES?
I MUST STOP THINKING ABOUT IT. OF COURSE I LOVE HIM--OR I WOULDN'T HAVE CONSENTED TO MARRY HIM. I MUST BELIEVE THAT.
HERE WE ARE, DARLING--- AFRICA AT LAST!
WHERE'S THE GUIDE AND CARRIERS WHO WERE TO MEET US?
2

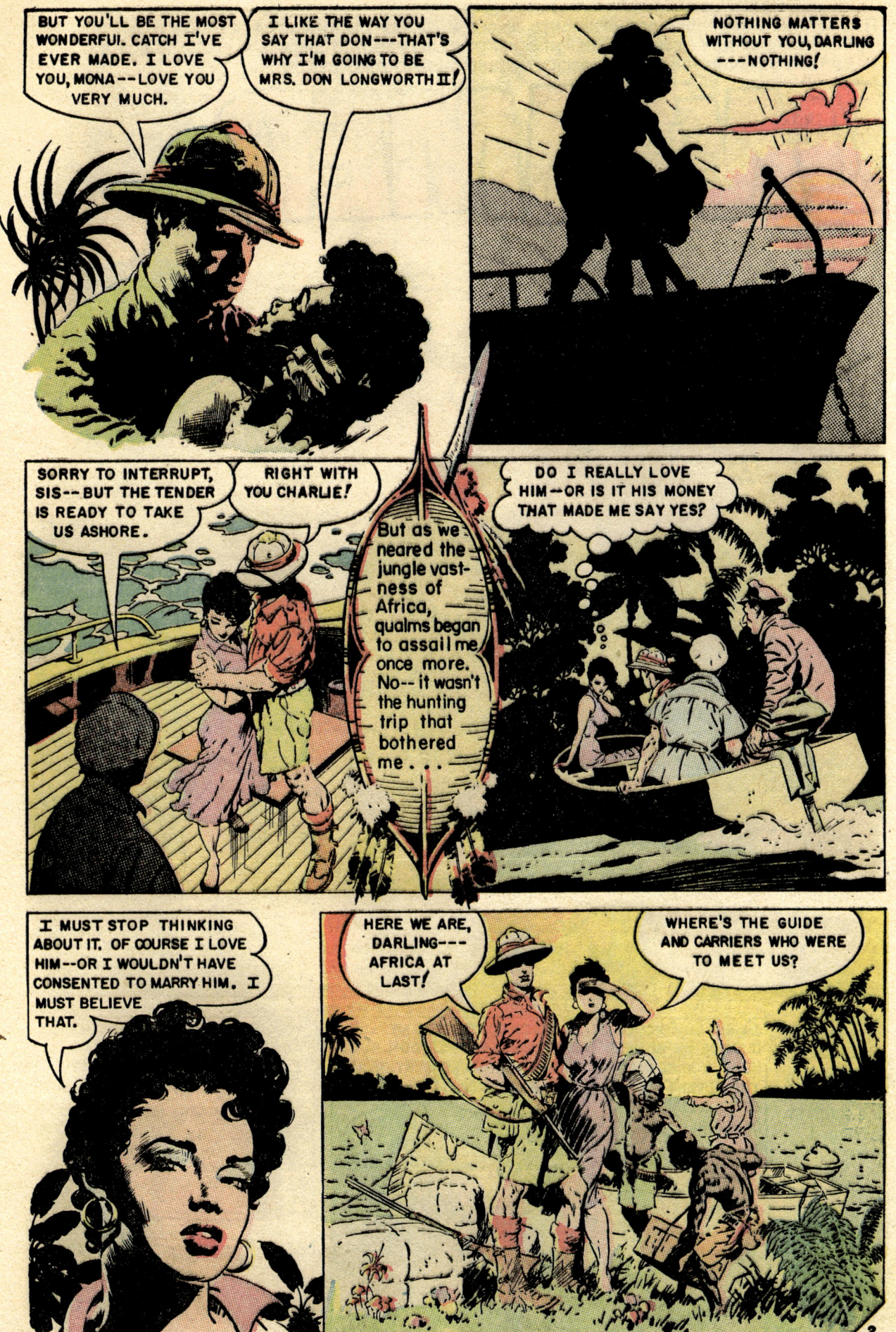

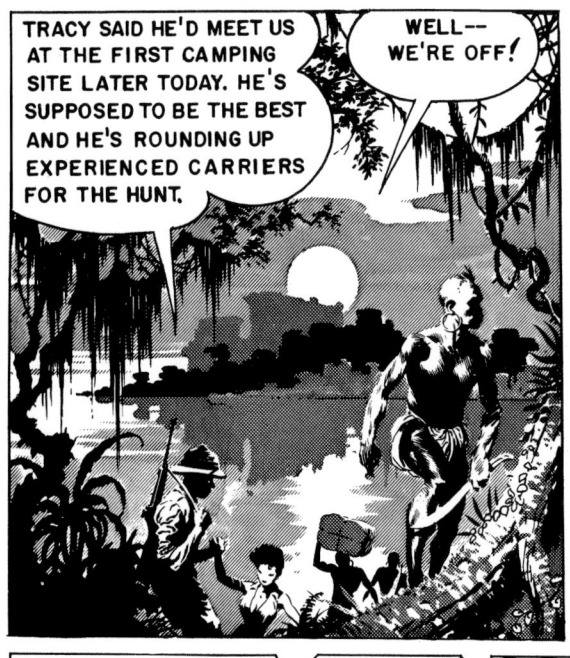

TRACY SAID HE'D MEET US AT THE FIRST CAMPING SITE LATER TODAY. HE'S SUPPOSED TO BE THE BEST AND HE'S ROUNDING UP EXPERIENCED CARRIERS FOR THE HUNT.

WELL-- WE'RE OFF!

It seemed that we walked endlessly that day and when we finally made camp that night, I felt exhausted...

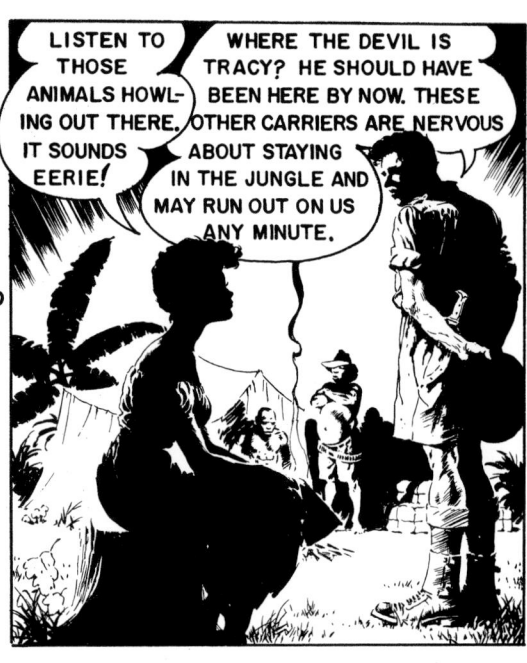

LISTEN TO THOSE ANIMALS HOWLING OUT THERE. IT SOUNDS EERIE!

WHERE THE DEVIL IS TRACY? HE SHOULD HAVE BEEN HERE BY NOW. THESE OTHER CARRIERS ARE NERVOUS ABOUT STAYING IN THE JUNGLE AND MAY RUN OUT ON US ANY MINUTE.

I NEVER SHOULD HAVE LISTENED TO HIM WHEN HE INSISTED WE MEET HERE. THEY TOLD ME HE WAS AN INDEPENDENT CUSS, BUT HE'S STILL WORKING FOR ME!

RELAX, DARLING. IF HE SAID HE'D BE HERE--HE WILL!

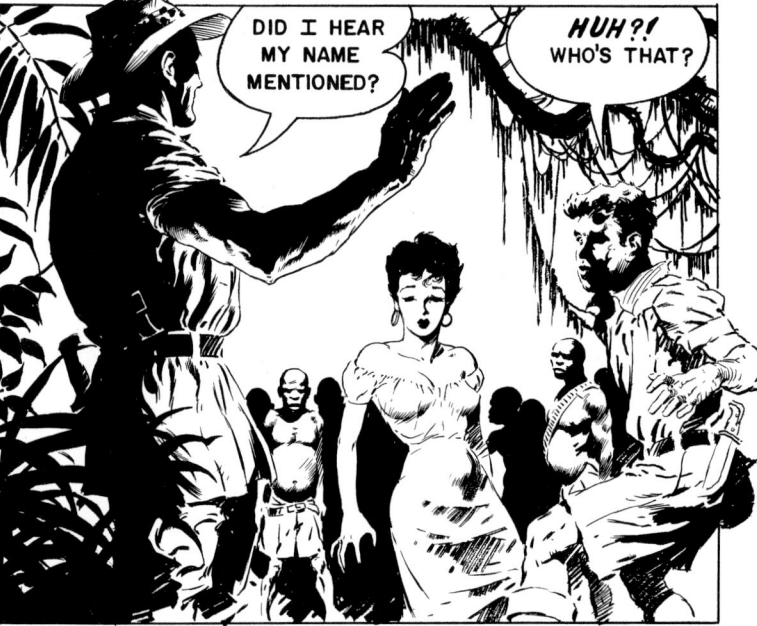

DID I HEAR MY NAME MENTIONED?

HUH?! WHO'S THAT?

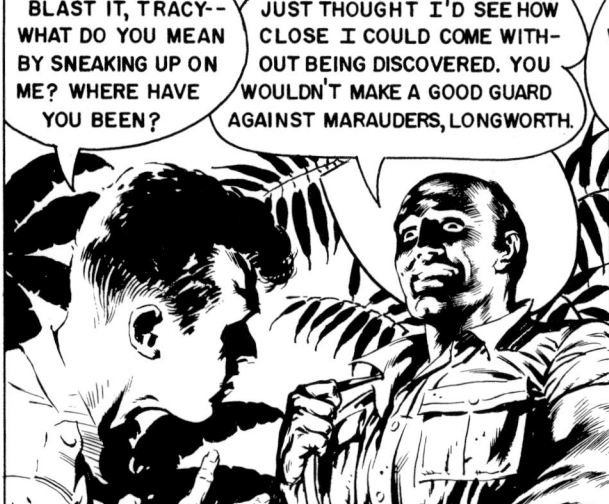

BLAST IT, TRACY-- WHAT DO YOU MEAN BY SNEAKING UP ON ME? WHERE HAVE YOU BEEN?

JUST THOUGHT I'D SEE HOW CLOSE I COULD COME WITHOUT BEING DISCOVERED. YOU WOULDN'T MAKE A GOOD GUARD AGAINST MARAUDERS, LONGWORTH.

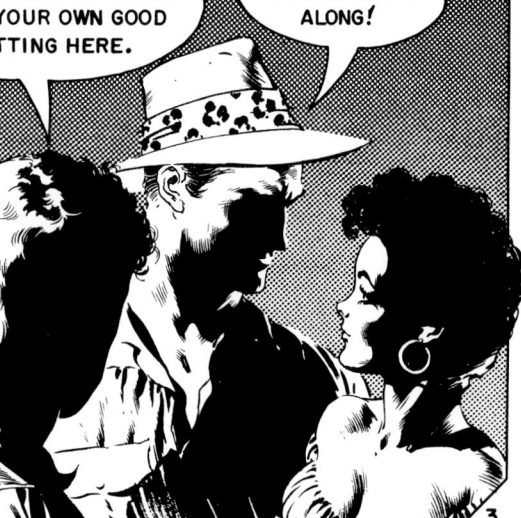

I'M PAYING YOU MORE THAN WELL FOR THIS TRIP, TRACY, AND YOU HAVE YOUR GALL TAKING YOUR OWN GOOD TIME GETTING HERE.

YOU DIDN'T SAY ANYTHING ABOUT WOMEN COMING ALONG!

3

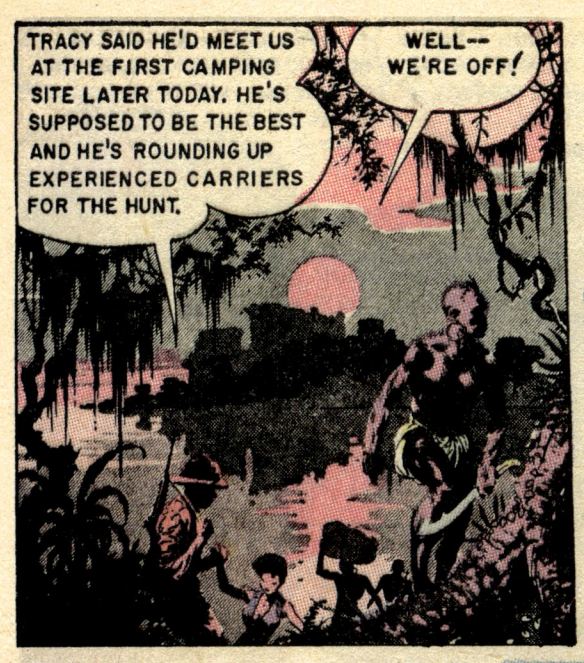

TRACY SAID HE'D MEET US AT THE FIRST CAMPING SITE LATER TODAY. HE'S SUPPOSED TO BE THE BEST AND HE'S ROUNDING UP EXPERIENCED CARRIERS FOR THE HUNT.

WELL-- WE'RE OFF!

It seemed that we walked endlessly that day and when we finally made camp that night, I felt exhausted...

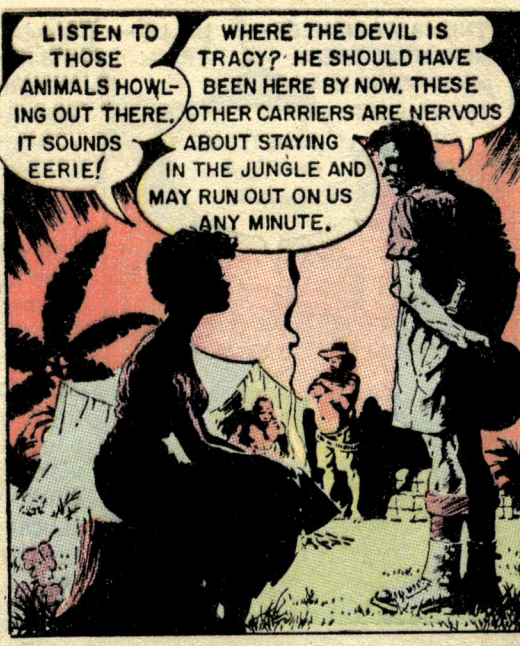

LISTEN TO THOSE ANIMALS HOWLING OUT THERE. IT SOUNDS EERIE!

WHERE THE DEVIL IS TRACY? HE SHOULD HAVE BEEN HERE BY NOW. THESE OTHER CARRIERS ARE NERVOUS ABOUT STAYING IN THE JUNGLE AND MAY RUN OUT ON US ANY MINUTE.

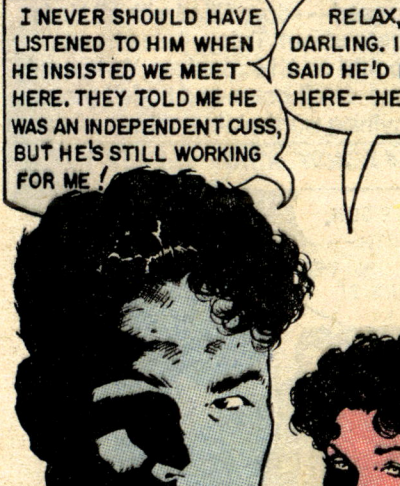

I NEVER SHOULD HAVE LISTENED TO HIM WHEN HE INSISTED WE MEET HERE. THEY TOLD ME HE WAS AN INDEPENDENT CUSS, BUT HE'S STILL WORKING FOR ME!

RELAX, DARLING. IF HE SAID HE'D BE HERE--HE WILL!

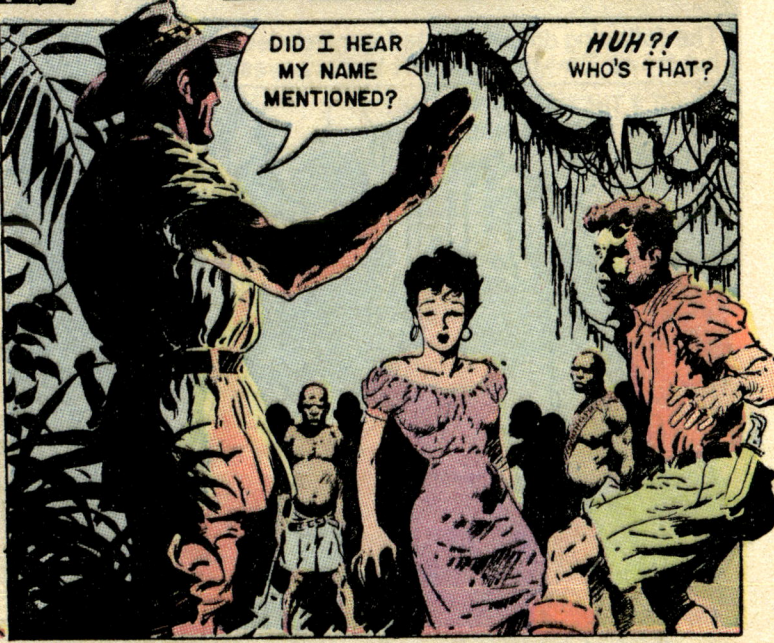

DID I HEAR MY NAME MENTIONED?

HUH?! WHO'S THAT?

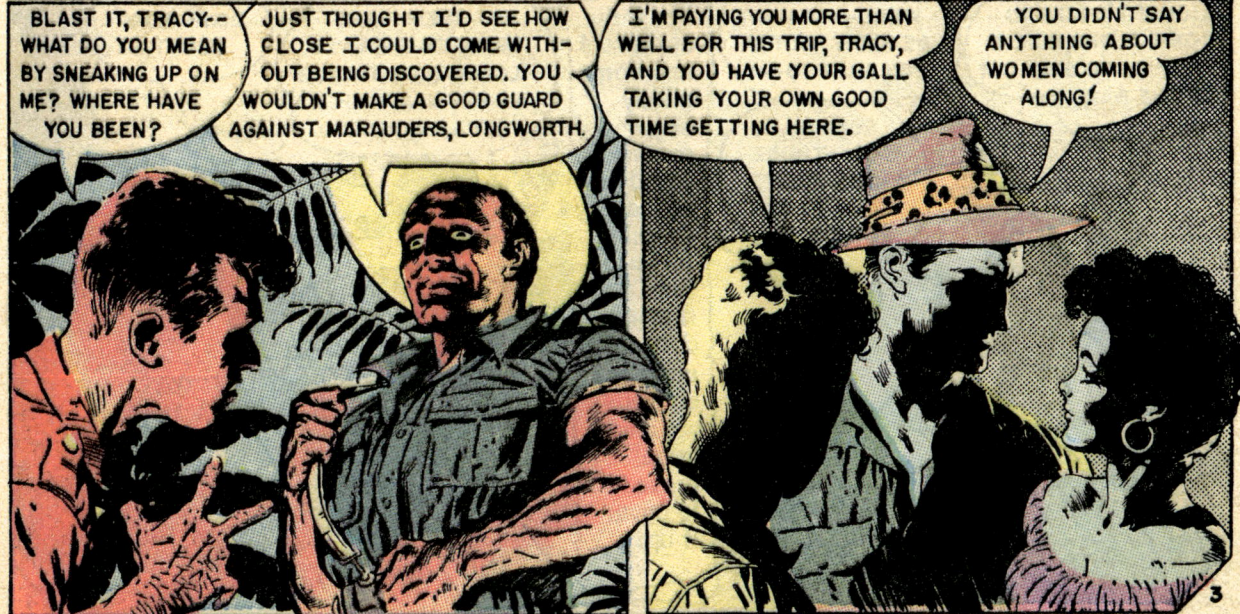

BLAST IT, TRACY-- WHAT DO YOU MEAN BY SNEAKING UP ON ME? WHERE HAVE YOU BEEN?

JUST THOUGHT I'D SEE HOW CLOSE I COULD COME WITHOUT BEING DISCOVERED. YOU WOULDN'T MAKE A GOOD GUARD AGAINST MARAUDERS, LONGWORTH.

I'M PAYING YOU MORE THAN WELL FOR THIS TRIP, TRACY, AND YOU HAVE YOUR GALL TAKING YOUR OWN GOOD TIME GETTING HERE.

YOU DIDN'T SAY ANYTHING ABOUT WOMEN COMING ALONG!

3

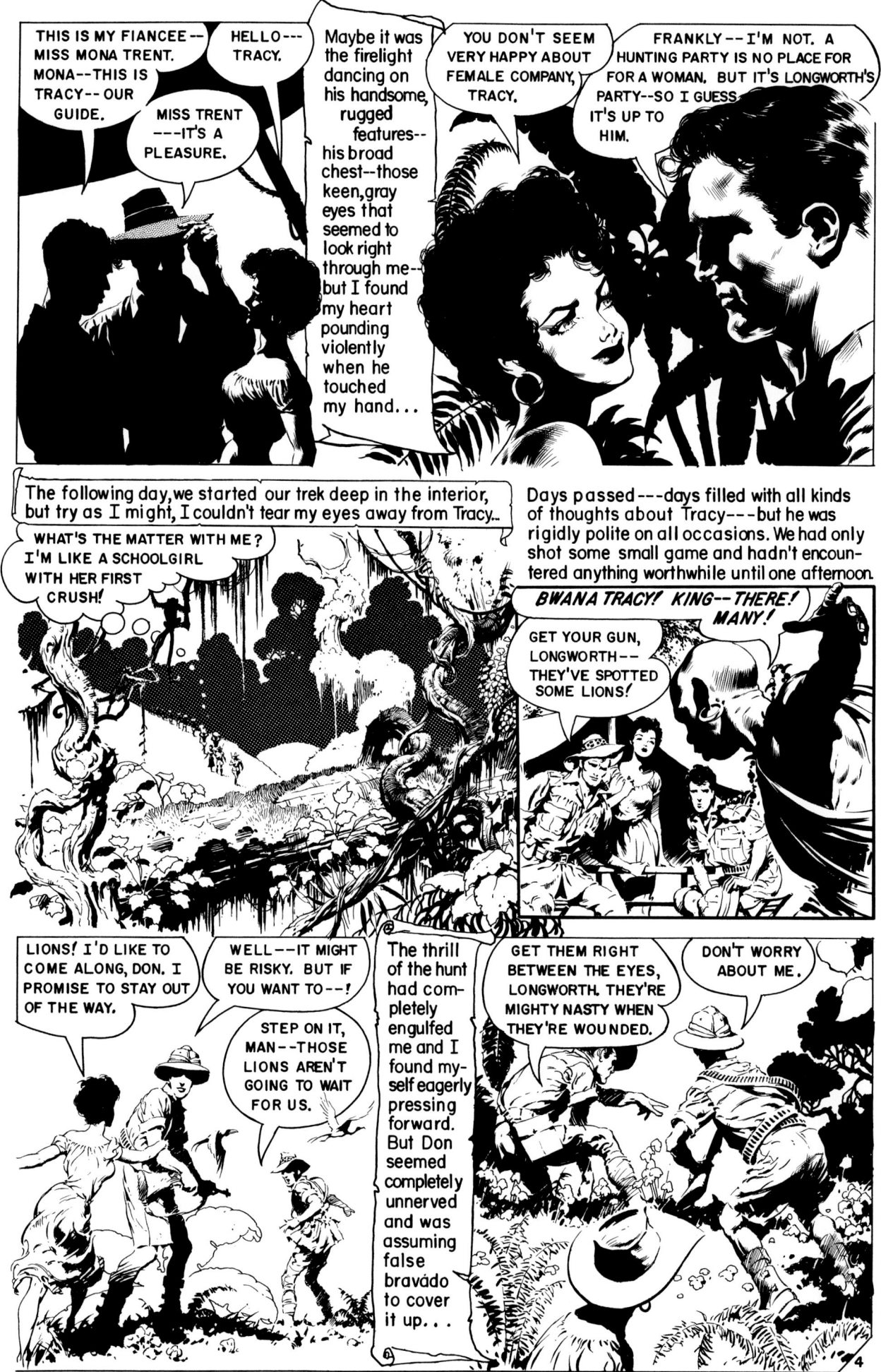

THIS IS MY FIANCEE-- MISS MONA TRENT. MONA--THIS IS TRACY-- OUR GUIDE.

HELLO--- TRACY.

MISS TRENT ---IT'S A PLEASURE.

Maybe it was the firelight dancing on his handsome, rugged features-- his broad chest--those keen, gray eyes that seemed to look right through me-- but I found my heart pounding violently when he touched my hand...

YOU DON'T SEEM VERY HAPPY ABOUT FEMALE COMPANY, TRACY.

FRANKLY--I'M NOT. A HUNTING PARTY IS NO PLACE FOR FOR A WOMAN. BUT IT'S LONGWORTH'S PARTY--SO I GUESS IT'S UP TO HIM.

The following day, we started our trek deep in the interior, but try as I might, I couldn't tear my eyes away from Tracy...

WHAT'S THE MATTER WITH ME? I'M LIKE A SCHOOLGIRL WITH HER FIRST CRUSH!

Days passed---days filled with all kinds of thoughts about Tracy---but he was rigidly polite on all occasions. We had only shot some small game and hadn't encountered anything worthwhile until one afternoon.

BWANA TRACY! KING--THERE! MANY!

GET YOUR GUN, LONGWORTH-- THEY'VE SPOTTED SOME LIONS!

LIONS! I'D LIKE TO COME ALONG, DON. I PROMISE TO STAY OUT OF THE WAY.

WELL--IT MIGHT BE RISKY. BUT IF YOU WANT TO--!

STEP ON IT, MAN--THOSE LIONS AREN'T GOING TO WAIT FOR US.

The thrill of the hunt had completely engulfed me and I found myself eagerly pressing forward. But Don seemed completely unnerved and was assuming false bravado to cover it up...

GET THEM RIGHT BETWEEN THE EYES, LONGWORTH. THEY'RE MIGHTY NASTY WHEN THEY'RE WOUNDED.

DON'T WORRY ABOUT ME.

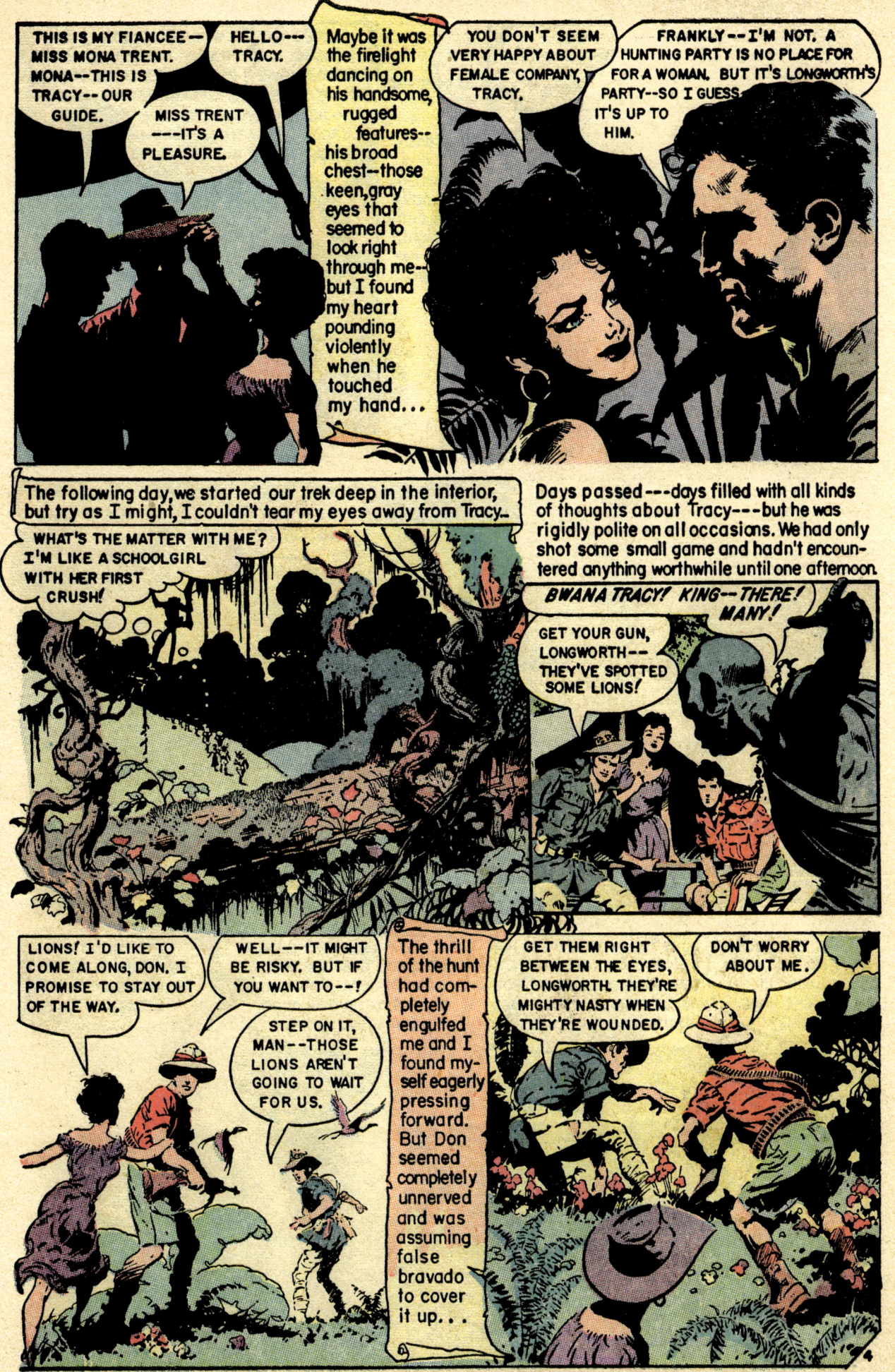

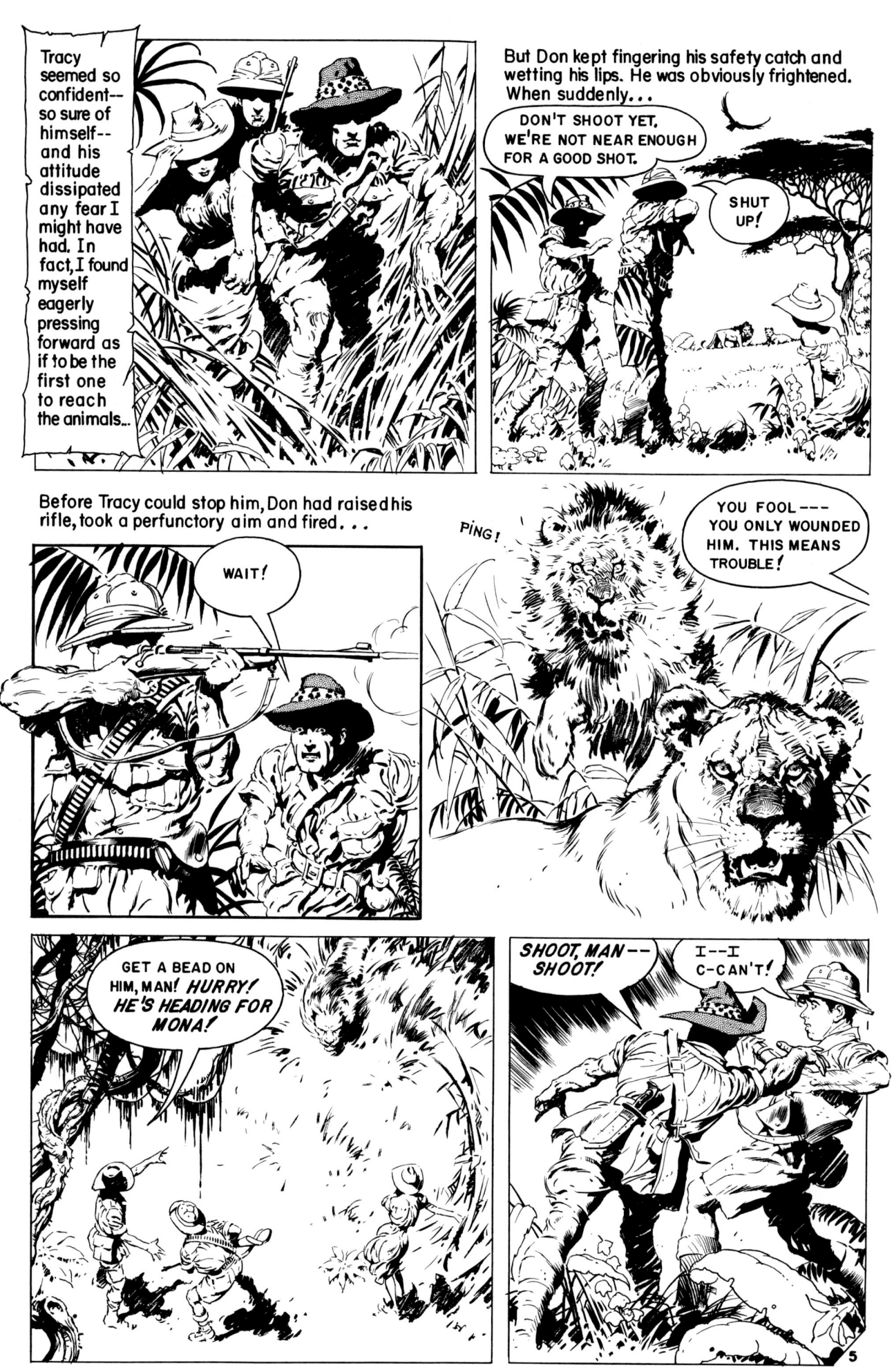

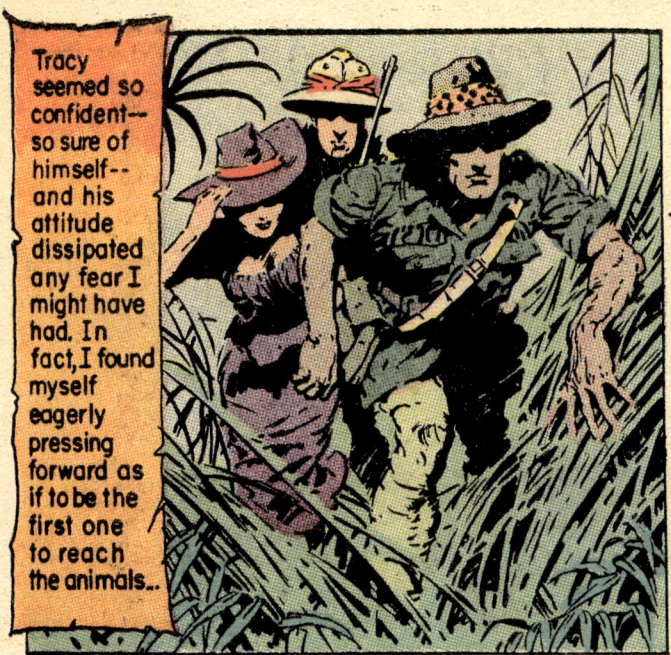

Tracy seemed so confident-- so sure of himself-- and his attitude dissipated any fear I might have had. In fact, I found myself eagerly pressing forward as if to be the first one to reach the animals..

But Don kept fingering his safety catch and wetting his lips. He was obviously frightened. When suddenly...

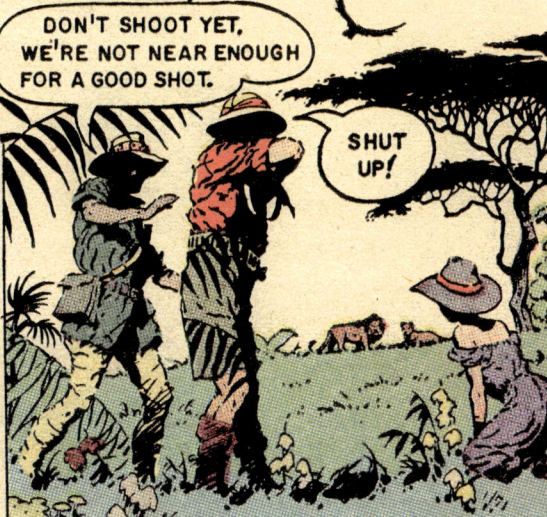

DON'T SHOOT YET, WE'RE NOT NEAR ENOUGH FOR A GOOD SHOT.

SHUT UP!

Before Tracy could stop him, Don had raised his rifle, took a perfunctory aim and fired...

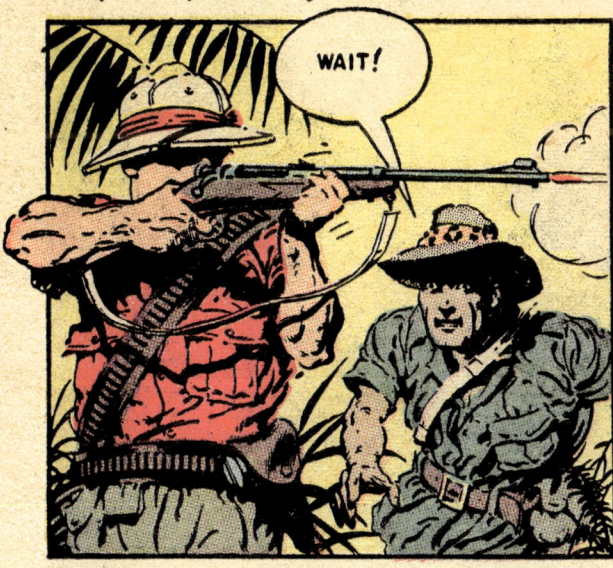

WAIT!

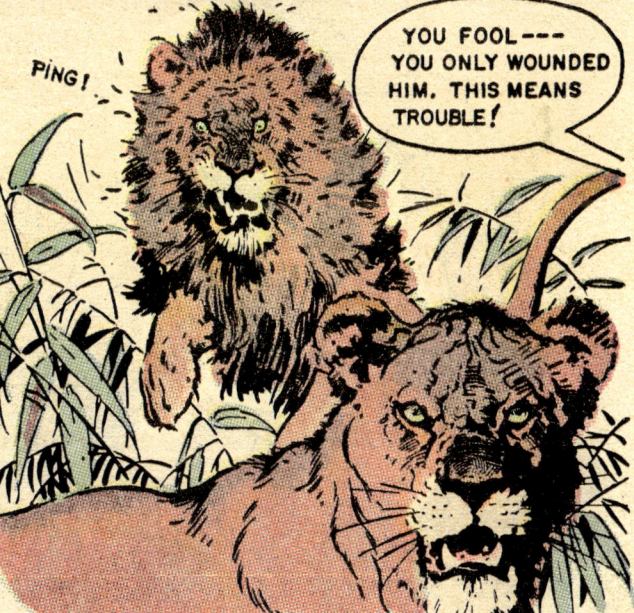

PING!

YOU FOOL--- YOU ONLY WOUNDED HIM. THIS MEANS TROUBLE!

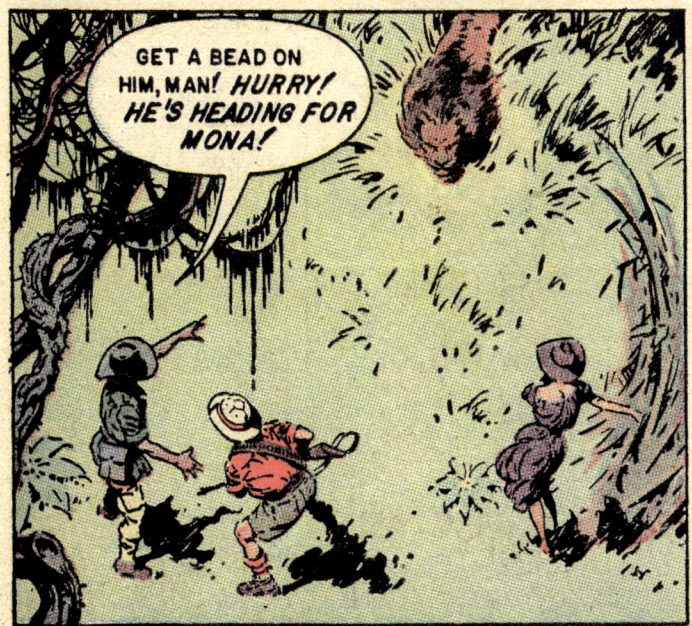

GET A BEAD ON HIM, MAN! HURRY! HE'S HEADING FOR MONA!

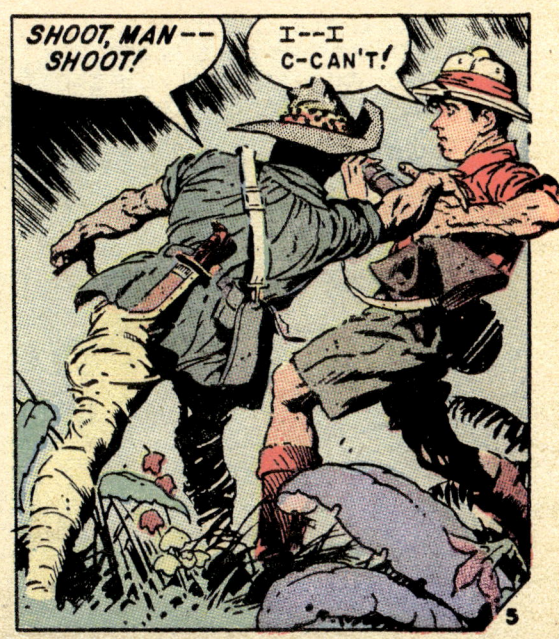

SHOOT, MAN-- SHOOT!

I--I C-CAN'T!

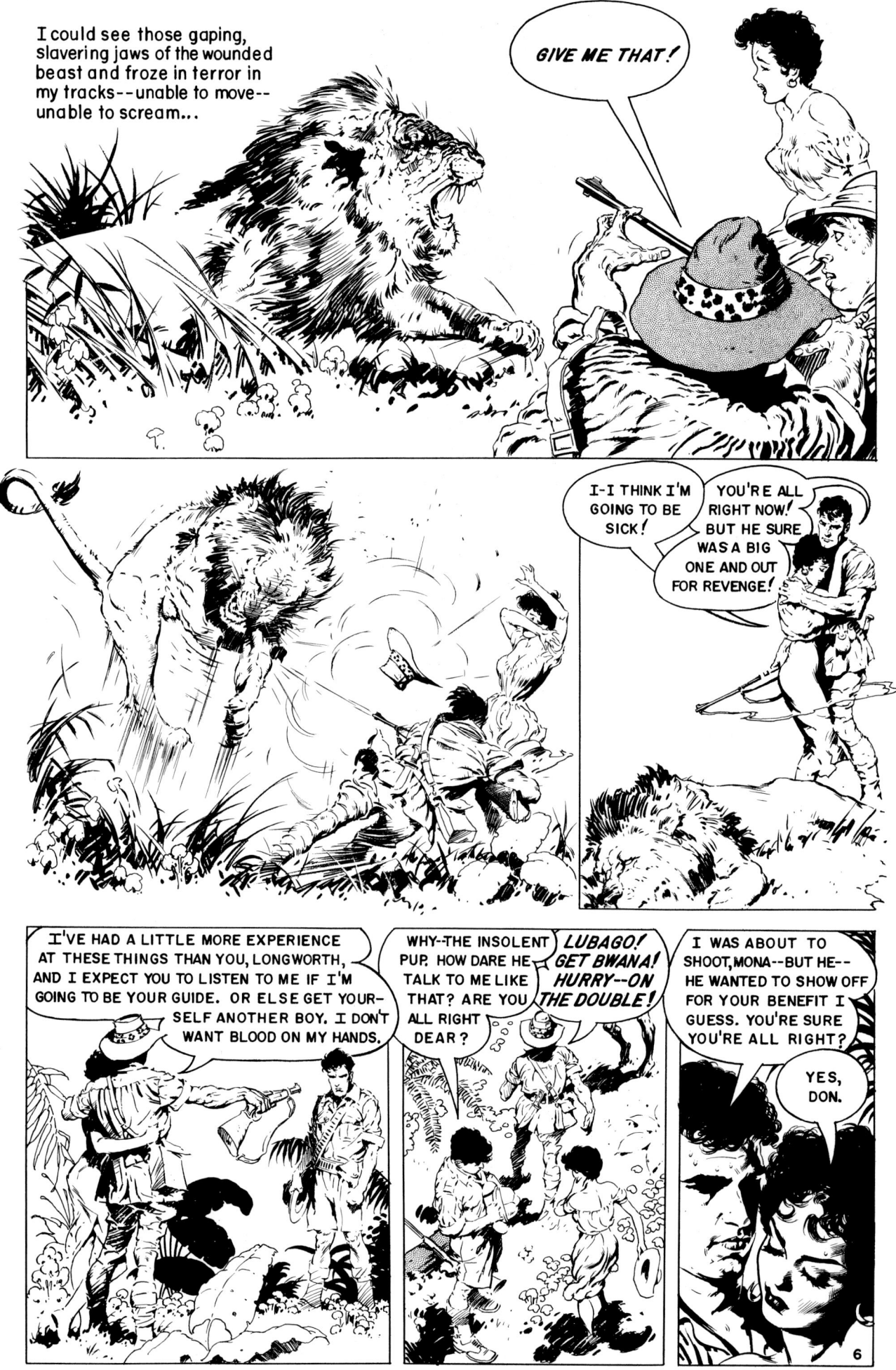

Personal Love #32 (Famous Funnies, April 1955)

I could see those gaping, slavering jaws of the wounded beast and froze in terror in my tracks--unable to move--unable to scream...
GIVE ME THAT!
I-I THINK I'M GOING TO BE SICK!
YOU'RE ALL RIGHT NOW! BUT HE SURE WAS A BIG ONE AND OUT FOR REVENGE!
I'VE HAD A LITTLE MORE EXPERIENCE AT THESE THINGS THAN YOU, LONGWORTH, AND I EXPECT YOU TO LISTEN TO ME IF I'M GOING TO BE YOUR GUIDE. OR ELSE GET YOURSELF ANOTHER BOY. I DON'T WANT BLOOD ON MY HANDS.
WHY--THE INSOLENT PUP. HOW DARE HE TALK TO ME LIKE THAT? ARE YOU ALL RIGHT DEAR?
LUBAGO! GET BWANA! HURRY--ON THE DOUBLE!
I WAS ABOUT TO SHOOT, MONA--BUT HE--HE WANTED TO SHOW OFF FOR YOUR BENEFIT I GUESS. YOU'RE SURE YOU'RE ALL RIGHT?
YES, DON.

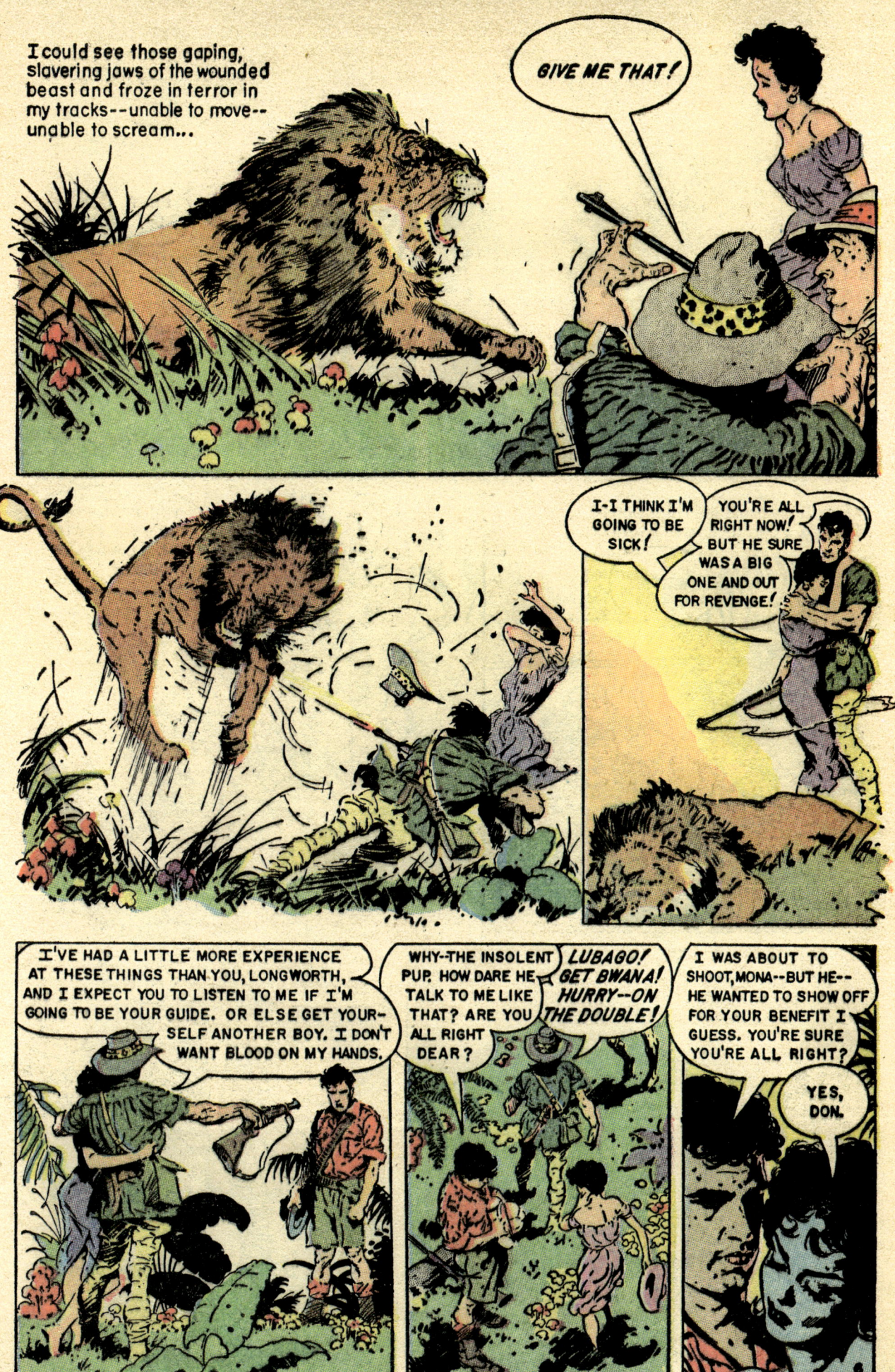

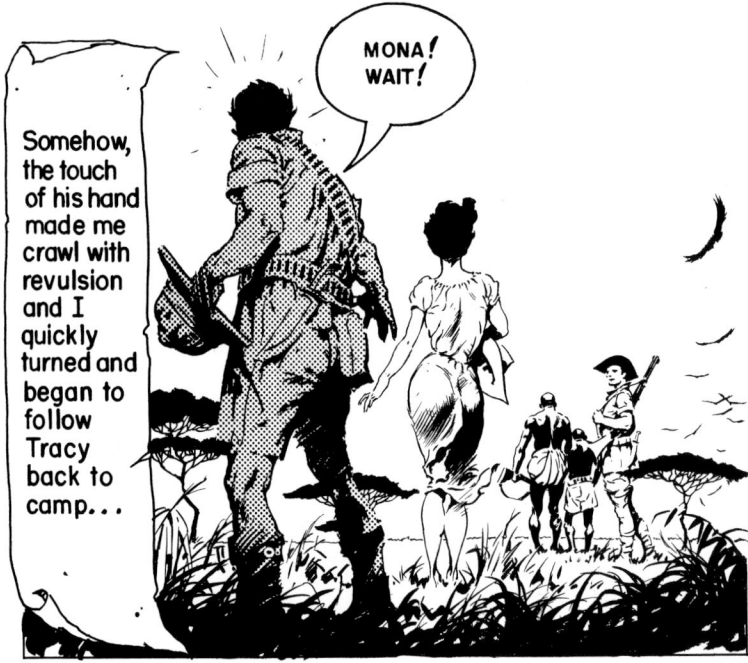

Somehow, the touch of his hand made me crawl with revulsion and I quickly turned and began to follow Tracy back to camp...

MONA! WAIT!

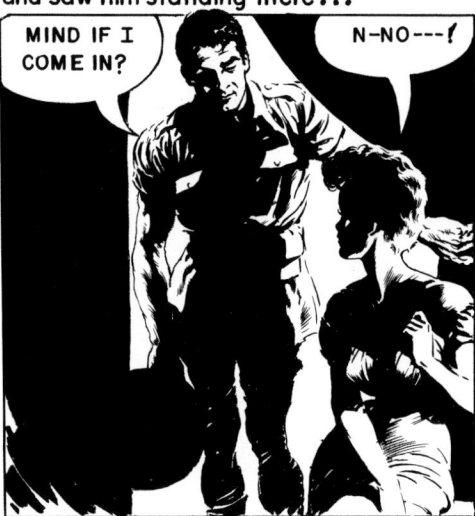

That night, as I sat alone with my confused, jumbled thoughts--thoughts that kept revolving around Tracy, I looked up and saw him standing there...

MIND IF I COME IN?

N-NO---!

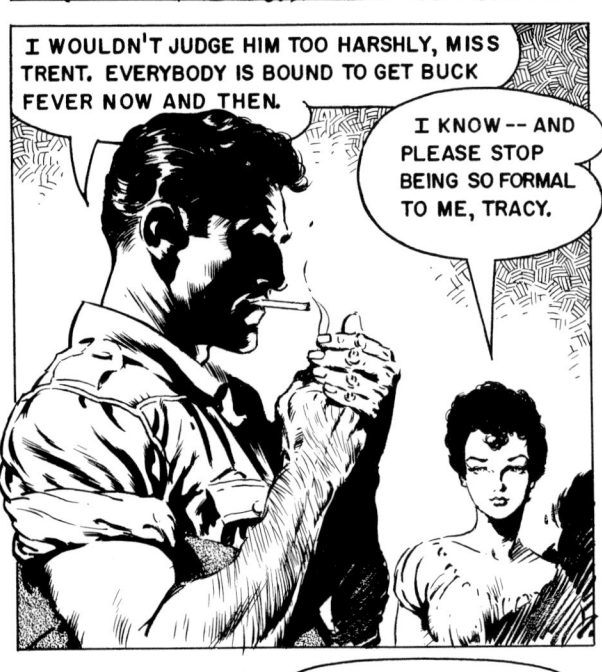

I WOULDN'T JUDGE HIM TOO HARSHLY, MISS TRENT. EVERYBODY IS BOUND TO GET BUCK FEVER NOW AND THEN.

I KNOW-- AND PLEASE STOP BEING SO FORMAL TO ME, TRACY.

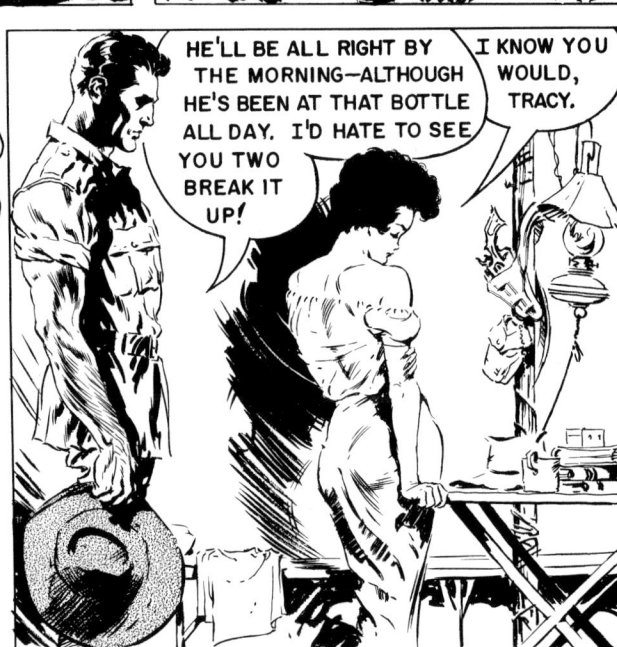

HE'LL BE ALL RIGHT BY THE MORNING--ALTHOUGH HE'S BEEN AT THAT BOTTLE ALL DAY. I'D HATE TO SEE YOU TWO BREAK IT UP!

I KNOW YOU WOULD, TRACY.

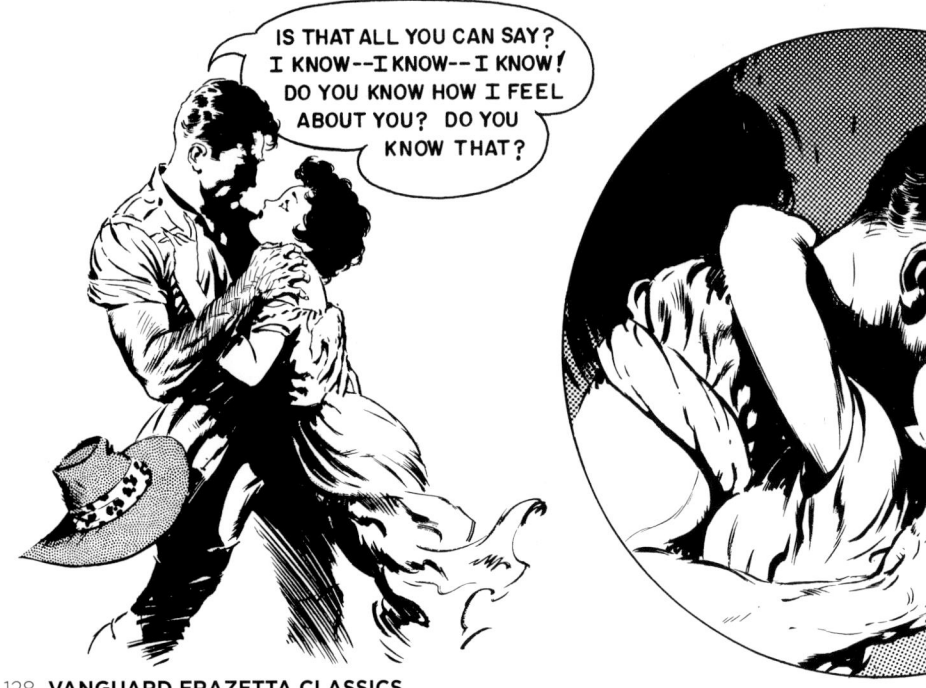

IS THAT ALL YOU CAN SAY? I KNOW--I KNOW--I KNOW! DO YOU KNOW HOW I FEEL ABOUT YOU? DO YOU KNOW THAT?

OH, TRACY-- I TRIED TO FIGHT IT!

7

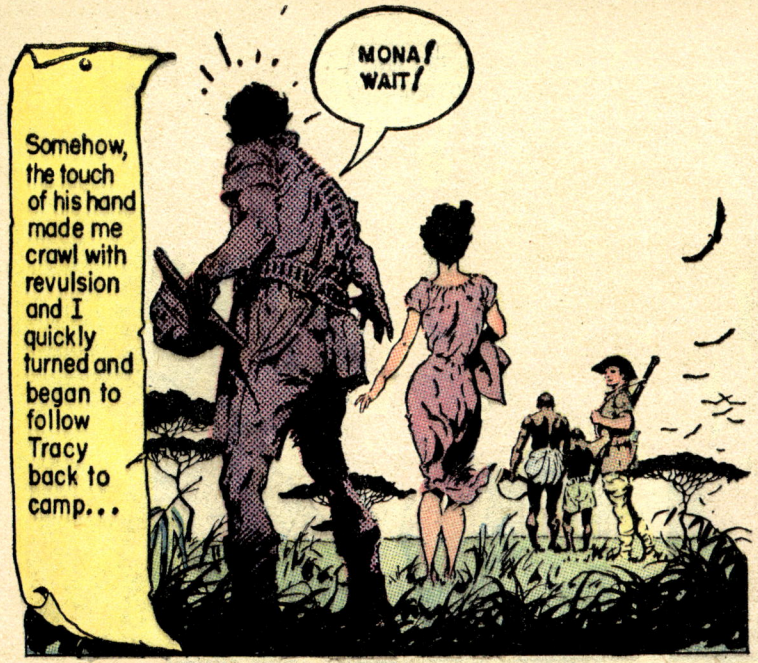

MONA! WAIT!

Somehow, the touch of his hand made me crawl with revulsion and I quickly turned and began to follow Tracy back to camp...

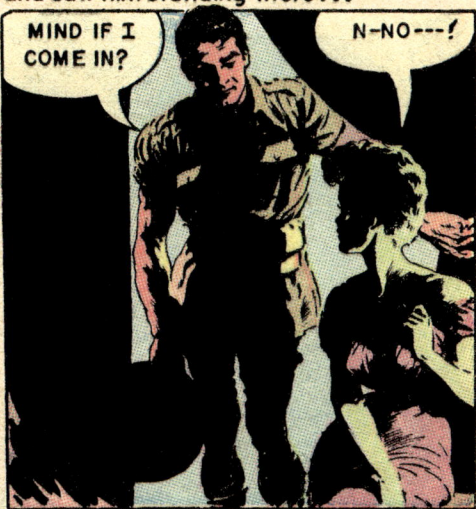

That night, as I sat alone with my confused, jumbled thoughts--thoughts that kept revolving around Tracy, I looked up and saw him standing there...

MIND IF I COME IN?

N-NO---!

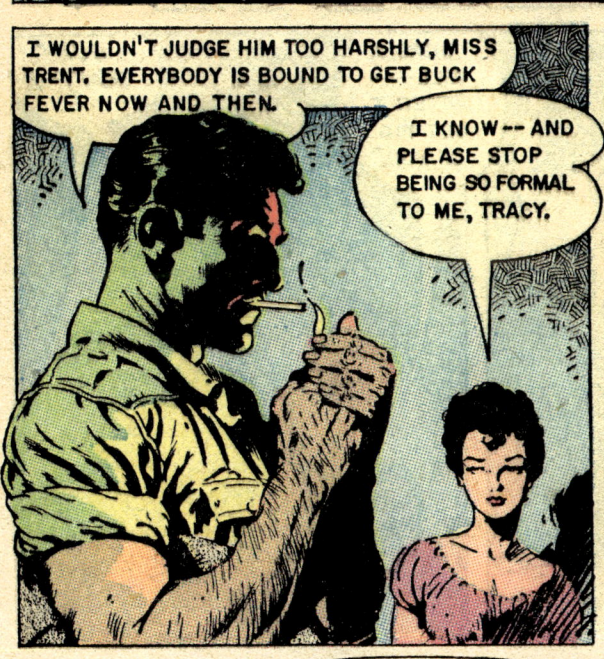

I WOULDN'T JUDGE HIM TOO HARSHLY, MISS TRENT. EVERYBODY IS BOUND TO GET BUCK FEVER NOW AND THEN.

I KNOW-- AND PLEASE STOP BEING SO FORMAL TO ME, TRACY.

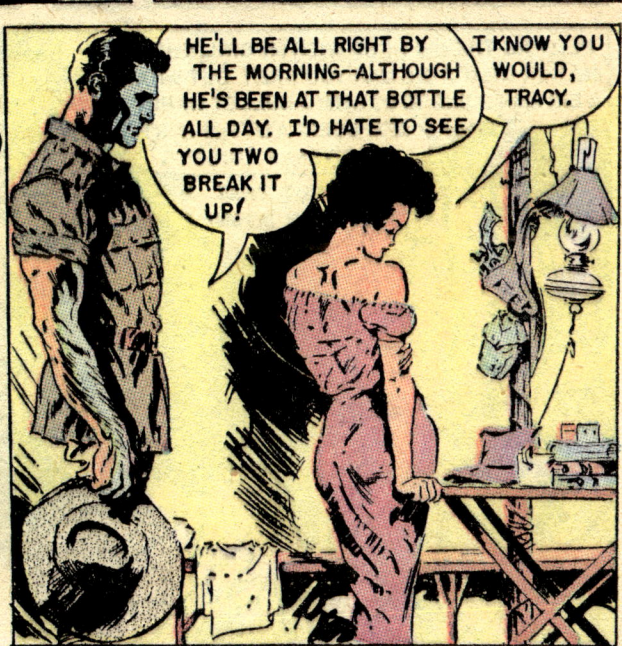

HE'LL BE ALL RIGHT BY THE MORNING--ALTHOUGH HE'S BEEN AT THAT BOTTLE ALL DAY. I'D HATE TO SEE YOU TWO BREAK IT UP!

I KNOW YOU WOULD, TRACY.

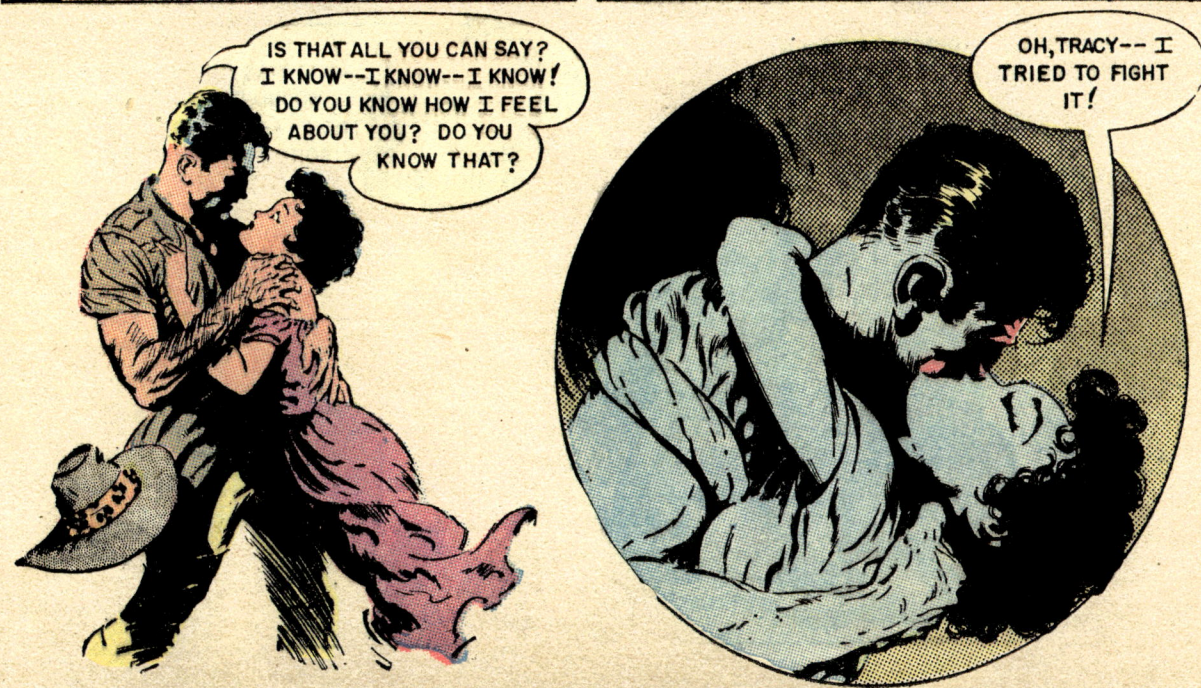

IS THAT ALL YOU CAN SAY? I KNOW--I KNOW--I KNOW! DO YOU KNOW HOW I FEEL ABOUT YOU? DO YOU KNOW THAT?

OH, TRACY-- I TRIED TO FIGHT IT!

WHEN I SAW THAT LION COMING AT YOU, I KNEW THEN THAT NOTHING ELSE WOULD EVER MATTER IF ANYTHING HAPPENED TO YOU.
I DO LOVE YOU, TRACY-- WITH ALL MY HEART!
A VERY PRETTY AND TOUCHING PICTURE INDEED!
DON!
PLAYING THE BIG HERO WITH MY GIRL, EH? SHOWING HER WHAT A BIG MAN YOU ARE! BUT WHAT'S A BIG MAN GOING TO DO WITH A BULLET IN HIM?
I'M DOING A LITTLE HUNTING MYSELF TONIGHT.
PUT THAT GUN DOWN!
SURE I WILL--- AFTER I GET RID OF YOU!
DON! DON'T--!
There was a loud explosion and a searing burn in my arm and then complete blackness...
Slowly, slowly--I came out of the bottomless pit to find Tracy kneeling next to me with a look in his eyes every woman recognizes...
IT WAS JUST A SUPERFICIAL WOUND, DARLING! HE'S GONE NOW--AND I GUESS PRETTY SORRY FOR WHAT HE DID. BUT WHAT ARE YOU GOING TO DO NOW?
STAY WITH YOU, MY SWEET--- FOREVER AND EVER.
THE END
8

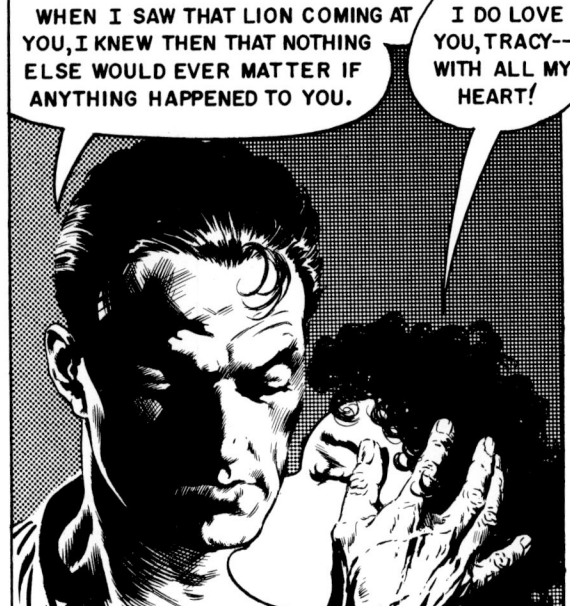

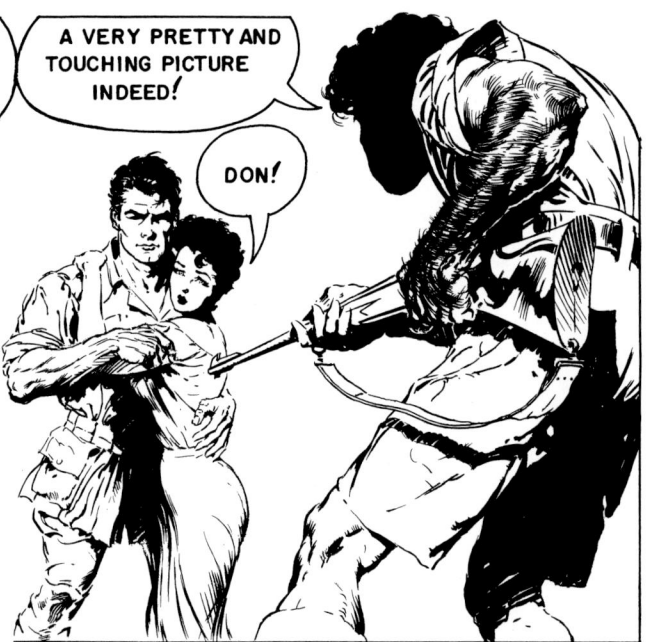

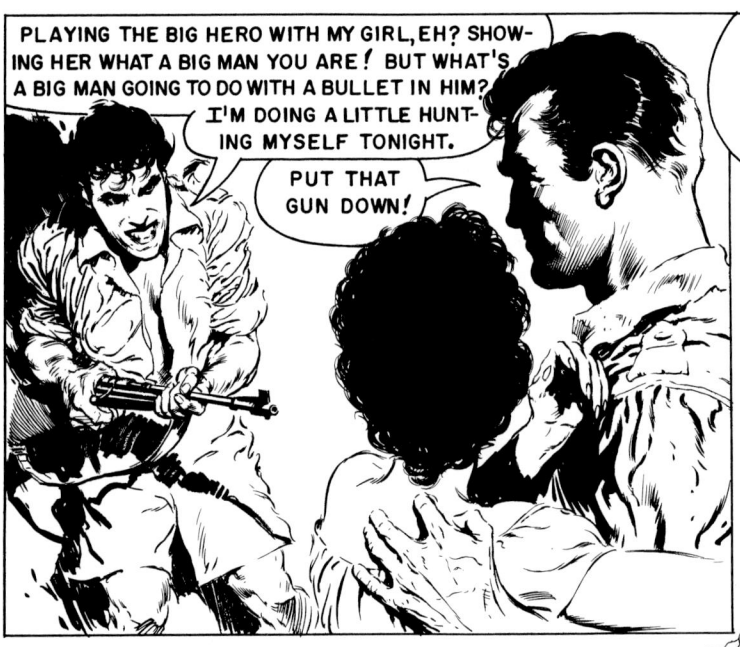

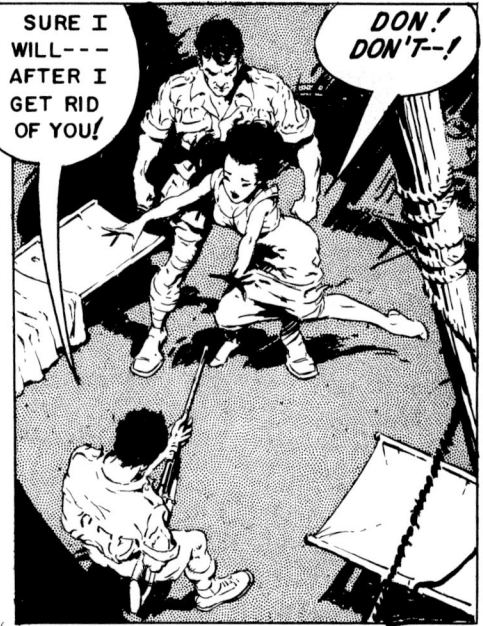

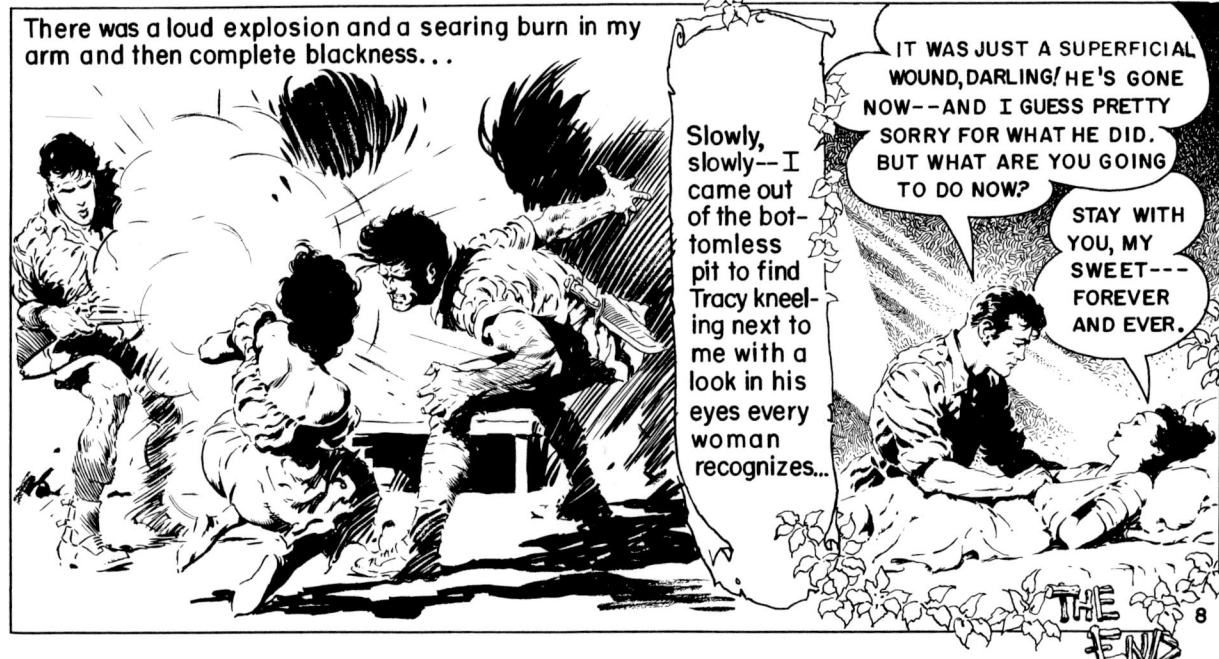

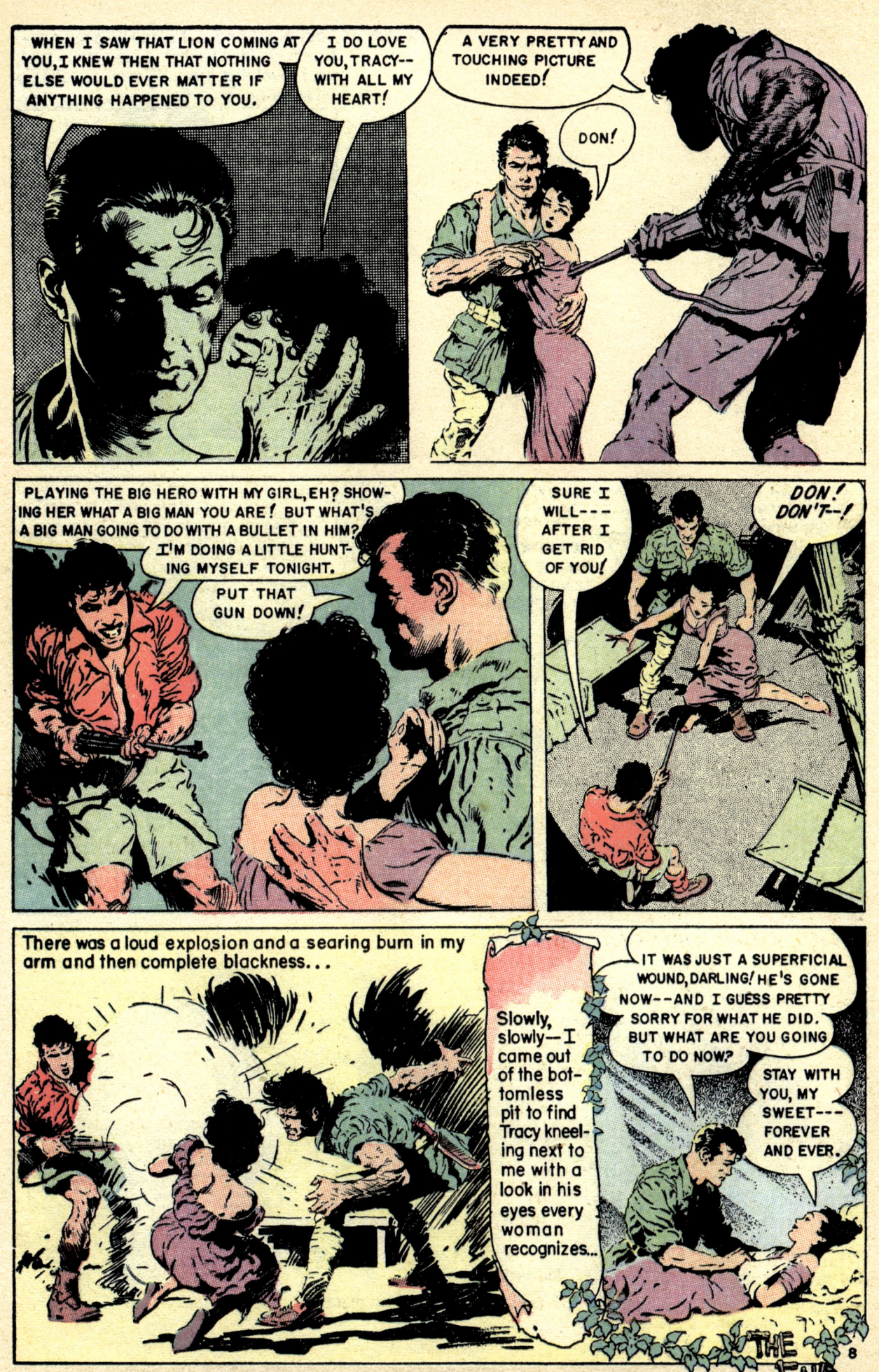

HEY! LOOK WHO'S RIDIN' THE BIG ONE... IN TANDEM! IT'S DAVE!

WHAT'S HAPPENING?! LAST TIME I SAW HIM, HE WAS A BOARDLESS HODAD LIKE YOU AND ME!

YOU'D DO WELL TO QUIT BURNING UP YOUR POCKET MONEY ON CIGARETTES! I DID AND BANKED THE CASH INSTEAD... YOU'RE LOOKIN' AT WHAT IT GOT ME!

...AND, MAN, I NEVER GET WINDED NOW!

MAKES SE A SMOKER A E T C

WHAT GIVES, CUT-BUDDY? HOW'D YOU DIG UP THE COINS FOR THIS MEAN HUNK OF WOOD?
A *CUSTOM JOB!* AND I'M DOING WELL TO KEEP MYSELF IN SMOKES!
IF YOU THINK IT LOOKS GOOD, WAIT'LL YOU TRY IT!
NOT NOW, DAD! TOO WINDED FROM THE SMOKE... I'D DO WELL TO PADDLE OUT THROUGH THE BREAKERS!
'D TRADE GH FOR LIKE ET'S T A MAYBE FEW NTHS...
SMOKING DOESN'T PAY!
FRAZETTA
5 CIGARETTES A DAY COST $32 OR MORE A YEAR!
10 CIGARETTES A DAY COST $64 OR MORE A YEAR!
20 CIGARETTES A DAY COST $128 OR MORE A YEAR!
WHY RISK YOUR HEALTH FOR CIGARETTES?

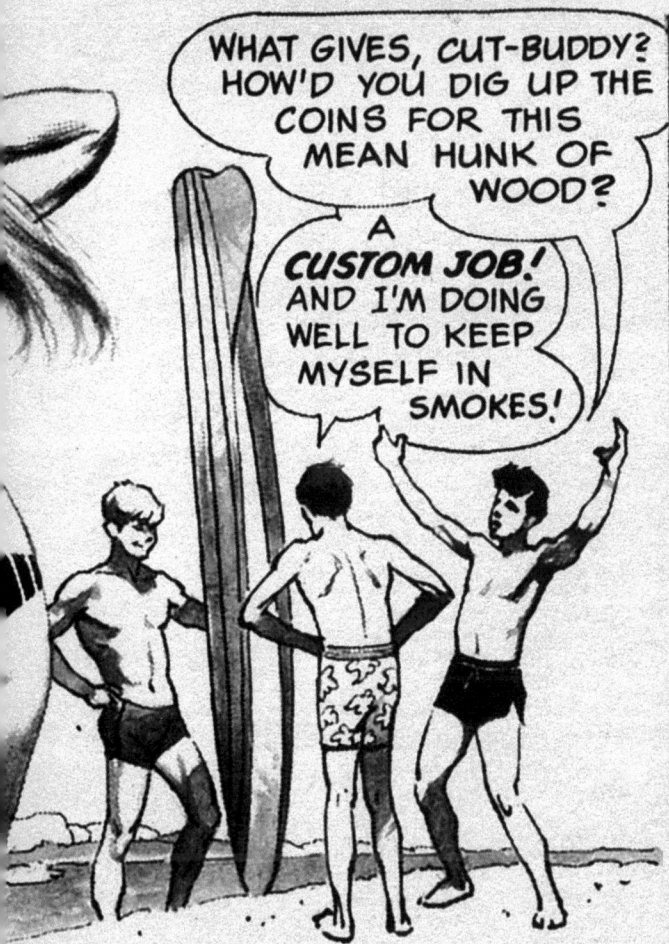

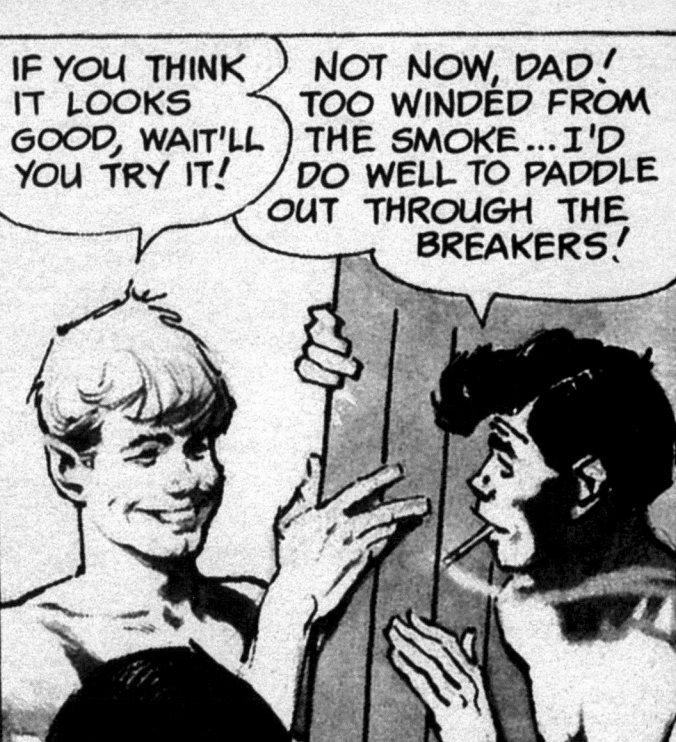

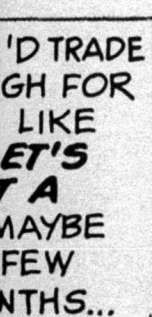

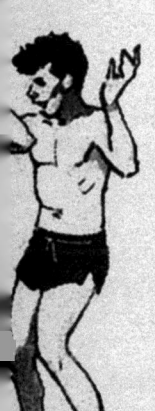

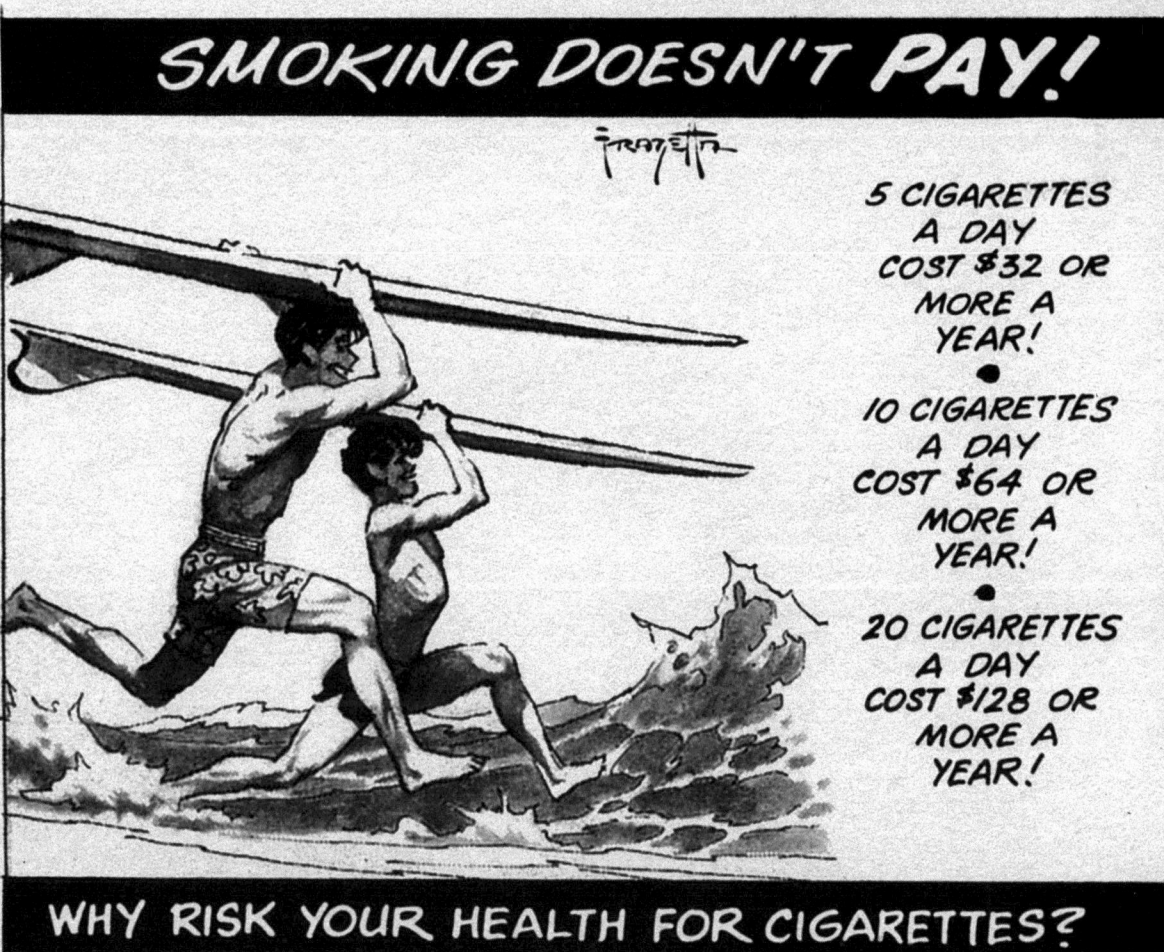

Little Annie Fanny
AND WILL ELDER
WITH JACK DAVIS & FRANK FRAZETTA
IT IS SAID THAT JUSTICE IS BLIND. NOT SO IN THIS STANZA. HAD JUSTICE INDEED BEEN BLIND, WE WOULD HAVE HAD NO STORY TO TELL ON THE DAY OUR LITTLE EYEFUL WAS BROUGHT BEFORE THE BAR IN A BATHING SUIT –
C-CAN I GET OUT NOW, S-S-SOLLY? THE REPORTERS WILL NEVER C-COME IN THIS WEATHER, JUST TO SEE ME S-S-SWIMMING.
SWEETIE - BABY ··· EVEN IF IT'S LENA THE HYENA, SWIMMING OUT OF SEASON ALWAYS MAKES PAGE ONE.
THINK OF THE PUBLICITY AND YOU WON'T MIND THE COLD.
–NOT (GULP) ANY-THING?
–LIKE WHEN YOU'RE HANGING TEN, LOCKED IN AND SQUEAKING THROUGH A RED-HOT TUBE ··· A WHIP-TURN WILL WIPE YOU OUT!
YOU'VE LOST YOUR BIKINI!
–A SHARP RAP, JUST BELOW THE CENTER OF GRAVITY HERE, AND –
RAP!
BONG!
FLAP!
TOOT!
I'M FREE!

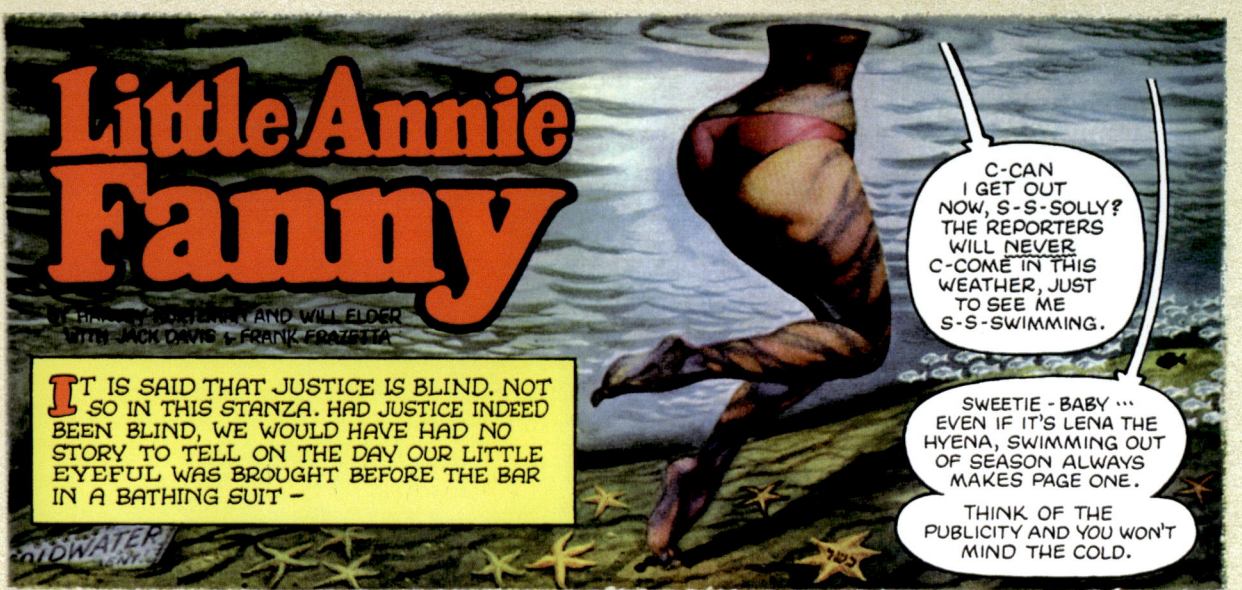

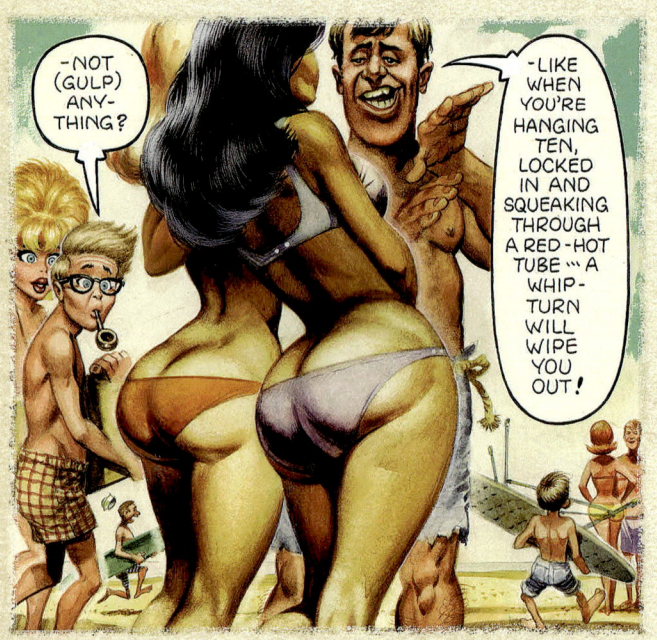

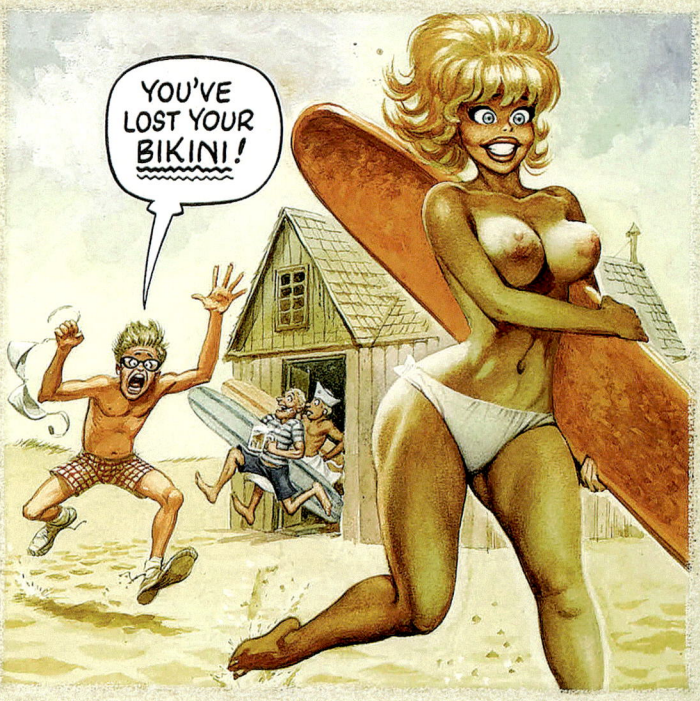

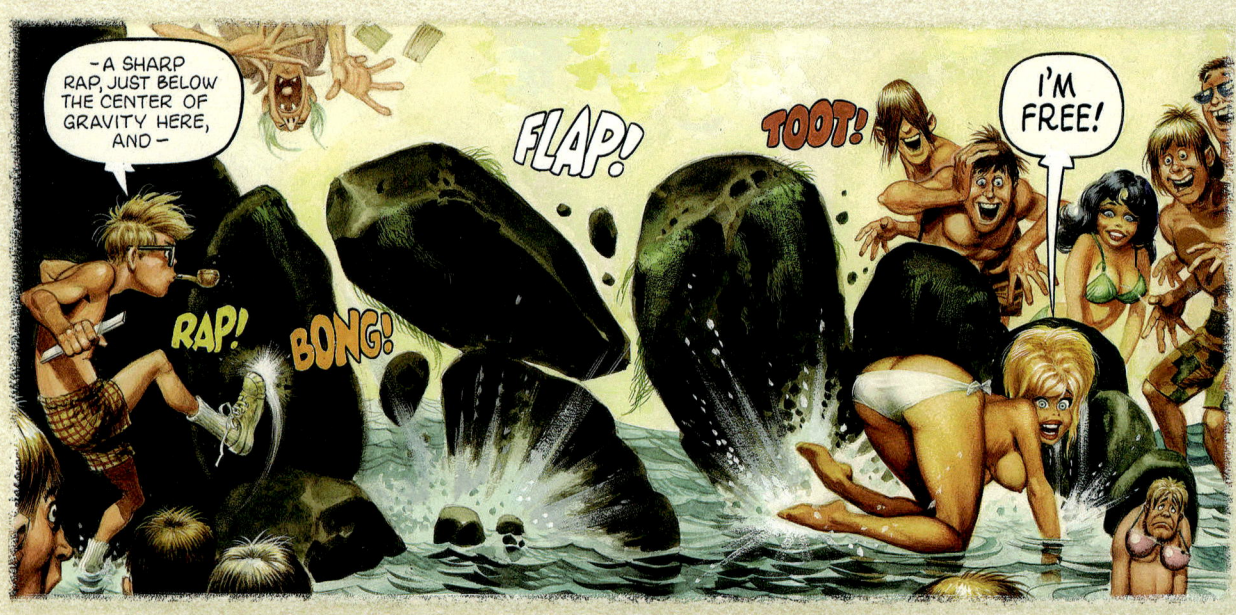

PRETTY FUNNY WOMEN

SEX IN A HUMOROUS VEIN

Though Frazetta is most famous for lavish oil paintings of voluptuous babes, barbarians, and beasts, perhaps surprisingly, one of his greatest talents and interests was humor. Frazetta's beautiful women and humor combined perfectly in various works including *Li'l Abner, Little Annie Fanny* and his 1960s major movie posters. Frazetta's career had started as a comic book artist with him working on a great range of diverse subjects from funny animal comics to humor (*Louie Lazybones*), science fiction, romance, westerns (*White Indian* and *John Wayne*), to EC Comics with his friend and collaborator Al Williamson, who introduced Frank to artist friends Roy Krenkel, Wallace Wood, Angelo Torres, Nick Meglin, and others. In 1951, Frazetta landed the auto-racing strip *Johnny Comet* written by champion Indy 500 driver Peter DePaolo and third-tier screenplay writer Earl Baldwin. The strip launched on January 28, 1952 but *Comet* struggled, ultimately changing its name to *Ace McCoy* shortly before it was canceled a year later. Then, *Li'l Abner* creator Al Capp contacted Frazetta, who was now a member of the National Cartoonist's Society. *Li'l Abner* was one of the biggest hits in comic strip history. It had 60 million readers in over 900 American newspapers and 100 foreign papers in 28 countries. In his 2011 *Southern Quarterly* article, M. Thomas

Inge wrote that Capp, "had a profound influence on the way the world viewed the American South."

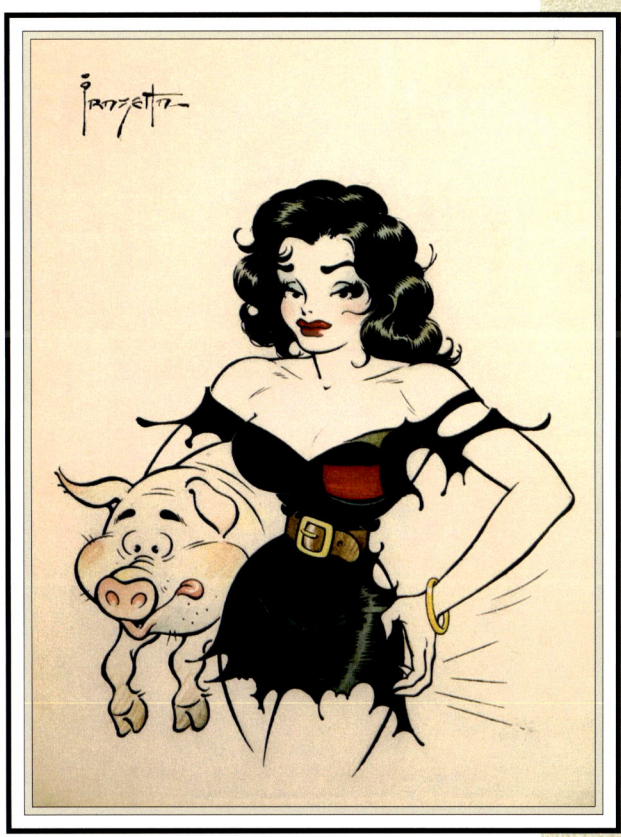

In many ways, Frazetta's dream of becoming a successful newspaper strip cartoonist had come true but he toiled for years as a "ghost" artist with Capp getting all the acclaim. Frazetta, interviewed by Russ Cochran in 1978: "Originally, Capp's idea was to have me do most of it. I would do the realistic figures like Li'l Abner and the beautiful gals. He even said that he wanted to see my style creep in, because he really

THIS PAGE:
Li'l Abner's Moonbeam McSwine, published as a greeting card in the 1950s by Superior Greeting Co. Inc.

OPPOSITE:
Selected Frazetta panels from LITTLE ANNIE FANNY, *published in three issues of* Playboy *from 1965.*

liked my stuff. But when my style crept in, the Syndicate got upset. They weren't being critical of my work, but it didn't look like Al Capp. So we had to go back to keeping it 'straight Capp.' They said, 'Frazetta is good in his own right, but it's not Al Capp anymore.' And, Al Capp was what they were paying for. So, I was forced to do it just like Capp, in his own style. You couldn't tell us apart after a while. It was dull, boring stuff, but I didn't care, because uppermost in my mind was the fact that I'm making big plans for me…I know what I'm going to do. Any day now, I'm going to quit this stuff and take the world by storm. But, it never happened. Nine years just slipped by — nine damn years."

"I had a good life, a better than average income, and all the goof-off time I wanted. Life was easy. I kept telling myself, 'This job allows me the time to sit and make great plans…to be a great painter.' I met Roy Krenkel, through Al Williamson, and he helped

• • • • • 66 • • • • •

I went up to Boston to work in [Capp's] studio. He had Andy [Amato] and Walter [Johnston] and Harvey [Curtis]. Then I found out one of the guys was crying that Al had cut the guy's salary so he could pay me. He was that kind of guy. I felt terrible. After a few weeks up there, we made [an] arrangement where he'd send a blank page that was just lightly stick-figured, and I would pencil the thing, wrap it up and mail it. And that was it for nine years.

— FRANK FRAZETTA

Interviewed by Gary Groth in 1994 for The Comics Journal

convince me that I could do great things. I didn't really need convincing, but he twisted my arm and pushed me a little. He called me a time-waster and a goof-off, and made me feel guilty about it. He introduced me to all kinds of great art through his collection. It was really inspiring! He's been an inspiration through the years in as much as he would be very critical — not always right, of course — and I enjoyed hearing his opinions."

"[Then, Capp and I] had a bit of a disagreement. He was insisting that I come to Boston one particular week, and I had just moved into a house and we were in a mess. One of his assistants was under the weather and he needed me. I said, 'Gee, I appreciate that, but my wife needs me here.' We'd just moved in, were in the middle of unpacking, and had a thousand things to do. He said, 'Well, you gotta come up!' So I said I'd talk it over with Ellie and see if she could hack it without me for a week. We discussed it and said we guessed we owed it to him, so I called him back and said okay and just added in passing that the price

PLAYBOY
ENTERTAINMENT FOR MEN

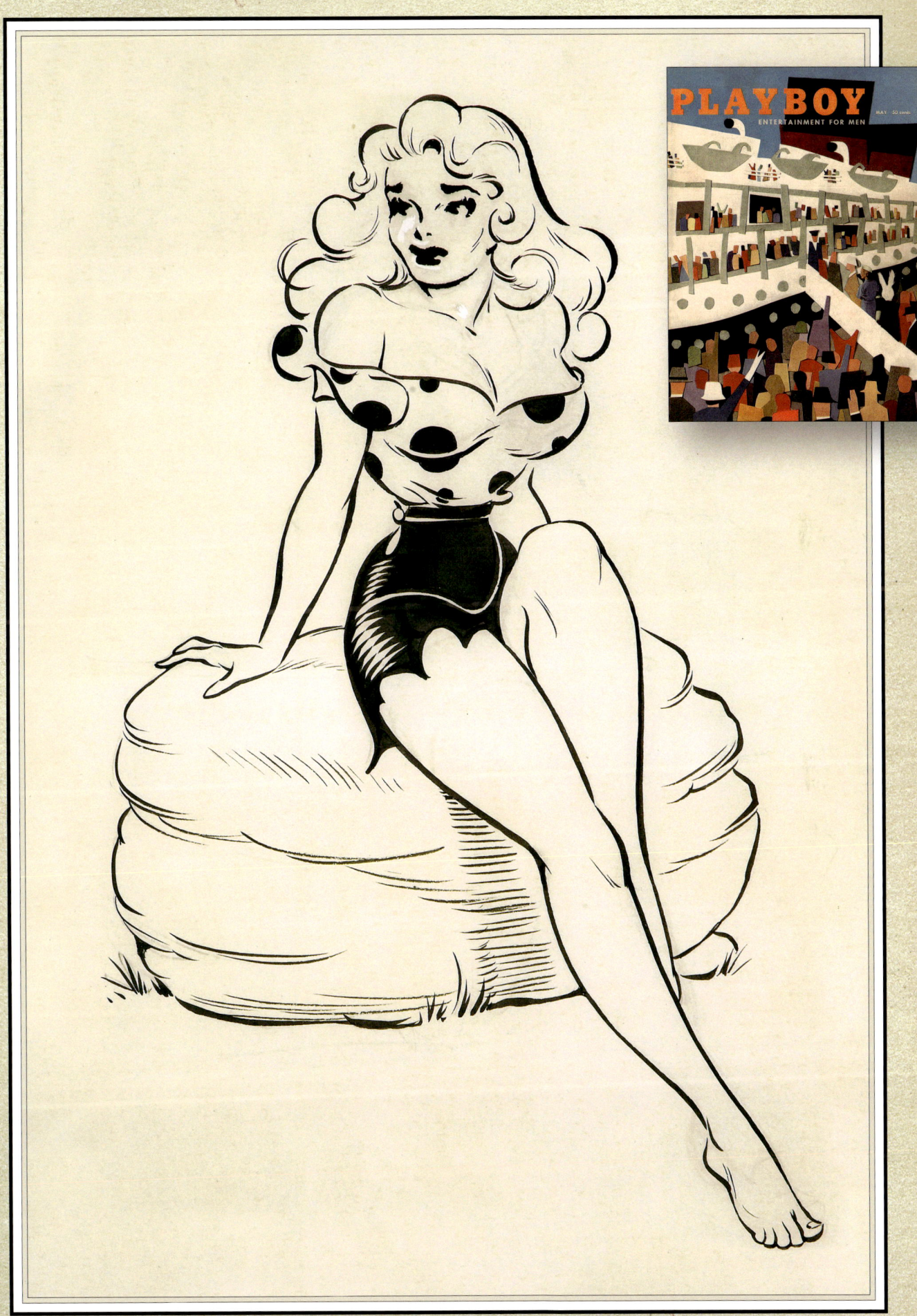

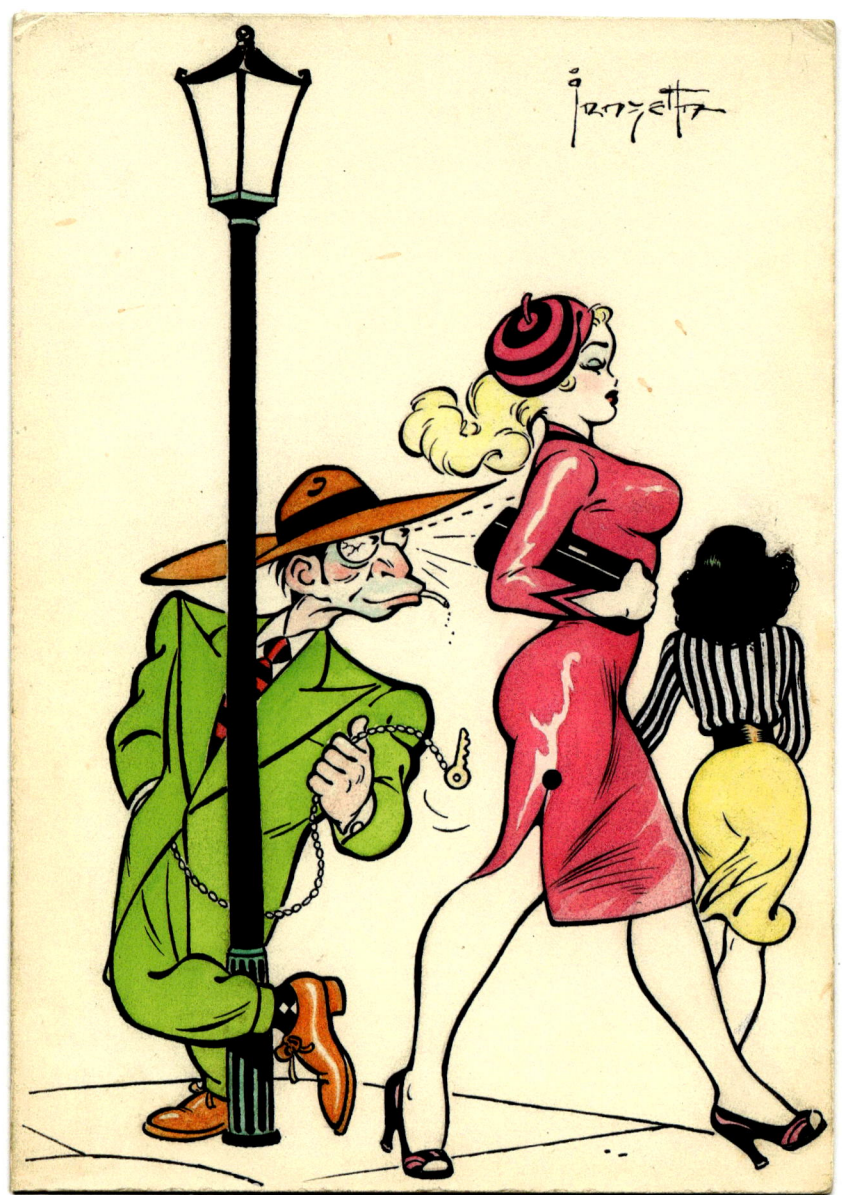

Li'l Abner's Evil-Eye Fleegle (6" x 8.5"); published as a greeting card in the 1950s by Superior Greeting Co. Inc.

would be the usual hundred bucks a day. 'Oh, no,' he said, 'Things have been tough.' Well, to make a long story short, he just decided that he would cut my salary in half, and at that point I decided he could go hang himself. I said, 'Goodbye, it's been nice knowing you.' Not only didn't I get a raise, not a nickel in nine years, mind you, I didn't even complain about it. He was ready to cut it back."

After leaving Al Capp, Frazetta had a surprisingly tough time. His old comic-book accounts were either out of business or had nothing for him. It's been said that either Capp had him blacklisted or the surviving comic-book publishers now thought Frazetta's work looked old fashioned.

Frazetta was scrambling. He picked up some men's magazine and risqué paperback illustration work, George Evans gave him some inking work on the comic book, *Frogmen*, and his dear friend Roy Krenkel was working to get Canaveral and Ace books to hire Frazetta to illustrate Edgar Rice Burroughs works when Frank heard

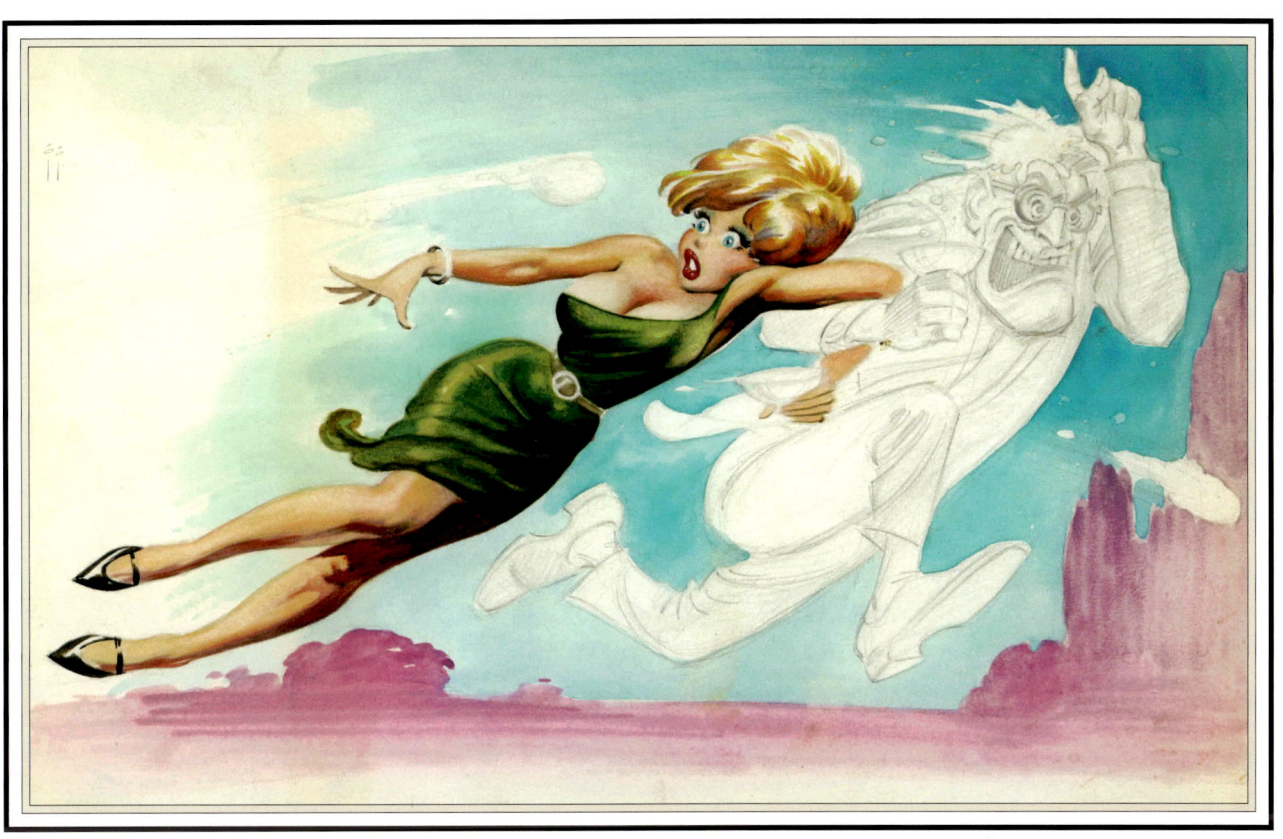

from another old EC Comics friend, *Mad* founding editor-writer, Harvey Kurtzman. Since leaving *Mad*, Kurtzman had teamed with *Playboy*'s Hugh Hefner on a few projects and was currently working with his closest associate, Will Elder, producing the hit, fully painted, sexy comics strip, *Little Annie Fanny*, which ran in *Playboy*.

Interviewed by Gary Groth in 1994, Frazetta said, "Harvey Kurtzman gave me some work on *Annie Fanny*. The only objection I had was [Kurtzman's] requirement — or maybe it was Hefner's — was that there were all these details in the background.

I didn't understand that at all. So I refused to do that. I said, 'You think I'm gonna paint 20 light bulbs in the background, and the doors and the floor and the table and the chairs….You can forget about it! I'll do *Annie Fanny*, I'll do her little boobs, and that's it.' So that's what I did. I did *Annie Fanny* for a little while. [But,] Hefner had no use for me. Hefner didn't like my *Annie Fanny*; it didn't look like Elder's. I can understand Hefner being a little upset because I suddenly changed the look of it. Harvey, of course, loved it. But Hefner got upset: 'It looks like a whole different version! It's not good, it doesn't work!' So that was that."

TOP:
Frazetta's tryout drawing of ANNIE FANNY *as proof to Hugh Hefner that he could draw women. (12"x 7.5")*

LEFT:
Stupefyin' Jones (8"x 12.5") used in Playboy, *May 1957.*

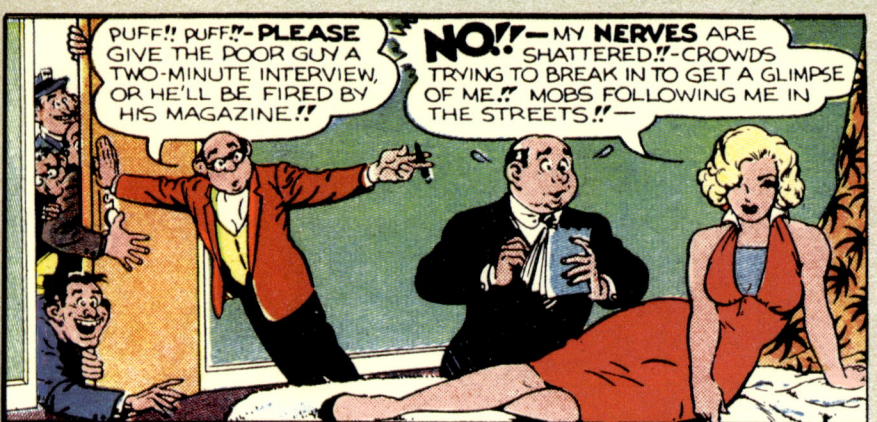
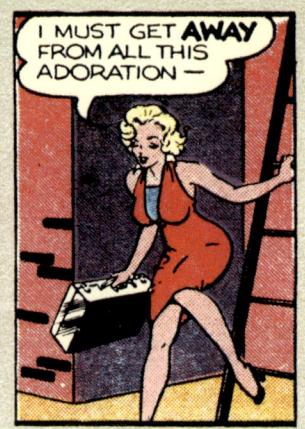
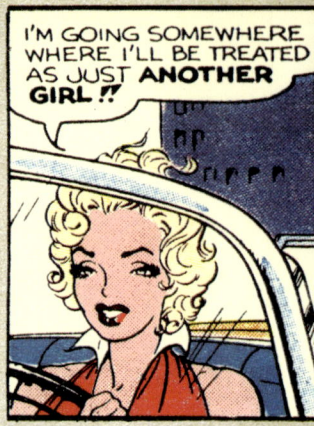
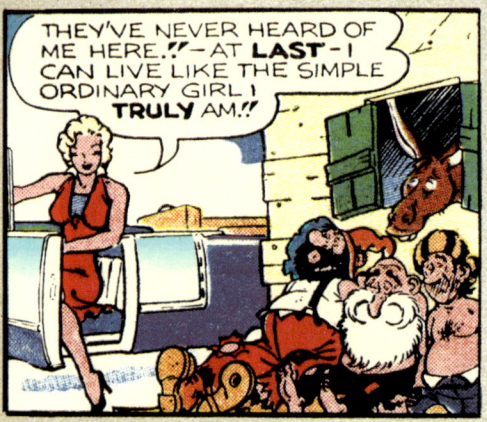
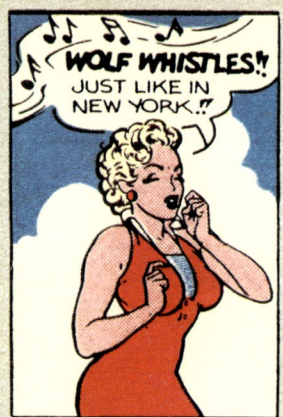
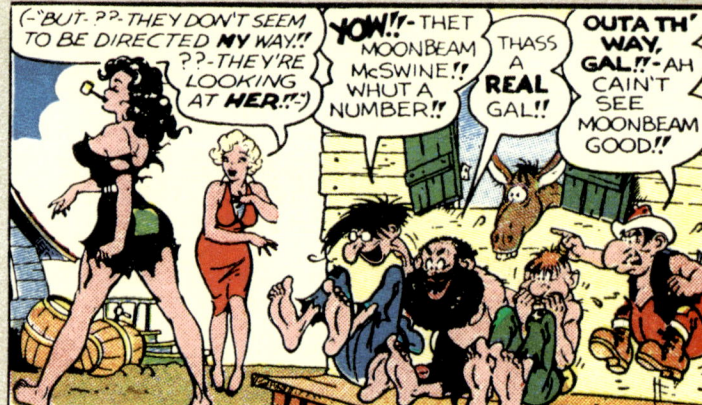
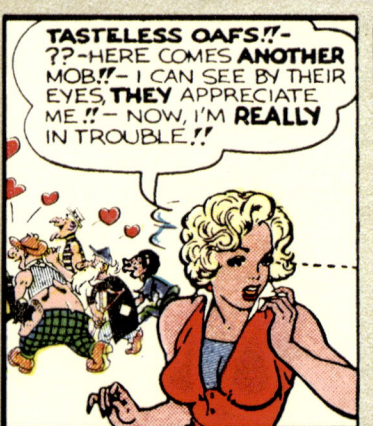
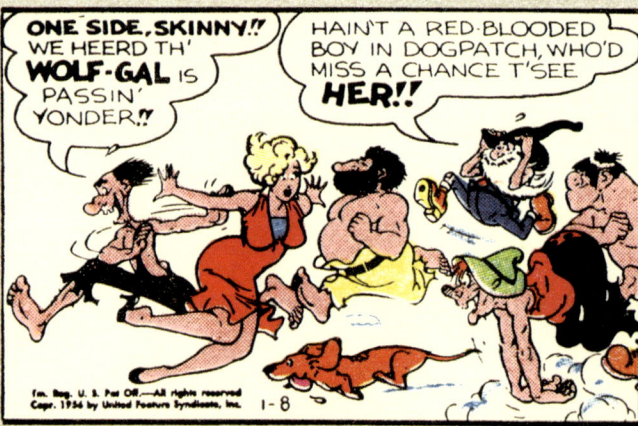
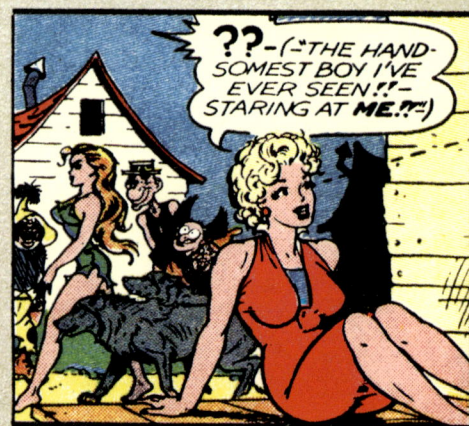
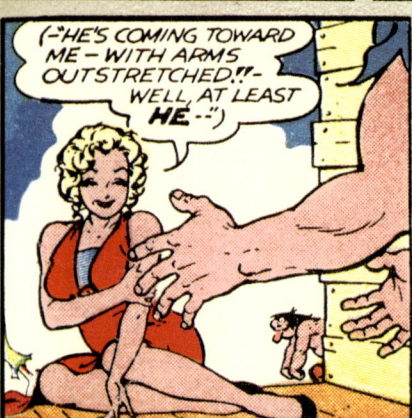
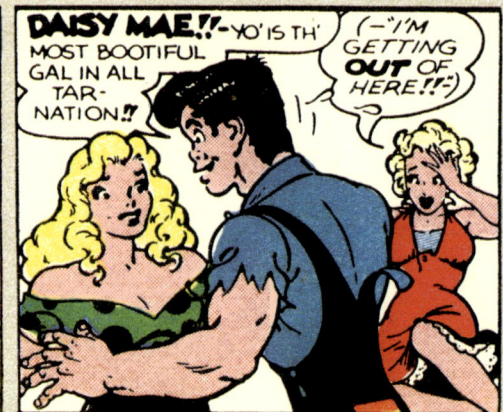
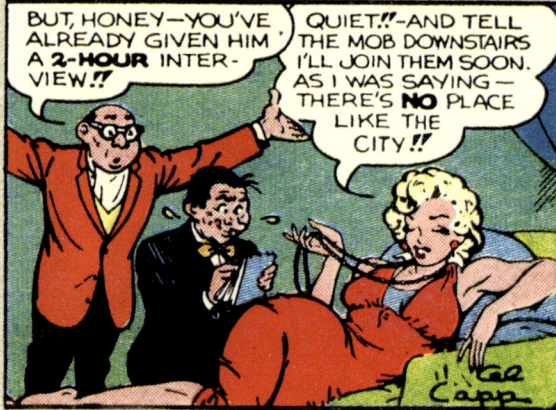

January 8, 1956 Sunday page for Li'l Abner *featuring Marilyn Monroe.*

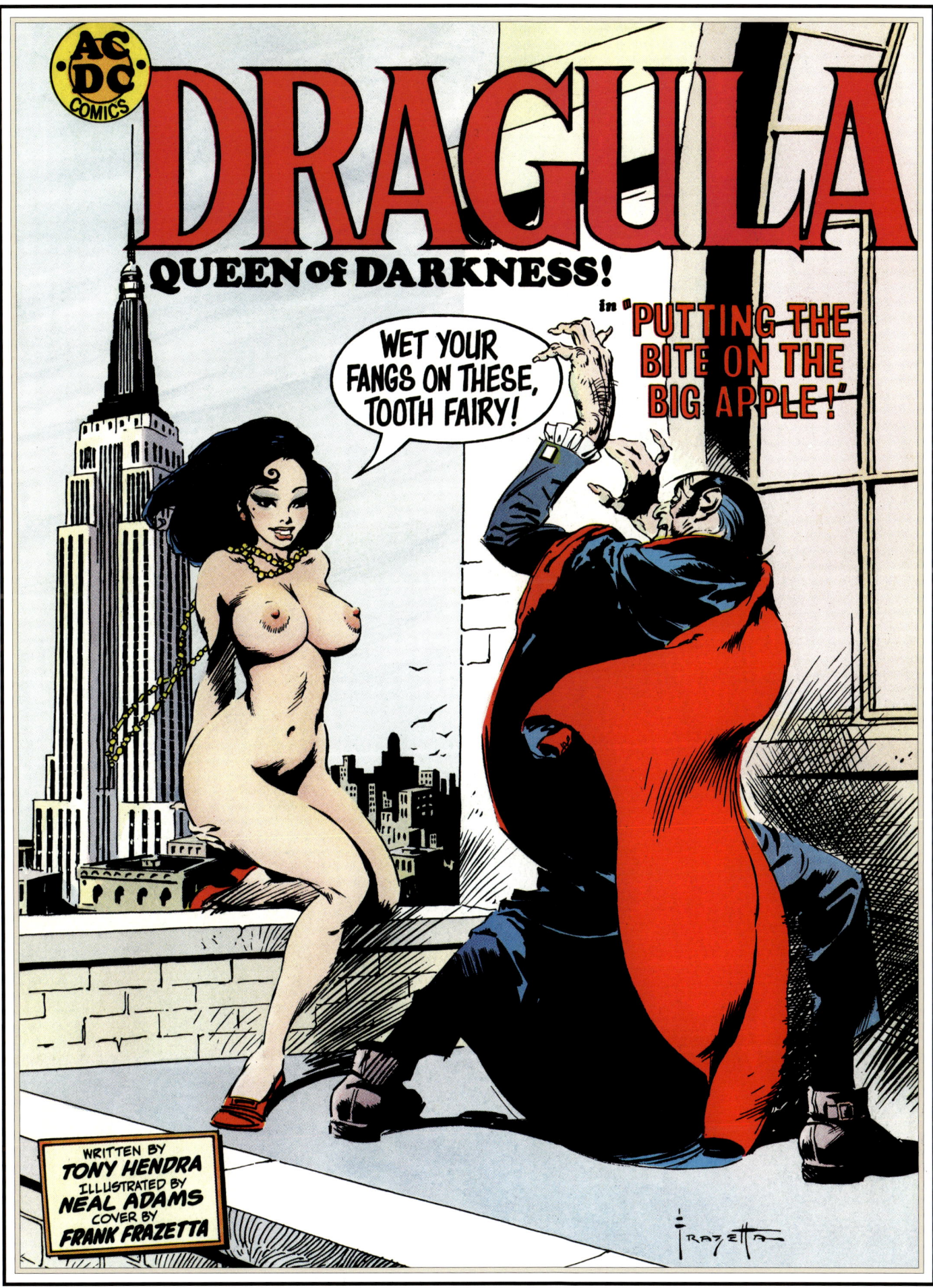

The vampire spoof DRAGULA, *from* National Lampoon #20, November 1971

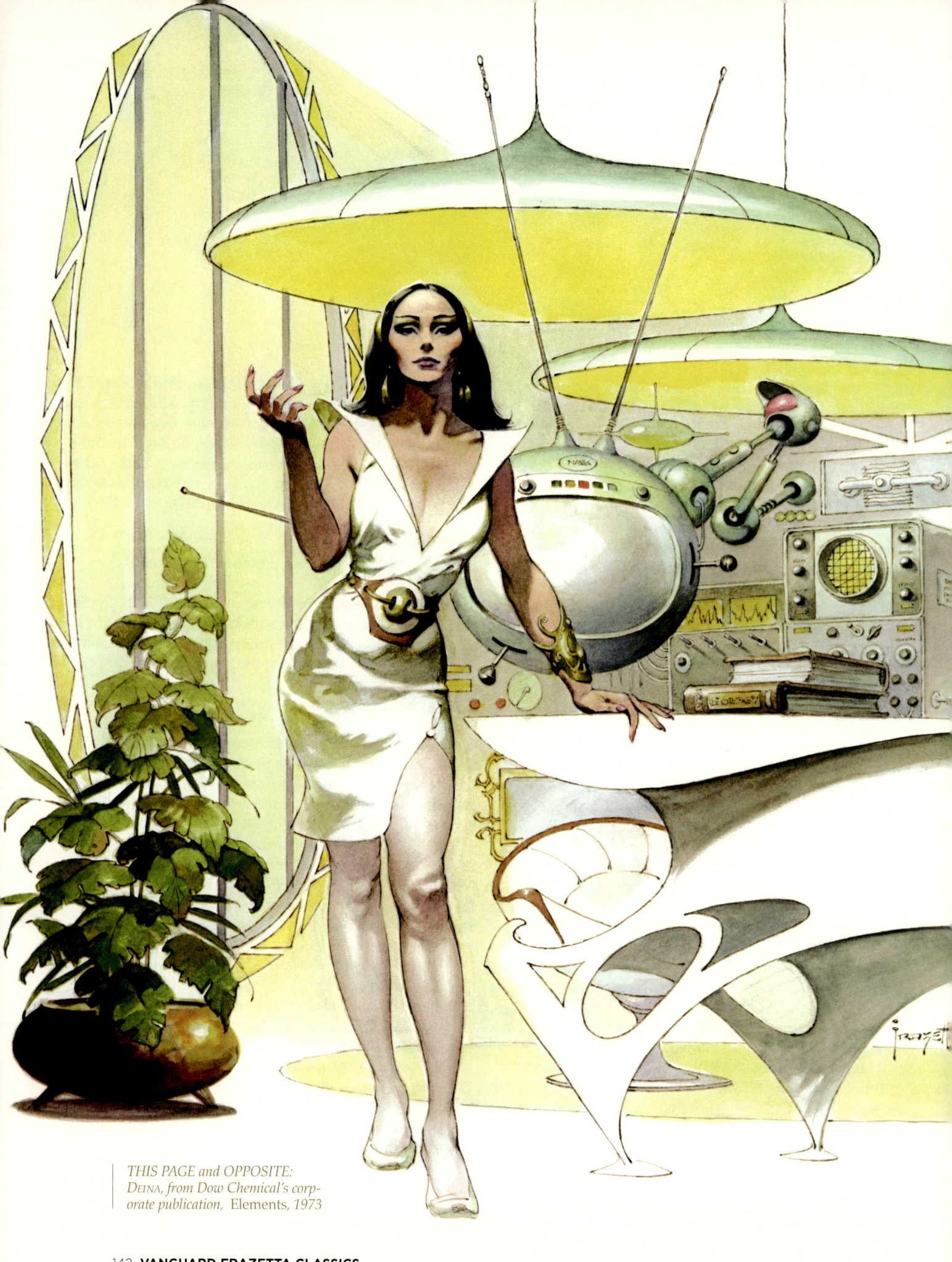

THIS PAGE and OPPOSITE:
DEINA, from Dow Chemical's corp-
orate publication, Elements, *1973*

CHAPTER FOUR
SAUCY STORIES
MEN'S MAGAZINE ART

Frazetta's first men's magazine work was his uncredited contributions to the "Li'l Abner's Gals" feature in the May 1957 issue of *Playboy*. But Hugh Hefner never knew Frazetta by name until the February 1965 issue of *Playboy*, in which Frazetta started his brief period assisting his old EC Comics friends, Harvey Kurtzman and Will Elder, on *Little Annie Fanny*. Unfortunately, Hef thought of Frazetta as the new guy who didn't paint *Annie Fanny* like Will Elder. Which is a shame as otherwise, Frazetta might have enjoyed a long relationship with *Playboy*. Still, Frazetta did do work for the competing risqué men's magazines, *Dude, Gent*, and *Cavalcade*.

For sexy publishers of the 1950s and '60s, it was a volatile industry and legal issues over varying local decency laws, could raise hell at any time. Publishers made a point to cover their tracks in an effort to keep an issue over one publication from bringing down their other publications and/or lines. This was accomplished largely by listing a different company name for nearly every magazine and as many different addresses as possible for those various company names. While these policies make it difficult to reconnect the dots now, 50 years later, our research shows that there were connections between Midwood/Tower, the risqué paperback publisher Frazetta created art for, and at least one of the men's magazines he worked for in the same, post-*Li'l Abner* period, mid-1962 thru mid-1964. Midwood/Tower Publisher Harry Shorten frequently partnered with various other publishers — including one or more of his long-time associates at MLJ/Archie Comics — for his different lines including Midwood Books, Tower Books, Belmont Books, and Tower Comics.

But the following evidence indicates Shorten was also the head of Skye Publishing (sometimes, Sky) at 505 Eighth Avenue in New York, which published *Cavalcade* magazine. The same address was associated with Tower Books, *Cavalcade* ran ads for Tower Books, and, although neither Shorten, nor any other individual, was named in *Cavalcade* as publisher, occasionally, Shorten's right-hand man, Marshall Dugger, was credited as Executive Editor on *Cavalcade*. Dugger was the contact Frazetta cited as being who he worked with at Midwood/Tower.

But while Frazetta only cites his work with Dugger for *Cavalcade* and Midwood/Tower Books, Frazetta's first work in the risqué men's magazine genre was actually for another outfit, Maurice Murray and Frederick A. Klein. The duo partnered together under company names including Dugent and Mystery Publishing Co. Inc., which published *Dude* magazine and *Gent* magazine, with offices at 48 West 48th Street in New York. Dude (or *The Dude*) was edited by Bruce Elliott who, under the alias Maxwell Grant, had famously written many pulp novels featuring The Shadow.

Interviewed by Gary Groth in 1994, Frazetta said, "I was just making the rounds. [Marshall] Dugger was the art director up at Tower, and he loved my stuff — he was the only one who loved my stuff! And

A Gentle Breeze sketch sheet #2 (11" x 13").

he gave me work, and even that started getting all kinds of response. They loved it." But how did Frazetta get to *Dude* and *Gent*? Frazetta's longtime friend, Dr. Dave Winiewicz recalled Frazetta telling him that it was Frazetta's *Famous Funnies* contact, Stephen A. Douglas, that referred Frazetta — to someone — for men's magazine work. Winiewicz said, "Al Williamson was the person who first introduced Frazetta to Stephen Douglas back in the early '50s. That introduction led to some nice jobs for Frank."

In *Comic Book Culture: An Illustrated History*, Ron Goulart wrote, "Stephen A. Douglas was one of many artists who made the transition from newspaper comic strips to comic books. However, as the art editor (and, really the effective day-to-day editor) for *Famous Funnies* from its inception to its demise, he [should] be regarded as especially significant. He was essentially the first editor of the first American comic book. Given that he implemented innovations such as printing wholly original work — in an era when the norm was to reprint material that had originally appeared in newspapers — he may be regarded as one of the 'founding fathers' of the American comics industry. Douglas occasionally signed his work with only his initials. This led to the probably intentional irony of a comic with the word 'Funnies' in its title bearing the word 'sad' on some of its covers."

In 1962, in search of work after quitting Al Capp and the Li'l Abner strip, Frazetta reached out to Douglas. But, *Famous Funnies*, like many of

Continued on Page 150

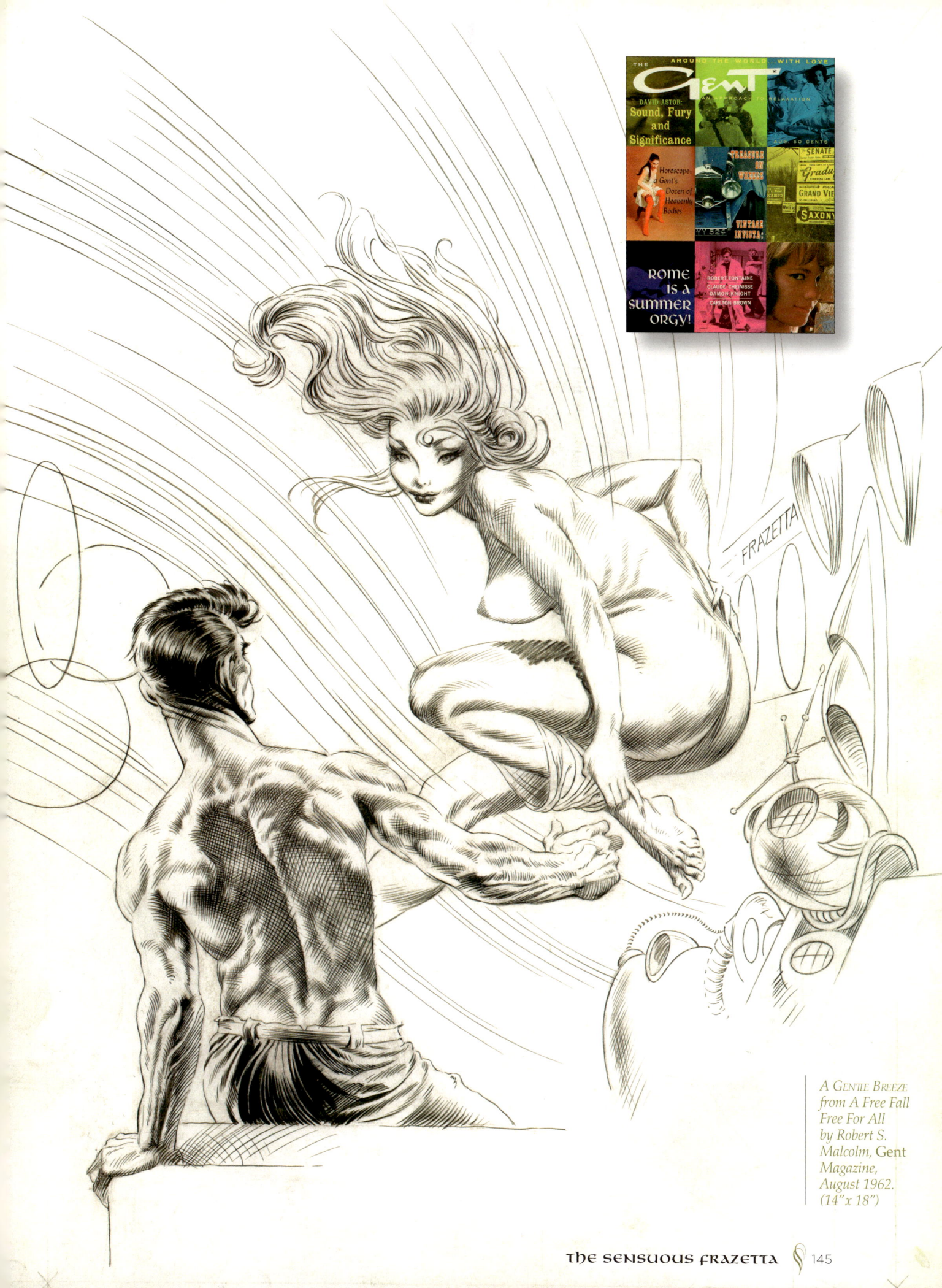

A Gentle Breeze from A Free Fall Free For All by Robert S. Malcolm, Gent Magazine, August 1962. (14" x 18")

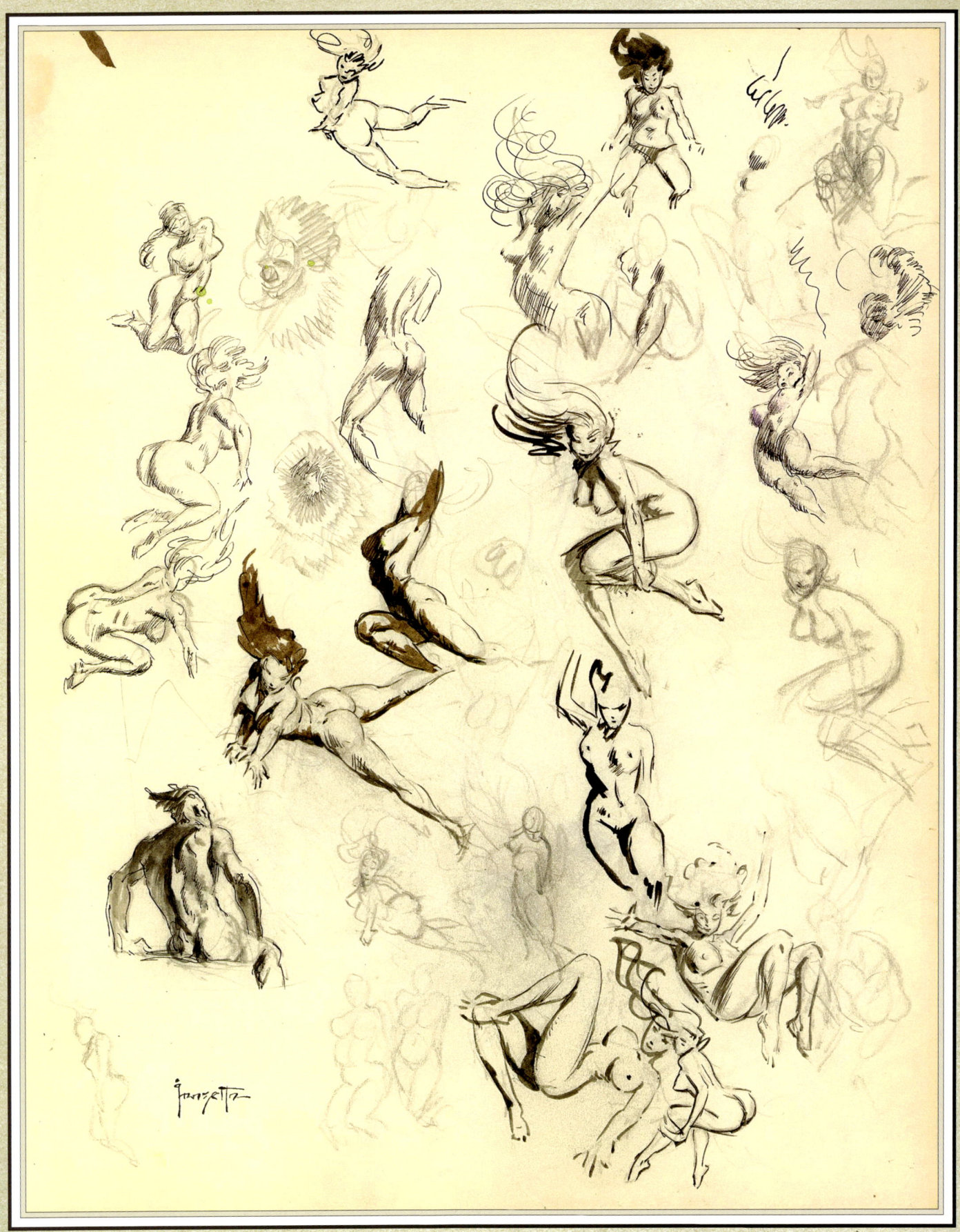

THIS SPREAD:
A Gentle Breeze sketch sheet #1 (11" x 13") —
and final published page from Gent Magazine, August 1962.

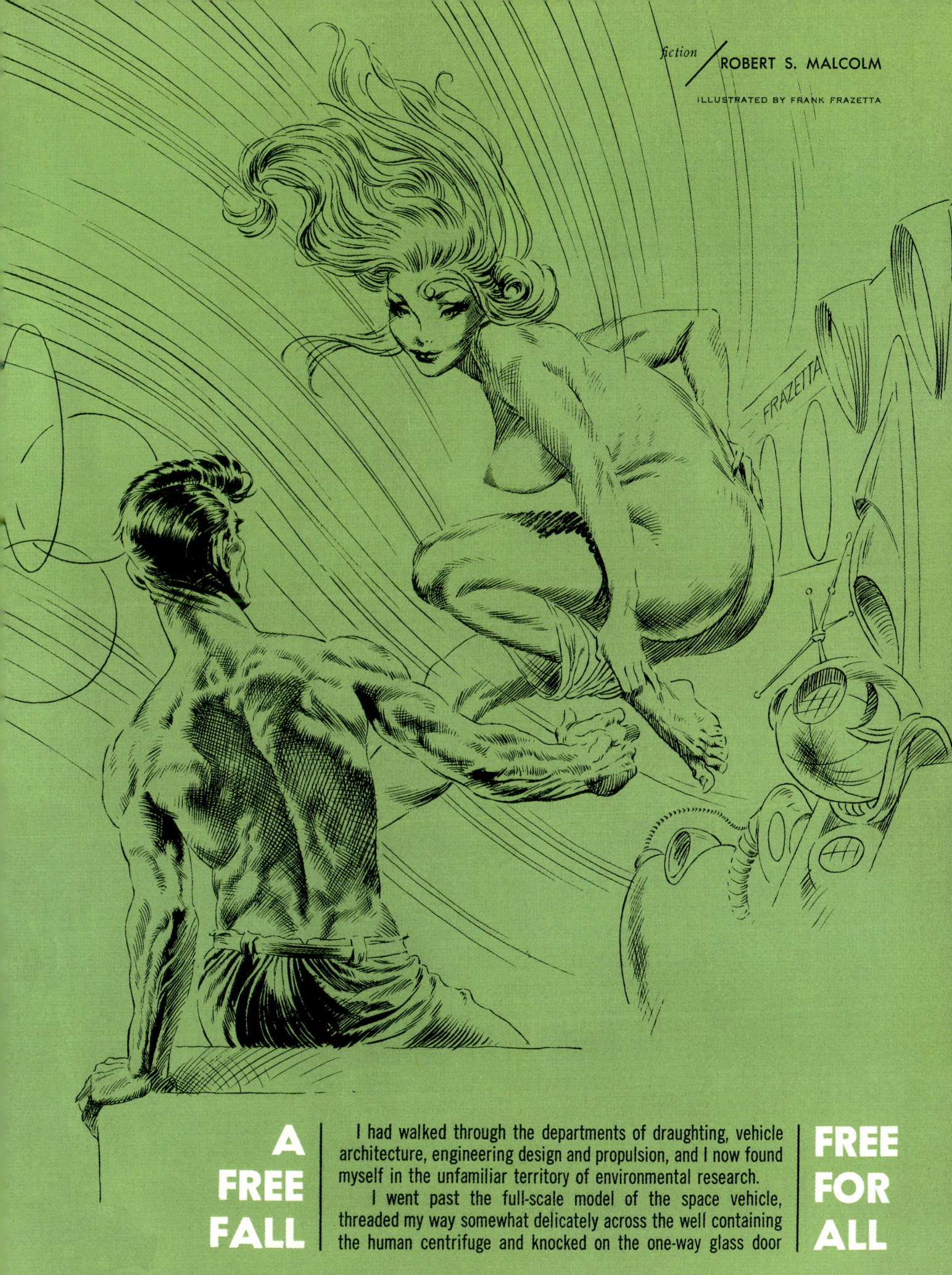

fiction / ROBERT S. MALCOLM

ILLUSTRATED BY FRANK FRAZETTA

A FREE FALL

FREE FOR ALL

I had walked through the departments of draughting, vehicle architecture, engineering design and propulsion, and I now found myself in the unfamiliar territory of environmental research.

I went past the full-scale model of the space vehicle, threaded my way somewhat delicately across the well containing the human centrifuge and knocked on the one-way glass door

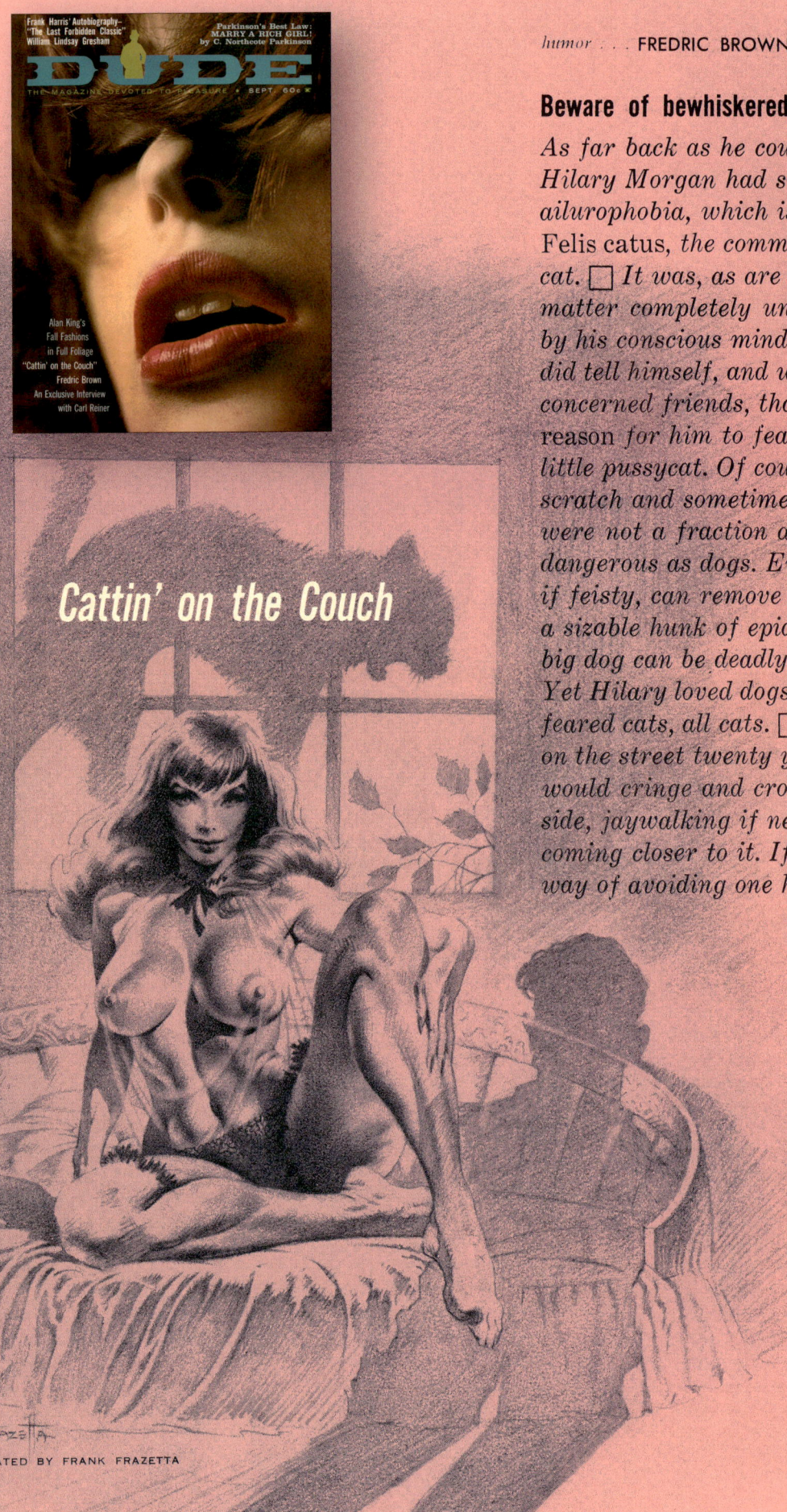

Cattin' on the Couch

ILLUSTRATED BY FRANK FRAZETTA

humor . . . FREDRIC BROWN

Beware of bewhiskered head-shrinkers.

As far back as he could remember, Hilary Morgan had suffered from ailurophobia, which is morbid fear of Felis catus, *the common or domestic cat.* ☐ It was, as are all phobias, a matter completely uncontrollable by his conscious mind. He could and did tell himself, and was told by his concerned friends, that there was no reason for him to fear a harmless little pussycat. Of course cats could scratch and sometimes did, but they were not a fraction as potentially dangerous as dogs. Even a small dog, if feisty, can remove quite painfully a sizable hunk of epidermis, and a big dog can be deadly. Cats? Phooey. Yet Hilary loved dogs, all dogs, and feared cats, all cats. ☐ If he saw a cat on the street twenty yards away he would cringe and cross to the other side, jaywalking if necessary to avoid coming closer to it. If there was no way of avoiding one he would turn

CATTIN' ON THE COUCH (as published in Dude *magazine, September 1962).*

Shall it be a light bite . . . or the big spread? ● humor / Robert Fontaine

I cannot believe that the problem of love on the lunch hour is a widespread one and yet I have had a number of puzzled lovers and would-be lovers bring up the matter with some concern and distress.

There seems to be a number of men for whom, either love at lunch time is the only safe possibility, or (while other possibilities present themselves at more con[...] to be the most ecst[...]dled.

I have [...] this problem, hav[...] beautiful creatu[...] the only time ava[...]

Obviou[...] s a long

evening of expectation and a sweet night of repose. Just the same we must not leave a single avenue unexplored. There follow, therefore, a few brief notes on the subject.

One of the disadvantages of love, cafeteria or lunch counter style, is that neither of you really dare consume enough liquor to set up for the moment of truth without the risk of going back to the office or the agency slightly vague and unsteady, or, at least, dreamy and confused.

On the other hand, a rendezvous in the cold light of noon without any romantic beverage, has an air about it of breeding Pekingese. My experiments suggested that a decent wine, a dry sherry or even a

(turn to page 66)

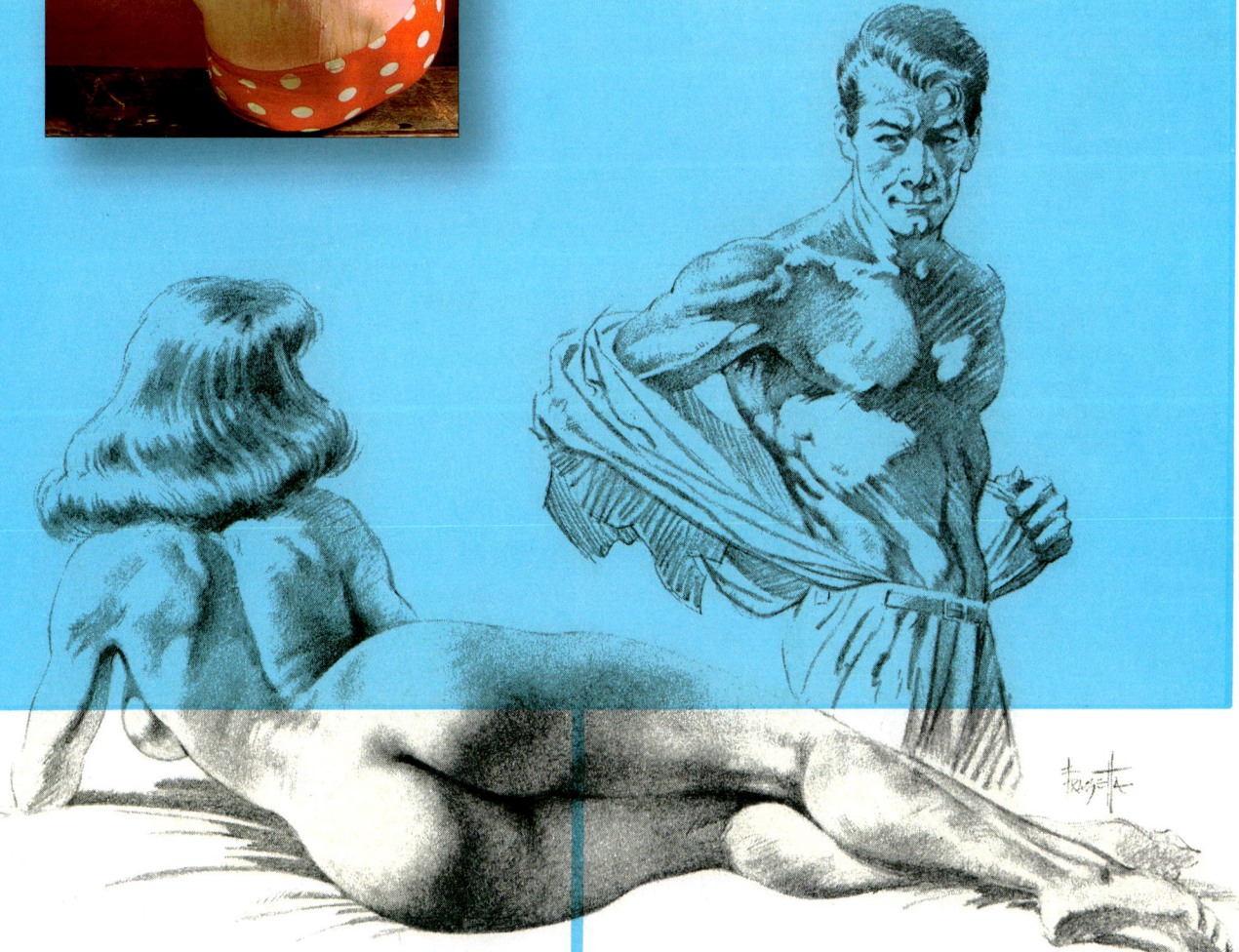

ILLUSTRATED BY FRAZETTA

a menu for . . . **SEX IN THE AFTERNOON**

Sex in the Afternoon by Robert Fontaine (as published in Gent magazine, October 1962).

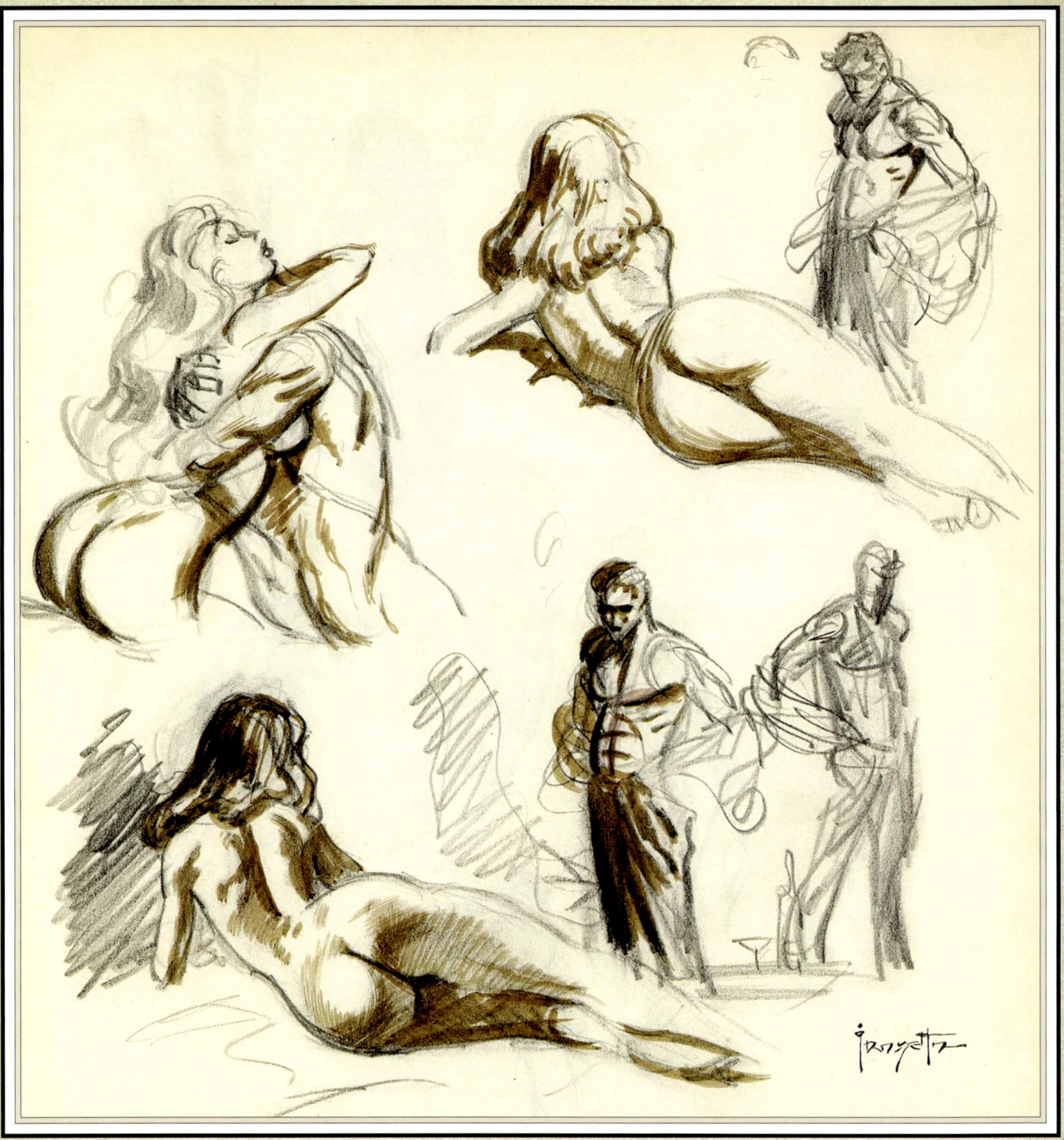

...continued from Page 144

Frazetta's old comic-book accounts, had shut down during a beaten and battered period for the comic-book industry in the mid-to-late-1950s. Still, Douglas was determined to help. Winiewicz continued, "Stephen had a ton of contacts and Frank said he made a few calls on his behalf, including the men's magazine people, which lead to those jobs. Frank had the highest regard for Douglas, as did Al

[Williamson] and Roy [Krenkel]. He was a good guy and honest. Frank said he respected him as a person, unlike most of the phonies and con-men he was used to dealing with."

So, either Steven Douglas referred Frazetta to the *Dude* and *Gent* publishers or to both companies. If Douglas only referred Frazetta to *Dude* and *Gent*, perhaps there was some slight connection between them and Midwood/

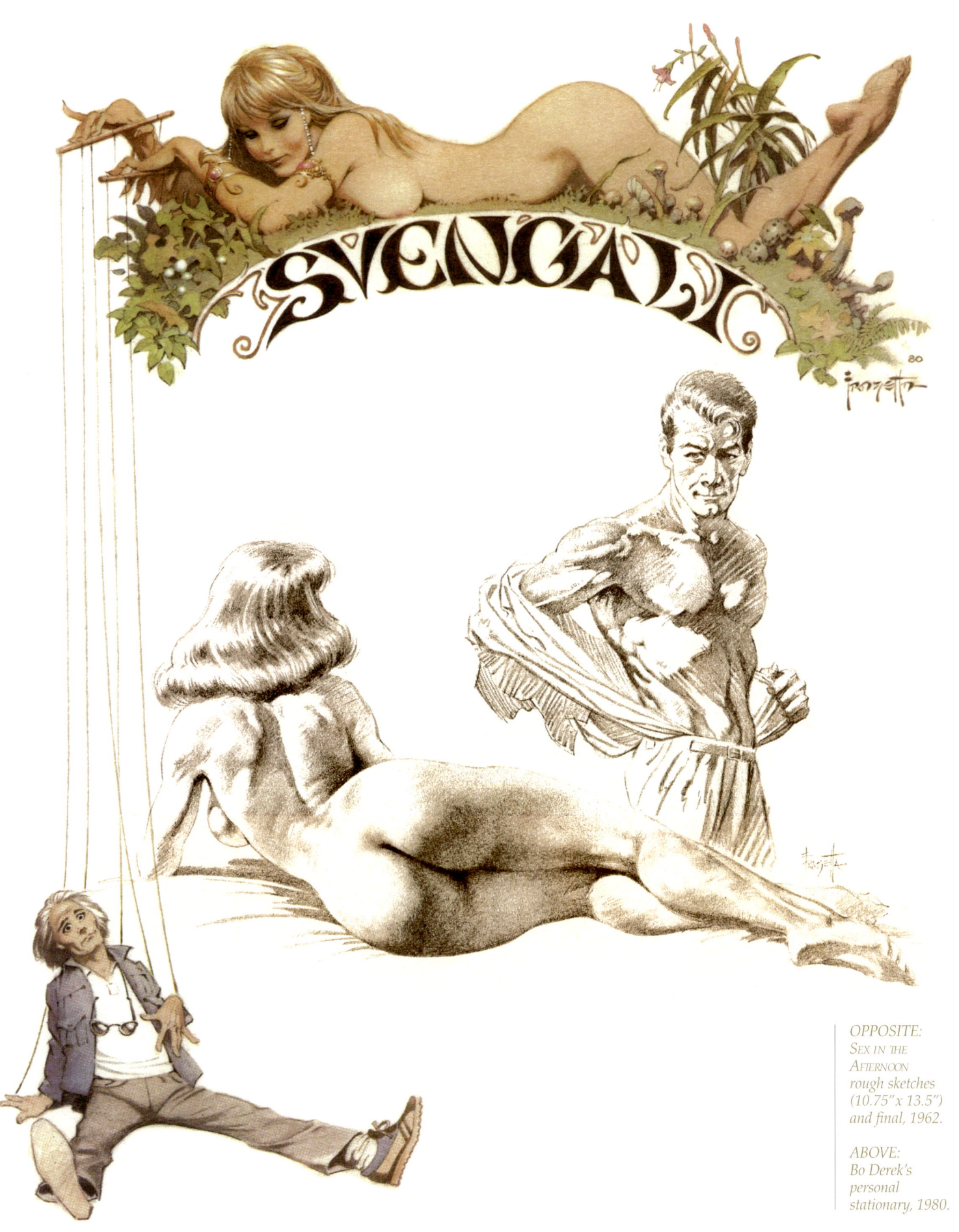

SVENGALI

OPPOSITE:
*SEX IN THE
AFTERNOON*
rough sketches
(10.75"x 13.5")
and final, 1962.

ABOVE:
Bo Derek's
personal
stationary, 1980.

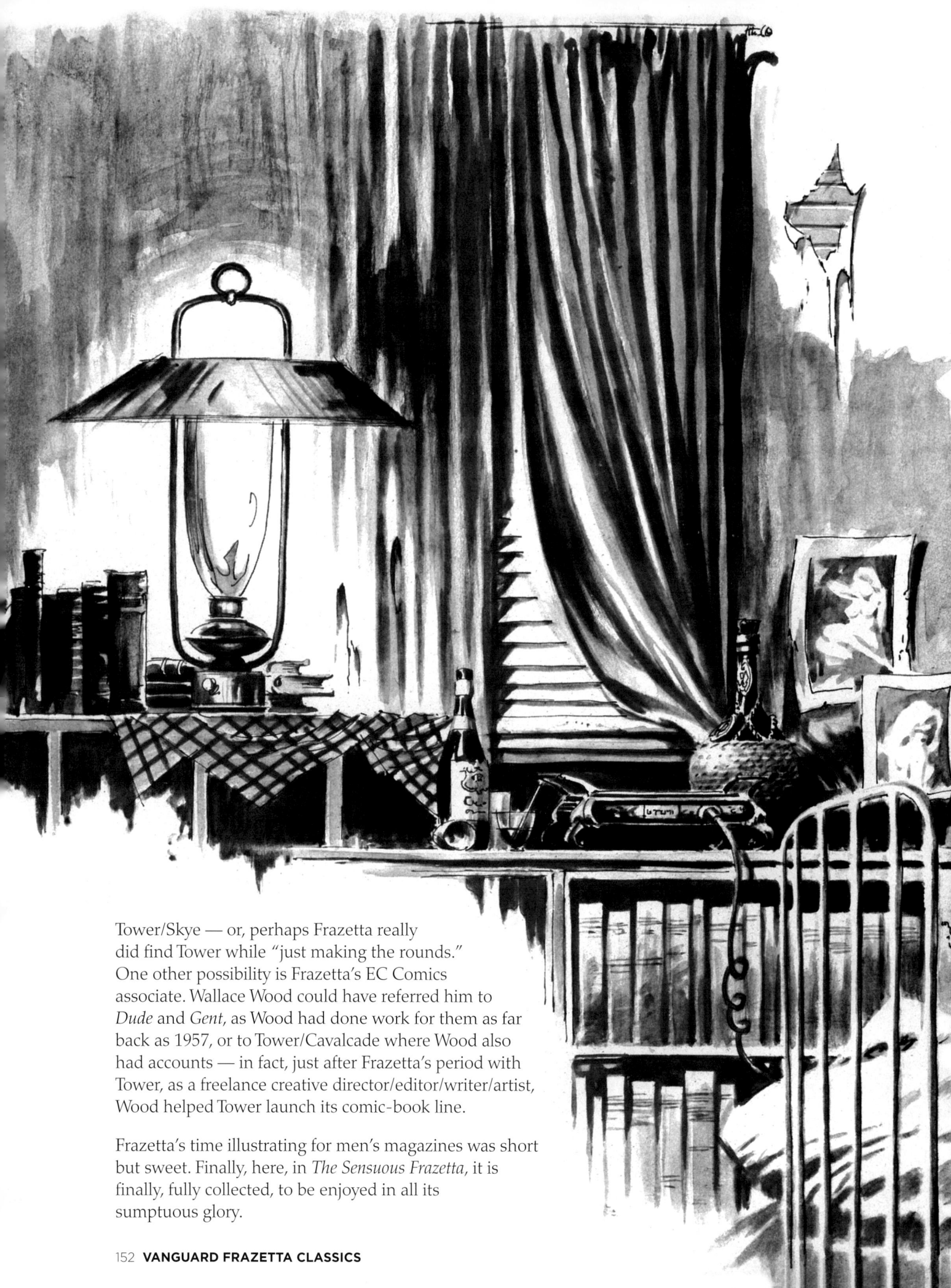

Tower/Skye — or, perhaps Frazetta really did find Tower while "just making the rounds." One other possibility is Frazetta's EC Comics associate. Wallace Wood could have referred him to *Dude* and *Gent*, as Wood had done work for them as far back as 1957, or to Tower/Cavalcade where Wood also had accounts — in fact, just after Frazetta's period with Tower, as a freelance creative director/editor/writer/artist, Wood helped Tower launch its comic-book line.

Frazetta's time illustrating for men's magazines was short but sweet. Finally, here, in *The Sensuous Frazetta*, it is finally, fully collected, to be enjoyed in all its sumptuous glory.

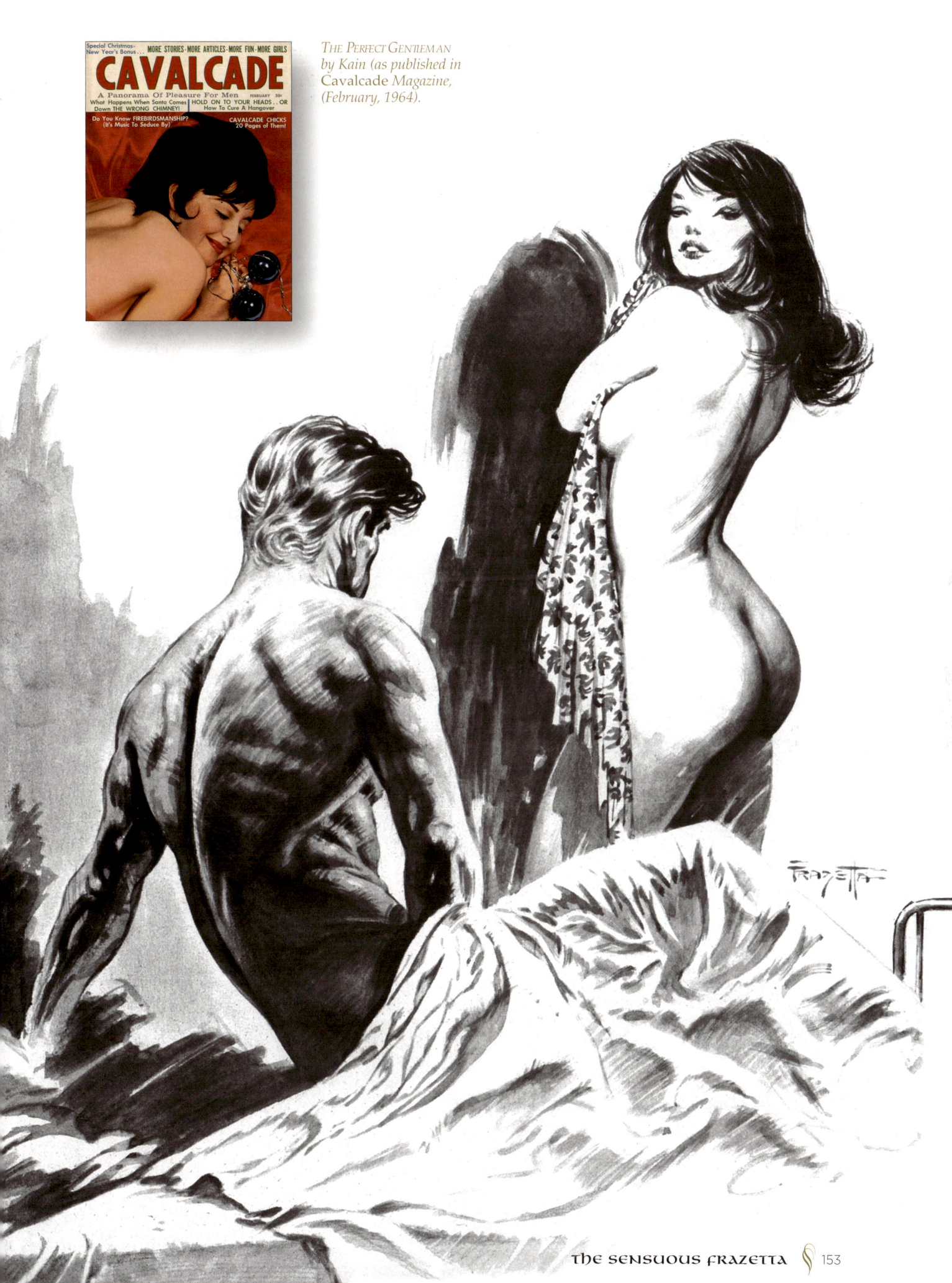

*The Perfect Gentleman
by Kain (as published in
Cavalcade Magazine,
(February, 1964).*

FRAZETTA

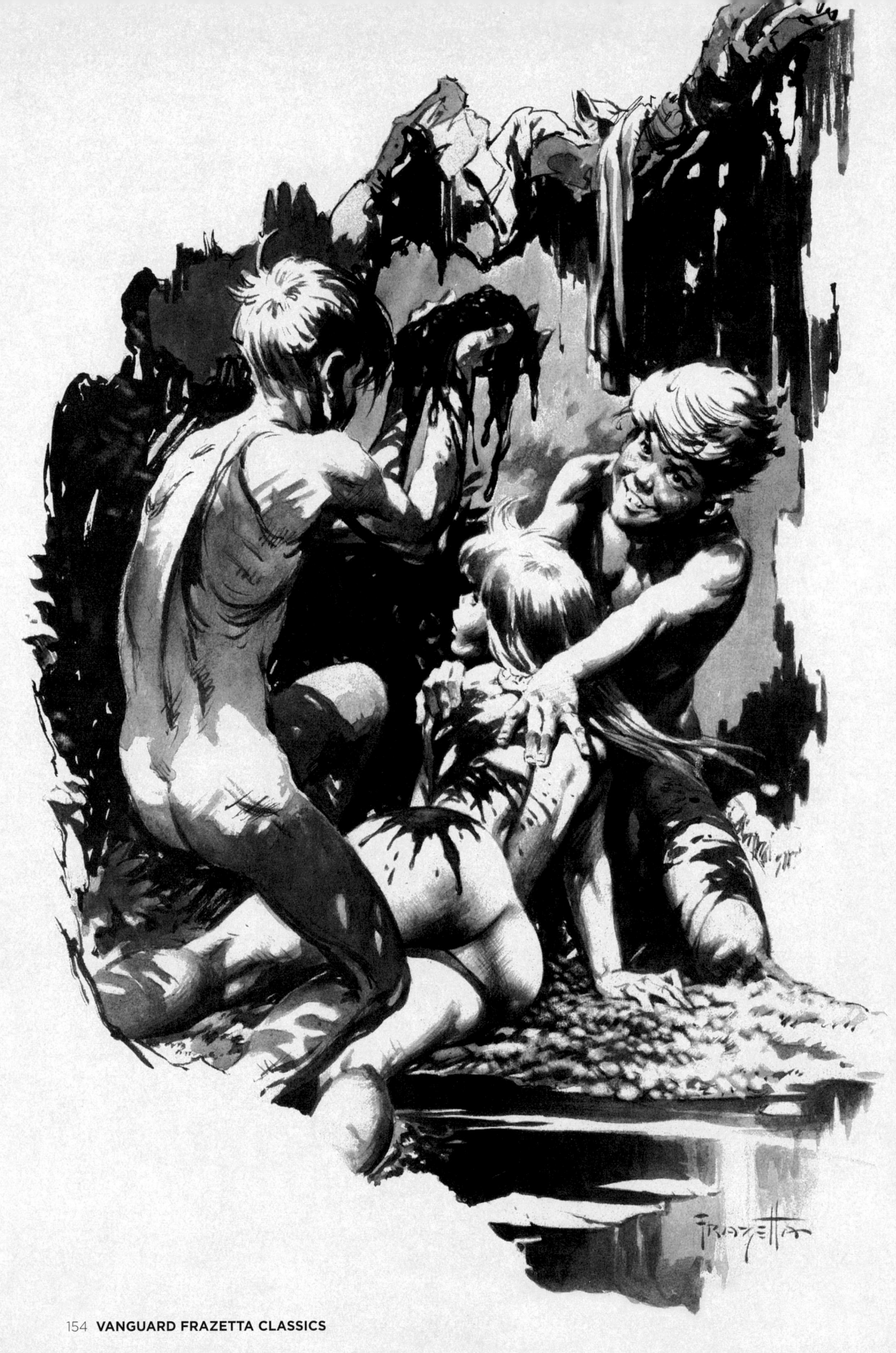

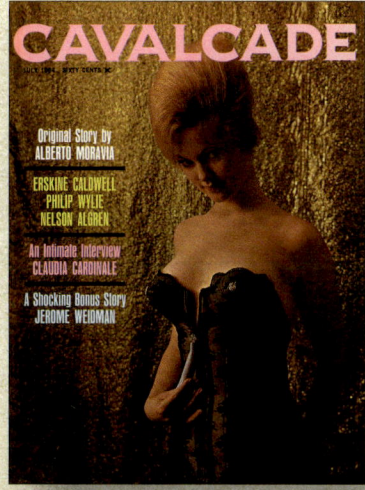

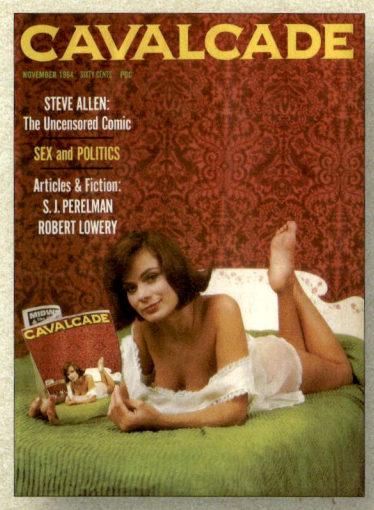

OPPOSITE:
Indian Summer
by Erskine
Caldwell (as
published in
Cavalcade
Magazine,
July 1964).

ABOVE:
The Giantess
preliminary,
1964 (5" x 4.75").
Final on
following
spread.

FRAZETTA

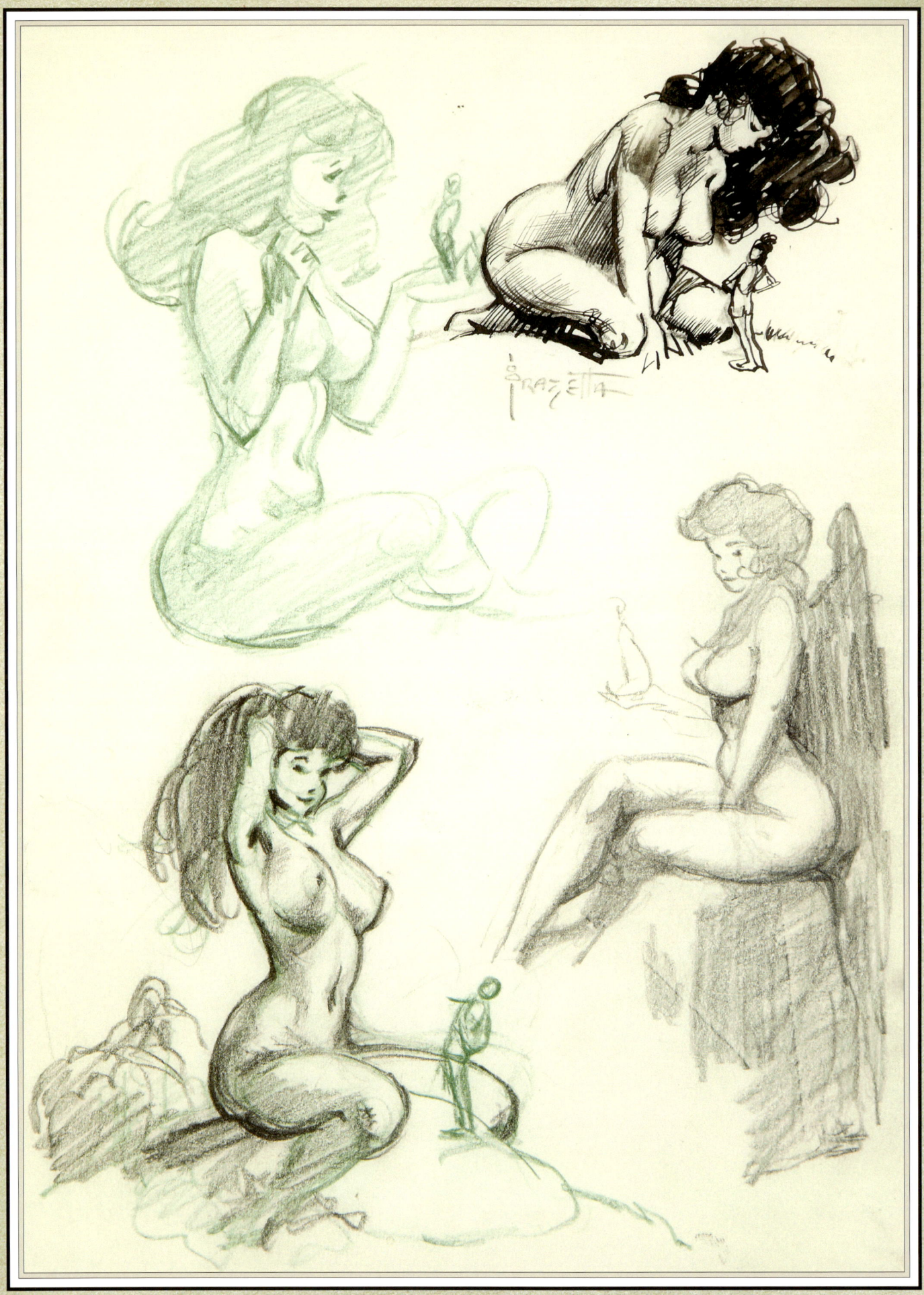

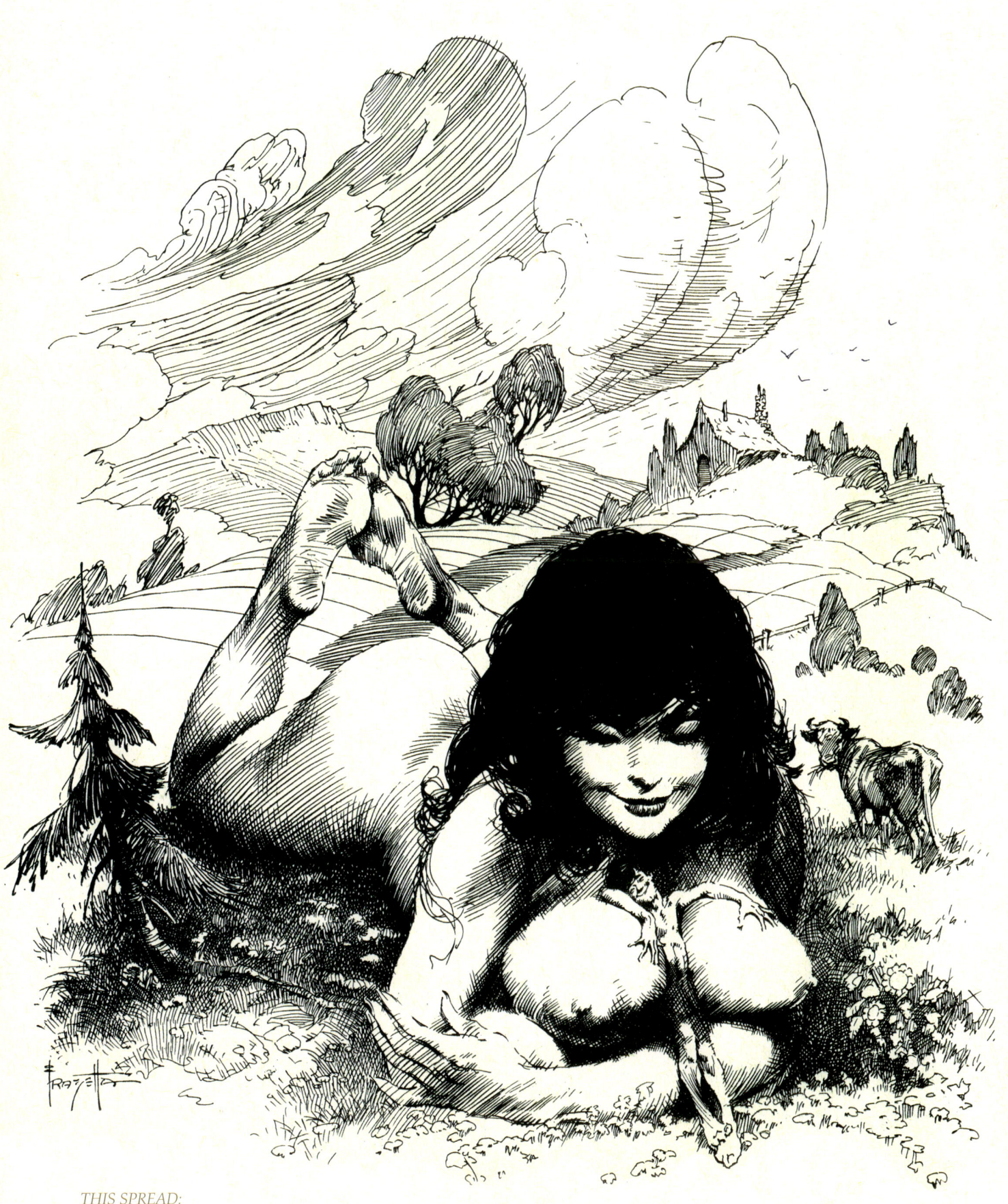

THIS SPREAD:
Another Giantess preliminary
(6.5"x 9.5") — and final, as published
in Cavalcade *magazine, November*
1964). Story by Charles Baudelaire.

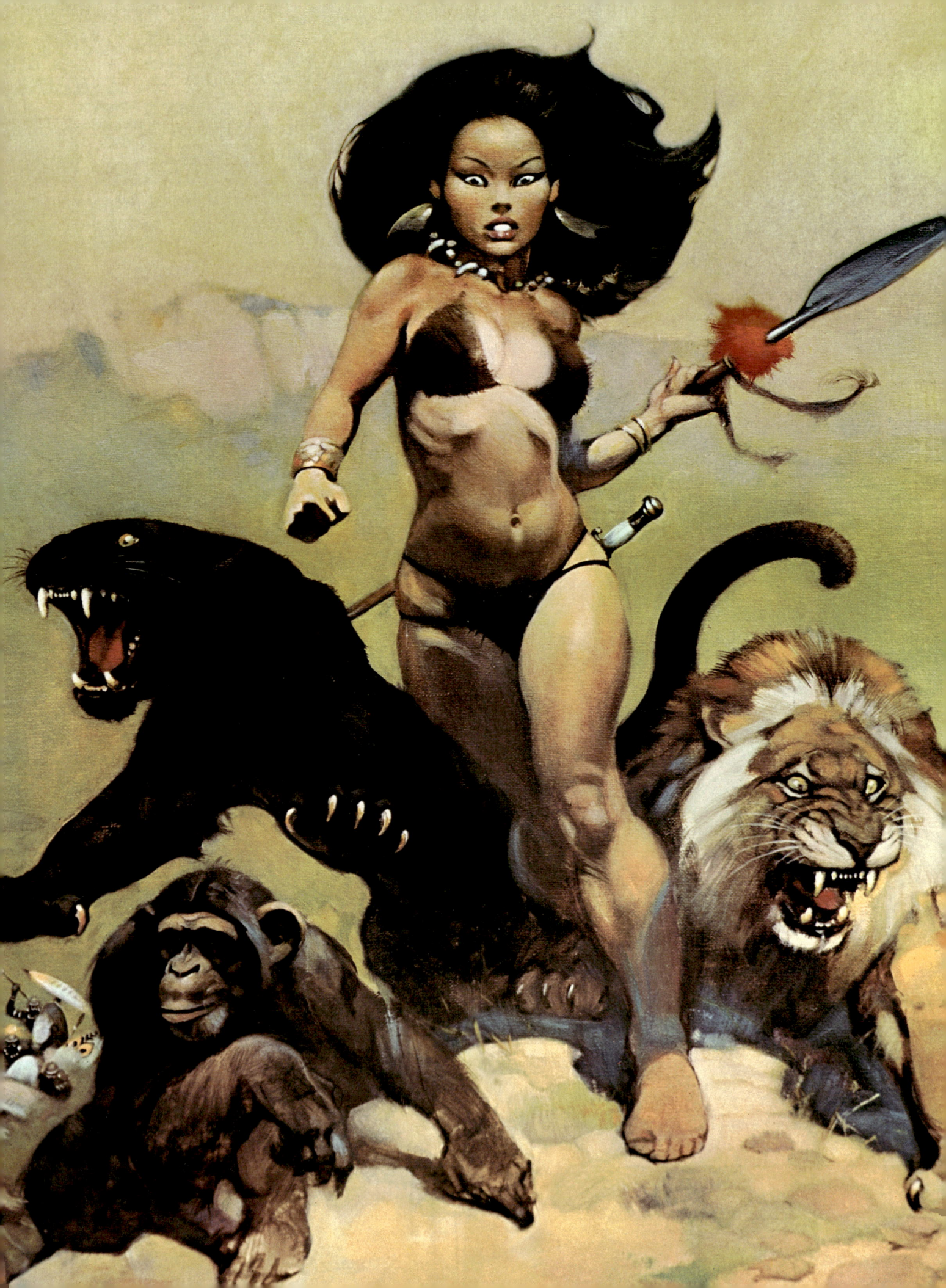

CHAPTER FIVE
From Casting Couch To...
HOLLYWOOD VIGNETTES

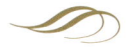

Mad and EC Publisher Bill Gaines had always highly valued Frazetta's work, and would have hired him but Frazetta hesitated because Gaines insisted on keeping the original art. This was a bone of contention for Frazetta. But in his early-to-mid-1960s period of struggle, just as Frazetta was let go from *Playboy's Little Annie Fanny* for not matching Will Elder's style, Frazetta gave in and did two back cover paintings for *Mad*. At the same time, thanks to Roy Krenkel, Frazetta began getting assignments painting covers for the Ace paperback line of Tarzan and other Edgar Rice Burroughs books. One of the *Mad* back covers was a take-off on Tarzan and the other was of Beatles drummer Ringo Starr, in a take-off on the then-prolific "Breck Girl" shampoo ads. Though fans were thrilled that Frazetta was beginning to do Tarzan and other Burroughs' character art, career-wise, the Ringo painting opened up a great door of opportunity for Frazetta.

The peak of the illustration business is major motion picture poster art. Inspired by the Ringo portrait, United Artists, MGM, Paramount, etc., started commissioning Frazetta for movie posters — likely, all through one agency. Overnight, Frazetta went from struggling to find work and being forced, under duress, to surrender his originals to feed his family, to producing top quality art for some of the biggest films of the time. These Frazetta posters were regularly humorous, caricature-based works including posters for *What's New Pussycat, The Busy Body, Yours, Mine and Ours, The Night They Raided Minsky's, After The Fox, Mad Monster Party*, and more.

Frazetta was painting perfect likenesses of such top stars as Victor Mature, Woody Allen, Peter Sellers, Ursula Andress, Paula Prentiss, Peter O'Toole, Britt Eklund, Shirley Jones, Stella Stevens, Alec Guinness, Gina Lollobrigida, Henry Fonda, Lucille Ball, and more. Frazetta was equal to any when it comes to likenesses, including Jack Davis and Mort Drucker, but his painting skills and use of color easily surpassed the competition. There was yet another absolutely unique quality Frazetta brought to his movie poster work; the unmistakable sensuality he imbued his female subjects with. Though many have written on Frazetta's film work, here, for the first time, we spotlight the sensuous side of Frazetta's Hollywood.

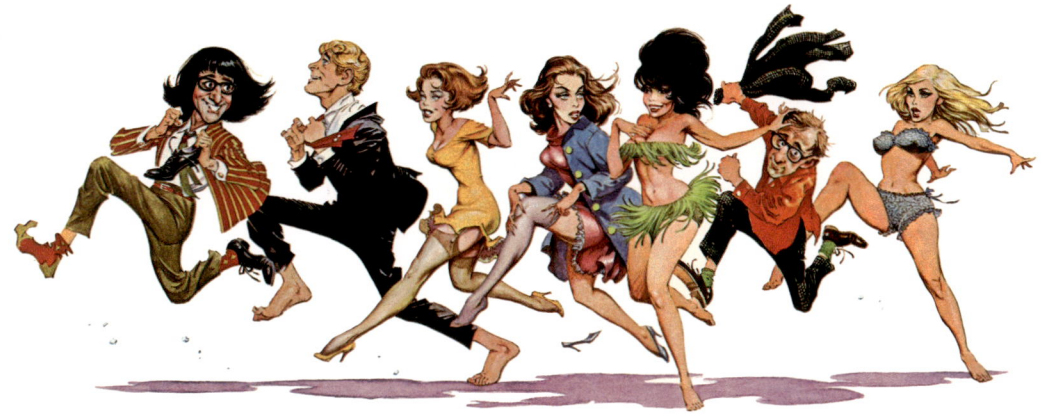

POLICE
BURLESQUE
MIDNIGHT SHOW TONIGHT

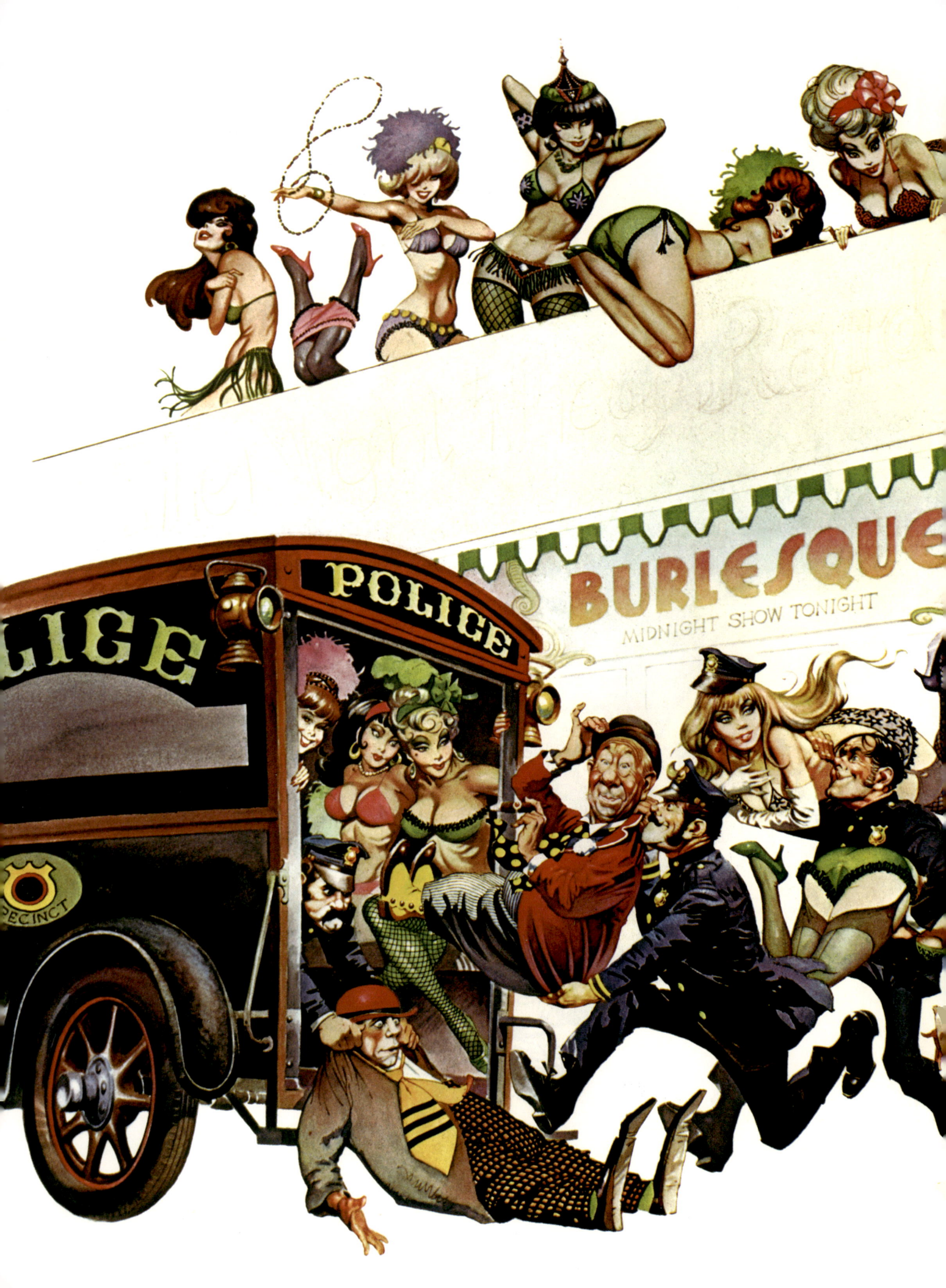

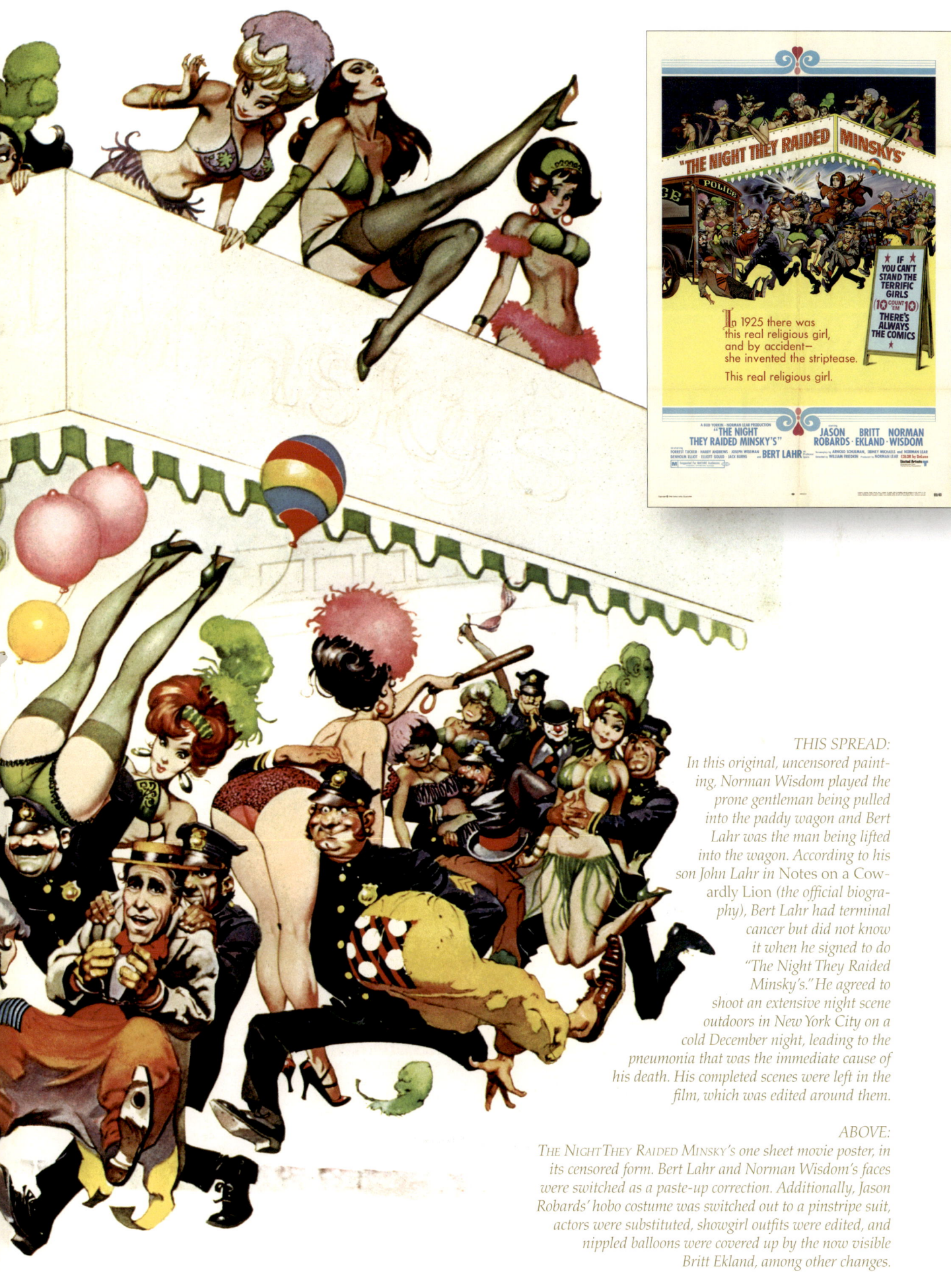

THIS SPREAD:
In this original, uncensored painting, Norman Wisdom played the prone gentleman being pulled into the paddy wagon and Bert Lahr was the man being lifted into the wagon. According to his son John Lahr in Notes on a Cowardly Lion *(the official biography), Bert Lahr had terminal cancer but did not know it when he signed to do "The Night They Raided Minsky's." He agreed to shoot an extensive night scene outdoors in New York City on a cold December night, leading to the pneumonia that was the immediate cause of his death. His completed scenes were left in the film, which was edited around them.*

ABOVE:
The Night They Raided Minsky's *one sheet movie poster, in its censored form. Bert Lahr and Norman Wisdom's faces were switched as a paste-up correction. Additionally, Jason Robards' hobo costume was switched out to a pinstripe suit, actors were substituted, showgirl outfits were edited, and nippled balloons were covered up by the now visible Britt Ekland, among other changes.*

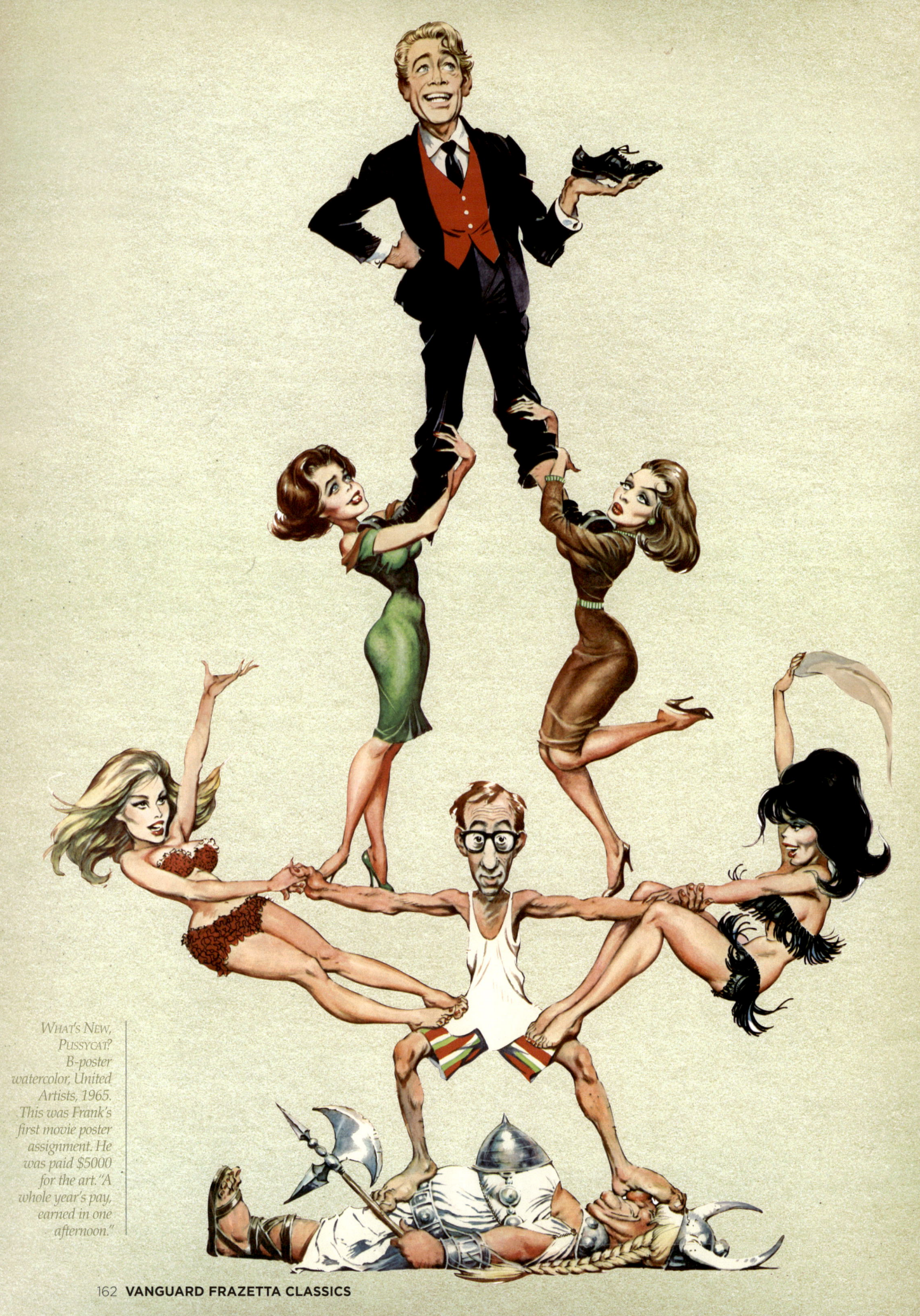

WHAT'S NEW,
PUSSYCAT?
B-poster
watercolor, United
Artists, 1965.
This was Frank's
first movie poster
assignment. He
was paid $5000
for the art. "A
whole year's pay,
earned in one
afternoon."

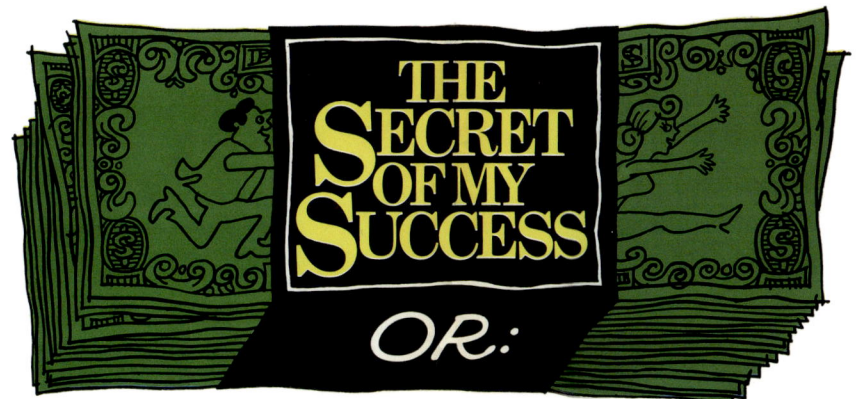

THE SECRET OF MY SUCCESS

OR:

how THREE Beautiful GiRLS Love for Fun-and MURDer for PROFIT

THE SECRET OF MY SUCCESS, one sheet poster watercolor, Metro-Goldwyn-Mayer, 1965. Starring Shirley Jones, Stella Stevens, and Honor Blackman. This was Frank's second movie poster.

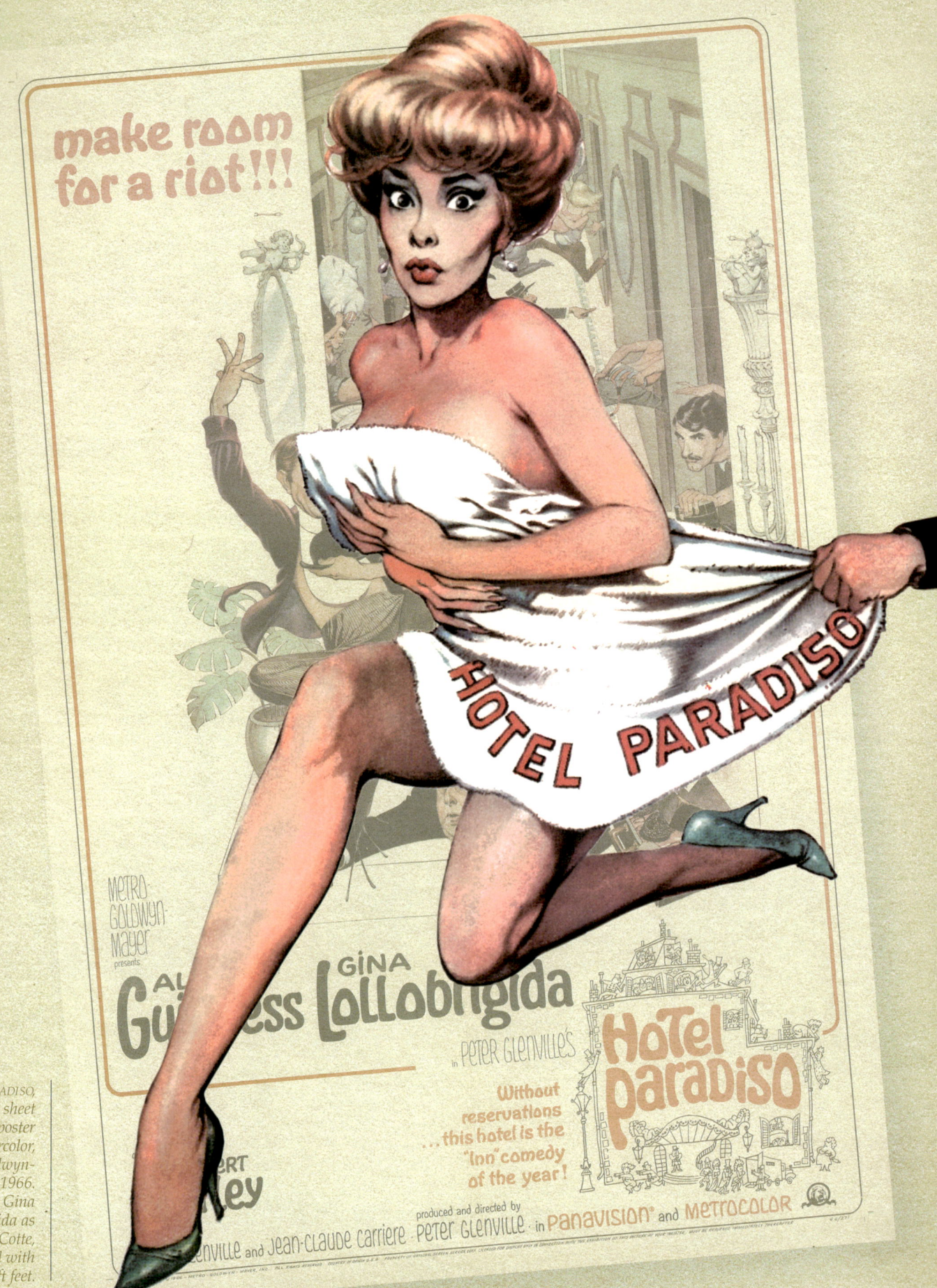

Hotel Paradiso, one sheet A-poster watercolor, Metro-Goldwyn-Mayer, 1966. Starring Gina Lollobrigida as Marcelle Cotte, painted with two left feet.

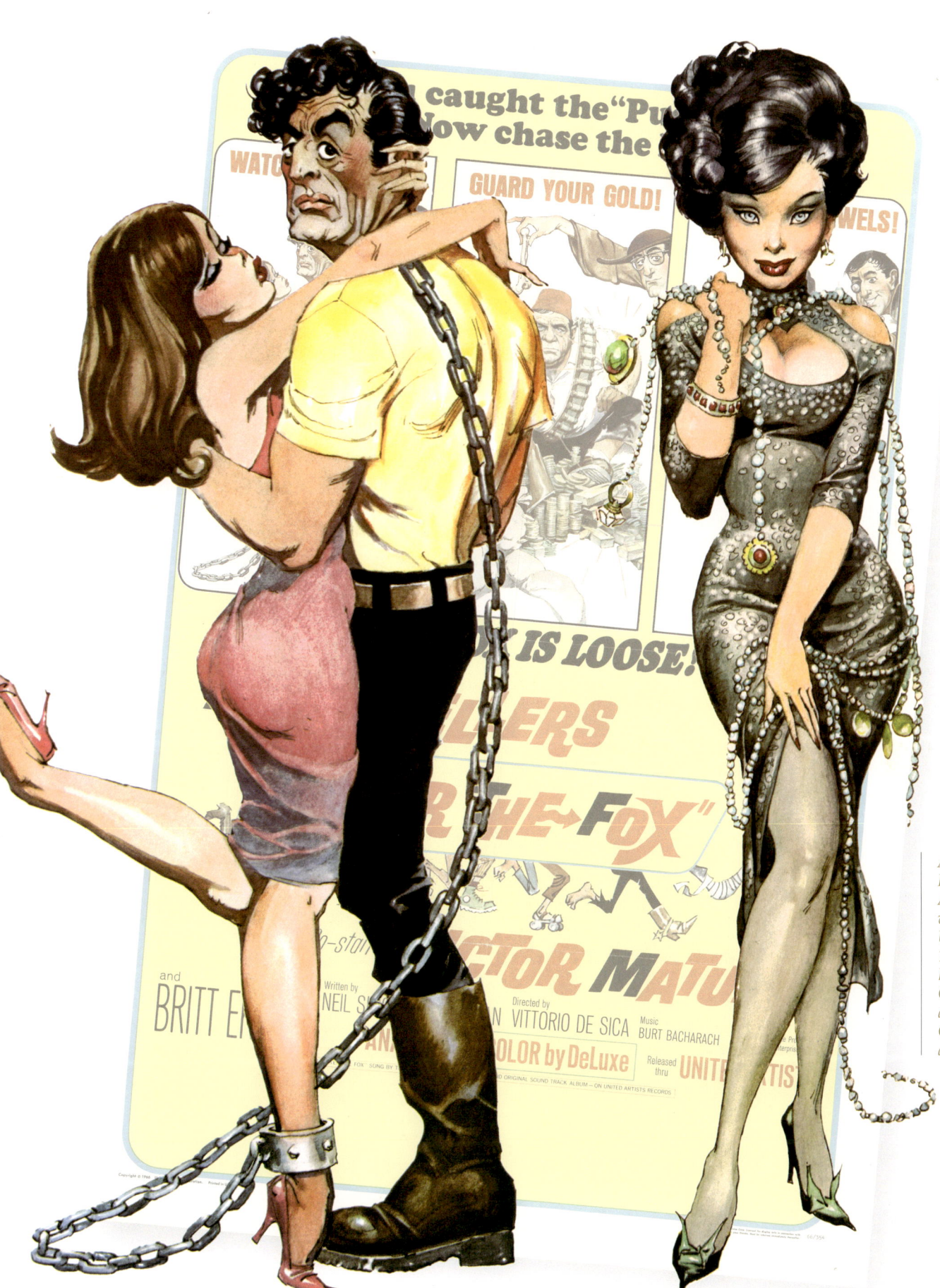

After the Fox, one sheet A-poster watercolor, United Artists, 1966. Starring Britt Ekland as Gina Romantica and Maria Grazia Buccella as Bikini Girl.

FRAZETTA
©1965

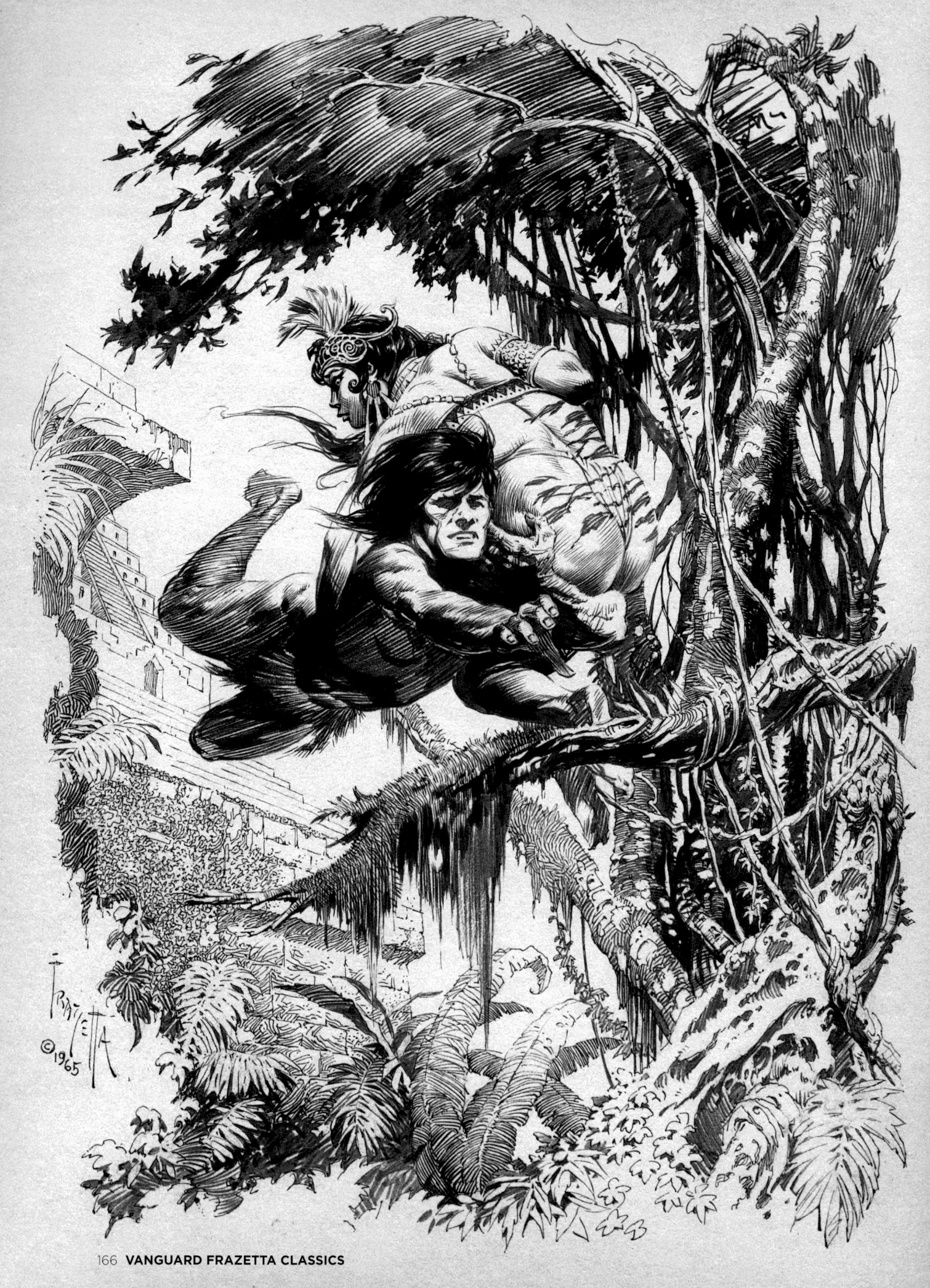

CHAPTER SIX
STARS IN HER EYES
THE ZODIAC CALENDAR

Regarding his 1960s men's magazine art Frazetta said to Groth, "It was trashy stuff. Not the sort of thing I would do now. I had no choice; I was going hungry [with] no work. [But] the girls are attractive and there's [nothing overt — just] a suggestion of some hanky-panky."

On the subject of sexism, Frazetta said, "My women are beautiful, [and while sometimes] they look vulnerable, certainly we're [portraying] heroic [subject matter], and generally the hero is saving the woman. On the other hand, you've got [my painting,] Cat Girl… I don't think there's anything sexist there. These are beautiful women that I truly adore. They're delicious, they're exciting, and I don't think I suggest that they're weak or being taken advantage of."

Frazetta continued, "The key word is 'taste.' And taste makes for beauty. When you start doing pornography, there ain't no way it can be in good taste. And for the most part, it isn't beautiful. I want to see the guy who can do it and make it beautiful. There's a difference between sexuality and pornography. Sex can be beautiful. You can suggest it and you can do it so it's not explicit, and yet it's sensuous as hell. You can get great joy and be more stimulated by that than some trashy stuff."

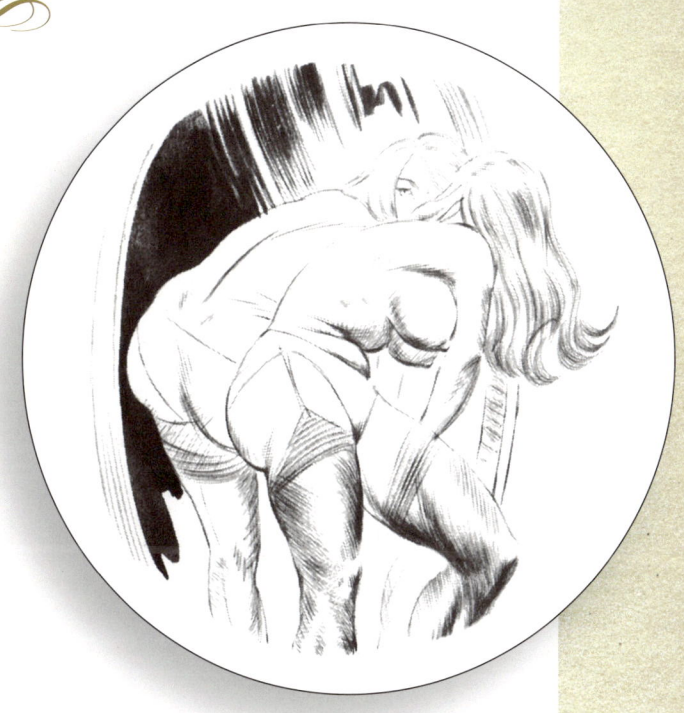

> • • • • 66 • • • •
>
> *Women are awfully sexy as it is. The name of the game is fantasy and if I can excite you… without anything explicit, what's wrong with that? It has an element of class to it; it's enduring; you could hang it in a museum.*
>
> — FRANK FRAZETTA

Frazetta: "[When drawing or painting,] I see the whole woman, right up to her kittenish eyes. I see the lighting; I see the way the buttocks play, one against the other; I see the shape of the calf; I see the little turns of the head; I just see more. It's all very personal; people don't have to agree with my interpretation. [I often] focus on certain areas [that] are more appealing to me. There are foot men and elbow guys, and ass men and so on. When I was very young, I had a calf fetish. I used to marvel at ballerinas with their wonderful legs. I don't know what it suggested to me — who can explain it?"

We wrap up *The Sensuous Frazetta* with a glimpse of his first men's magazine work, from the August 1962 issue of *Gent* magazine. Here, we see Frazetta's famous sensual touch being adapted to a different kind of Zodiac calendar.

THIS PAGE: Aquarius (as published in Gent *Magazine, August 1962).*

OPPOSITE: Tarzan Carrying Itzl Cha from Tarzan and the Castaways *(Canaveral, 1965).*

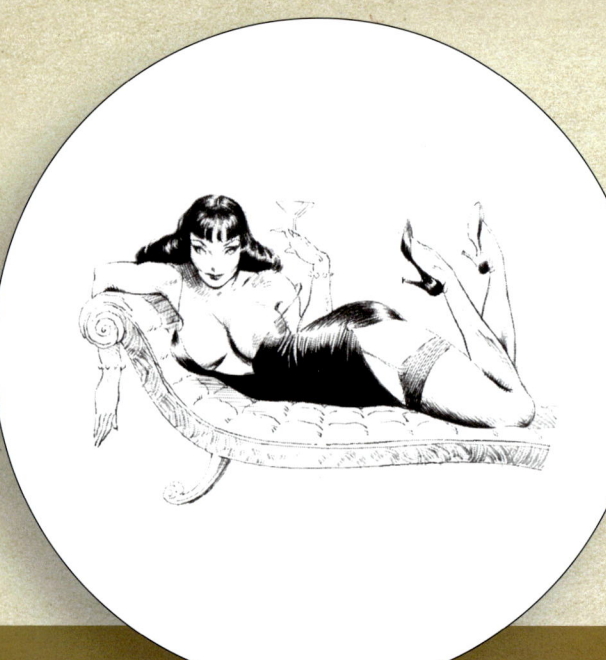

PISCES — "THE FISH"
(February 20-March 20)

She's easier to catch when high.
Impulsive, possessive, she clings to you,
And all of her secrets she'll bare...
But when she lets go,
And you think that she's through,
It's only to come up for air!

ARIES — "THE RAM"
(March 21-April 20)

The Aries girl is often sweet.
She'd sooner meet a man than eat.
It's romance that she's dreaming of,
But a girl's got to live —
She likes some comforts with her love.
Her password? Give and let give!

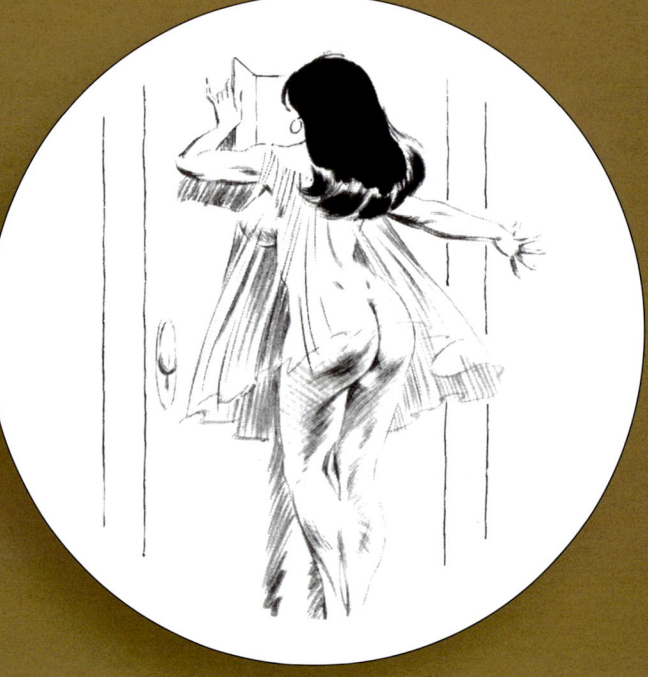

GEMENI — "THE TWINS"
(May 22-June 21)

Two souls make their home in the breast
Of double-jointed Gemeni.
Take the one that suits you best,
And leave one for a later try.
Remember, when you meet her,
She's got a way with sex.
Be careful not to cheat her —
Or you'll pay out double checks!

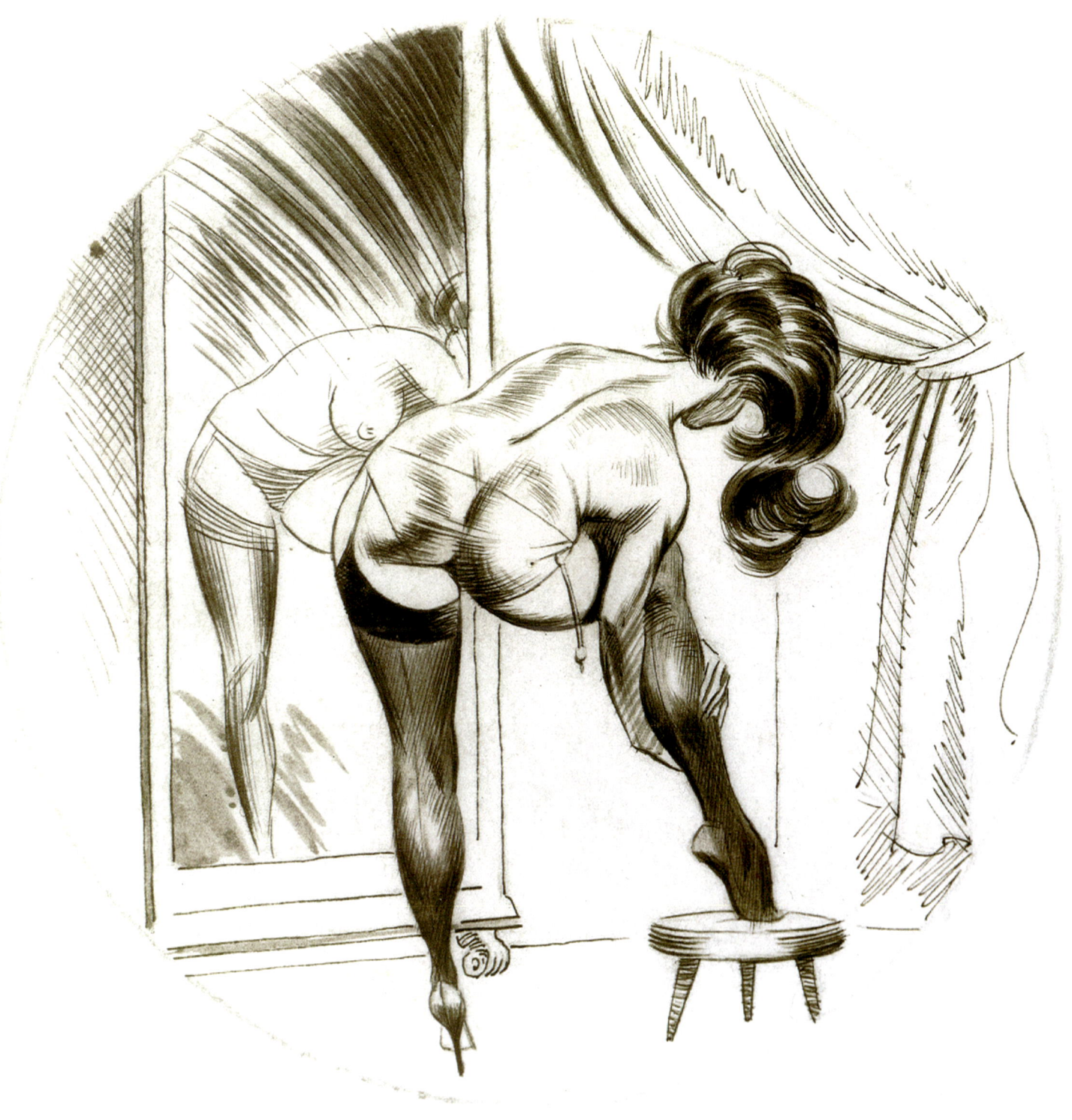

AQUARIUS — "THE WATER-BEARER"
(January 21-February 19)

Calm, cool and collected,
That's how the Aquarian works.
First you'll get dissected,
Then she talks about her quirks.

For instance, while undressing,
She quotes from "Arabian Nights."
Then hints she wants caressing,
And turns on all the lights!

AQUARIUS,
alternate
drawing,
previously
unpublished.

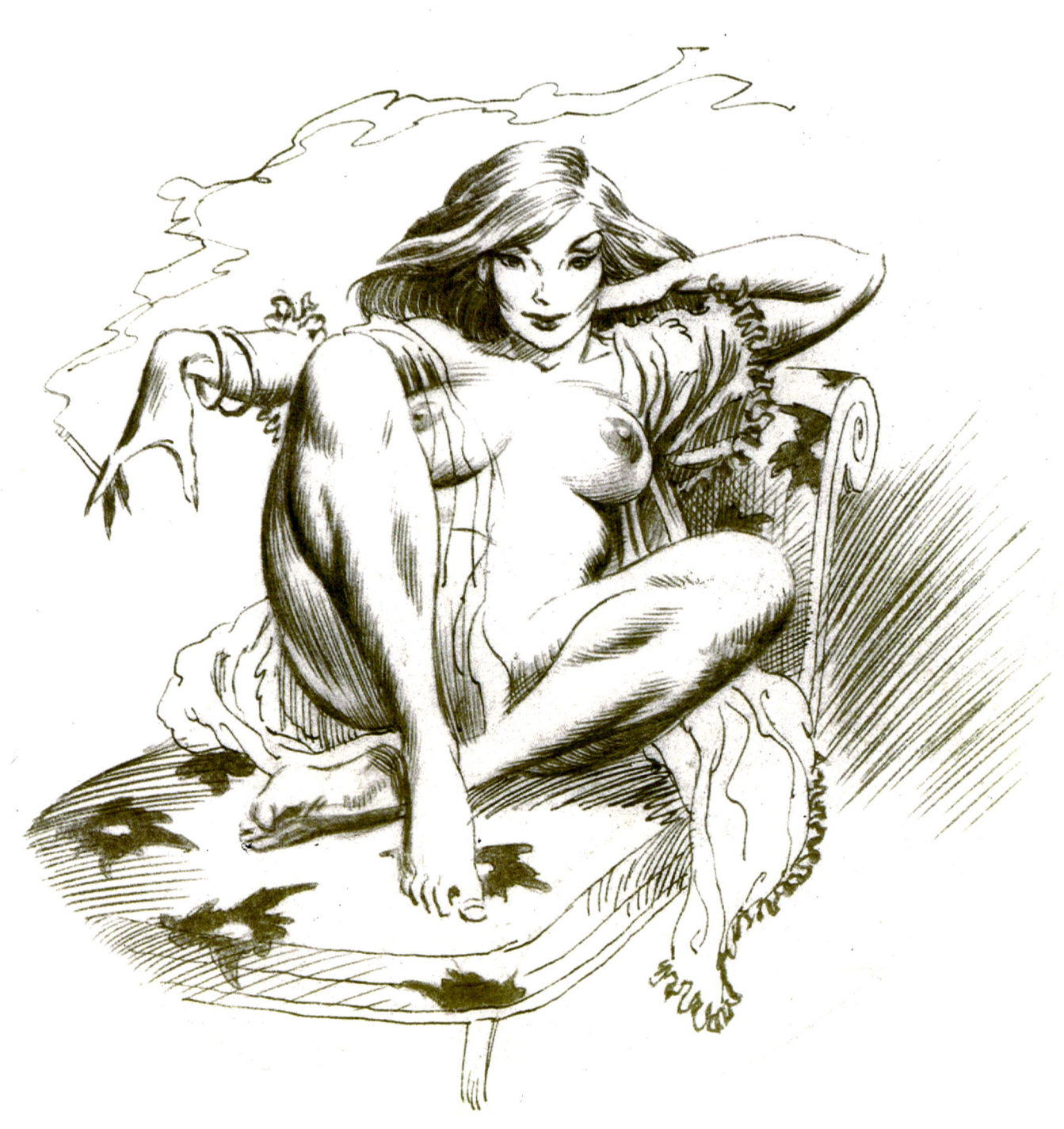

TAURUS — "THE BULL"
(April 21-May 21)

This lovely lass was born when Taurus ruled.
A lamb — but seldom shorn and never fooled.
She's stubborn over things of great concern
And asks of all she knows how much they earn.

Her habitat most often is the bed,
But leading men she picks don't lead — they're led.
She chooses all her victims with great care —
And marries them! So, bachelor, beware!

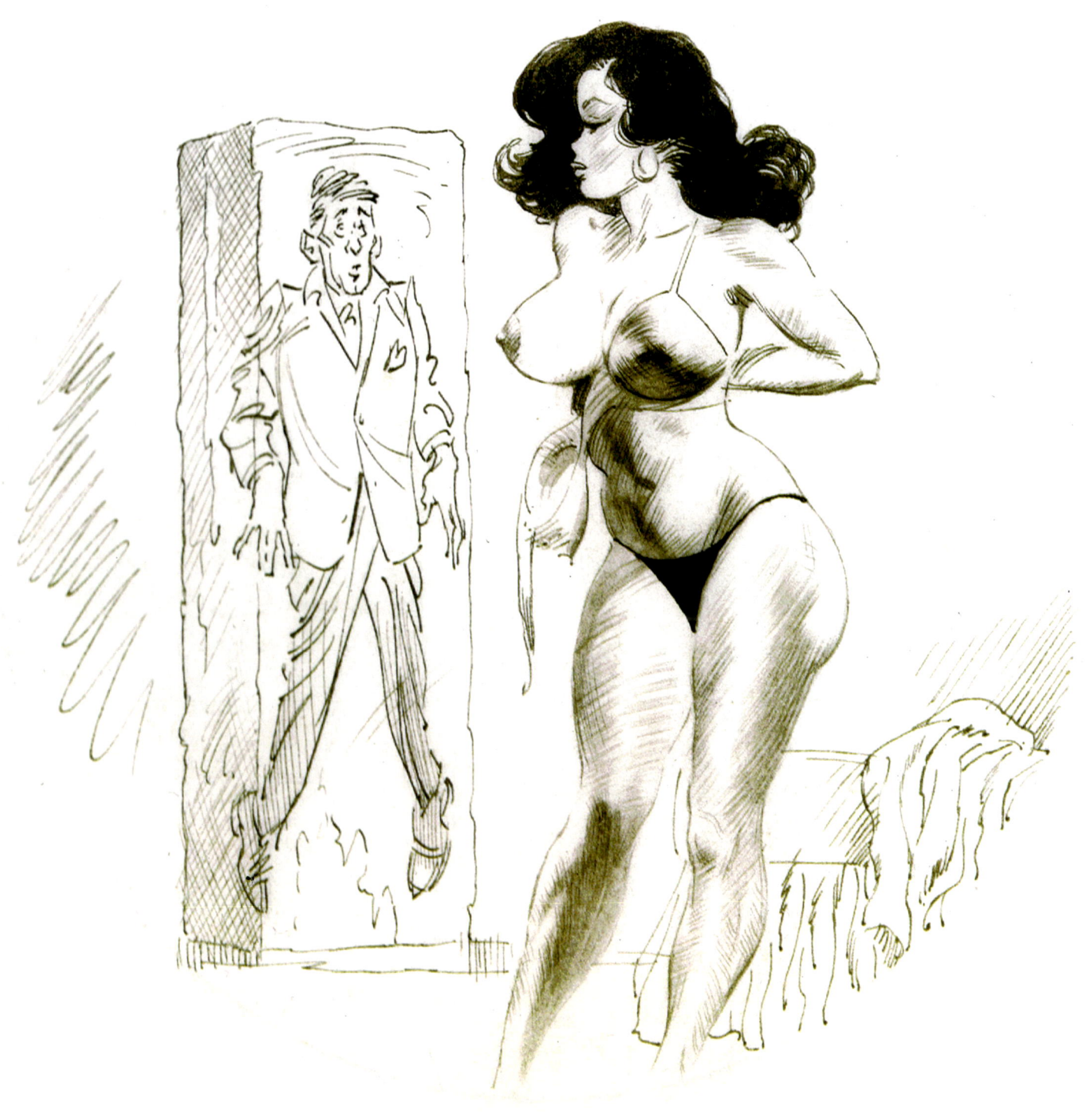

VIRGO — "THE VIRGIN"

(August 24-September 23)

The best of everything is barely good enough,
For Miss Virgo, who likes to sleep in buff,
So do your best and give her a bit more —
And she will never leave your bed — and bore.

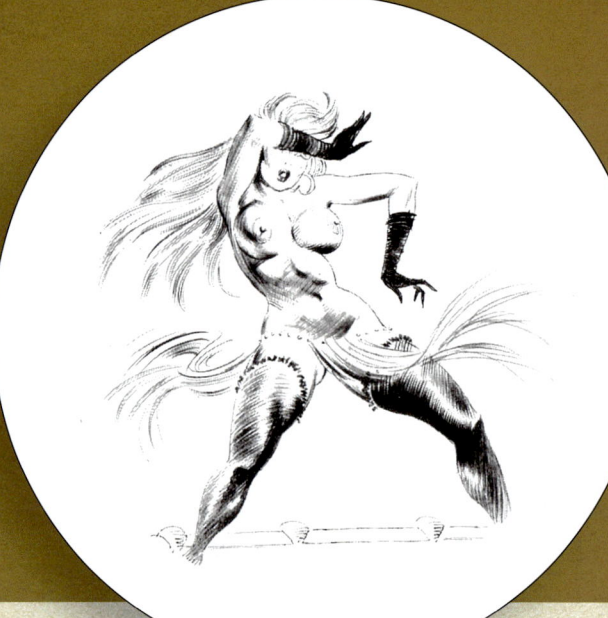

CANCER — "THE CRAB"
(June 22-July 23)

Quick-tempered is the word for Cancer"
And only for friends is yes her answer.
One moment it is do or die,
The next time you're a bore —
So if there's one you wish to try,
Feel out her moods before!

LEO — "THE LION"
(July 24-August 23)

The Leo gal is rarin' to preen
Hot-blooded, she thinks she is a queen.
When she's upset, she's even hotter,
And then the lioness shows through.
So be wise — be a plotter.
Into the shower — cool off with you!

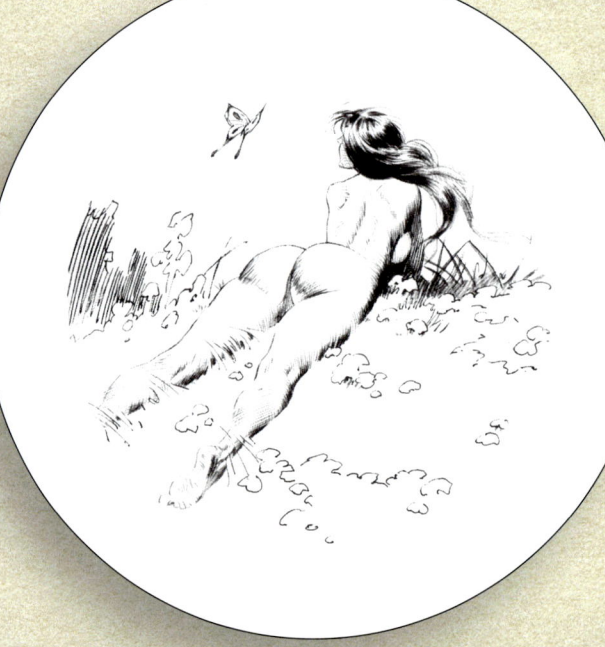

LIBRA — "THE SCALES"
(September 24-October 23)

The Libra girl in fancy clothes is best,
Although she's most expansive when undressed.
Though Libra stands for balance — let her purr,
You'll lose your balance quickly over her!

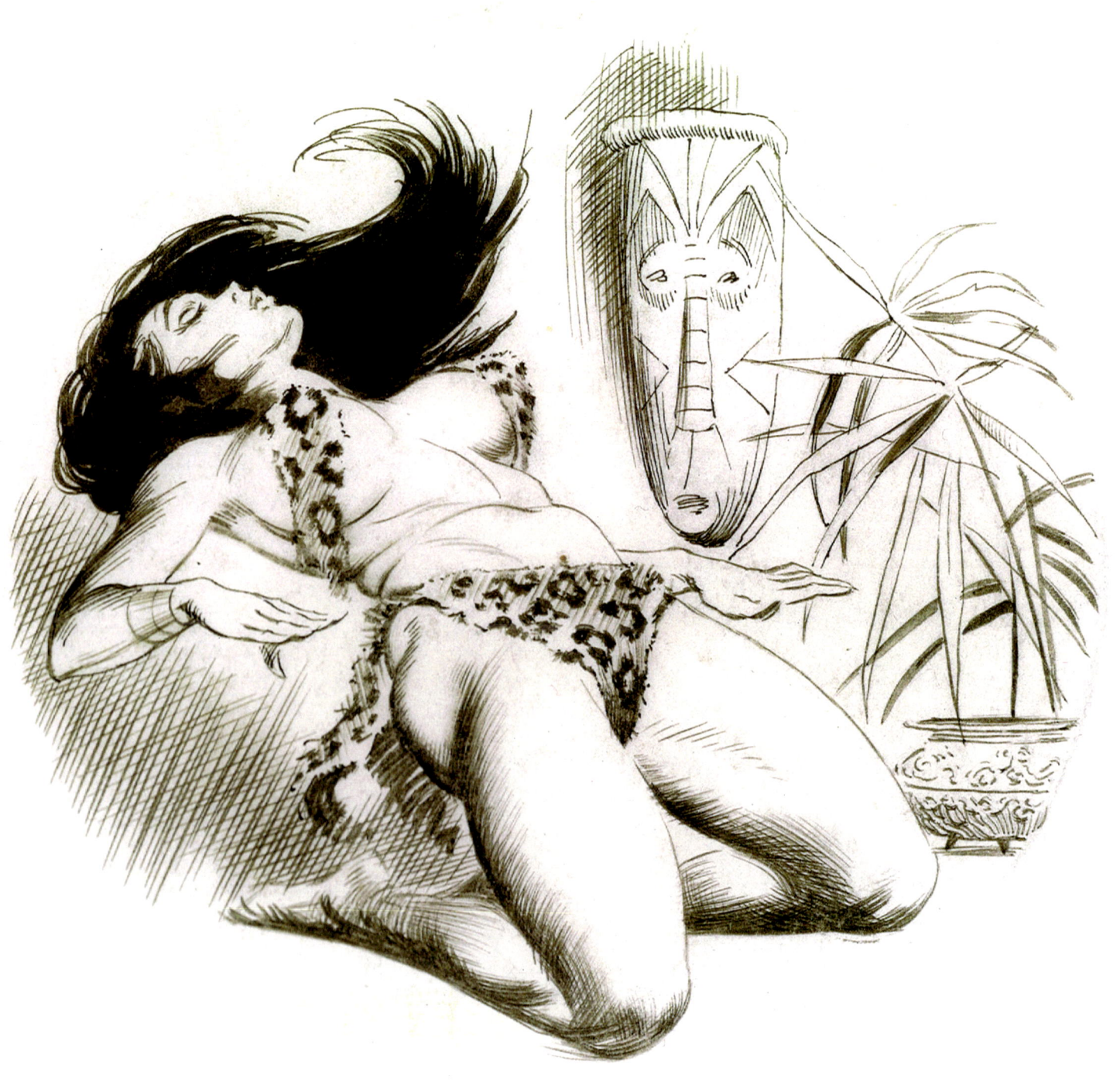

SCORPIO — "The SCORPION"
(October 24-November 22)

The Scorpio gal likes off-beat stimulation,
Like bullfight music to be romanced by.
So when you're set for an investigation,
Be sure the lights are low — and you're in high.

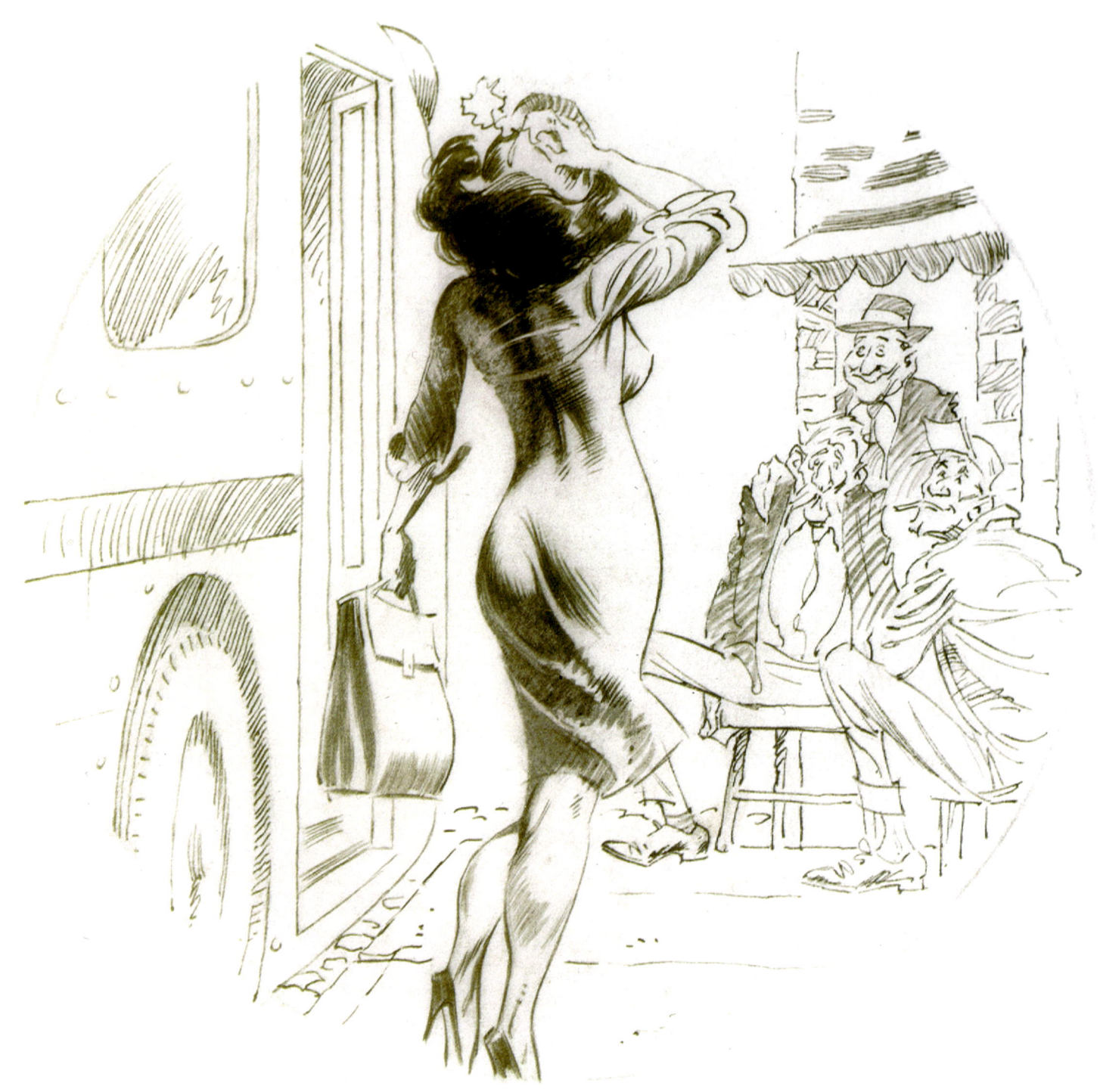

SAGITTARIUS — "THE ARCHER"
(November 23-December 21)

Adventurous Sagittarius likes to roam,
Though every young man's house is not a home.
She is the very life of any party,

If you're the party, things will not be dull.
Her prose is picaresque, her dress is arty.
They say she is the storm before the lull!

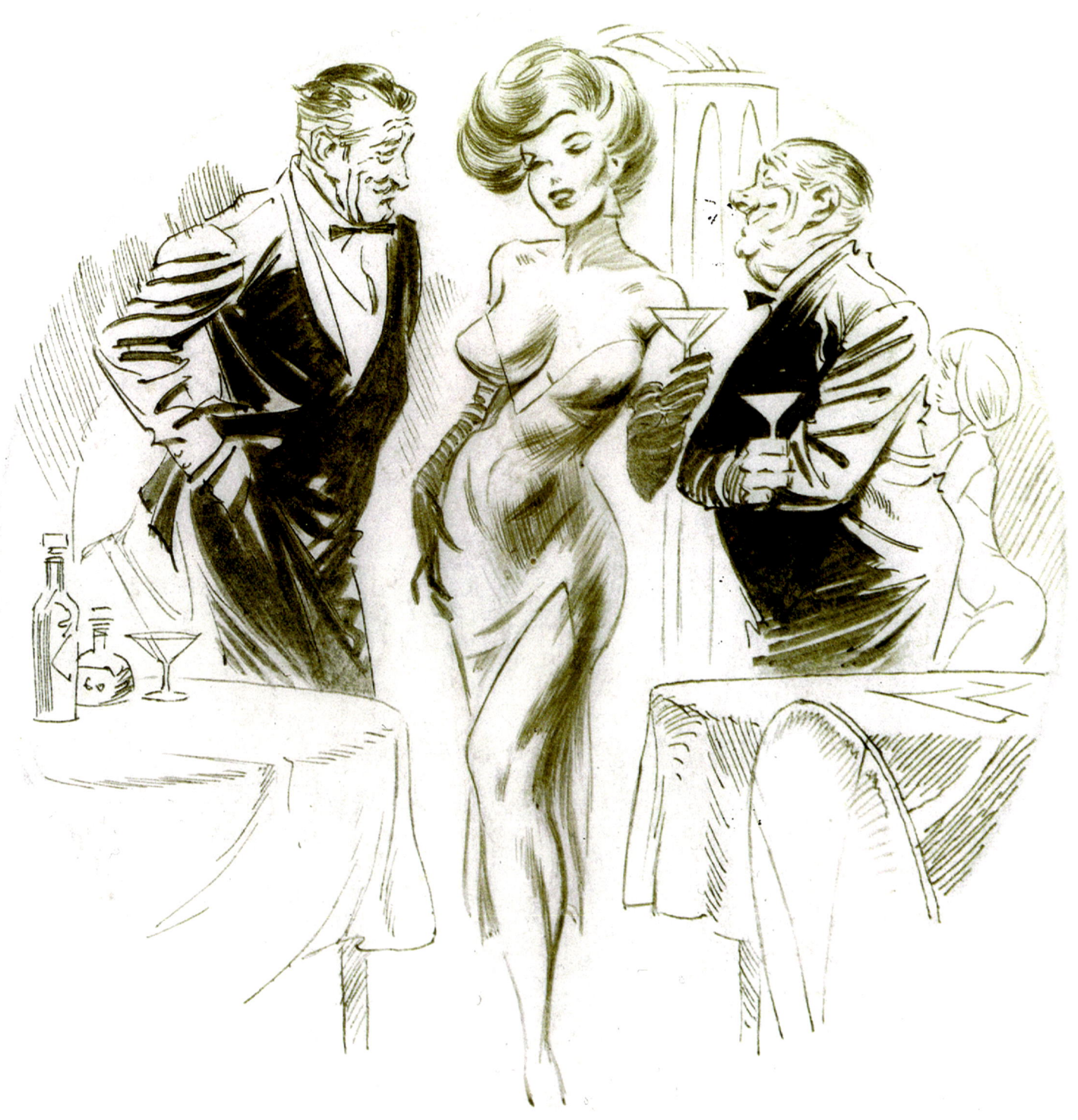

CAPRICORN — "THE GOAT"
(December 22-January 20)

Capricorn's conjugal, but frugal with her charms,
Unless a wedding band comes with your arms.
She has a sense for business, though, as well,

And while the sun shines, Capricorn makes hay.
So if you really do know how to sell,
A little sample goes a long, long way!

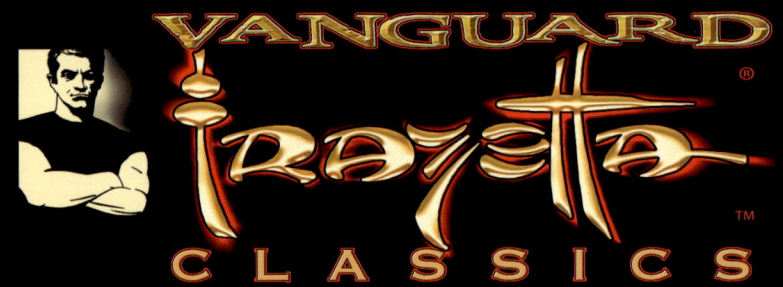

VANGUARD Frazetta CLASSICS ™

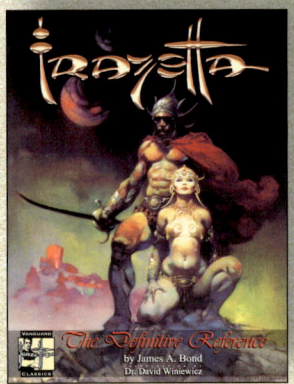

Definitive Reference

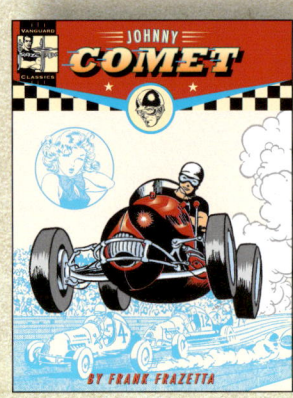

Johnny Comet SC

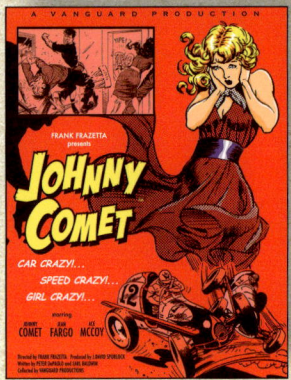

Johnny Comet DLX

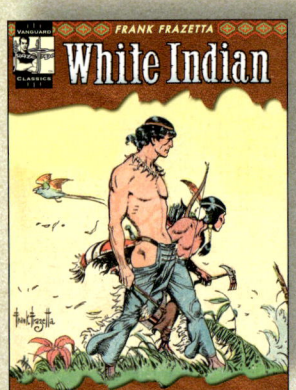

White Indian SC

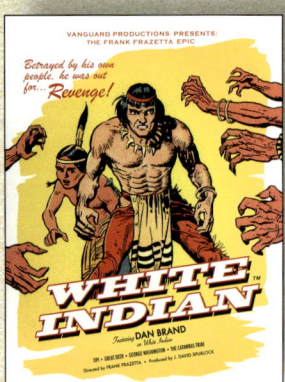

White Indian DLX

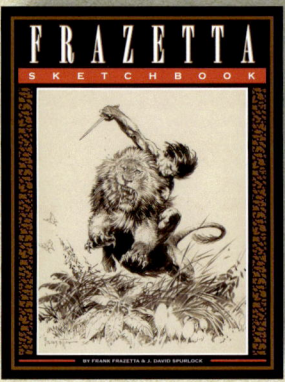

Sketchbook I SC

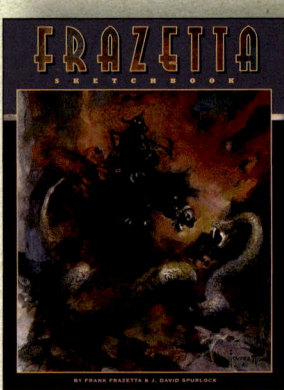

Sketchbook I DLX

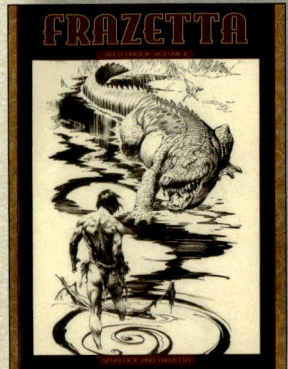

Sketchbook II SC

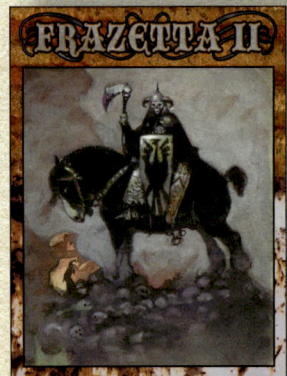

Sketchbook II DLX

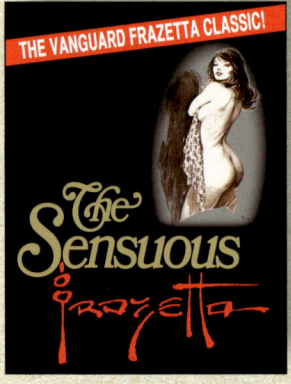

Sensuous Frazetta SC

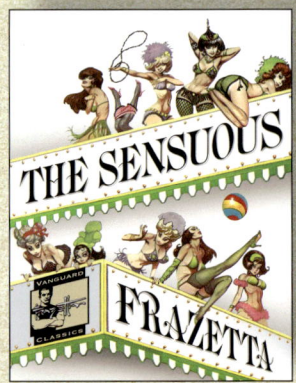

Sensuous Frazetta DLX

www.VanguardPublishing.com

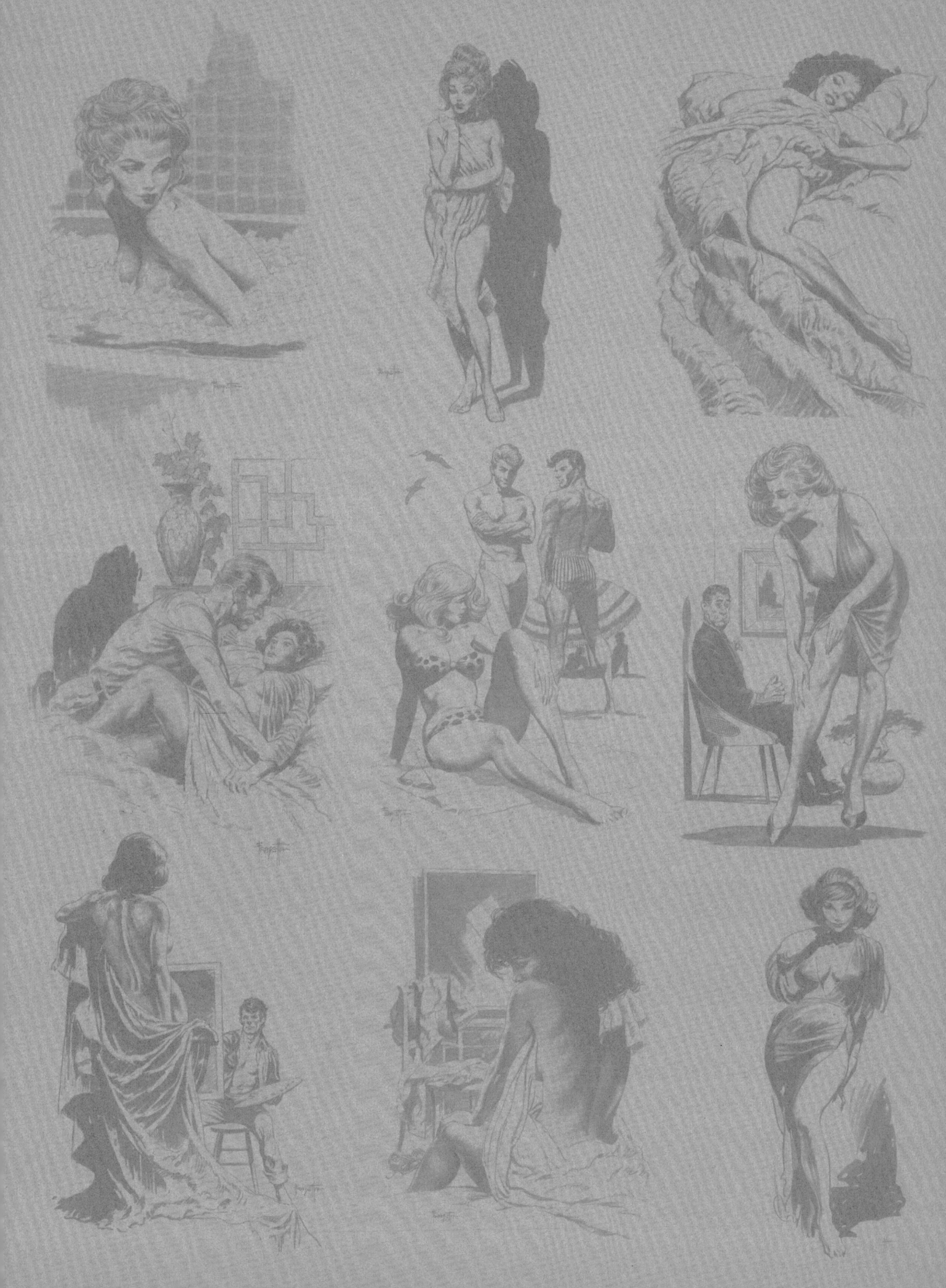